By Laurie J. Marks from Tom Doherty Associates

Earth Logic
Fire Logic

Earth Logic

Elemental Logic:
Book Two

Laurie J. Marks

TOR®
fantasy

A TOM DOHERTY ASSOCIATES BOOK
NEW YORK

EARTH LOGIC: ELEMENTAL LOGIC: BOOK TWO

Map by Jeanne Garnoll, Union Street Design, LLC

A Tor Book
Published by Tom Doherty Associates, LLC
175 Fifth Avenue
New York, NY 10010

www.tor.com

Tor® is a registered trademark of Tom Doherty Associates, LLC.

ISBN 0-765-34838-1
EAN 978-0-765-34838-8

First edition: March 2004
First mass market edition: June 2005

Printed in the United States of America

0 9 8 7 6 5 4 3 2 1

For the people of Melrose, Massachusetts—especially the baristas, poets, counselors, babies, delivery people, firemen, illegal parkers, students, parents, photographers, coffee drinkers, jaywalkers, and neighbors. And also for the people who love snow, plant flowers, hang Christmas lights, and refuse to put vinyl siding on their beautiful Victorian houses. And for their dogs and cats, and for the crabby snapping turtle I rescued from the middle of the road one afternoon, and for the flocks of geese that fly by overhead.

Acknowledgments

For four or more hours a day, for more than a year, I sat writing in the front window of a downtown coffee shop, in sun and snow, warmth and chill. The people of Melrose came and went before and around me—and gradually they began waving hello, chatting, and inquiring about my progress. I am grateful to them—and I am equally grateful to the smiling young baristas who concocted my lattes, visited my table to see if I needed a refill, and stayed to ask questions about writing, language, and education. Thanks also to the friends who suffered through my incoherent first draft, the members of my writing group, the Genrettes—Delia Sherman, Rosemary Kirstein, and Didi Stewart. And, when this book had—with their help—moved beyond its early confusion, even more people read the manuscript and helped me to see how to finish it: Amy Axt Hanson, Diane Silver, Jeanne Gomol, Debbie Notkin, Deb Manning, my agent, Donald Maass, and my beloved Deb Mensinger. As my life is so filled with kind, intelligent, generous friends, it's no surprise this book is filled with them as well.

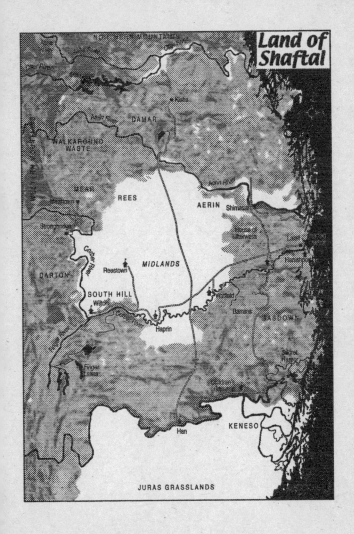

Land of Shaftal

Part 1

❧

Raven's Joke

✣ ✣ ✣ ✣ ✣ ✣ ✣ ✣ ✣ ✣ ✣ ✣ ✣ ✣ ✣ ✣

One day, Raven was bored. He left his home in the cliff that can be found at the end of the world and went flying back and forth over the forest, until he noticed a woman sneaking through the trees. The woman was trying to shoot a deer to cook for her three daughters, who had big appetites.

Raven flew up ahead of the hunter until he saw the deer, which was lying in the cool shade waiting for sunset. Raven shouted, "Run away, deer, as fast as you can, for there is a hunter's arrow aimed at your heart!" The deer jumped up and ran into the forest. Then the hunter was very angry and cried, "You are an evil bird, for because of you my daughters will go hungry!"

Raven was ashamed of himself and said, "You are right to be angry with me. So take your bow and arrow and shoot me, and take me home for your daughters' supper." So that is what the hunter did. She killed the Raven and cooked him in a soup.

Even though the girls ate the soup, they were still hungry, and no matter how much they ate, they stayed hungry. And the hunter, their mother, who was tired because she had been hunting all day, stayed tired no matter how much she rested. And their neighbor, who was very old and sick, never died. And the summer never turned to autumn. And the harvest never ripened. And nothing ever broke, but the things that already were broken could not be mended.

One day everyone in the world came to visit the tired hunter and her three hungry daughters. "Did Raven trick you into killing him?" they asked. The tired hunter told them exactly what had happened. Everyone became very upset with her and said, "Didn't you know that Raven is the one who decides everything? He may be mischievous and hard-hearted, but without him we cannot go forward with our lives. You should have thought of what you were doing. Now we will never see our children grow up, and whatever we are now, that is what we will always be, and nothing will ever change."

They all thought and thought, and then the hunter's youngest and hungriest daughter said, "I know where Raven's bones are." So they dug all Raven's bones out of the ashes of the fire. The middle daughter took some string and glue and put all the bones together the way they were supposed to be. Then, the oldest daughter found all the Raven's wing and tail feathers and glued them on the bones. Finally, the hunter took the arrow that had killed the Raven and smeared the bones with the blood that was still wet on the arrowhead. And then, all the people of the world began to laugh. "Hey, Raven," they said, "that was a pretty good joke!" Raven, of course, could never resist a good laugh, so began to laugh too. "Ha! Ha!" he said. "That was a good joke!" And then he flew on his bone wings to the river to eat frogs and snails until he got fat and looked like himself again. The hunter shot a deer and her daughters were no longer hungry. The harvest ripened, the old neighbor died, and the world continued its journey as it should, from summer to winter, from life to death, and from foolishness to wisdom.

� � � � � � � � � � � � � �

Chapter One

The woman who was the hope of Shaftal walked in solitude through a snow-muffled woodland.

Dressed in three shirts of threadbare wool and an ancient sheepskin jerkin, she carried an ax in a sling across her back, and dragged a sledge behind her, in which to pile firewood. She might have been any wood-cutter setting out between storms to replenish the woodpile.

The season of starvation had brought down another deer. It was frozen in a bed of churned-up scarlet snow, and the torn skin now lay in stiff rags. Rib bones gleamed with frost, the belly was a hollowed cavern, and a gnawed leg bone lay at a distance. The woodcutter scarcely glanced at this gruesome mess as she strode past, breaking through the snow's crust and sinking knee-deep with every step. But the ravens that followed behind her uttered hoarse shouts of discovery and swooped eagerly down to the feast of carrion. They stalked up to the deer's remains, sprang nervously up into the air, and landed again. After this silly ritual of caution they began to bicker over the best pieces.

The woodcutter, having selected a tree, unslung her ax. As the sharp blade bit into the trunk, clots of snow were shaken loose from above. The ravens paid no heed, not even when the tree fell with a spectacular crash.

The woodcutter gazed with satisfaction at the fallen trunk. Her cut had revealed the tree's sick center, the rot that would have soon killed it. Breathing heavily, she took off her bright knit cap to cool herself, and her wild hair sprang up like the tangled branches of a thicket. "It's cold enough to freeze snot," she said.

The ravens, apparently easily amused, cackled loudly.

The woodcutter let her gaze wander upwards, across the treetops, toward a distant smear of smoke, nearly invisible against the heavy clouds. "Scholars! They'd die of cold before they noticed they were out of firewood."

"Ark!" protested a raven, as another stole a tidbit right out of his mouth. They scuffled like street children; feathers flew.

"Uncivilized birds!" The woodcutter struck her ax into the stump.

The birds looked up at her hopefully as she approached the dead deer. Using a knife that had been inside her coat, she trimmed back the deer's stiff skin and sliced off strips of meat, which she fed to the importunate ravens. The birds were not yet sated when she abruptly rose out of her squat and turned toward the northeast.

She was tall: a giant among the Midlanders. Still, she could not see over the treetops, yet she seemed to see something, and her forehead creased. A raven flew up to her shoulder. "Another storm is coming," the raven said.

"Of course," she replied. "But there's something else. Something strange. And terrible."

"In the village," said the raven, as though he knew her mind.

"Something has come," she said.

"No, it has always been."

"Not always. But a long time. Longer than I've been alive."

"Waiting?" croaked the raven. "Why?"

She shrugged. "Because some things wait."

"The Sainnites came thirty-five years ago. Is this thing theirs?"

"Yes, they brought it with them."

After this firm declaration, raven and woman both were silent. Then, she took a deep breath and added heavily, "It is my problem now."

"Ark!" exclaimed the raven with mocking surprise.

"Oh, shut up."

"Coward," he retorted.

With a sweep of the hand she flung the bird off her shoulder. He landed in the snow, squawking with laughter.

"Tell Emil what I am doing," she told him.

She left her ax and strode off through the snow, between the crowded trees. She could see the storm coming: a looming black above, trailing a hazy scarf of snowfall. She walked toward it.

In the attic of the nearby stone cottage, Medric the seer dreamed of Raven, the god of death. "I will tell you a story, but you must write the story down," said Raven. Medric went to his battered desk and found there a fresh candle burning and a newly trimmed pen, which he dipped into an inkwell. "What shall I title this story?" he asked.

"Call it 'The Raven's Joke,'" said the god, and began: "One day, Raven was bored . . ."

Downstairs from the seer's book-filled attic, a little girl was very busy. She had been induced to take a bath that morning, but now had smudges of dirt on her wool smock, and a spider web, complete with dead bug, tangled in her hair. The woman who sat on the hearth studying a book paid no attention as the girl rummaged through cupboards and closets, while conversing with the battered stuffed rabbit whose head poked out of her shirt pocket.

A man came into the parlor, looked vaguely around, and said to the woman on the hearth, "You're letting the fire go out."

The woman reached for a log and put it onto the coals without taking her eyes off the stained page of the ancient book. Her dark skin, hair, and eyes; her narrow, sharp features; and her long, complexly braided hair identified her as a *katrim* of the otherwise extinct Ashawala'i people. The book she studied was written entirely in glyphs; few could have made sense of the arcane text.

"Leeba, why have you taken my ink?" the man asked the little girl.

"I need it," she declared.

"I need it also. What do you need it for? You have neither paper nor pen."

"I need it for my journey. When I reach a place, I'll ask the people there if they need anything. And if they need some ink, I'll sell it to them. By the time I come home, I'll have a hundred pennies."

"A hundred pennies? Well, let's see. How much were you going to charge for this lovely bottle of ink?"

There followed an impromptu numbers lesson. The woman on the floor rubbed her eyes, for the fireplace was smoking. Finally, she looked up from her book to push the split log further into the fireplace, and to blow on it vigorously until the flames caught. The man went out, and came back in with a sheet of paper and a pen. He said to his daughter, "Loan me some ink, I'll make some pennies to pay you with."

The woman studied the page, frowning—or, perhaps, scowling—with concentration. A few of the numerous slender plaits of her hair had slipped over her shoulder and looped across the page like lengths of black yarn.

The man paid for his bottle of ink with fifteen paper pennies. "Zanja," he said.

"Don't bother me," the woman said.

He bent over to examine the symbol at which she glared. "My land! What are you reading?"

"Koles."

"The poet? No wonder you're surly. The poetry students at Kisha University used to swear he had randomly copied glyphs out of a lexicon."

"There's always a pattern. Even if the poet himself didn't believe he had a reason, or didn't know what his reason was." Her voice trailed off into abstraction, and she abruptly reached for something that she expected to find dangling from her belt. "My glyph cards!"

"Leeba!" said J'han, horrified.

Leeba interrupted her cheerful humming. "Thirty pennies," she demanded.

"Oh, dear," said J'han, as Zanja uncoiled upward from her seat on the hearth.

But the little girl looked up fearlessly as Zanja plucked a pack of cards from her collected goods. "Your daughter is a thief," said Zanja to J'han.

"I'm your daughter too," Leeba protested.

A smile began to do battle with Zanja's glare. "You are? How long have I had a daughter? How did it happen?"

Leeba clasped her by the knees, grinning up at her. "Thirty pennies!" she demanded.

"Extortion!"

"I'll buy them for you," said J'han hastily. "In gratitude. For not strangling her. Thirty pennies, Leeba?" He began counting paper pennies.

Zanja protested, "It's too much. Look at these worn-out old cards! They've been dunked in water, smeared with mud and grease, and—this is a bloodstain, I believe."

"There must be some sweat-stains too," said J'han. He paid his daughter, took the cards out of Zanja's hand, and then presented them back to her. "A humble token of my esteem and gratitude."

Zanja was still smiling as she knelt again on the hearth, tugged the book safely out of range of the crackling flames, and began laying out glyph cards.

Leeba, who came over to watch Zanja lay out the cards, said eagerly, "It's a story!"

"It's a story with half its pieces missing. In fact—" She shuffled through the deck. "Did you take one of the cards? A picture of a person standing halfway in a fire?"

"No." Leeba sat beside her on the hearth and leaned against her. "There's a girl," she said, pointing at the card called Silence. "Why is she so sad?"

"Maybe she has no one to play with."

Through this method of question and answer, the sad girl's story was revealed: how she got herself in trouble due to the lack of a playmate, and how her toy rabbit came alive after being fed a magical tea from a miniature teapot. Leeba leapt up and ran out of the room. J'han, who had been drawing again, commented, "I certainly hope that Emil's traveling tea set is well hidden. Is this a suitable replacement for the missing card?"

He handed her a stiff piece of paper, on which he had carefully drawn the glyph called Death-and-Life, or the Pyre, in the lower left hand corner. Above and around the ancient symbol, he had drawn an anatomically convincing picture of a person half in, half out of a burning fire. The half that was in the fire was skeleton; the other half was a very muscular woman with what appeared to be a bush growing on her head.

Zanja gazed at it until J'han began apologetically, "It's not very artistic."

"It looks like Karis," Zanja said.

"It does?" He looked at his own drawing in surprise. "I guess that makes sense. It is the G'deon's glyph, after all. It's natural I would draw her."

In the kitchen, there was the distinct familiar sound of disaster, followed by the equally familiar sound of Norina losing her temper. J'han rose from his squat, saying mildly, "Hasn't Leeba learned not to drop a kettle when that mother is in the room?" He went off to make peace in the kitchen.

Zanja said to his back, too softly for him to hear, "Karis is everything. But she's not the G'deon."

The parlor windows, double-shuttered against the cold, shut out the light as well. J'han had drawn his pictures by lamplight, but he had thriftily blown out the flame as he left. Now gloom descended, and silence. By flickering firelight, Zanja studied the newly drawn glyph card in her hand. She felt no pity for the woman paralyzed in the flame.

The glyphic illustrations often gave Zanja a path to self-knowledge, but at this moment she was reluctant to acknowledge that she might be pitiless and impatient. For four-and-a-half years—Leeba's entire life—Zanja and Karis had been lovers. Yet Zanja understood Karis less with every passing year. Like the woman in the pyre, who was neither completely consumed nor fully created, Karis remained inexplicably contented. Zanja was the one who could not endure this inaction.

She heard Emil return from his weekly trip to town. With much stamping on the door mat, he announced unnecessarily that it was snowing, and added that according to his watch, which he knew was accurate since he had just set it by the town clock, it was time for tea. Leeba loudly demanded magic tea for her rabbit. The racket brought Medric blundering sleepily down the stairs, to plaintively ask for help finding his spectacles.

"I'm afraid Leeba took them," J'han said. He called rather desperately, "Zanja!"

"I'm coming." She extricated both pairs of Medric's spectacles from Leeba's pile, and forced herself to leave the quiet parlor and step into the chaotic kitchen. There Medric, even more tousled and beleaguered than usual, stood near the stairway peering confusedly into the cluttered room, where Emil fussed over the teapot, Norina sliced bread for J'han to toast, and Leeba managed to be in everyone's way. Zanja set a pair of spectacles onto Medric's nose and put the other into his pocket. "Wrong!" he declared, and, having exchanged the pair in his pocket for the pair on his nose, asked, "Do you think there might be something a bit disordered about our lives?"

"We've got too much talent and not enough sense."

"Really? Is that possible? Well, if you say so." He added vaguely, "Your raven god has been telling me a story about himself. Why is that, do you suppose?"

"Whatever Raven told you," Zanja said, "don't believe a word of it."

Medric managed to appear simultaneously entertained and offended. "I'm not a complete idiot. Not more than halfway, I shouldn't think. I certainly know an untrustworthy god when I meet one!"

Medric had spoken loudly in his own defense, and everyone in the room stopped working to stare at him. Norina displayed her usual expression of unrestrained skepticism, which was only enhanced by the old scar that bisected one cheek and eyebrow. Emil gazed at Medric with amusement and respect. "That is a bizarre pronouncement."

"Isn't it?" An underdeveloped wraith of a man, Medric had

to stretch to get his mouth near Zanja's ear. He whispered, "Raven's joke: nothing changes."

She looked at him sharply, but he had already swept Leeba up in a madman's dance dizzy enough to put all thoughts of magic tea right out of the little girl's head.

The last time Zanja heard the Ashawala'i tale of Raven's Joke, she had been huddled with her clan in a building much more crowded than this one, while the snow, piled higher than the roof, insulated them against the howling wind of a dreadful storm. To her people, the tale had made sense of the maddening stasis of winter. Now, perhaps Medric's vision was admonishing her for her impatience. Or perhaps it was congratulating her for it.

"Where's Karis?" asked Norina.

Emil looked surprised. "You don't know? A raven told me she had gone to town, though I didn't see her there."

The toast was buttered, the tea poured, and the letters distributed from the capacious pockets of Emil's greatcoat. All three men had received letters, for they each kept up a voluminous correspondence. Today, even Norina had a letter, which she viewed with doubtful surprise and seemed disinclined to open. Zanja helped Leeba with her milk and spread jam on her toast, then lay out the glyph cards again.

Once again, she studied Leeba's sad girl, the glyph called Silence. To Zanja, silence signified thought, but to Karis it might signify inarticulateness. What has Silence to do with the Pyre, Zanja wondered? In the Pyre, death becomes life; life becomes death. But if nothing changes, the fire cannot do its work of transformation. Thus the person in the pyre is trapped between death and life, and cannot speak at all, not even to say, Help me.

In the hush, it almost seemed Zanja could hear the snowflakes floating down and settling outside the door. She was aware that Medric, across the table from her, was only pretending to read his letter. Then Norina, who had finally broken the seal of her letter, uttered a snort, Emil grunted, and J'han folded up a letter with apparent satisfaction. "The trade in smoke appears to be in a serious decline," he announced.

"Of course it is," said Emil. "Haven't you healers cured almost every smoke addict in the land, now that you know how to do it?" He tapped his own letter with a fingertip. "Here's something downright strange. Willis, from South Hill—do you recall him?"

Medric had known of Willis but had never met him, Norina had met him only once, and J'han might not remember who he was and what he had done. Zanja responded, though, as if Emil's question had been directed to her. "Willis? Wasn't he the one who shot me, beat me, imprisoned me, called me a traitor, and nearly had me killed? No, I had completely forgotten him."

"I am extremely surprised to hear that," said Emil gravely. "Listen to what my South Hill friend wrote to me: 'We have received some word of Willis at last. He claims to have had a vision of the Lost G'deon! Apparently, he has formed a company of his own, for he believes he has been chosen to single-handedly lead the people of Shaftal in a final battle that will eliminate every last trace of the Sainnites from the land.'"

There was a long, amazed silence. Zanja sat back in her chair and began to laugh. "Oh, Emil, write a letter to Willis and tell him exactly where the Lost G'deon is, and what she is doing."

"Wouldn't you rather tell him yourself?" asked Emil with a grin.

"My letter is just as peculiar," said Norina. "Listen to this: 'I must speak with Karis on a matter of some urgency. I beg you, in the name of Shaftal, to convince her to meet with me as soon as the weather permits travel, in a place of her choosing. Signed, Mabin, Councilor of Shaftal, General of Paladins.'"

Emil, who had just picked up his teacup, set it down again rather sharply. "I don't believe it."

Norina passed him the letter. He examined it closely. "Well, it appears to be Mabin's handwriting."

Norina said, "If Mabin thinks Karis will even be in the same region with her—"

"Mabin must think you can change her mind."

Norina snorted. "Well, the councilor is under a misapprehension."

Medric, to protect his unstable insight, did not drink tea and avoided both fat and sweets, so he had nothing to eat but a piece of dry toast that he had torn into bits. He now sat very quietly with his palms together and his fingertips against his mouth. He returned Zanja's glance, and his spectacles magnified the intentness of his gaze. Even without the seer's expectant look, all these significant letters would have seemed like portents to Zanja. At last, something was going to happen!

Then, they heard the sound of Karis stamping the snow off her boots outside the door. Leeba leaped up, shrieking with joy, making every mug and cup on the table rattle ominously. A flurry of snow followed Karis into the house. The door seemed disinclined to shut, but could not resist her. Karis let Emil help her out of her coat, and bent over so Leeba could brush the snow out of her tangled thicket of hair. The room had shrunk substantially; the furniture looked like toys; even lanky Emil seemed reduced to the size of a half-grown child. If Karis had stood upright, her head would have dented the plaster. But it was not the mere impact of her size that made the house seem to stretch itself, gasping.

Perhaps Karis was immovable, thought Zanja, but she also was unstoppable.

Karis's kiss tasted of snow. "Zanja, the ravens would have told you where I had gone, but you didn't venture out the door. What was I to do? Send a poor bird down the chimney?"

Emil had pulled out a chair for Karis. The chair groaned under her weight, and groaned again as Leeba crawled into her lap. Zanja pushed over her own untasted toast and untouched cup of tea, both of which Karis dispatched before Emil could bring her the teapot and bread plate.

"There's an illness in town," Karis said. "And there's going to be a lot more of it. And not just here." She tapped a forge-blackened fingertip on the tabletop. "Here," she said. "Here. And here."

J'han examined the table's surface as though he could see the map of Shaftal that to Karis was as real and immediate as the landscape outside the door.

"And here," Karis added worriedly, tapping a finger in the west.

Leeba peered at the tabletop, then up at Karis. "What's wrong with the table?"

"Illness doesn't spread like that," J'han objected. "Not in winter, anyway. Sick people can't travel far in the snow—so illness doesn't travel far, either." He frowned at the scratched, stained surface of the table.

"It was already there," Karis said. "It was waiting."

"Then it could be waiting in other places, too."

"Yes."

J'han stood up. "I'll start packing."

Karis nodded. She said belatedly to her daughter, "Leeba, there's nothing wrong with the table."

"You said the table is sick!"

"No, it's Shaftal that's sick."

Leeba looked dubiously at the tabletop.

Emil, busy smearing jam on toast almost as fast as Karis could eat it, gave Zanja a thoughtful, level look. He was worrying about Shaftal—he always was. *How will this illness affect the balance of power in Shaftal?* He was probably wondering. *Will it show us a way to peace?*

Zanja plucked a card from her deck, but the glyph her fingers chose to lay down on the table did not seem like an answer to Emil's unspoken question. It was the Wall, usually interpreted as an insurmountable obstacle: an obdurate symbol that in a glyph pattern often meant utter negation. She could not think of what, if anything, the glyph might mean at this moment.

From the other side of the table, Medric said, "That glyph looks upside down to me."

"Maybe you're upside down," Zanja said.

"Maybe you are," Medric replied solemnly.

Zanja considered that comment. If it was intended as a criticism, it certainly was gentle enough. She said to Karis, "I'm coming with you and J'han."

Before Karis could reply, Medric said, "Pack carefully,

Zanja. I'll go copy a few pages of Koles for you to bring with you. It'll keep you preoccupied for months."

"For months?" Karis asked sharply.

Medric waggled his eyebrows. "Oh, and I've thought of another book you had better bring along." He headed back upstairs to his library. A notorious waster of time, he could be quite efficient when he had to be.

Norina said, "Karis, you have to look at this letter and tell me what to do with it." She pushed it across the table.

As Zanja left the kitchen to start packing, Karis was already reading Mabin's letter. A moment later, Zanja heard her utter a sharp shout of laughter.

❈ ❈ ❈ ❈ ❈ ❈ ❈ ❈ ❈ ❈ ❈ ❈ ❈ ❈

Chapter Two

In the hot kitchen of the Smiling Pig Inn, Garland had finished feeding everyone and was starting the stock for tomorrow's soup when the serving girl bustled in and informed him that a dozen people had just arrived. They had taken all the places closest to the fire, which had left the regular customers feeling put out. Garland had to make a lot of fried potatoes, and the girl nagged him to hurry up. "Give them some soup," he told her. "You know they'll complain even louder if I serve them scorched raw potatoes."

"No one's fussier about their food than you are," the girl said, and Garland took that as a compliment. She filled bowls with bean soup and would have forgotten to sprinkle them with bacon crumbs and caramelized onions if Garland hadn't stopped her. She complied, rolling her eyes with exasperation.

"They're already asking about tomorrow's breakfast," the girl reported when she returned with the empty bowls. "They have to leave at first light, they say. And they want to carry dinner with them when they go."

"First light? Who's in that big a hurry at this time of year?"

"They're skating the ice road all the way to the coast, and the old timers are telling them the ice will break up any day now."

Garland's heart sank. When the ice broke up, it would be spring. And what would become of him then?

"The potatoes are done," he said. "Take those plates out of the warming oven, will you?" He served, swiftly, slices of crispy roast pork, mounds of crackling fried potatoes, and scoops of steaming pudding, all in the time it took the girl to ladle out the boiling applesauce. Five months Garland had been cooking in this kitchen, from first snow to last, and no one had yet complained that their food was cold. In fact, no one had complained at all, and many had asked for more.

"Help me with this!" the girl said impatiently. Garland glanced around to make certain there was nothing on the stove or in the oven that demanded his immediate attention, picked up a tray, and followed her out into the public room.

The room was crowded, and everyone huddled as close to the fireplace as they could get. It might have been nearly spring, but that didn't prevent the wind from blowing hard and bitter enough to find a way in through stone and mortar. People had taken off their coats and gloves, but tucked their hands in their armpits and loudly demanded that another log be added to the fire.

"Here's supper," the girl called cheerily. "Sizzling hot! Take the cold right out of your bones!"

"Is that the cook?" someone asked. "That was a fine soup."

The newcomers crowded the trestle table. "Yow!" cried one young woman as she burned her tongue on a piece of potato. It seemed an unlikely group to be taking such a long, fast journey together, Garland thought as he distributed the hot plates. Members of a farm family usually bore a regional resemblance to each other even if they were only related by marriage, but these people did not look much alike. And in any case, it would be unusual for so many members of a single family to travel together like this. Garland had learned a little about farming during his years of wandering: a farmstead that missed spring planting time because its farmers were on a trip was surely heading for disaster.

The way they passed the plates to each other revealed a peculiar hierarchy. Among Shaftali, the hierarchy should be determined by age, but here the man most fussed over was not the oldest. While fetching salt cellars and mustard pots, Garland kept glancing at him surreptitiously, noting how everyone fell silent to listen to his trivial remarks.

Back in the kitchen, Garland cubed the leftover pork and mixed it with parboiled vegetables to make a filling for turnovers. He put together a sturdy dough—a tricky business to make a dough strong without making it tough—and seeded it with dried rosemary before breaking it into fist-sized balls and rolling them out.

The girl came in, and before she opened her mouth Garland said, "Bring them slices of dried apple pie. There's clotted cream in the pantry." He crimped the edges of the first turnover, and sprinkled it with a bit of salt.

"Is that for their dinner tomorrow?" the girl asked as she got the pies out of the warming oven. "Will it taste good cold?"

"Well, I'm spicing it up a little more than I would if it were eaten hot, and if those people have got any sense they'll keep their dinner inside their coats so it doesn't freeze."

Garland flinched as the girl lost control of the pie server and wrecked what would have been a lovely slice of pie. "Who cares what it looks like?" the girl said impatiently.

Garland said, "So what do you think about those people? Are they Paladins?"

"They must be." The girl frowned with concentration as she served out the dollops of cream. Garland had tried to teach her how to make each spoonful a work of art, but the lesson didn't seem to have taken hold.

"That looks nice," he said, to encourage her.

"You're an odd sort of man," she replied irritably, and then added, "It's peculiar to see Paladins traveling at this time of year, don't you think? Usually they winter with their families, don't they, like ordinary people?"

This comment may not have been intended as a criticism of Garland's irregular status, but he didn't reply, and pretended to be having difficulty with the turnover dough. The girl finally said apologetically, "I guess some people don't have families."

A person who lacked a family was assumed to be at fault, and so most vagabonds made some effort to counteract this social disapproval by concocting ornate tales of family tragedy or betrayal that made them look like victims or heroes. However, Garland did not know enough about Shaftali families to be able to conduct such an elaborate pretense, so he always declared that his past was too painful to talk about. For nearly five years, that approach had kept people from prying, but it also had kept them from even considering offering Garland a permanent home. He was lucky to have this temporary position, lucky that the innkeeping family had found themselves unexpectedly short-handed when Garland happened to be wandering through last summer. But two young people would be marrying into the innkeeping family come spring, and both of them were reported to be competent cooks.

Garland sometimes wondered what would happen if he told someone he was a Sainnite. It seemed to him the truth should earn him sympathy, but he thought it much more likely the truth would get him killed. Those Paladins out there in the public room, for instance, who even now were gobbling up his delectable pie, they would nod with satisfaction, belching as they washed his blood from their hands. "One less monster in Shaftal," they might say. "Too bad he was such a good cook."

Later, with the pots washed, the leftovers in the cold cupboard, and the next morning's bread dough rising in the lingering warmth of the oven, Garland finally got around to serving himself a little supper, and went out into the public room to eat it. Most of the guests had left for home or gone to bed, but the twelve ice travelers remained; some huddled by the good oak fire still trying to get warm, while others took turns sharpening their skate blades. Garland went to sit at an empty table, but someone called, "Hey, cook!"

It was the Paladin commander, beckoning him over. "No, bring your meal and join us. It's warmer over here."

Garland protested to no effect. One of the Paladins had already risen to make room for him, and he found himself seated beside the commander. His appetite evaporated. He knew his Shaftalese was as good as anyone's; he knew his appearance was nothing extraordinary, both language and appearance having been given him by his Shaftali mother. But he did not particularly trust his ability to tell believable lies.

"You're awfully thin for a cook," the commander commented. "Are you just getting a chance to eat?"

"It's been a busy night," Garland said. He took a spoonful of the soup, and though he analyzed its construction—the onions were bitter, but that couldn't be avoided at this time of year— he did not actually enjoy the taste. He glanced sideways at the commander. Older than Garland, probably in his forties, the commander had a rough look about him: a face burned to leather by wind and sun, an untrimmed, grizzled beard, and tangled hair. Garland noticed no piercings in the man's earlobe. He looked again to make sure, and accidentally caught the man making a similar survey of him.

"I'm Willis," said the commander, and introduced some of the others nearby.

"I hear you're skating to the coast," said Garland.

The others energetically recounted tales of their journey, and in the telling made their chilly, effortful trip seem more adventurous than miserable. Garland managed another sneaking glance at the commander. He did not even have scars on his earlobe from old piercings. Most Paladins were irregulars, recruited into the war after the Fall of the House of Lilterwess some twenty years before, but Garland had often heard that Mabin would promote to commander only those who had taken Paladin vows, as this man apparently had not. So these people were not Paladins after all. But what were they?

Willis turned to Garland, who hastily jammed a chunk of meat into his mouth. "We hear you're not one of the innkeepers. You're a wandering man, taken in for the winter."

Garland nodded, chewing.

"You've put some fine food in front of us tonight—" He looked around, and his companions uttered enthusiastic confirmations—excessively enthusiastic, Garland thought.

"Thank you," he mumbled, and stuffed in another bite.

"So what is it you're seeking? What would it take to end your wandering?"

It was a shocking question, and not only because Garland realized he was being recruited. He swallowed, and said carefully, "Sir, fact is I'm a coward."

Garland had surprised Willis in return, he saw, and this was not a man who liked to be surprised. "Cowardice? There's no such thing! People who believe enough in what they're doing, that belief overrides fear. That's what bravery is. You just need something worth believing in."

The serving girl had gone to bed and wasn't around to come to Garland's rescue. If he suddenly declared he had to check something in the kitchen, it would raise suspicions rather than fool anyone. Garland said, "I do believe in something: food. And I'm still a coward."

Willis apparently decided Garland had to be joking, and uttered a hearty laugh that all his sycophants echoed just as heartily.

"Give me your hand, brother," said Willis. Helpless to refuse, Garland reluctantly let his hand be clasped. Willis's hand was warm, rough, his grip strong. "I'm going to tell you something that happened to me," said Willis. "And when I'm done, you'll have something to believe in."

For a single, dreadful moment, Garland felt himself begin to slip. These people wanted him. And wasn't that, after all, what Garland sought? He wanted it so badly he almost could believe it was possible he could belong with these—but what were they? Garland applied himself desperately to his plate, thinking that the sooner he finished, the sooner he could claim exhaustion and take himself off to bed.

It quickly became apparent he would run out of food before Willis ran out of words. "I was a wandering man like you, once," Willis began. "You remember all that business in South Hill, five years ago? Well, you must have heard about the Wilton garrison being burned down, at least."

Garland had heard about it, all right. That had happened in his first months as a deserter, the first summer that Cadmar had been general. Garland hadn't yet learned to trust his ability to disguise himself as Shaftali. People's anger at the Sainnites had been running high that year, and with every reported atrocity in South Hill, it had risen even higher. Never mind that the Sainnites had taken as bad a beating as they had given—their garrison practically burned to the ground, and who knows how many seasoned soldiers killed or disabled. Of course Garland could not ask someone to explain to him why, if the violence in

Shaftal was such a terrible thing, no one became outraged at, or even mentioned, those dead Sainnites.

Willis had been telling him about his own involvement in the events in South Hill, and Garland didn't want to care or pay attention. Now Willis was saying, "And that was cowardice. That commander was always holding back. And Mabin, backing him up, that was cowardice too."

Garland looked up from his nearly empty plate, shocked. Even among the Sainnites, Councilor Mabin was a legend. Someone else at the table said swiftly, "Oh, Mabin is a great leader, no doubt about that! But perhaps she has lost her vision. Thousands of fighters she's got at her command—maybe not as many as there are soldiers, but close enough—and yet she won't let them take offensive action. A few decisive blows is all that would be required!"

"She doesn't believe enough," someone else murmured. "She doesn't believe in Shaftal enough."

These other voices fell immediately silent as Willis took up his tale again. "So I left South Hill. And for a good long while, I confess I was giving in to despair. I don't know how long you've been without a family, but for me a year was nearly enough to kill me. There I was, half frozen in an inn like this one, begging someone to spare me a penny so I could eat a bit of bread. Well, you know, it leaves a person thinking that he really is of no account. And that was when I heard the story of the Lost G'deon."

Garland looked around himself. Everyone at the table appeared transported by devotion. After all this talk of courage and belief, Garland belatedly realized what these people had actually meant. They believed—he'd never seen anything like it before—and what they believed in was a story. Garland had heard the story, of course, but when he had heard it the first time—that same winter, apparently, that Willis had first heard it—he had given it no importance. He had thought that this wild tale of a big woman piercing Mabin in the heart with a steel spike was just another legend about the Councilor's astonishing ability to survive. But eventually Garland had figured out why Shaftali people were enthralled by this story, a reason that several people at the table were now repeating in an eager chorus: "Only the G'deon can spike someone's heart and leave the heart still beating. Only the G'deon can do it, without a trial, to put that person's life in the G'deon's hands."

"And a question came to me," said Willis, his voice more and more taking on the sonority of speechmaking rather than conversation. "I thought to myself, if there's a G'deon in Shaftal, then why does she not act to free us of the Sainnite curse? Why does she spike the heart of our brave, much admired general? And then she came to me, the Lost G'deon herself."

"You've met her?" Garland cried.

"A vision," impatiently muttered the woman at his left. Apparently, this was not the proper time to interrupt Willis.

"She came to me," continued Willis. "And she said, 'Don't you see, you fool? Mabin has failed Shaftal. And so have you,' she said to me. 'But I'm giving you one last chance. Act decisively! Rid Shaftal at last of the Sainnites that befoul the blessed land! Eliminate the Sainnites, and I will come at last. Do not make me wait!'" Willis's voice had risen to a shout; now he lowered it to a murmur. "That's what she said. And I was pierced by her words, I say, pierced to the heart. And from that day on I've lived only to do the G'deon's will."

He turned to Garland, no doubt to check the effect of his words before he delivered the final persuasive speech that probably had convinced each of his devoted followers to join the company.

Garland stood up. "Good luck to you!" He fled, even leaving his dirty plate behind. He ran full tilt up the stairs to his bedroom in the chilly attic, and bolted the door for the first time since he had become a resident. They could easily kick down the door, of course, but the innkeeper family would surely not stand for that. Surely not!

His sweat was ice cold. He was shaking so he could hardly stand, but was too terrified to sit. His ears ached with listening, but he heard only the sound of the roof creaking the way it always did on a windy night.

After some hours he finally convinced himself to get into bed, and, some hours after that, to fall asleep. His dreams were full of bloodshed. He ran and ran, but wherever he fled, his mother's people and his father's people were in battle with each other. And then Shaftali and Sainnite both turned on him crying out, "No one of your heritage will ever cook for us!" "So what?" he replied, absurdly. "At the rate you're killing each other, there soon will be no one to cook for!"

He awoke late, with an innkeeper pounding on his door, and by the time he stumbled downstairs, Willis and his people were long gone.

※ ※ ※ ※ ※ ※ ※ ※ ※ ※ ※ ※ ※ ※ ※ ※

Chapter Three

A soldier's life swings between boredom and terror. Even though Lieutenant-General Clement had endured thirty-five dull winters in Shaftal, she still preferred the boredom. But oh, she yearned for sunshine—though not for the renewal of conflict that would accompany better weather.

Surely I am old enough to know that there's no point in wanting anything, she thought.

As she stepped into the spare quarters that housed the General of Sainnites in Shaftal, she could hear the hollow clangor of the midday bell. Cadmar, though he had even less to do at this time of year than Clement did, was just getting around to shaving. Peering into a tiny round mirror, he deftly turned his face this way and that to follow the track of the razor. His chin glimmered with a white frost of stubble where he had not yet shaved, and he had to stretch his sagging skin for the razor. "Well?" he said, without looking at Clement.

"Nothing to report, General."

He grunted and gestured with his razor in the direction of his table, on which sat a dented, soot-smeared tea kettle. Clement crossed the chilly room to the even chillier bay window, where one shutter hung open to let in what passed for light. Soldiers desperate for something to do had recently refinished Cadmar's battered table, and its surface now shone like ice and was just about as slick. As Clement poured herself tea, the heavy pottery mug nearly slid over the table's edge.

The tea did not steam as it poured, and no warmth seeped from the mug into Clement's cold-numbed hand.

"Do you want some tea, Gilly?" she asked the general's lucky man, who sat like a blasted crow on his stool.

"Not if the tea is cold," Gilly said, without looking up. He turned a page, squinting in the dim light.

"You need spectacles."

Cadmar, still peering into his tiny mirror, uttered a snort. "Spectacles wouldn't help his appearance any!"

"They couldn't hurt," said Gilly absently.

Gilly was a hideous man. His face and form might have been put through the wringers in a laundry and then frozen in that twisted, crumpled state. His face was crooked, his eyes uneven, his ears out of level, his shoulders hunched in a position of permanent furtiveness, his spine so contorted it seemed amazing he could stand, even with the support of a sturdy cane. However, Clement was oblivious to Gilly's ugliness except when Cadmar amused himself by pointing it out. Cadmar had plucked the ugly beggar boy out of a Hanishport gutter thirty years ago, but it was Clement who, by defending him from the soldiers' abuse, had won his lifelong friendship.

The Sainnites had still believed then that every winter in Shaftal would be their last. Any day now, they believed, they would conquer this land of stubborn farmers, and offer the subjected country to one of the lords of Sainna as a bribe to let the exiled soldiers come home. In the early years, none of them could have imagined that they would die of old age in a still-unconquered land.

Clement drank the cold tea and half listened to Cadmar's tedious account of the various bouts he had fought in the training ring that morning. Fortunately, Clement's smaller size had always excused her from being the big man's training partner. Though she often wished to pummel him, it was more likely to be the reverse: no one admired Cadmar's acumen, but his prowess as a fighter was beyond doubt.

Cadmar began telling old, often repeated jokes that he had heard in the men's bathhouse. Gilly finally looked up from his

book and rescued Clement with a comment about the storm
that was approaching. They argued amicably about whether or
not this winter was lingering longer than the last, until Cadmar, impatient with any conversation that was not about him,
dismissed her.

"Gods be thanked," muttered Clement after the door was
shut behind her.

However, she had nothing else to do. She had tended the
flower bulbs that bloomed on her windowsill; her quarters
were pristine, her uniforms clean and mended, and she had
bathed herself and changed her bed linens only yesterday. That
morning she had attended the gathering of the garrison's senior officers, who were themselves desperate to create new
projects to divert the soldiers from picking fights with each
other.

They were all half mad with cold and confinement and the
bad humors that move like evil spirits from one barracks to the
next. But Clement doubted that anyone had more cause for
wretchedness than she had. For five years, she and Gilly had
conspired to keep a dreadful truth secret from everyone but
Cadmar. And Cadmar sustained his own equanimity by listening selectively or, when that failed, by re-shaping the inconvenient facts into a comforting new form.

The man was a marvel, really.

Clement started down the hall. She would take a walk before
the storm confined her indoors again. At the front door, she
found that the soldiers on watch duty had already taken shelter
in the anteroom. "It's gotten awfully cold out there,
Lieutenant-General," one warned. Clement set her teeth and
stepped out the door into the rising wind. By the gods, it was a
bitter day! Surely, if the Sainnites had arrived at Shaftal in
winter rather in summer, they would have simply expired
of cold.

Winters in their homeland, Sainna, had been little more than
interruptions in the growing season. In Sainna there had been
lush croplands, vineyards, fat cows in green fields. And there
had been soldiers, fighting in the service of one or another
bloodthirsty lord, killing each other over possession of one or

another tract of land. In Sainna, Clement had been born in a child-crowded hovel outside a garrison, and had never been certain which of the four constantly pregnant women had given birth to her. She regularly saw her siblings sold to soldiers, then one day was herself sold to a new mother, Gabian, who took her into the garrison to become a soldier. A couple of years later, their entire battalion was forced to sea, and they became refugees.

Clement remembered riding on her mother's back as they ran for the docks with an army at their heels. She had been eight, or maybe nine years old. She did not know she was screaming with fear until her mother put her down on the ship's deck and slapped her to make her be quiet. After that, a blur of seasickness, bad water and worse food, and a single clear memory of being brought above deck to see some gigantic fishes, bigger than the ship. Their ship had run aground on the rocky, inhospitable coast of Shaftal, and Clement arrived in her new land by being heaved out of a longboat and dumped onto the sand, along with several other children and a great pile of armor, weaponry, and supplies. One of the soldiers who rowed that boat repeatedly through treacherous waters so as to unload the wrecked ship of its supplies and passengers had been as a god to her: a big, golden-haired young man whose great muscles gleamed with freezing spray, whose blue eyes glinted with joy when a jagged rock or towering breaker challenged his strength. That man had been Cadmar.

It had been high summer then, but the Sainnites had soon learned the bitter facts about Shaftal's weather. Today, the wind felt sharp enough to trim the skin off Clement's face. She pulled the muffler up to her eyes, jammed her hat down over her ears, and set out across the sand-strewn ice. She walked briskly, giving every appearance of having a destination, exchanging greetings with the few soldiers unfortunate enough to have outdoor business. Most of the five hundred here in Watfield Garrison would be in the barracks, huddled together under blankets rather than using their day's ration of fuel, grumbling, arguing, gambling, and telling each other the same worn-out stories over and over again.

Clement walked a half-circuit of the garrison. At the edge of a wasteland of snow, she perched on an ice-encased stone bench and tried to imagine the garden that would emerge here in the spring. The flower bulbs she had inherited from her soldier mother were planted under this snow. That they would soon bloom seemed unbelievable.

The cold had taken hold of her very bones when the gray sky blithely began scattering stars of snow across her lap. She broke her own torpor by cursing the weather, and then, because it made her feel better, continued to curse as she walked, starting with her enemies, but not neglecting her friends and herself. She cursed everyone in Shaftal while she was at it, and everyone who had ever been born, and only stopped short of cursing the gods because her angry, snow-kicking perambulation had finally brought her near enough to the gate that one of the guards might have noticed and been perplexed by her behavior.

The gate, just then being shoved open to admit a new arrival, contained the city beyond in an illusory cage composed of its heavy iron bars: the narrow street, the high, steep-roofed buildings that seemed ghostly and restless in the falling snow. In those buildings, the people of Watfield did whatever they did—tirelessly busy, indifferent to weather, oblivious to the threatening presence of the garrison. Artisans, shopkeepers, builders, brokers—they worked hard, ate well, lived comfortably, and followed rules or laws that Clement simply could not comprehend, no matter how often Gilly explained them to her.

Clement walked over to the gate captain and pulled aside her muffler so he could see her face in case snow had obscured the insignia on her hat. He saluted casually—after five years it was generally known that Clement didn't share Cadmar's obsession with protocol—and said, "It's a messenger from Han."

"Han? That's a journey of a good twelve days."

"In good weather," said the captain, "on a clear road. But it took this soldier some twenty days, she says. She sure walks like she has a case of frostbite. Here, you, soldier!"

The limping messenger blundered her way to the captain

and made a vague gesture that might have been a salute. The captain said, "This is Lieutenant-General Clement. You can give your message to her."

The messenger peered at Clement, apparently snow-blind, and asked hoarsely, "You're Clement?"

Clement had once known every soldier in Han Garrison, but she did not recognize this woman. "I'm afraid I am. Have you got a packet somewhere inside all those clothes? Let's get you out of this weather, eh?"

"Take her in the barracks," said the captain, gesturing so Clement would know which barracks he meant. "They're having a birthday party on the men's side, if you don't mind a bit of noise."

"Whose wretched luck was it to be born in this dreadful month?"

The captain grinned. "Eliminate all the dreadful months and you wouldn't have many left for people to be born in."

Clement took the messenger by the elbow and led her to shelter. In the cold trap it was not much warmer than it was outside, but further inside, the coals in the fireplace still gave off a little heat. The room was plain, low ceilinged for warmth, with its windows caulked shut and insulated with straw and burlap. The neat room, crowded with beds, smelled as bad as might be expected, of dirty linens, unwashed chamber pots, and used blood rags. The messenger took a deep breath of the stink and said hoarsely, "Home."

"Knock some of that snow off your clothes, will you, and I'll get these coals to flame a bit."

On the other side of the dividing wall, the company was enthusiastically, if tunelessly, thumping and shouting their way through the last verse of a particularly raunchy birthday song. The cake they ate would be gluey at best, since Cadmar had driven away Watfield Garrison's talented cook some five years ago.

When Clement commanded Han Garrison during the three years she had managed to get herself out from behind Cadmar, the entire garrison had turned out to sing to her on her birthday every year. Then the old general died, Cadmar was elected to replace him, and he gave Clement her unwelcome promotion. Now, no one cared when it was her birthday.

"I'm glad to see you," Clement said to the exhaustion-addled messenger, now the fire was burning. "You've distracted me from poisoning myself with pity."

"Eh?" the messenger said. "It's dark in here, isn't it?"

Clement brought the messenger to the fire, unbuttoned her coat, and sat her down on a stool. "Can you see my insignias now? So you believe who I am?"

The messenger peered blurrily at Clement's hat. "All right." She plucked a packet from the inner pocket of her coat, releasing with her movements a stink of sweat and another smell that reminded Clement unpleasantly of rotten meat. The woman handed Clement the packet, then toppled messily off the stool.

Startled, Clement felt the woman's greasy skull to make certain she hadn't cracked her head open. Her head felt scalding hot. She left the woman collapsed on the hearth, head pillowed on stone and one leg still tangled in the stool, and shouted out the door at a passing soldier to fetch a medic. Then, she broke open the packet and read its contents by the dim, glittering light of the snowstorm.

Commander Taran had written with the unapologetic terseness of extreme duress. "An epidemic has overcome the garrison, a hideous illness so swift and vicious I fear for all our lives."

"Gods of hell!" Clement cried. She dropped the letter, slammed her fist through the thick skin of ice over the water in the bucket, and plunged in both her hands. A yellow bar of soap lay nearby; she whacked it on the floor to break it loose from its dish, and began vigorously scrubbing her hands. But she could not think how to scrub the woman's contaminated breath out of her lungs.

"An epidemic could do us in," she muttered. "Bloody hell!"

The stricken woman uttered some ugly, choking sounds and flailed her arms vaguely. The fetor of the room was overlaid by the appalling stink of vomit.

"Did you have to be such a hero?" Clement asked her. "Couldn't you have died on the road?"

The woman's aimless movements stilled. Clement slammed open the barracks door and again shouted for help. The snow, falling heavily now, swallowed her voice, but eventually a shape approached out of the white curtain, and she told the soldier to fetch the guard captain.

"The entire gate watch goes into immediate isolation," she told the captain. "Send someone who had no contact with the messenger to inform Commander Ellid."

"You'll have to be isolated too, Lieutenant-General."

"Aye," she said glumly. "Better inform the general of that fact."

The stricken messenger died before the day was out. When the dead woman was undressed, the medic found a horror: a gruesome sore in the armpit that seeped pus and stank of rot, and black marks like the footprints of a fell creature that had marched across her belly and thighs. They burned the body, the clothing, and everything the messenger had touched, and the entire contents of the barracks in which she had collapsed. The company that had lived there was relocated, and Clement and her unlucky fellows were locked in, without even a window through which to watch the world melt its way from depressing snow to appalling mud. For twenty days they endured each other's company, playing cards or listening to Clement read out loud Gilly's wry and witty daily letter, which he illustrated with unflattering caricatures of people they all knew.

At first, the confined soldiers were so anxious that every sneeze or cough seemed a death knell, and to complain of an itch or a pain was to be condemned to days of avoidance—not easy in these cramped quarters. However, after a few days in which none of them experienced a worse affliction than boredom, they began making a joke of this enforced idleness. Clement gave up fretting over Han Garrison, since there was nothing to be done. Often, she found herself actually enjoying the company of her fellow soldiers. She had not slept in a barracks in at least twenty years, but the members of this company had lived together for so long that they had blunted each other's sharp edges years ago. Though Clement, along with the medic, got the usual courteously distant treatment accorded outsiders, the conviviality was still comforting enough to make her nostalgic for the days when the members of her company had constituted her entire world.

By the end of her confinement, five more messengers had arrived bearing news of garrisons devastated by illness. The messengers were all quarantined in a dank basement, where two had died, while the other three idled away the time and complained about the food. In the quagmire of the garden, bright green spikes had broken through, and Clement, along with most of the soldiers in the garrison, checked every day to see if any bulbs were blooming yet. It rained, and rained, and rained.

Seeking Gilly in the archives, Clement trotted through a downpour with a packet of papers inside the oiled leather of her coat to protect it from the wet. The archives were in a massive storeroom near the stables: a dusty, cluttered, mildewed space in which the shelves crowded so close together that it was almost impossible to pass between them. Gilly had visited the archives only once before and had declared the place a hopeless trash pile of worm-eaten paper. Now, Clement found him crouched miserably in the dank room at an unsteady table, leafing through hundreds of deteriorating documents with a girl soldier fresh out of the children's garrison to do his fetching and carrying.

"All the messengers are still well today," said Clement, as she sat beside Gilly. Gilly hushed her, jerking a thumb towards a lamplit corner, where his young assistant was shuffling papers. In a low voice he asked, "And no one in Watfield Garrison is sick yet?"

"No. Nor anyone in town, either, I'm told. But in some towns, as many as half the people are sick."

"And it's an ugly way to die." Gilly stretched his crooked back, grunting with pain. "Look at this, will you?" He opened a leather-bound book and showed her how an enterprising mouse had made herself a cozy nest inside some garrison's old logbook. Six naked mouse babies lay in the hollow chewed out between the covers, curled in a bed of shredded paper. "Sometimes I think this is all these books are good for," said Gilly. "But I have learned a few things—nothing very useful, yet. You soldiers probably brought this illness with you from Sainna. I've learned that."

"But this thing is killing Shaftali people as well."

"Do you think an illness can pick and choose between you and me?" His bitter gaze mocked her.

"But we came from Sainna over thirty years ago. Where has this illness been hiding?"

"What do you expect of me, Clem? If you need expert understanding, you'll have to bring a Shaftali healer back from the dead to consult with."

For Clement to actually be able to resolve one of the problems that were her unfortunate responsibility was a rare event. "As requested," she said, gloating as she put the thick packet in front of him.

"What? What is this?"

"Well, I can't read it, since it's in Shaftalese. But someone handed it through the gate at first light, and told the guard it was from a healer, and that it's about this terrible illness. Cadmar is suspicious, of course. I myself am wondering why a healer would help us, if that's what this is."

"To keep healthy Shaftali from being infected by sick Sainnites," said Gilly, studying the first page. "That's what the healer writes here."

He scanned the documents. "Look: a drawing of a person's insides. This healer is a bit of an artist." Later he said, "Well, here's the answer to why it might take thirty years for the illness to reappear. It's an illness of rats, he says, and only occasionally does it get transmitted from rats to people. Through flea bites. Now I wonder how the healer figured that out."

"A rat illness, carried by fleas? It's bizarre!"

Gilly, apparently fascinated by the healer's exposition, turned back to the anatomical drawing. "This healer says that if a sick person gets big, painful boils here or here"—he pointed at the groin and the armpits—"then the sickness can only be passed from the sick person to the well person by fleas. But if there are no lumps, then the illness is in the lungs, and can be transmitted by the sick person's breath. These are the people who must be quarantined, and they almost certainly will die within a few days of falling ill. The others can be cared for in the infirmary, so long as it's free of fleas, and half of them may survive."

Clement gazed at the drawing in horrified fascination.

"I think this is no fabrication," said Gilly. "This healer writes from a knowledge that far exceeds mine."

"Or maybe it's the healer's imagination that exceeds yours."

"That, too," said Gilly enviously.

They sat in silence for a while, then Gilly called loudly, "Kelin! Come out of your dark corner!"

Clement looked up as a slim girl, bearing a lamp and an armload of documents, approached out of the darkness. Half a year ago, when Kelin was first released from the children's garrison, Commander Purnal, who was usually irascible, had acknowledged her potential with what passed for him as eloquence: "Keep her from getting herself killed." Clement had assigned Kelin to a particularly reliable company, right here in Watfield Garrison. She had wanted to keep an eye on her, for young soldiers did have a way of getting themselves killed. Even though Captain Herme immediately assigned a veteran of his company to look after Kelin, Clement had forbidden the girl to go outside the garrison. Throughout the winter, Gilly had given her an actual education in reading and writing and also in speaking Shaftalese, none of which Commander Purnal bothered to provide his young charges.

In six months, Kelin had never ceased to interest and even delight her guardians. She was eager, high spirited, and unrestrainedly curious. After half a year, the young soldier had an entire battalion of hardened veterans watching out for her as obsessively as any devoted parent. Never had a young woman been more coddled and worried over. Naturally, Kelin complained about it: she was fearless, and could not imagine what her battle-scarred elders were protecting her from.

Kelin stopped short when she saw Clement, and apparently was confused by the problem of how to salute with her hands full. "You can always greet me," Clement said.

"Good afternoon, Lieutenant-General."

"Good afternoon, Kelin. I have been receiving good reports of you."

"I hope so, Lieutenant-General."

"Why don't you put that lamp down before you drop it and set us all on fire?"

"Yes, ma'am." Kelin set down her burdens and said apologetically to Gilly, "Most everything is eaten by bugs or covered with mold."

"Oh, ours was a doomed project from the beginning," said Gilly lightly. "But it's kept us out of the rain, eh? And now the very thing we were looking for has been sent to us by a healer."

Gilly showed Kelin the document, which she studied with interest even though she could read Shaftalese no better than Clement could.

"I thought we killed all the healers," Kelin said.

"Tell me, Kelin," said Gilly. "If there were five hundred healers scattered across Shaftal who looked and dressed exactly like everyone else, and if everyone you talked to was determined to keep their identity and location secret, how exactly would you kill them all?"

"One at a time," said Kelin. "And I wouldn't give up. Or lie about it."

"Never give up, and always tell the truth," said Clement dryly. "It's amazing we didn't try that."

Kelin was more than relieved to be released from the moldy prison, even though it just meant she'd go back to being bruised and humiliated and rolled in the mud by her bunkmates, who were unrelenting in their efforts to improve her weapons skill. With some difficulty, Clement and Gilly con-

vinced Cadmar that following the mysterious healer's recom-
mendations could not cause any harm, and Gilly and the company clerk spent a day copying and re-copying a complicated
general order that, among other things, detailed the care of the
sick, defined methods for killing fleas and domestic rodents,
and recommended that the commanders populate the garrisons
with house cats. In due time, the responses returned that these
measures had proven effective, but that cats were nowhere to
be had. Kittens, one commander reported, were sold before
they were even born, at exorbitant prices. Besides, commented
another commander, what do soldiers know about keeping
cats?

If the soldiers had known something about keeping cats,
thought Clement angrily as she pored over the duty rosters,
maybe the illness wouldn't have reduced their force by another
three hundred irreplaceable fighters. Maybe it was time they
learned.

❈❈❈❈❈❈❈❈❈❈❈❈❈❈

Chapter Four

That year's spring mud was a tortuous season: rain fell and stopped, the roads firmed up, then rain fell again. Many a farmer, thinking the rain had ended, went out to sow the fields, only to watch the precious seeds wash away. Many a wanderer thought it was time to travel, only to be stranded by renewed flooding and boggy roads.

Norina had been spared such frustrations, for though only a water witch could control the weather, an earth witch like Karis could at least predict it. Norina was able to sandwich her journey neatly between rainstorms, and arrived dry and cheerful at her destination. The same could not be said about Councilor Mabin, who arrived on horseback several days later, muddy and wet, taunted by the sunshine that after four days of rain once again rent through the storm clouds and set the sodden fields to sparkling.

Norina had last seen Mabin the year Leeba was born. Since then, the councilor's hair had gone to white, and her vigorous frame had begun to shrink. Her face, however, was no more or less hard and embittered than it had ever been.

The councilor was escorted by a half-dozen black-dressed, gold-earringed Paladins—a rare sight these days, for most of the surviving true Paladins had put on plain clothing and were commanding companies of Paladin irregulars, as Emil had done for fifteen years. Some of these who served Mabin were Emil's age, and they seemed to know of Norina's connection to him, for their inquiring glances asked questions about him:

What has become of our brother Paladin? Why will he not explain his sudden retirement? These sharp looks were puzzled, impatient, but not condemnatory. Just as a Truthken's duty was to judge, a Paladin's was to suspend judgment. With Mabin avoiding putting herself in a position where she would have to answer questions, and with Emil maintaining a bland silence, the Paladins apparently had simply suspended judgment of him, and of Mabin, for five years now.

It was a remarkable exercise of philosophy, Norina thought, and wondered briefly how this paralysis of silence might finally come to an end. Mabin was both an air blood and a Paladin, a rare combination that condemned her to a life-long duel between flexible ethics and rigid principles. The principles won, of course, for one's natural elemental logic would always prevail, and as a result Mabin was often in the exceptionally awkward position of having to ethically justify acts that were grounded in unexamined prejudice. The Paladins in her command certainly would not overlook such intellectual sloppiness. The pain of a steel spike in her heart—that Mabin could bear with equanimity. But the inability to explain how and why it had happened, that must have been almost beyond endurance.

Norina had stood silently without greeting Mabin for some time, and Mabin had neither spoken nor dismounted. The exercise of politeness was an expression of status, after all, and Norina wanted to establish that she was not under Mabin's command as badly as Mabin wished to establish that she was. Norina was about to turn her back and walk away, which certainly would force Mabin to accede, when Mabin said nastily, "Well, Norina, everyone in the region could tell me where to find you. Though I suppose if I had asked the Sainnites in their garrison, they would have been surprised to learn that their region is ruled by a Truthken."

"Oh, no," Norina said. "The Sainnites have put a price upon my head, which goes up every year, much to everyone's amusement."

Mabin dismounted stiffly. The farmers, who had gathered around with their tools in their hands, curtsied unnoticed.

Their work-dirty children stared; only the chickens took no interest in the living legend that had trampled through their muddy farmyard. The family elders invited Mabin into the tea room.

Mabin greeted them, though Norina could see behind the gracious mask to the councilor's resentment at having to waste her time and energy on people she had no use for. Mabin was too canny a campaigner to forget that when the Sainnites left the Paladins devastated, it had been the farmers who had taken up arms and given her an army to command. But when she was finished with courtesy, she muttered, "Little do the farmers suspect that you should be as much an outlaw to them as you are to the Sainnites!"

Norina found this comment no less entertaining for the fact that Mabin apparently believed it true. However, Mabin's truths were extraordinarily difficult to read, for the disguises she cast over her secret motivations were several layers deep. So now, to keep testing her own judgment, Norina said, "Shall we tell these farmers what happened four-and-a-half years ago, and let them judge between us? I will admit that I violated a councilor's edict—never mind that a Truthken isn't much use if she can't challenge and refuse an unlawful command. But you must admit in turn that you tried to murder the vested G'deon."

"I acted for Shaftal's sake," said Mabin.

"You nearly killed Shaftal."

They were about to step through the common house door. Mabin paused and looked at Norina—a deliberate look, deliberately revealing, and no less surprising for all that. "I tried to murder the vested G'deon," she said. She spoke as a repentant criminal, as sincerely as possible, considering that she was not actually convinced of the wrongfulness of her actions.

Norina said, "Councilor, you cannot be hoping to deceive me. But you certainly are surprising me."

An anxious child helped Mabin remove her boots and coat, and Norina showed the way to the tea room, which the family had spent two days cleaning. Now, the new-painted walls glared with reflected sunlight, the rare old Ashawala'i rug's bright colors and ornate pattern had been released from a prison of dust, and the heat of a brisk fire in the scoured fireplace competed with a cool breeze coming in the open window. The sideboard was spread with an extravagant array of morsels: savory dumplings, dried fruit compote, sausage rolls, a steaming loaf of bread and golden pat of butter, a half dozen bowls of jam. But Mabin, noticing none of this, stopped short in the doorway and said sharply, "Where is Karis?"

"Shut the door," said Norina. When Mabin had complied, Norina leaned out the open window. "Raven!"

The raven, who had been lingering at the top of a nearby tree, flew down and landed on the windowsill. "The councilor wants to know where Karis is," Norina said to him.

The raven said, "She is with Zanja and J'han, in the Juras grasslands."

Pretending she had not noticed Mabin's rigid surprise at being confronted with a talking raven, Norina said, "Tell the councilor why she is there."

"Karis has been eradicating a plague, town by town. And now she is fighting the illness among the Juras people."

Norina turned to Mabin. "My husband believes that some half of the people in Shaftal would have been dead by summer's end if Karis hadn't acted so quickly. No one knows to thank her, either, not even the healers, who are winning the battle because J'han has written to all of them to tell them how. So," Norina added, "there's your lesson, Councilor, should you choose to learn it. Do you care to take some tea?"

The silence lingered as Norina poured, offered a cup to Mabin, who appeared not to notice, and sat down at the table with a filled plate. She gave the raven, a big, unlovely bird, a meat dumpling to eat.

Mabin finally said, rather unsteadily, "What is that bird?"

"The raven is Karis," said Norina. "He is her eyes, her ears, her thoughts."

The raven took a pause from gorging itself to ask, "Why did Mabin want this meeting?"

"To berate you," Norina said.

"No, I'm here to be berated, apparently," said Mabin.

"I've always admired your ability to recover from surprise," said Norina politely. "Are you certain you don't want some tea? These dumplings are really quite good."

The councilor came to the table, picked up the teacup Norina had poured, tasted it, then added a half spoonful of sugar. Stirring the cup, she said to the raven, "Tell Karis that what I have to say to her deserves to be said in person. But of course I admire what she is doing, and I don't doubt that it's more important."

"Half true," murmured Norina. "At best."

Mabin said coolly, "Will you be satisfied for once, Madam Truthken? Half truths are all you ever get from anyone." She tasted her tea again and appeared to be considering more sugar. "Karis is acting like a G'deon," she commented.

"Karis is doing what she cannot help but do. She is acting like herself."

There was a silence. Mabin said again, "In acting like herself, she acts like a G'deon. Why does she not call herself what she is?"

Twenty years ago, almost immediately after being vested with the power of Shaftal, Karis had been forbidden to act as G'deon, a decision that could only be reversed by Mabin herself. Yet Mabin was in no position to prevent Karis from doing what she liked, so her question was not quite so absurd as it at first seemed. Norina said, "Are you demanding that she explain herself? Or are you simply sick of trying to anticipate what she'll do?" This strategy of listing possibilities and observing the reaction was usually sufficient to get a reluctant witness to reveal her secrets. But Mabin did not particularly react. "Why are you here?" Norina asked. "It's early spring; the Paladins are sharpening their blades and grinding fresh gunpowder. You have work to do." Now, at last, a momentary trembling of Mabin's disguises. Norina said swiftly, "But you can't do it, can you? No, you can't, and though you've come all this way to ask Karis for her help you can't bring yourself to ask for it. Councilor, why must you make my business so difficult!"

Mabin drank half her cup of tea in a swallow, and didn't flinch. "Perhaps you already know this, but I doubt you understand it. The rumor of a Lost G'deon has inspired a new uprising."

"Are you referring to Willis of South Hill and his little band of fanatics?"

"I'm told he has fifty followers, which means he really has at least two hundred. And most of them are veteran Paladin irregulars, like him, not the kind of people I would lightly dismiss."

Mabin paused, perhaps expecting that Norina would use this opening to continue to accuse and challenge her. "Do continue, Madam Councilor," Norina said.

"If Karis were to join these people who call themselves Death-and-Life, their numbers would immediately swell to thousands. An irresistible army. The Sainnites would be defeated."

Now it was Norina's turn to use her teacup as a prop to make herself seem unsurprised, and even indifferent. But the raven spoiled the effect by uttering a harsh caw of laughter.

Norina said, "And yet you want to prevent this from happening? I thought you wanted to rid Shaftal of its Sainnite scourge."

"Has Karis thought of joining them? She must have heard that they believe the Lost G'deon will appear to them."

"I'll answer you, if you tell me why it would be so terrible if she did. Because you yourself would be put out of power?"

Mabin said quietly, "Although these people call themselves Death-and-Life, they have no alliance to the old ways. They would dismiss the orders, the law, the code—" She paused. "Madam Truthken, I am an old woman, and sometimes I am very tired. Inevitably—soon—I will be put out of power by someone, or by death. But I do not want to die in a land I loved and could not save from destruction."

"Truth!" said Norina, amazed.

Mabin gave her a wry look. "How can you waste such talent?"

"It's no waste to serve Karis, I assure you."

"Who also wastes her talent."

"She's saving the land from being devastated by plague."

"Saving it for what?"

"This is a fruitless argument," Norina said.

"Will she join these people who call themselves Death-and-Life? Or not?"

"Of course not. They are war-mongers, and war makes her sick."

But Mabin did not seem relieved. She set down the empty teacup on the table, and took a breath. "I want Karis to know that I regret that she was hurt by the way she was treated in the past. I thought I was acting for the best—"

"I listen to people try to justify themselves all day long," Norina said. "I wish I might meet one who could do it with brevity."

"What I did was wrong," Mabin said. "I wish to ask Karis to come to me, to the Lilterwess Council, and take her rightful place in the G'deon's chair."

A long time Norina gazed at her, but, although she was not certain what had caused this amazing reversal, she could see no sign of dissimulation. Even the raven stared at her, speechless. "The last time I saw you," Norina said, "you declared that Shaftal would never come into the hands of a Sainnite pretender, the smoke-addicted daughter of a whore. Those are your words, exactly as you uttered them."

"Karis no longer uses smoke. Her mother was of an ancient, respected people. I would wish Karis a non-Sainnite father, but so might she." Mabin seemed to realize how self-serving these corrections on her past statement might sound, and added, "I'm very sorry for those angry words. I was mistaken. And I was wrong."

Norina turned to the raven in astonishment. "Did Karis think she'd live to see this day? How shall I reply? Does she want to know why Mabin has changed her mind? Or does it even matter?"

The raven said, "Give her the note."

Norina found herself reluctant. "The councilor has made a sincere apology."

"Give her the note."

Karis had written the note many weeks ago, shortly before she, Zanja, and J'han stepped into the snowstorm. She had not asked for Emil's advice on how to deal with Mabin's request. She had simply written three words on a piece of paper, which Norina took out of a pocket now and handed to Mabin. "Leave me alone," Karis had written.

Mabin read the note and then crossed the room, threw it into the fire, and watched it burn. When she turned back, though, she seemed calm enough. She said to the raven, "Haven't I already left her alone, these four years? And not because I feared this." Her hand briefly touched her breast, where Karis's steel pierced her heart. "She'll regret making this choice. What is happening in Shaftal is worse than a plague."

"There is no choice," the raven said.

Mabin turned to Norina, who read in her face an honest desperation. "Will she give up Shaftal to Willis, rather than give up her anger against me? Will you knowingly allow her to do so? And will even Emil fail to intervene? Does every one of Karis's followers think loyalty must be blind?"

"We are not her followers, and we argue with her and with each other incessantly. I don't know how Emil would advise Karis, but he certainly would disagree with you about the way you have conceived these choices. We air bloods are always drawing neat lines through everything, as though dividing good from bad and right from wrong were a simple business. When I first began to live with three fire bloods, I feared their chaos of possibilities would drive me insane! My companions live courageously, in doubt and loss and desperate uncertainty, and I've come to tolerate their thinking and even to admire it sometimes. But your way, Councilor, is too simple. If Karis refuses to restore the old order, and also refuses to embrace the war-mongers, why does that mean she has no other options?"

There was a silence. Mabin said, "I used to have arguments just like this with Harald. Might as well argue with a wall. Shout all I want, the wall is unmoved." She turned away as though to leave the room, and then turned back. "Karis is the hope of Shaftal. How can she refuse?"

Norina said wearily, "When I was young and knew no better, I delivered Karis to you, and betrayed her without knowing it by pressuring her into obedience. I am fortunate that she forgave me for it. But she is in her full power now, and even I don't know exactly what that means. Only a fool would trifle with her—and I am not a fool anymore."

"I'm not asking you to betray her, just to remind her," Mabin said. "When the day comes that she can leave her bitterness against me behind, remind her that I said I would acknowledge her."

"I will remind her, Mabin, though a reminder will not be necessary."

When Councilor Mabin had left the room, taken her leave of the farmers, and ridden off with her attendants down the muddy road, Norina said to the raven, "I had to promise Mabin something or I would not have gotten rid of her. Are you still hungry, raven?"

The raven flew away with a sausage roll in its beak. Norina tossed her cold tea out the window and poured a fresh cup, but then sat without drinking it. She was expected in a nearby town to judge an accused murderer—and, if necessary, to execute him. But she was considering what a relief it would have been to her had Karis simply accepted Mabin's offer. And then she considered how little she would admire Karis had she accepted.

�ежеѕежеѕежеѕежеѕежеѕежеѕежеѕеже

Chapter Five

Zanja's clan brother, Ransel, had been dead for years, yet every day she missed him. They had been born in the same lodge within a month of each other, and as infants they had nursed at the same breasts and slept in the same cradle. Inseparable as children, they had remained scandalously close into adulthood, and the gossips were always examining Zanja's shape, hoping to be the first to discover that she was concealing an incestuous pregnancy. The fire clan of Tarwein was mostly known for its skilled, artistic rug weavers. Only occasionally did the clan produce a person like Zanja whose elemental talent, and the confirmation of the owl god Salos'a, destined her to be a crosser of boundaries. But Ransel also had become a *katrim*, and served the raven god—Raven in his trickster aspect—for Ransel's relentlessly lighthearted delight in the world had seemed inextinguishable. Nearly six years after the Sainnites killed Ransel, what Zanja remembered most vividly was his wide grin and his loud laugh—both rather shocking among a people of such emotional restraint.

Zanja had survived without him—a bereaved twin, uncertain how to know herself without her alternate self to measure by. And then she met Emil. Now, Shaftali people, whose big, loose families accommodated every kind of coupling imaginable, occasionally referred to Emil as Zanja's husband—which startled and embarrassed her, but inspired Emil to laugh. He'd say, "We fire bloods are always arguing about words because they're so inadequate. That's a good example: husband."

After five years with Emil as her commander, teacher, father, brother, and friend, Zanja could predict both what he would say and what he would be thinking. During their long summer separations, Zanja conversed with Emil in her imagination, and would discover, months later, that Emil remembered those talks as though they had actually occurred.

Now she plodded through thick mud in a merciless rain, with J'han suffering silently behind her, and Karis finding the way by dead reckoning through a woodland of sparse trees and dishearteningly dense thickets. Karis often resorted to simply forcing through the bushes, dragging Zanja and J'han behind her. Thorn-pricked, twig-scratched, rain-soaked, mud-coated, and unspeakably weary, the three of them were about to chase the springtime plague right out of Shaftal.

"You're crossing the boundary," Emil commented in Zanja's head.

"A boundary of thorn bushes," Zanja responded crabbily. "Another one. And another one after that."

"No one ever promised it would be easy."

Ahead of Zanja, Karis had paused to sense the land ahead, stretching to her full height to see over an obstacle that Zanja was too exhausted to trouble to identify.

Emil said in that quiet way of his, "She seems so ordinary."

"In all these months, no one has paid her much heed, other than to remark on her size and strength. She goes steadily from one task to the next, until the impossible project is completed. Her persistence is what is supernatural. Her imperviousness is what's supernatural—her imperviousness to discouragement, her strength of will."

"These qualities are both admirable and maddening," commented Emil. "What do you think she'll do next?"

"I don't know! She wants to serve the land as she is serving it. But Shaftal needs a leader, not a servant."

"Does it?" Emil said thoughtfully.

Karis was pushing through a thicket again. Zanja pressed up against her to use her as a shield. Still, the thorns grabbed hold of her; her ragged rain cape made a ripping sound; she was snagged. Then Karis reached casually back and jerked her loose, out of the thicket into the abrupt, surprising flatness of a new land.

"How about that!" said J'han, as Karis pulled him loose in turn.

They stood at the southern edge of Shaftal. At Zanja's back lay the woodland. Ahead lay flat, featureless sand, as far as could be seen. The rain was falling so heavily now it seemed a wonder they were not swimming. Karis pointed a wet finger at the nearly invisible horizon. "That way," she said.

The sand seemed to last forever. Unintimidated, Karis began to cross it.

Four days later, Zanja awoke from an exhausted, uncomfortable sleep to the sound of rain falling on the oilcloth of the makeshift tent. Karis, sound asleep, clenched her arm across Zanja's chest in a grip it would not be easy to escape. Curled against Karis's back, J'han uttered a small snore. The three of them had slept like the dead in a makeshift tent, in wet clothing, under wet blankets, in a flat and featureless land devoid of tree or stone. It had been a dreary, disorienting journey across the sand, with no sight of the sun or stars to reassure them that they were not walking in circles.

J'han snored again, and Zanja heard another sound as well: faint and distant, but distinctly familiar. She lifted an edge of the sagging oilcloth and peered out. A low sky swallowed up the flat horizon, rain pelted the sand, and a haze of sprouting grass seedlings quivered in the watery assault. There was nothing else to see. Mumbling a complaint, Karis hauled Zanja back under the blankets.

But J'han had awakened. "Did you see something?"

"I saw an inn," Zanja said, "with smoke rising from the chimneys and bread hot from the oven."

J'han groaned. "No, you saw sand, grass, and water. Why do you torture me?"

"I heard a goat."

"A goat?" J'han shook Karis roughly by the shoulder. "We're taking this tent down!"

"Cruel healer," Karis mumbled. "Let me sleep!"

With some effort, Zanja extricated herself from Karis's powerful grip, and she and J'han began rolling blankets. Not until they had put on the rain capes that formed the tent, so that the downpour was falling in Karis's face, did she get up, heavy and reluctant as an old bull. "Why don't we just let them all die?" she suggested grumpily. But when she took a deep breath, she smiled. "I smell smoke. What do you suppose the Juras eat for breakfast?"

"Sand porridge," said Zanja. "With bits of grass for flavor. Made with rainwater, of course."

"So long as it's hot!" said J'han.

They had not walked far before the sand turned quietly to stone. The clouds lay down and kissed the earth, and Karis had to grab Zanja and J'han by the capes to keep them from stepping over the edge of a cliff. Below them, beyond this dramatic step in the land, where the sand began again, lay the Juras camp at last: an unassuming cluster of circular huts with walls of rubble and roofs of skin, and smoke seeping out from holes where the radiating poles met the lodge pole in the middle. Some small piles of hay remained of the haystacks that in autumn must have garrisoned the camp, supplementing the great wind block of the cliff.

As Karis found a path and led the way down the cliff, Zanja noticed that the base of the cliff was riven with wide cracks where dun goats crowded. One of the goats spotted them, uttered a warning bleat, and soon all the goats were shouting an urgent clamor, like townspeople at a fair who all shout "thief" at once. By the time they reached the bottom of the path, a half dozen giants had come out of the huts: people in their prime, as big as Karis, though not quite so powerfully built, their hair bleached almost white by sun, and falling in locks like orderly strands of yarn, with eyes like polished chips of lapis lazuli.

One of them, at least, spoke Shaftalese. He said, "We cannot offer shelter. We have a sickness here." His voice was deep and sweet as a pipe organ.

All six of them had glanced curiously at J'han and Zanja, but it was on Karis that their gazed lingered. Her voice, damaged by years of smoke use, was no more musical than a file on wood. "We have traveled far to cure this illness."

J'han added, "I am a healer."

The man spoke to the others, and the others spoke back. Zanja shut her eyes and listened. The rich, deep voices seemed to almost sing: question and answer, a harmony complex with adjectives. She said in a low voice, "This language is not conducive to quick decisions. We'll be standing in the rain for some time."

J'han said, "After studying their language in a book for a couple of months, you are able to understand them? You will never cease to amaze me."

The book Medric had slipped into Zanja's pack had proven to be a grammar of the Juras language, the life work of a long-dead scholar who had probably never imagined his dry study being put to such serious practical use. Zanja said, "Well, an hour or two of listening would help a great deal—"

"An hour!" said J'han.

"An hour?" said Karis. "Someone is dying!" She dropped her pack, and stepped briskly past the head-crackers. Fortunately, they proved indecisive about wielding their knob-headed sticks until she was past them. Then, one uttered a cry that seemed intended to give courage, and they drew themselves up to attack.

Zanja said sharply, in the Juras language, "She is *sham-re!*"

They turned to her, startled, their lifted sticks beginning to lower. "A witch?" said the man in Shaftalese, as though he thought Zanja had spoken a word of his language by simple accident.

"Your people are singing someone into death, are they not?" Zanja had noticed the melancholy murmur of sound, but until she spoke she had not known what it signified. "The *sham-re* will save that person's life."

The man spoke to his companions, not translating, but announcing in his own convoluted tongue that these three strangers were sent by the gods. "Well," Zanja said to J'han, "I think they might let us come in now."

"But will they feed us sand porridge?" he asked.

* * *

It was porridge, sure enough, made not from sand but from some kind of ground seed that looked fit for chickens, with bits of dry goat meat mixed in it, and chunks of something chewy and sweet that Zanja did not attempt to identify. In a storage hut hastily converted to guest quarters, Zanja and J'han contrived a laundry line and hung their blankets and clothing over the dung fire to dry. Karis returned, consumed a great bowl of the chickenseed porridge, and lay down on a pallet of goat hides. "The place is crawling with vermin," she said. "The people are so crowded together they can scarcely find room to separate sick from well. They kept handing me their babies— babies the size of calves! They know what an earth witch is good for." Karis shut her eyes. "I'll kill the fleas," she promised, her words already blurred by sleep. "Why am I so tired?"

"Zanja and I will manage," J'han said.

They went out again into the rain and found the six head-crackers, crowded with two dozen others into a bursting hut where the only people not talking were wailing children. The din fell still as the two of them ducked through the skin-hung door. The fetor was overwhelming. Zanja said to the man who spoke some Shaftalese, "You must help me to explain something to your people. They are in great danger, and we have come to help them. This illness has traveled to you from the north, and we have followed it. We know it well. We have seen it kill entire families."

The man sat still, his big hands folded. "That may be so," he said. "This *sham-re* who healed Si-wen-ga-sei-ko-che-ni-so-sen. She is a Juras woman-born-outside-the-plain? Whose child is she?"

"She does not know her mother's name. She was born among strangers who did not care to remember her mother for her. Please, I know that you are curious, but your people are in danger. Do you understand?"

The man said, "You want me to speak to my people. But

they will not hear my words until they know this woman's mother-name."

J'han murmured at Zanja's elbow, "Your people also had peculiar ways, didn't they?"

"And many's the time I wanted to scream at them, too," Zanja muttered. "Perhaps you could barge your way into the sick room without being invited."

She gave him the bags of supplies she carried, and watched him walk out of the door before she turned again to the man and explained, "Karis did not know her mother or her mother's name."

"Ka-ris, that is her name? And has she had no life since she was born?"

The people within hearing repeated, "Ka-ris!" And then the din began to rise. At least they were not a gesticulating people like the Midlanders, but their big voices filled the hut. They argued among themselves and shouted questions that the man was hard put to translate, and Zanja to answer. Was Karis born in the autumn, they asked, and how many years ago, and had her mother been enamored of sweets, and what had her mother been so ashamed of, to run away from the comforts of the Ka clan? A gray-haired woman rose and began to chant what seemed to be a list of names all beginning with "Ka," which Zanja realized must be a genealogy, frequently interrupted by other elders who seemed to be arguing that this or that could not be Karis's particular branch, for reasons Zanja could not decipher.

"Huh!" said her translator at last. "I guess she owns a lot of goats."

"Goats?" Zanja said in some bewilderment.

"They say her mother must be Ka-san-ra-li-no-me-la, the eldest daughter of Ka-ri-sho-ma-do-fin-brae-kon, the eldest daughter of . . ."

Zanja interrupted as politely as she could. "And this Kasanra, what happened to her?"

"She had a restless heart and ran away."

"Karis's mother died when Karis was born, thirty-five years ago."

He turned and spoke at length with several other people. Zanja sat upon her heels. She could tell Karis her mother's name! And, apparently, though Kasanra had not been remembered by anyone in Lalali, she had lived long enough to name her infant, and that name had been remembered. So now that name alone was enough to give Karis a clan, a genealogy, and even living relatives.

The translator turned to Zanja and said, "Yes, Ka-ris is rich! Her mother's sister's eldest daughter, Ka-mo-le-ni-da-he-fo-so, is holder of the goats, but everyone thinks they belong to the daughter of Ka-san-ra-li-no-me-la."

"I doubt Karis wants those goats, though. Kamole can continue to keep them."

This statement excited much comment, for Kamole had a fine herd and any of them would certainly want those goats. And Kamole was overly self-important, and perhaps deserved to lose her herd to a stranger. Their eyes danced at the possibility.

"Ka-ris does not want them for her daughter, and her daughter's daughter?" said the translator.

Zanja gathered that these people would not count Leeba as a daughter, and said, "Karis can bear no children of her own body."

At this, the gathered people groaned and cried as though someone had died. The translator explained, straining the limit of his vocabulary, that the Ka women were good breeders, but the clan had long thought the Ka gift had died out, for in three generations there had been no *sham-re*. That Karis could not pass on her talent to her own children was a dreadful tragedy.

The people demanded to know why Karis could not breed and what the names of all her parents, friends, and lovers were, in the order that she met them. "Shouldn't Karis tell you this herself?" Zanja asked, but gradually it became clear that to tell one's story was the duty of one's *shu-shan,* which the man confusedly translated as "the people of her name."

"Her clan?" she asked, using the Juras word.

"No, no, her *shu-shan.*"

Zanja was getting tired, and the camp's fleas had worked their way to her skin by then, and she was not enduring the discomfort of their sharp bites with a stoicism that would have made her teachers proud. She said, "Am I in her *shu-shan*?"

"You know her story, don't you?"

She rubbed her eyes, which were burning from the smoke. The rain pounded on the stretched hide roof, and leaked into some well-placed containers. She said, "Karis cannot bear children because her womb was injured. Her father's name she does not know. I do not know the names from Karis's childhood, for she has chosen to forget them. The first one to befriend her was named Dinal, whom she calls her mother, though she did not know her long. Dinal's foster daughter, Norina, became her first and oldest friend. I am her first and only lover, Zanja, of the Tarwein clan. And then her friends all came at once: J'han, the healer who is with us now, his daughter, Leeba; Emil, our elder; and Medric, a wise man. That is her entire *shu-shan*."

The man, diverted by curiosity, asked, "Your clan-name is your second name? Do your people do everything backwards?"

"I come from the furthest northern borderland of Shaftal, and the Juras live in the furthest southern borderland. My homeland is as wrinkled as yours is flat, and the mountains are so high that some of them at their peaks have stars shining on them in the middle of the day. Your people are large and fair and full of noise. My people were small and dark and full of silence. You Juras seem backwards to me!"

The translator grinned at her. His curiosity and humor would make him a fine ally, Zanja thought, as he turned to participate in the rapid, complicated discussion that Zanja could not follow. The fleas continued to bite, and Zanja practiced her deep breathing, while the people talked interminably. She understood that they were still, after all this time, arguing about Karis's name. She put herself into a listening trance, and came awake only when the man said, "Tar-wein-zan-ja, does Ka wish to continue to be known as Ris?"

"Of course. Why wouldn't she?"

"Ris is a lost-name, a wilderness name. And now she has come home."

Zanja said, "Would it be wrong for her to remember that she once was lost?"

"No, no," he said. "It is her choice, but she may ask her clan to give her a new name, now that she has come home." The people talked some more. The man asked Zanja how many of the people she named were dead. When she told him that Dinal had died in the Fall of the House of Lilterwess, the translator shook his head morosely. "Then Ka-ris's name is too short."

Zanja named some of the still-living people who had befriended Karis in Meartown: the forge master Palo who taught her all he knew, and Mardeth who had watched the gate and reminded Karis to eat. More argument ensued, but at last the people gathered there seemed satisfied. "We will call her Ka-ris-ri-lo-seth-ja-han-il-ric-ba. It is a very short name for a woman her age. But since she has a child in her *shu-shan,* perhaps she will avoid losing her name entirely as her friends die."

"I will urge her to increase her *shu-shan,*" said Zanja gravely, though in her opinion Karis was not doing so badly for a woman whose life had hardly begun until five years ago. Unlike Karis, Zanja would have had a very lengthy name if the Sainnites had not killed her entire *shu-shan* in a single night's work. Now her Juras name would be shorter than Karis's. She knew from harsh experience that it was indeed a dreadful fate to be, by Juras standards, nameless, for so she had been for the months after the massacre, before she met Karis and her own *shu-shan* began to increase. Then she smiled a little, realizing that despite the fleas and smoke and weariness, her fire logic had not failed her, and she was starting to understand these people. She said, "Will your people hear what I have to say now?"

"They are listening to you, Tar-wein-zan-ja." Indeed, the people had all fallen silent, and even the children had ceased to fret.

"I will tell you a story," she said in the Juras language. Her pronunciation, she knew, could only be atrocious, and the vocabulary provided in the book she studied had not taught her even half the words she needed to know. She did what she had always done: she improvised, while her ally aided her by re-saying the words she terribly mispronounced, or offering other words that carried her meaning more clearly.

"There was a tiny man who wore a black coat and was named Little-Biting-Dust. I am afraid I cannot tell you all his names, for his *shu-shan* is very great, and saying his name would take all day. One day, Little-Biting-Dust found a dark magic in his dinner, and he ate it. Though he was just a tiny man, so tiny that he hardly could be seen, this dark magic made him powerful, for from that day forward everyone he bit with his little teeth sickened and died. You see, the dark magic had become part of his blood, and when he bit someone, the magic went into their blood too, and killed them.

"Little-Biting-Dust boasted to his *shu-shan* that although he once had been almost nothing, now he was a man of great importance. They begged to know his secret, and he said, 'You must follow me, and watch. When I bite someone, wait for that person to fall sick. Then you bite that same person, and the dark magic will go into your blood, and you will be as powerful as I.' So his numberless *shu-shan* all did as he said, and soon they all had his power. His clan became the most important people in the north. People came and bowed down to Little-Biting-Dust and gave him everything they owned, even their clan goatherd, in exchange for his promise not to bite them. But as you can tell, he was a very evil man, and he broke all his promises, and he bit everyone.

"Soon, Little-Biting-Dust's clan began to starve. They had killed every person and animal in their town, except for the rats, and now they had nothing to eat, for even they would not eat rats. 'What shall we do?' they cried.

"'We must go to a new town,' said Little-Biting-Dust. Now, as I said, these people were very small, so they could ride the rats to the next town. Soon, the people in that town also began to sicken and die. There was nothing they could do to fight back, for Little-Biting-Dust's people were so small and fast that nobody could catch them.

"But then one day, there came into that town a woman with

a short name who had a lot of goats she did not want, who had the gift of the Ka-clan and was a *sham-re*. Her magic was stronger than Little-Biting-Dust's magic, and soon the people who were sick began to get better, rather than dying. Little-Biting-Dust was angry, and he jumped onto her leg to bite her, but she reached down and caught him by the coat collar. 'Now I have you, you evil little man,' she said, and she put him in her mouth and cracked him open with her teeth. And so died Little-Biting-Dust, and not a day too soon!

"But by now, Little-Biting-Dust's *shu-shan* were numerous as the blades of grass that sprout up during the spring mud, and they all fled the wrath of the short-named woman, riding on the rats. Some went east and some went west, and she chased them and found them and killed them all. But some went south and they hid in a place they thought they never would be found: a good place where the skies are big and the people sing with loud voices, a place far away from the short-named woman's home. 'She will never find us here,' they said, and they started to bite the people, and the people began to fall ill. 'That *sham-re* will not stop us from becoming the most important people in the world!'

"But then one day the *sham-re* arrived, for Little-Biting-Dust's relatives had settled in the home of the short-named woman's mother. And there was nowhere left for the little people with the dark magic to run, for after the grassland come the steppes, and after the steppes comes the waste, and no one has ever crossed the waste alive. So they all prepared for a great battle, and today that battle begins."

Zanja awoke from a long nap and found herself alone beside a smoldering fire. Her sleep had not relieved her weariness, but instead had sent it deeper, into the center of her bones, where it filled her marrow with lead. Yet, like all her weary awakenings during this long winter and spring, she awoke satisfied. At last she had something to do, and it required all her faculties, body and mind. She got up, groaning but not complaining.

The rain had eased, and the Juras had built a bonfire in

which they were burning everything that might shelter a flea. The children danced; the young people wildly flung objects into the fire. The old people sang: a wild, big noise that issued from the deep of their chests and made Zanja feel giddy and powerful. Inside the main hut, she found a pot of something and helped herself to it, then ducked outside to avoid the dust of cleaning. A woman told her that J'han was in the sick hut, but Karis had gone away. Zanja's informant gestured vaguely.

Bringing their rain capes, Zanja climbed the cliff and looked out over the empty land, where the sky still hung so low she felt that she could touch it with her hands. Karis was easy to spot: the tallest thing between Zanja and the horizon. As Zanja drew closer, she saw that Karis sat beside a long, shallow stretch of standing water. An ecstatic cacophony of toad voices croaked the praises of this temporary pond. A pair of long-legged birds, white as clouds, stalked through the clear water, snatching up the love-frenzied toads to feed their own hatchlings.

Zanja squatted down beside Karis, who sat with her knees drawn up to her chest. The toads cried. "Water here! Come make babies! Beware the toad-eater!" The clouds, which had seemed so still, revealed themselves to be in motion—or else the earth itself was moving. The grass rustled, growing so quickly that Zanja thought she could see it. At times like these, she almost understood the land as Karis did. *How impatient I must seem to her,* Zanja thought.

Karis said, "Such big people! So loud, and crowded! They are exhausting."

"They keep each other warm, I guess."

The sky spit rudely at them. Zanja unrolled their rain capes, which smelled of dung smoke now. She wrapped one around Karis. Looking into her lover's face, she saw an unfamiliar strain. She said, surprised and concerned, "What is it?"

Karis dug a hand into wet sand. She said, "When there are no words for what I know, how am I to explain myself?"

"I'll teach you words from other languages. Or I'll make words up for you."

"Must there be words? I just want my toolbox, so I can whack away at something for a while."

After a silence, Zanja said, "You're tired of people. I'll leave you alone."

Karis's hand, wet and gritty, took hold of hers. Zanja subsided, leaning against Karis's shoulder, and watched a white bird stalk into the grass with a hapless toad dangling from her beak. Zanja told Karis her mother's long name, her own short name, and the name of her cousin who owned such a quantity of fine goats. Karis listened in silence.

"The Juras people will all gather together in a few weeks, and you'll be able to meet your entire clan then, if not before."

Karis nodded. "That would be worth doing, I guess. But they are not my people, not like the Ashawala'i were to you. You already understand the Juras better than I ever will, and you'll spend our entire time here explaining them to me."

"That's true," said Zanja. "Is that too bitter a truth for you?"

"It's not bitter to know that my mother Kasanra named me," Karis said. "I assumed she just dropped me in the street like a dog drops her litter." She took a harsh breath, and turned her face away. "But do I want to know that bearing a child broke her heart?" Her wrecked voice sounded worse than usual. "If every truth is bitter, then we're better off with lies, aren't we?"

"Without the truth, we'd never solve a single problem."

"Without the truth, we'd have no problems. Or at least, we wouldn't know we had them."

"What darkness there is in your heart today."

Karis uttered a weak laugh. "I'm just talking like a smoke addict. A single breath of that stuff and all pain went away. How easy it was!"

Zanja had never feared that Karis would return to using smoke, and now she simply nodded without comment. Their love had been conceived in the midst of pain, and so they had always allowed room for each other's sorrow. But Zanja could not guess what made Karis so wretched now. While Zanja had napped, Karis had probably wandered the Juras camp, killing fleas, giving immunity to the healthy and making certain none of the sick would get the illness in their lungs. She had done the same in every town they had passed through, and in her wake some people died, the rest recovered, and the illness disappeared. It was a normal sequence of events by now.

"Something new has happened," Zanja said at last. "Something the ravens know, perhaps."

"Yes. I can't explain it."

Zanja could feel Karis's bulk, her muscle, and even some bone now that she had gotten thin with travel. But Zanja could feel her sturdiness also, and a physical warmth that kept the chill and damp at bay. "You'll tell me when you can," she said.

Karis let go of her hand, and wiped a palm across the sand to smooth it. Then, she began to shape the wet sand into a map, complete with geographical features. Even though Karis had never seen those places, the map would be accurate; where she went, the land was never strange to her. "There's ten more infected camps," she said, and marked them with her fingertip. "Seven to the east of us and three to the west. When do the Juras gather together, do you know?"

"After the spring rains have fallen, when the grass is deeply rooted enough that the goats can be allowed to graze, there's a white flower that blooms at around the time the goats drop their kids, and that's the time that the Juras people gather to sing to the stars and to make marriages." Zanja gasped for breath.

"That was an unspeakable statement," Karis observed.

"It's how they talk. They have big lungs."

"Well, the goats will start dropping kids in about twenty days."

Zanja studied the map. "How far apart are the camps?"

"About a day's journey. The herds need a lot of room." Karis frowned. "If the infected people go to the gathering, bringing their fleas with them—"

"You and J'han need two or three days in each camp. I'll have to run ahead, and persuade those people to stay where they are."

Karis gave her a look of despair. Confused, Zanja said, "For years before I met you, I was a solitary traveler, so I am fairly skilled at it."

"I never forget that," said Karis hoarsely.

"Well, it's too bad we couldn't bring a raven, but still, you'll always know where I am—" Zanja let her voice trail away. "What do you mean by that?"

Karis was trembling. "What's wrong with me?"

Zanja felt a sudden horror. She put her hand to Karis's forehead, and it was like putting her hand into a crackling fire. "Dear gods. You can protect everyone—"

"I'm sick?" Karis sounded blank. "Why am I sick?"

Zanja tried to speak calmly. "Little-Biting-Dust wanted revenge, I guess. Someone must have told him that you can't heal yourself."

"War makes me sick. Norina said so."

"War only makes you sick at heart," said Zanja. "Get up. I'm taking you to J'han."

Chapter Six

Zanja knelt on the floor of pounded sand, near the edge of the crowded, stinking hut where after a feverish night the sick had lapsed into exhausted silence. An old man had died during the night, and as soon as the sun rose, J'han had gone out with the weary volunteers to expose his body to the sky, which was the Juras way of disposing of the dead. J'han would have preferred to burn the bodies, but the closest firewood lay four days journey to the north. Lomito, the translator, had assured Zanja that Juras tradition would keep people away from the body while the scavengers did their work. Now, the volunteers began to come back in: all old people whose names were getting short. They lay down on their pallets with groans of exhaustion; like Zanja they had been awake all night. They muttered among themselves about the danger that the old man's ghost might haunt them because they had been too tired to sing him properly into death, but soon they fell silent.

All night, while Karis lay restless and muttering with fever, Zanja had sponged her with cool water. Now Karis lay quiescent, pallid, stark. The distinct marks of Little-Biting-Dust's dark magic had become visible in her flesh, mysterious bruises that J'han said were battlegrounds. Feeling how cool Karis was now, Zanja covered her with a blanket.

Karis opened her eyes. "Are you still here?" she said accusingly.

"Karis—"

"You have to go!"

"I can't bring myself to leave you."

Karis looked at her: a strange look, resolved, not particularly tender. "A solitary traveler," she mumbled.

"That life is over."

"No. It is your gift." Her broken voice cracked. Her bruised eyelids closed.

Zanja sat back on her heels. In four or five days' time, J'han would be able to say with some confidence whether Karis would survive. But by then Zanja should be far away, with no raven messenger to tell the news. If Karis lived, she wouldn't forgive Zanja for remaining with her while a whole people was devastated by this awful plague. And if Karis died, Zanja's presence or absence would make no difference in the outcome. But she could not make herself stand up and go.

The hut was dim, but outside the heavy clouds allowed in a promise of sunshine. The people within breathed in and out, some snoring, others mumbling vaguely in their sleep. Zanja took out her glyph cards and whispered a question. "If I leave, will Karis and I be separated forever?"

She looked down at the card her fingers had picked. It was Unbinding-and-Binding, with its illustration of two people tied at either end of a rope looped around a rock, hanging helplessly from a cliff. For one to climb, the other must fall. Zanja put the card back into the deck. She felt very strange: empty— so empty she felt almost light—and giddy, though not with joy. She stood up and went out.

J'han was asleep with the others, but Lomito was waiting outside near her pile of gear to bid her farewell. J'han would remain with Karis while Lomito traveled west and Zanja east, to teach the Juras how to prevent the illness and how to care for those who were already sick, but above all to persuade them to avoid the gathering.

Lomito said, "Be at peace, Tar-wein-zan-ja. There never was a *sham-re* of the Ka clan that could be easily killed."

"Thank you," she said distantly. She felt like she was falling; Lomito was far away, and Karis was even farther. "Safe journey," she said to him. She picked up her gear, and walked away.

* * *

From one crowded Juras camp to the next, as the rain gradually let up and the earth began to warm, Zanja traveled, told her story, saw the people institute J'han's plan for killing fleas and preventing infection, and traveled on. It took fifteen days for the clouds to break apart and drift away. That day found Zanja alone as the vivid green plain unrolled before her feet like a bolt of green silk. Blue sky met green horizon, featureless and flat in all directions, and only Zanja's own shadow could tell her which way she was going. She had spent much of her life alone, but never had she been without a tree or hill to inform her of her place on the world. Now, as she walked, her interior spaces remained empty as the plain and the sky: disconnected, all her ties illusory, all her hopes a vacancy. She became convinced that Karis was indeed dead, and wept as she walked, dazed by sorrow, dazzled by light, through a thick steam that began to rise as the sun warmed the wet sand.

The air even smelled of death: a faint, sweet stink that gradually became overpowering. She wiped her eyes and looked around herself, for she had gotten completely disoriented and might have been walking in aimless circles for all she knew. Ahead of her, a sturdy caravan rose out of the mist, still and derelict as a wrecked ship lying askew on the shore. A broken axle, Zanja thought, but her nose told her that something worse than a mere mischance had befallen this house on wheels.

When she drew close, she saw the remains of the dray horses, dead in their traces, half eaten by scavengers before the winter cold froze the remains. Now, fat flies blew up in a cloud as Zanja approached, and vultures fled in great, ungainly hops through the calf-deep grass. The message of the dreadful scene was not too hard to read: the horses, trapped by the broken wheel, had died of starvation with grass just out of reach. But what of their driver?

The caravan door was tilted skyward, and the wood had swollen from the long rain. She levered the door open with her knife blade, and then fell back, gagging from the stink. She caught only a glimpse of what lay within: a man's dead body, rotting in a tangle of ruined trade goods. Holding her nose, she kicked the door shut, and fled beyond range of the smell to collect herself. No wonder her very thoughts had been infused with the stink of death.

In the warmth of the afternoon, the steam began to burn away, and Zanja noticed that underfoot, beneath the shelter of the grass leaves, a second plant was thriving and had almost completely matted over the sand's surface with its small, lobed leaves. Looking closer, she saw the tiny green buds swelling. In a few more days, the sand would be decorated with flowers. She spotted a small eruption in the sand, and there emerged a fat black bee the size of her thumb tip. He basked in the sunshine after his mead-sipping winter underground, buzzing his wings occasionally, no doubt planning what he would do when the flowers came into bloom.

So Karis now sat, somewhere on this same empty plain, with the sunshine in her face, thinking how to restore her life after the ravages of illness and the hardships of that winter. Zanja sat back on her heels, beside the sleepy bee, and let her fear and sorrow go. She had chased Little-Biting-Dust across the plain, from one Juras camp to the next, and in each camp she had found fewer sick and greater surprise at her urgent message. Now, she had reached the end: a dead man, a peddler, with illness carried in his trade goods, and perhaps in stowaway rats as well. Here the plague's journey had finally ended.

She slept for a while beside her buzzing companion until she was awakened by goats bleating in the distance. She followed the sound to the flock, which meandered its lazy way across the grassland, driven, or perhaps merely followed, by a loose cluster of heavily laden Juras. The giants lightly carried their children, their early kids, their furniture, and their very houses upon their backs. When they spotted Zanja's approach, they stopped dead in their tracks, staring. One of them said, "Look: it is a very small person made of shadow." Some rather ostentatiously loosed their clubs, which they generally used only to defend the goats from predators, but they relaxed quickly enough when Zanja gave proper greetings to the headwoman. She explained that they should give wide berth to the wrecked caravan in the distance, and eventually, when she had explained enough, they gave her some provisions, and loaned her a small ax, which she promised to return when she found them again at the gathering of the Juras.

With this ax she chopped apart the rolling mausoleum and used its wood for fuel with which to build a pyre. By noon the next day only black skeletons of wood and bone remained.

Zanja's boots had fallen apart at the seams, and she arrived at the gathering of the Juras barefoot. She had let her long hair out of its braids to dry, and had never bothered to plait it up again. As she made her way among the gathered flocks of goats, where many a goat lay in labor or nursed her newborn kids, the old does kept a close and hostile eye on her. At the center of this tremendous goat gathering lay the camp, where several hundred goatskin tents stood like tan sails on a green sea. Here, the Juras people sat in the sun, and talked, and sang, and roasted fresh meat on open fires. For once, it was not goat, but buffalo, and it smelled delicious. Like the goats, the people turned in astonishment to watch Zanja pass.

When she returned her borrowed ax, the children of that household followed her through the camp, asking question after question and begging to be allowed to touch her hair. They trailed behind her like a pack of enthusiastic but clumsy puppies, until at the very heart of the camp they suddenly disappeared. She lifted her gaze at the sound of a familiar, hoarse croak. A lone raven had landed on the tip of a tent pole. "Raven, is Karis here?" she cried.

"Follow me," said the raven.

He led her to a tight circle of tents, where she found a big Juras woman sitting among her cousins, with her hair cropped short and tied in tiny bunches all over her skull. Karis's face had gotten more alien as well: pale and hollow, gaunt with illness. She listened attentively to an elderly woman as though she could understand her, while at her shoulder Lomito struggled out a framework of Shaftali words, with all the heart stripped out of them.

Zanja knelt behind Karis and asked quietly, "Is this your mother's relative?"

"Her aunt," Karis said, without turning her head.

Zanja took over the translating, which seemed a relief to Lomito. The old woman said, "Do you know, there are some goats that cannot be watched. The moment the herders turn their back, this goat sets forth from the flock. The wise goats call to her to come back, and warn her that there are places without water, and places where hungry lions roam. But they cannot convince her, and so we find her later, dead or injured. And if she lives to be returned safely to the flock again, she sets forth again, sooner or later."

Karis was nodding. "Yes, yes," she said in the Juras language, which was probably the only word she had learned.

"My sister's daughter was like that goat: restless, heedless, deaf to advice. After she came into her womanhood, she only grew worse: she often disappeared for days at a time, and nothing could keep her at home, or make her contented with her mother's fine flock. At last, she disappeared entirely, and never was seen again."

"Was it in the spring?" Karis asked. Karis knew all about the springtime restlessness that sets the feet to roaming.

"It was in the spring, during the gathering. I remember that Man-in-Rolling-House came, and we traded winter wool for fat and sweets to make a feast. Perhaps Kasanra went with him, hidden in his house. My sister Karisho had no other daughters, only sons, and so the goats went to my other sister's eldest daughter, Kamole. Kamole was born before Kasanra disappeared."

"Do I look like Kasanra?" Karis asked.

The woman studied Karis's face. "I think you look as your mother would have, had she not killed herself with foolishness. You look somewhat like Kamole, who now has three children, and her eldest bore a child this winter. Here is Kamole now."

Karis murmured, astounded, "My cousin is a grandmother?"

Everyone in the circle was rising to their feet. Zanja stood up as well, but Karis only looked up politely as a big, angry woman came into the circle. Zanja, her hand on Karis's shoulder, said, "This woman is your enemy, I'm afraid."

"She does look grim. You should tell her they carried me here in a litter, and I am too weak to stand."

"What are you doing here, then?" Zanja asked, appalled.

"Oh—trying not to waste any more of my life. Look at me: no goats, no grandchildren . . ." She was smiling, but her hand closed over Zanja's as Kamole towered over her. The supposedly peaceful Juras told tales of wrestling matches between rivals, and it was rivalry over goats as often as it was over lovers. Kamole certainly seemed to be in the right mood, and Zanja hoped she wouldn't have to draw her dagger in Karis's defense.

Zanja said in the Juras tongue, "Karis apologizes that she is still too ill to stand."

Kamole gave Zanja a startled look, as though she were a goat that had abruptly spoken. "What are you?" she demanded.

"I am a crosser of borders, a speaker of languages, a reader of signs. I am Zanja na'Tarwein."

"Huh," said the woman. "The gathered Juras talk only of the *sham-re* daughter of lost Kasanra. You must be the one of her *shu-shan* who tells stories."

Zanja said to Karis, "Well, she is unimpressed with us, and implies that anyone who admires us is frivolous."

"What's to admire?" said Karis. "I am too weak to stand, and you don't even have shoes. But perhaps you'd better reassure her that I don't want her goats."

"And insult her by implying that her goats are not desirable?" Zanja spoke to Kamole. "Karis says that everyone has spoken highly of the daughter of her mother's sister, whose goatherd is the finest in the southern plain. She is glad to finally meet you." She instructed Karis, "Look glad. Clasp her hand."

Karis did, and everyone but Kamole relaxed and sat down.

Kamole said, "Why have you come here? We prefer that the people of the forest lands leave us alone."

Karis said, "This illness we have chased here would have

killed so many Juras that perhaps the tribe might not have recovered."

Kamole replied obstinately, "Every other stranger brings grief to the Juras. We have not forgotten how the forest people brought their sheep onto the plains and let them graze before the grass was properly rooted, and so laid waste the land that our goats began to starve and the grassland turned to desert."

Karis grumbled, "That was forty years ago. Neither one of us was even born then."

"I won't translate that," said Zanja.

"Well, remind her that Harald G'deon intervened, and forbade Shaftali people to graze upon the plain, and replanted the grass, and sent wagonloads of hay to feed the goats. And remind me to thank Emil and Medric for forcing me to learn so much history."

After Zanja had reported this history, Kamole replied, "That may be what happened. But now this illness was brought to us by evil fleas, and none of the Juras brought those fleas to our land. I know this is true."

Zanja said, "It's true that Man-in-Rolling-House brought the fleas here, inadvertently, and now he is dead."

"So!" said Kamole.

"And we have come to cure it," Karis said. "The healer will remain with the Juras as long as you need him—will you refuse him hospitality?"

No, Kamole did not plan to turn away a resource so valuable as J'han, despite her objections to strangers. And it would have made no difference if she had, for the fourteen Juras clans were fiercely independent, and would give J'han shelter no matter what Kamole said. Zanja wondered if Karis would ask hospitality for herself, but she did not, and if she were hoping it might be offered voluntarily, she was disappointed.

As the sun began to set, Karis, leaning on Zanja, walked slowly out of the great camp, among the goats upon the open plain. There they drove a staff into the sand for the raven to perch on, and spread their blankets in the grass. Karis lay for a while with her face in the sand. But then she turned onto her back and looked up at the sky. That broad expanse, unbounded by tree or mountain, had unnerved Zanja, for in the high mountains, with all the world below her, she had never felt so exposed. But now the sky was a glory. "We'll watch the stars come out," Karis said.

They watched, huddled together for warmth, Zanja with her head resting in the hollow crook of Karis's bony shoulder. The goats closed in, and wheeled around them in a benign examination. The fearless kids, with the remains of umbilical cords still hanging from their bellies, came right up and stared them in the face. The sky's colors slowly cooled, and stars pricked through the blue like distant lamps. Zanja told Karis of her travels. Karis said she could not remember being ill, and when her delirium had passed she wondered why her hair had been cut. Lomito had returned from his trek by then, and explained it was bad luck to have tangled hair.

Zanja said, "If they had cut my hair I would think they were making me an outcast."

"Well, they just want to make me seem more like them. Untie the knots, will you? I don't care if I offend them."

Zanja worked by feel to undo the knots of yarn. "J'han remained in the sick camps, I assume. Why did he let you go to the gathering?"

"He sent me away to get some rest."

"You were healing people?"

"I couldn't help it," Karis said, and added, "You're laughing at me."

Zanja put her fingers through Karis's springy hair. Her own hair kept getting in the way. Karis lifted away the hair curtain and clasped it in a fist at the nape of Zanja's neck. Zanja kissed her. Karis's mouth opened under hers; she uttered a small sound. The goats that had lain down around them looked at them in some surprise.

There was an amazing sound, a swell of loud, sweet, deep voices. The Juras had begun singing to the stars, which filled the sky in a brilliant crowd of lights. Karis was crying hoarsely, undoing buttons ahead of Zanja's mouth and tongue, and kept getting herself tangled in Zanja's loose hair. The voices rose; the empty sky blazed with light; the sand vibrated with sound. Karis gasped, uttered a small shout. A newborn kid asked its dam a sleepy question. The Juras sang glory into the sky.

Later, Zanja put Karis's clothing back on her so she wouldn't get chilled. When she finished doing up shirt buttons, she discovered that Karis's face was silvered with wet starlight. "What?" Zanja said gently. Karis put her arms around her, but was too weak to hold on for long. Resting on Karis's breast, Zanja said, "I thought the cards told me you would die. I should know better than to ask them a personal question."

Karis rubbed a sleeve across her face. The Juras were still singing, but softly. Perhaps it was a lullaby for their children and their goats. Karis said, in a rush of ragged words, "Just before I fell ill, Mabin apologized for her wrongs, and asked me to sit in the G'deon's chair. Norina says she was sincere. But I did not accept."

Zanja thought, *I must not flinch*. But she already had.

"I could not accept!" Karis's voice was raw—not just fatigued, but fearful, agonized.

Zanja rested her forehead against Karis's shoulder. After such sweet intimacy, to confront the fact of their increasing estrangement seemed unendurable. "Karis, if I've made you feel like you have to justify yourself to me . . ."

"Fighting the plague has been a joy to you," said Karis. "Now the fight is over, you'll be aggrieved again."

Zanja wanted to contradict her, and could not do so. She said painfully, "If I could choose not to be angry or disappointed, I would make that choice with all my heart."

"And if I could choose to make you happy—"

"My happiness is not your responsibility."

"Oh, but your unhappiness is."

"Dear gods, is that what you think? That I blame you for my own failure to be contented?"

Karis's big hand had lifted to clasp Zanja's shoulder, but now it slipped down again and she said fretfully, "I can't hold you."

"You don't have to," Zanja said. She raised her head. "For five years I've shaped my life by waiting, though you never said that you would ever say yes to Shaftal. So my impatience is my own fault."

Karis's hand lifted again, and again it fell weakly to the sand. She said hoarsely, "The plague is over. But the land still cries out to me for healing. Do you—does everyone—think I am deaf to that? I know I must do something. But I cannot act. It's not a choice. I have no choices. I have no choices." Her voice was blurry with fatigue.

Because she could not say she understood, Zanja said, "You need to rest." Then she lay beside Karis, silent.

Then Juras sang—such an astonishing song!—and the stars whirled wildly in the sky. Karis had fallen asleep. The goats slept around them, a field of goats that spread as far as could be seen. Zanja blinked—she had been dozing, and in her sleep she heard Medric warning her not to put too much importance on the plague. "Nothing changes," he whispered in her ear. "Nothing changes."

The cards had not been wrong. Zanja had asked if she and Karis would be separated forever—and the dreadful answer was that they would not separate at all. They were bound together on the side of the cliff, trapped there, each of them unable to choose to let the other one fall. And there they were destined to remain.

Chapter Seven

"I'm weary of looking at your glum faces," said Cadmar one evening at the peak of the spring bloom, and he dug the whisky from his footlocker and started pouring drinks. Gilly, who had already taken his evening draught of opiates, perched like a hunched crow upon his stool, sipping from his glass and uttering grave witticisms that no one would remember in the morning. After downing three glasses, Cadmar turned garrulous and started reminiscing, though there was nothing Gilly and Clement didn't already know about his illustrious life.

"Drink," he urged. "Drink and be cheerful."

Clement drank, and pretended to be cheerful.

"Those were good days," Cadmar concluded with a sigh. Gilly, as though to contradict him, dropped his glass and, slowly at first but with increasing speed, slithered off his stool. Cadmar caught him and dragged him across the floor to the bed. "The man can't hold his drink." He fumbled with Gilly's shoes. "How do these come off?"

Clement helped Cadmar put Gilly to bed, and checked that he was still breathing, for the medics had warned that combining his drugs with liquor could kill him. As she stood looking down at her misshapen, sardonic friend, her heart hurt in a way that no soldier could ever admit to. Without him, her life would certainly be unendurable.

"Are we drunk yet?" Cadmar asked.

"Drunk enough," she said unenthusiastically.

"Well then, let's find ourselves a trull. Like we used to do."

"General—"

He held up a hand. "You are *not* drunk enough." He filled her glass and supervised until she had emptied it. Her eyes watered; her stomach protested; she felt more ill than drunk. But it seemed apparent that Cadmar would keep filling her glass until she either passed out like Gilly or began feigning a cheerful mood more convincingly.

As they made their way to the garrison gate, she couldn't help but ask, "Aren't we too old for this?" She certainly felt too old.

"Not too old. Too dignified, maybe."

"Well then—"

"But we are soldiers, by the gods! And who else are we to lie with, eh? We've got no bunkmates and we outrank everybody!"

She said, "But you've got Gilly." She realized only then that she was truly drunk, though not pleasantly. That Cadmar still sometimes made his way to Gilly's bed was something she was not supposed to have noticed.

"Gilly's getting old too." Cadmar patted her with clumsy affection. "But you've got no one at all, old or young. How long has it been?"

"More than five years," she admitted.

"Five years! No wonder you are so glum."

The gate captain coped so calmly and expertly with the phenomenon of the general setting forth in search of a prostitute that Clement realized this could not be the first time. The captain summoned a detail of a half dozen soldiers and included herself in the impromptu escort. It was a very quiet night. After spring mud came the short summer season in which the year's food was planted, grown and harvested, while the bulk of the business and commerce was also done. From now until autumn mud, the Shaftali would work every moment of the rapidly lengthening days. Now, the shop shutters were closed, the windows were dark, the streets echoed with the guards' hob-nailed footsteps, and Cadmar's cheerful voice seemed very loud.

They would go to a woman who did not call herself a prostitute, and made her services available only to officers. Clement felt a certain relief: prostitutes were usually smoke addicts, and she did not enjoy their company.

"I understand the whore isn't pregnant," said the captain. "Not at the moment, anyway. But she makes some officer a father almost every year."

"She sells them her children, you mean," muttered Clement.

"She claims the officer is the baby's father."

"Of course she does. If she's paid enough."

Cadmar gave Clement a reprimanding push. The captain said with strained cheer, "This is the place. I'll ring the bell and see if you can be accommodated."

They had reached a modest townhouse, the only building on the street with lamps still lit. A stout, plainly dressed woman answered the door, and soon the escorting soldiers had been shooed down a narrow hall toward the kitchen. Meanwhile, the stout woman left Clement in a tasteful drawing room while she showed Cadmar up the stairs.

At least there had been no unseemly argument over who would go first. On the small room's delicate side table, a sweating wedge of cheese and a dry loaf of bread reminded Clement that she had drunk her supper. She ate, which did not settle her rebellious stomach, and then began to be bored. She shuffled a deck of cards that lay on the table, trying to remember the solitary card games she had not played in years. But then she noticed that the backs of the cards were decorated with a variety of pornographic pictures, and she leafed through them. She had never seen such a subject portrayed both explicitly and artfully before.

Cadmar came down the stairs, looking composed and extraordinarily complacent. "Listen, Cadmar," Clement began, planning to excuse herself from the trip upstairs.

But he clasped her hand jovially, saying, "That woman has talent! I've paid her for us both, so don't pay her again."

It was hopeless. While waiting to be summoned, Clement diverted him with the pornographic cards. She decided she would go upstairs, sit by the courtesan's fire, and let herself be enter-

tained for half an hour by empty-headed conversation. Cadmar
would never know his money had been wasted. The servant
came to fetch her, and at the top of the stairs Clement stepped
through an open door that was quietly closed behind her.

She smelled flowers, very delicate and faint, and her eye
sought out the source: violets, she saw, and daffodils—homely,
early-blooming flowers tucked into crystal vases. The room
was warm, lamplit, painted coral pink so that Clement felt inti-
mately embraced though the woman who was to entertain her
sat on the far side of the room beside a quiet fire, with a piece
of needlework in her hand. The big bed lay demurely shadowed, though its covers were folded back to advertise the pristine whiteness of the sheets.

Clement could smell not even a hint of old sex. It was a neat
trick, she thought, as though she were watching a magician at a
fair. The courtesan, eyebrow raised, gazed at her with some
amusement. "Lieutenant-General, I understand you're here
against your will. The general gave me some rather strict orders, however."

"Fortunately, he is not your general."

"Yes, it is fortunate." The courtesan smiled, her hands busy
making stitches that only a close observer might realize were
haphazard. "Do come in and sit by the fire. I will not throw
myself on you, I assure you."

Clement walked across soft carpets and sat, and the chair
embraced her. The courtesan served her a hot drink, sweet and
milky, gently spiced. Clement sipped and felt her stomach settle, finally. This comfortable, intimate room was not what she
had expected. That she hungered for this comfort, this quiet,
she also had not expected. Oh, she was weary of being who she
was! "Call me Clement," she said desperately.

"Clement, I am Alrin."

The courtesan was not young; nor was she intimidatingly
beautiful. The loose silk robe she wore outlined in folds of
light and darkness a heavy thigh, a lush breast, a body as comfortable as the chair in which she now curled, setting aside her
fancywork and smiling as though she had a secret. She and
Clement spoke of commonplace things: the town, the weather.

Clement felt as if she had entered a different world, where all was mundane and not even a prickle of violence and politics could be felt. To leave the embrace of the soft green chair and enter the embrace of slippery silk and lightly perfumed skin was not so hard to do. It happened. Alrin made it happen by waiting and hinting and smiling that secret smile. Eventually, the pristine bed was put to use.

The homely flowers of spring bloomed in every crack where a bit of earth might be shoved atop a bulb. The barren garrison's snowdrifts were replaced by drifts of flowers that the occasional Shaftali visitor had no little cause to wonder at. The soldiers could coax a flower to bloom anywhere, and would sooner risk injury than step on even the edge of a flowerbed. Clement supposed there was something contradictory about the Sainnite love of flowers; certainly, the Shaftali found it peculiar. Clement's mother had filled her coat pockets with bulbs on the way to becoming a refugee. Clement went to the garden every day to watch her mother's flowers bloom.

Now it was summer, and as the last of the spring blossoms shriveled in the warmth, Clement's sudden romance with Alrin abruptly failed. "You've gotten gloomy again," commented Gilly one warm day, as the two of them were making the final plans for Cadmar's annual tour of the garrisons.

She grunted discouragingly, but the ugly man had set his pen aside. "Are we now strangers, you and I?"

"That's an odd remark," she said.

"It's you who have gotten odd, friend."

"Well." She sighed. "I notice that Alrin's belly has gotten round, and now I hear that half a dozen officers are bidding against each other to be named the baby's father."

Gilly raised his eyebrows. "You were pretending she's not what she is?"

"Don't make fun of me. I've seen your foolishness often enough."

"I can't deny it. So you'll visit her no more?"

"It was a waste of money."

"By your gods, I'd pay for it myself! A waste of money it was not!"

Clement muttered, "So all it takes to make me happy is an hour with a trull? I can hardly be proud of that."

That night she went late to bed, not because she was up carousing, but because with warm weather came the war, and death, and the cursed duty roster. She lay awake, of course, uncomfortable on her lumpy mattress, which wanted re-stuffing. She had propped the windows open to the moonless night, and a little bat flew in on the trail of a moth, and flapped around the room a couple of times, practically soundless but for a dry rustle like leather in a breeze, and a squeak so shrill it was little more than a scratching in the ears. Perhaps she actually slept, for when she saw a dandelion pod of fire explode against the stars, she thought it was a dream.

She stared at it, bedazzled, mystified, too astonished to feel afraid. Surely it was a sign from the gods, perhaps a sign directed only to her, a promise that her life's purpose soon would be revealed. The fire faded, leaving a glowing trail behind. And now she heard a sound: an animal whine that became a scream the like of which she had only ever heard on the battlefield. In a few wild steps, she stood naked at the window, watching a soldier below dance a madman's dance as his arm and shoulder burned like fatwood.

Getting dressed took only a moment. To run down the stairs to Cadmar's quarters took another. But Cadmar was already gone: while Clement sought enlightenment, he had already realized that the garrison was under attack, and he was ahead of her, out of the building already, where the fire falling from the sky could burn him alive. "Gilly!" she bellowed, running full tilt down the hall to pound on his door. "Wake up, damn you!" She heard the muffled murmur of his drugged voice, and left him to save himself. He was no soldier, but he knew how to keep out of harm's way.

She ran out the door and found the burned soldier moaning, charred, scarcely conscious where he had been dragged into the shelter of the eaves. The sky exploded with fire. All across the garrison there were shouts: alarmed, astonished, and terrified. She shook the burned soldier brutally and shouted, "Was it the general who helped you? Which way did he go?"

The man said something, and perhaps he thought it was intelligible, but to Clement it meant nothing. She left him and ran down the nearest road, toward the rising shouts and the glow of fire now burning the rooftops. As she ran, she heard a captain blow his horn in the distance, signaling his disordered company to follow him into battle. Cadmar would chase that sound like a hound chases a rabbit—and just as mindlessly, she thought grimly. She ran after him, her pistols unloaded and her saber banging on her leg, with the sky exploding overhead and the garrison erupting below, and as she ran she cursed Cadmar, and cursed even louder at the beauty of the deadly explosions that filled the sky.

She reached a chaotic knot of soldiers who seemed to be trying to fight the fire that threatened to burn their barracks down, though the flames were mostly out of reach of the water they tossed at it. She found their captain and shouted at him to give up and find the source of the explosives instead, but he gave her a dazed look as though he had lost his mind or thought she had lost hers. He shouted that he had not seen Cadmar, which meant nothing.

She heard the distant horn again, and ran, and above the rising sound of chaos she thought she heard gunshots. It was a satisfying sound: at least someone had found something to do besides gape disbelievingly at the fire that exploded all around.

Rockets, she thought suddenly. Rockets, like the ones that five years ago had burned down a garrison in South Hill, supposedly invented by a now-dead Paladin named Annis. "Annis's Fire," the people had called the deadly stuff that dripped out of the sky, igniting whatever it landed on with flames that could not be extinguished by water. Sand would work, but there was not enough sand in the entire city to save this garrison from burning.

Her lungs ached. Cadmar was not quick-footed, and she should have caught up with him by now. She slowed her pace; she had lost him.

She heard a horn close by. Ahead of her were flares of ig-
nited gunpowder, pistol shots, the shouts and cries of battle.
She had run almost onto the heels of an organized company of
soldiers, and they in turn had run into an ambush. She ducked
into a doorway as a pistol ball plunked into wood, and finally
took the time to load her weapons. When she peered out, she
saw little more than shadows, but then a flaring fire nearby lit
up the street in garish light and she could see. Some people lay
wounded, and they soon would burn to death if no one dragged
them to safety. Beyond, blades flashed as soldiers and
strangers endeavored to kill each other hand-to-hand. One soldier, sapling-thin and giddy with excitement, was briskly rescued from her foolishness by a big, laconic woman whose
saber moved so quickly it scarcely seemed to move at all.
Clement recognized both of them: the big woman was her frequent training partner, one of the best blade fighters in the garrison. The sapling was young Kelin.

"Get that child out of danger!" she cried. "She is too young
for battle!"

Of course it was absurd: in the screams and shouts, the clash
of blades and the explosion of gunfire, with the flames roaring
in the nearby roof, Clement's voice was like the squeak of that
evening's wayfarer bat. The sapling girl and the laconic soldier
plunged side by side into the dark tangle of blade and ball.
Clement ran after them.

A shout. She used her saber to cut her way through a man
she presumed to be her enemy. A white face, she remembered
later, garishly lit by flame, with black marks on his forehead.
The flash of gunpowder, the whine of a projectile. She flung
herself flat, and rolled, and saw gobbets of fire raining down,
and got to her feet and ran. The sapling and the soldier had
ducked into the shadows of the eaves to avoid the deadly rain.
Clement coughed smoke and chased them, shouting hoarsely,
but if they heard her they gave her cry no importance. Apparently, they thought they were heroes.

Perhaps these two had been following Captain Herme's signals, but now they had left the company behind. The three
women appeared to be alone in the strange night, the fighting

left behind them now, the buildings here seeming empty and not yet burning. Ahead lay the garden, strangely lit with lamp flame and with—oh, Clement saw it now—the fiery rise of rockets. So this was where the rocketeers had set up their base. And did those two heroes think that it would be left unguarded? Or that they alone could end the attack? Apparently, they did.

Gasping now, for she had run across the entire garrison, Clement shouted weakly, "Beware sharpshooters!" Even as she cried out, there was a flash and the tall woman quietly folded herself up in the middle of the street, like a uniform on a shelf. Clement could already see her name, written in a company clerk's bold handwriting. Another dead soldier with no one to replace her.

Kelin did not even seem to know what had happened. She would be eager, too drunk on excitement to be wise, imagining herself as the one who would save the garrison from certain ruin. The girl ran straight to the garden fence and climbed it. She seemed to hesitate only a moment as she looked back and realized she had lost her companion. Perhaps she was surprised to learn that death was possible after all. Perhaps she even remembered that Captain Herme had commanded her never to do anything alone. Perhaps it occurred to her that she should wait, for the rest of her company would soon break through the battle line. But there was no glory in waiting, was there?

She dropped down the other side of the fence. Clement reached through the bars to grab for the booted heel that had already begun to run across the grass, toward the garden's fiery center where, with a shower of sparks, another rocket went arcing across the sky. Clement watched her go. She dared not shout after her, and could only watch, clenching the iron fence like a prisoner, as Kelin all but flew to the garish ritual. A half dozen giddy people seemed to dance and bow, with flaming lucifers in their hands, and then they all went dancing back. With a deep sound like a rushing wind or waterfall, the light flew fiercely up into the sky, trailing sparks and a gently glowing smoke. And then Kelin was on them, swift, blithe, oblivious.

Perhaps she managed to injure one—it was hard to tell in the tricky light—and then she was cut down.

Clement groaned as though the swordcut had entered her own pounding heart. Her eyes ached with smoke and from peering into the shadows. The rocketeers' dance went on: in and out, matter-of-fact. Another rocket burst into the sky.

Clement's head began to clear. She had gotten a few good breaths of air, perhaps, or perhaps she was simply too inured to battle to weep for long. She had begun to plan the attack on the rocketeers before she even realized it, and when Herme's company, now missing two members, came running down the street, she was ready to tell them what to do.

Hours later, Clement finally located Cadmar. Having himself never gone near the battle, he chastised her for her hotheadedness. She had commanded the company that eliminated the rocketeers, and had, after all that, emerged unscathed. Only Cadmar, whose temper came mostly from envy, could have failed to appreciate what a hollow victory it was.

When he had used up his anger, he sent her to locate Commander Ellid, a task that wasted what remained of the morning. Clement found the garrison commander at last, standing before the smoking ruin of a barracks, with her hair singed and her face black with soot. Clement would not have recognized her if not for the insignia on her hat and the messengers that circled her like bees around their hive. Ellid was a strongwilled, short-tempered old veteran who enjoyed good food and had never forgiven Cadmar for driving away her excellent cook. But today she seemed relieved to learn of the general's safety.

"He was fighting fires all night," said Clement. "Now he's visiting injured soldiers in the infirmary. He's no worse hurt than you are."

The commander looked ruefully at her singed uniform. "A few burns." Her voice was a hoarse rasp; like Clement she had been breathing smoke and screaming orders all night. "The general," she added, "was supposed to go to safety should the garrison be attacked."

"Surely you know that he will never be so prudent. But it was my duty to escort him to safety, if any safety could have been found last night, and I could not even find him, and ended up in danger myself. It's been a stupid night."

"That's true enough. Well, it's over, eh?" Ellid lifted her head and surveyed the smoking ruin of her garrison with swollen, red-rimmed eyes. "Though I can't believe what I see," she muttered.

"The refectory is still standing, anyway, though the kitchen is gone. The general requests that you meet him there. Surely the cooks will soon manage to produce something to eat."

Ellid made a soldier's gesture, simultaneously acknowledging, agreeing to, and delaying compliance with an order. One of her lieutenants was approaching, and she turned to see what he wanted.

Again, Clement limped slowly down cobbled streets turned black with ash, past smoking ruins of charred timbers. Soldiers sprawled here and there, the dead difficult to distinguish from the exhausted living, all dressed in ashes and masked with soot. At a well where the ground was still awash from the spilled water of a fire line, some soldiers took turns dunking their singed heads into a bucket of water. Clement joined them, took a turn with the cake of soap, and looked up from rinsing the grime away to find the gathered soldiers giving her demoralized salutes. One of them took her hat and polished the soot from her insignias. "Lieutenant-General, the Lucky Man says anyone who sees you is to tell you he's in the general's quarters."

She went there. Gilly had taken over Cadmar's table, since Commander Ellid's quarters had burned to the ground. He and the garrison clerk had opened the log and rosters, which, being singed in places, apparently had been snatched out of the flames. Soldiers came and went, to tell the clerk and secretary the names of soldiers dead or wounded. Soon it would be Clement's turn to deal with that dreadful paperwork. Perhaps this would be the disaster that finally forced Cadmar to close a garrison for lack of soldiers. And then the Paladins would realize the Sainnites' secret weakness.

"Come with me," she said desperately to Gilly.

She brought him his cane and helped him to his feet, and walked him past a newly arrived soldier, who was so tired he could scarcely tell the clerk the name of his fallen comrade.

As they walked down the hall, Gilly, leaning more heavily than usual on his cane, said admiringly, "The clerk actually ran into a burning building to save the records. If she hadn't, we would be in quite a tangle."

Clement looked at him in disbelief. Gilly's ugly face twisted with an ugly grin, and Clement began to laugh. Laughter whooped out of her aching chest: mad, mysterious. She laughed until she choked, and Gilly, still grinning his dreadful grin, pounded her too roughly on the back. She sopped up the tears that were running down her face. "Gods! Don't do that to me again today! It's been a hellish night!"

Gilly grunted. "The soldiers think we were attacked by magic."

"Cadmar did too, until I reminded him of Annis's Fire. They say that Annis was a genius with explosives."

"Was?"

"Apparently, even her family believes she's long dead, accidentally killed by Paladins. Her rockets and her fire haven't been used since she died, but I guess she told someone her secret after all."

They found Cadmar holding the clenched hand of a woman whose face had been burned to the bone. The infirmary stank of burned meat and sounded like a nightmare. The medics went around with smoke pipes to quiet the agony of the ones they judged were dying, but those that might live continued to scream.

"By the three gods!" cried Cadmar in a fury, once they were outside. "The Paladins will regret this cowardly attack!"

They had nearly reached the refectory before Cadmar had

raged himself into silence. Clement then ventured to say, "Commander Ellid will have enough to do just solving the practical problems of recovering from this attack. Let me handle the counter-attack. We must have a strong reaction—an intolerable one."

Cadmar said, "You'll need a detachment to serve under your command."

As they entered the refectory, Gilly muttered to Clement, "You think the Paladins won't target you now? You could be dead before midsummer."

"I'd rather be dead than have to deal with the duty roster after this disaster."

"What kind of revenge do you have in mind?"

"I'll take their children," Clement said, "and raise them to be soldiers."

Gilly looked stunned. But later, as they ate gummy gray porridge with Ellid, her lieutenants, and some of her captains, and Cadmar's resilience began to display itself in energetic conversation, Gilly leaned over to Clement and said softly, "It's brilliant! But if we start stealing children, you'll put that courtesan of yours out of business."

The commanders were piecing together a chronology of the night's events, all of which Clement already knew or had surmised. Cadmar announced that anyone who knew anything about the attackers was to be sent to Clement. They decided to go as a group to view the sites of the heaviest fighting.

The ten of them made slow progress across the garrison. Teams of soldiers methodically sorted the living from the dead, and the streets that before had been littered with bodies were now busy with exhausted soldiers being herded to food and shelter, injured soldiers being carried to the infirmary, and old veterans with buckets of soapy water, washing the faces of the dead so they could be identified. They passed an improvised paddock, where hysterical horses rescued from the burning stable were being soothed and treated. Shock had already given way to efficiency.

Gilly was obviously in pain, and seemed glad to have to pause again to let some litter bearers pass. He was accustomed to pain, and it only seemed to give his sharp mind a certain ruthlessness. He said, "This troubles me, this attack. It's not like the others. It goes against Mabin's directives, and the local Paladins' own disinclination to do anything that might lead to retaliation. They pride themselves on their long view, don't they? And on their caution."

Cadmar and Ellid had paused ahead of them, and Captain Herme was narrating how the well-armed attackers had lain there in ambush and had—he seemed reluctant to admit it— defended their position with determination and courage. Some ten of their bodies lay tossed contemptuously into a pile. Did the officers care to view them?

"What for?" asked Cadmar.

But Gilly had already limped over to the pile of dead bodies. "They are so young," he said. "This also is not right."

Clement stopped looking at the wounds and turned her attention to the faces. "And Paladins sneer at us for sending children to war," she said.

"What is that on his forehead? Wipe off his face, will you?"

Clement had nothing to wipe anyone's face with, but Gilly produced a voluminous handkerchief, and she bent over to smear away the soot and gore from the young man's forehead. What remained was a mark, painted in what appeared to be black ink. Gilly examined it silently and intently, and then stood back, looking first bemused and then unnerved.

He said to Cadmar, who grimly waited, "I would guess these fighters all have the same mark on their foreheads. It is a glyph, the one that is called the Pyre, or Death-and-Life."

"What does it mean?" asked Cadmar.

Gilly shook his head, his ugly face unreadable now. As they resumed their progress, Clement tucked a hand under his elbow to give him some help in walking. She said, "You suspect something."

Gilly said, "Councilor Mabin herself wrote in her book that she was at Harald G'deon's side when he died. She observed that he did not vest a successor. These rumors we've heard about a Lost G'deon—Mabin has to be certain they are untrue."

"So?" Clement felt nearly hysterical with exhaustion, and

strangling Gilly seemed better than listening to him recount irrelevant history.

"So I must conclude that these people who attacked us last night could not have been Paladins. That glyph on the dead man's face is the sign that used to be carried through Shaftal whenever an old G'deon died and a new one was vested: Death-and-Life, meaning that the G'deon burns in the pyre and yet the G'deon lives. Mabin would never allow her people to display that sign."

Clement was silent. She had paid little attention to the rumors of a lost G'deon, and was trying now to remember when she first had heard them. It had been less than five years ago, but Harald had been dead for twenty. "You think these people who attacked us believe Harald vested someone before he died?"

"That big woman who supposedly pierced Councilor Mabin's heart with a spike—perhaps they are fighting for her." He paused, then said one more word, but it reverberated in Clement's scrambled thoughts. "Fanatics," he said.

Later, they stood together in the scorched garden, looking down at the slender soldier who had run in such glad foolishness to her own pointless death. The soldiers had separated Kelin's body from the others, had wiped the soot and blood from her young face, and had covered her ugly wounds with a blanket. But they could not put the vibrancy back into her slack face, or the liveliness back into her blank eyes. Clement looked away from the girl's body. Gilly fumbled for his sooty handkerchief. *He should have known better than to become fond of a young soldier,* Clement thought bitterly. *All Sainnite children die in war. As fast as we send them into battle, they die. We might as well just kill them when they're born and save us all the trouble of raising them.*

Part 2

How Raven Became A God

When Raven was young, he had three friends: a grasshopper, a sparrow, and a wolf. They all were restless troublemakers, the shame of their clans and the scourge of their tribes.

One day, the bird gods appeared to Raven and said, "We have been watching you a long time, and we think we might make you into a god. But first you must make something that has never been seen before, to prove to us that you are clever enough to be a god."

Of course, Raven wanted to be a god, but he had no idea how to make something that had never been seen before. So he asked his friend the grasshopper for advice. The grasshopper said, "Well, I know one thing that has never been seen before: it is the soul of my clan, that lies at the center of the village, in a hut that nobody enters."

Then Raven went to the sparrow for advice, and the sparrow said, "Well, I know one thing that has never been seen before. It is the soul of my clan, that lies at the center of the village, in the hut that nobody enters."

Then, Raven went to the wolf for advice, and the wolf said, "Well, I know one thing that has never been seen before. It is the soul of my clan, that lies at the center of the village, in the hut that nobody enters."

So then Raven called together his friends. He said, "I have thought of a wonderful joke. We will go to each of your villages and make a great noise, and they will think they are being attacked. They will all run about like the ant clan, and we will hide in the woods and laugh at them."

They all agreed that this was a fine plan. So they waited for the dark moon, and on that night they all met outside the sparrow's village. They each had brought all the whistles and rattles they could find, and they spread out along the edge of the village and each commenced yelling and whistling and shaking their rattles. Soon, the sparrow warriors came running out of the village to find their enemy, while the sparrow elders and children hid in the huts. The three friends all slipped into the woods, laughing. But Raven sneaked into the center of the village, and found the hut that has no door, and with his claws he cut a slit in the wall and slipped in. There in the hut he found the soul of the sparrow clan.

Now, no one except Raven has ever seen a soul, so I can't tell you what the soul looked like. But Raven bit off a piece of it with his sharp beak and put it in his satchel. Then he slipped out of the hut and sewed up the opening he had made in the wall, so no one would notice, and he went and found his friends in the woods. "Wasn't that fun!" he said. "Let's do it again, this time at the grasshopper clan."

So they did it again, at the grasshopper clan and then at the wolf clan, and each time Raven sneaked into the village and stole a piece of the clan's soul. But after the wolf warriors had run into the woods looking for their enemy, they encountered the sparrow and grasshopper warriors, who were all searching the forest. They each thought that the other clans had banded together against them, and a huge battle began.

In the morning, Raven's friends found him in his camp, where he lived by himself. They all were sick with horror. "The warriors of our people have all killed each other, and now our clans will hate each other for many generations!" they cried.

But Raven didn't care. He had a pot of stew and he offered each of his friends some, but they were too upset to eat. So Raven ate it all himself, and his friends went away in disgust and never talked to him again.

Now, the stew was made out of the pieces of soul the Raven

had stolen from each of the clans. After a while, he started to have a stomachache, but he endured the pain, for he wanted very badly to be a god. And then at last he put piece of leather on the ground and he defecated on it, and there lay a raven's turd made of the digested souls of the three clans. No one has ever seen a soul-turd except for Raven, but you can imagine it wasn't pretty to look at.

Raven packaged up that turd and took it to the gods. "Here you go," he said. "Here is something that has never been seen before." The gods all looked at the turd, and then they looked at each other, and finally one of them said, "I can't believe that you have done this! But we have no choice except to make you a god. Considering all the havoc you have wreaked, I think we will make you the god of death." And that is how Raven became a god.

As for the turd, it was so disgusting that they buried it. A year later, Raven went back that way, and where the turd had been buried, a new clan had risen up out of the ground, and were living in a new village. They farmed and sang love songs like the grasshopper. They were clever and hardworking like the sparrow. And they were loyal and brave as the wolf. Raven took a special liking to them because his turd was the soul of the clan. They were the first human people.

Chapter Eight

The farm family, having been shouted out of their beds, huddled together as far as they could get from the heavily armed, impatient soldiers that crammed the dark parlor. The farmstead's many children had been made invisible behind a fortress of resolute adults. But one man, cut out from the crowd with a screaming child in his arms, faced down the hardened fighters that surrounded him. "You will not take the child," he said.

By the flickering light of the lantern held up by the signalman, Clement distantly examined the stubborn father. He did not seem old, but he was desiccated, his hair molting, his eyes set in shadowed hollows, his body sagging as though his muscles were coming detached from his bones. To admire his hopeless courage was a poor strategy, but as a nearby soldier eagerly lifted his club, Clement forestalled him with a raised hand. She said quietly to the man, "Your daughter's last memory of you will be of your death."

The man's hand protectively cupped his daughter's skull as she hid her face in his shoulder. Obstinately, fearlessly, he said, "You will not take her!"

They had just one night to round up forty children—Clement could waste no time in argument. She began to lower her upraised hand, and like a puppet the soldier again lifted his club.

"Wait!" An old woman stepped into the light, jerking herself loose from the hands that reached out to restrain her. "Take me instead."

"No!" cried the farmers. But the old woman, trailing a blanket snatched from her bed, gestured dismissively at them.

"Take the old woman," Clement said to the soldiers.

They laid hands on the old woman; they hurt her until she cried out. A grinning soldier pricked her throat with a dagger.

Now the little girl's father looked panicked. Good. Clement said, "We'll kill the old woman first. And we'll kill the rest of your family, one at a time. And with all of them dead, you'll still lose the girl."

The man said dully to his hysterical daughter, "Davi, you go with these people. Be a brave girl."

"No!" she shrieked. "They scare me!"

Clement jerked the girl out of the man's grip, and handed her, flailing and screaming, to the soldier behind her. The father uttered a shout and flung himself after her. A sharp crack on the head, and he fell. The old woman, released, cried bitterly, "We will never forget this!"

Out in the yard, which was crowded with war horses, they dumped the screaming child into the closed wagon, where her cries revived those of the other children previously snatched from other farms where other farmers had offered the same outraged, disbelieving resistance. It had become a routine. So far Clement had managed to convince the families of her seriousness without killing anyone. In Sainna, the parents would have begged her to take the children so they'd have one less mouth to feed.

"That's fourteen kids," said the sergeant in charge of guarding the wagon.

"Mount up," said Clement.

"Mount up!" cried the captain, and the signal-man led the way, with his lantern.

It was a gorgeous, soft night: spring's swift bloom had given way to summer; winter's bitter winds and drifting snow were nearly impossible to remember now. Stars crowded the sky, and Clement could almost imagine what the Shaftali found to

love in this unforgiving land. The children's muffled cries settled to whimpers, and Clement could hear bird calls and a din
of frogs at the pond they were passing. She pretended to herself that she was serene enough to appreciate this lovely ride.
Forty children for forty dead soldiers: a grueling night.

She had let the people of Watfield and the surrounding countryside wait for retribution. Immediately after the fire, the local
Paladins had been mustered, and for a long time had hovered
just outside the city, where they made themselves a nuisance
by interfering with lumber deliveries. Occasionally, Ellid, to
boost morale, had sent out a company of angry soldiers to fight
with them. When Cadmar, Gilly, and a select company of soldiers had ridden out to begin the tour of the garrisons, they reportedly had enjoyed a brisk clash of arms as they passed
through the Paladins' perimeter. Now, nearly a month after the
fire, the Paladin alert had relaxed. That night, Clement and her
detachment had slipped out of the city unnoticed, and so far
had done their work unhindered.

Clement could not predict how long it would take for the
Paladins to converge on them or how much the presence of
children would inhibit them from attacking. The attackers
would probably try to force the soldiers to abandon the wagon,
and Clement had trained the detachment accordingly. The soldiers had enjoyed the playacting, which was easier and more
interesting than clearing rubble. Clement had needed the dis-
traction, for she felt that she lived in the shadow of doom, and
Gilly was not there to jolt her out of her dark mood with his
acerbic commentary.

They rode into an empty farmstead. The soldiers searched
the house and reported bed covers flung back and clothing
tossed about. After they were on the road again, the captain
rode up beside Clement and said, "I suppose there's a farmer
galloping ahead of us on a fast horse."

In the past, farmers could have warned their neighbors or
summoned help using bells that were hit with iron poles, but
they had long since been broken of that habit by Sainnite retribution. Clement said, "Farmers don't have fast horses. They're
probably running from farm to farm in relay. Let's hurry our

pace, skip a couple of farms, and see if we can get ahead of the alarm again."

By this method, Clement's detachment managed to acquire a couple of more children, but then they found only empty beds again.

"Signal fire," the captain said in disgust.

Clement had also noticed light flaring on a hilltop, and knew that soon several more scattered hilltops would be aflame. "Return to Watfield," she said. "Quickly. No need to spare the horses now. And let's hope no one in town notices the signals."

In the city, her soldiers broke down the doors of two and even three houses at once. Even though Clement insisted that they take only one child from each household, the total quickly mounted by ten, fifteen, twenty more children before the fore-warned parents began hiding their children from the soldiers in cellars, woodsheds, and attics. The soldiers, forced to extricate cowering, hysterical children from dark and cluttered places while holding back and sometimes fighting desperate parents, began to lose their tempers. Clement, supervising from the street, heard reports of blood spilled, of a child injured. She listened to the city rousing: dogs barked as a ripple of door pounding and warning shouts spread down the streets from her operation.

"How many recruits do we have?" she asked the sergeant in charge of guarding the wagon.

"Recruits!" He laughed as though he thought she was joking. "Thirty-six."

"Close enough to forty. Signal-man! Retreat to garrison!"

The night was no longer quiet. From the water gate Clement could see a distant beacon, its flames subsiding now but still bright in the distance. The roused city echoed with the angry clangor of pots being banged. A mob had gathered at the garrison gate, and all watches had been mustered to guard the wall. Periodically, Ellid's bugler sounded a signal, which received an orderly answer from each of the scattered companies. The signals told Clement that there had been some few skirmishes, but so far no emergencies.

Clement was feeling very tired. The signal-man told her the time; soon dawn light would start to extinguish the stars. Clement rubbed her face vigorously and shouted at the stable sergeant, "How long does it take to change horses?"

"It's hard to get the harnesses buckled in the dark, Lieutenant-General," he said apologetically.

At last, the fresh horses were in their traces, and they were led down the ramp onto the barge, pulling the wagon-load of children behind them. The wheels were secured. As the wagon swayed with the movements of the water, Clement could hear children whimpering again. They would quickly learn not to cry, just as Clement had when her soldier-mother came to take her away from the only home she had known.

The barge was loose; the dray horses on shore leaned into the traces. Clement watched until the barge had been towed through the water gate and was picked up by the river's sluggish current. It would reach a garrison down river by mid-afternoon and from there the wagon would travel to the children's garrison. She turned away, sighing with relief. Her operation had been a success.

Some six days later, the gate remained blocked by a restless crowd that banged their pots and uttered ugly shouts every time the garrison bell rang. Food supplies came in by the water gate, but three times Paladins had cut barges loose from their tow-horses to be carried away and eventually wrecked by the slow current. Now, as far away as the western borders, lumber mills refused to sell at any price if they suspected the lumber was going to Watfield garrison.

"We can't manage without wood!" In a temper, Commander Ellid paced Cadmar's quarters, stepping over and around the clutter of sleeping pallets and gear. Most of the garrison's officers were sleeping in Cadmar's quarters at night; four companies slept in shifts in the hallways, and Clement slept with half a company in her own room, while another half occupied it in the daytime. Since the fire, solitude could only be found out of doors.

Clement got up from Cadmar's table, where she had been going over the duty roster, and took Gilly's book of maps from its shelf. "We'll send a company from another garrison to take over a lumber mill," she said. "Show me where the wood is coming from."

They discussed logistics, and Clement wrote an order in her own hand, which she had done a lot lately. The harried company clerk arrived, mixed a fresh bottle of ink and trimmed several pens, and left again with a sheaf of paper under her arm. She was not doing duty as a scribe anymore, for she was the only person in the garrison who could cipher well enough to produce reliable measurements for the building plans. "No workers," grumbled Ellid, still in a temper. "No materials, no facilities, no plans—" The door opened to admit an aide carrying a tray. "No edible food!"

Clement glanced at the unappetizing mess the aide set down on the table. There was a distinct smell of scorched potatoes.

Ellid continued, "And in these conditions I'm to rebuild a garrison in three months' time? I can predict now that we're spending the winter without a roof over our heads."

Clement said, "I would apologize that my operation has made yours more difficult, but since there's been no more rocket attacks, it seems justified."

"You did what you had to, Lieutenant-General." Ellid sat down to stir a spoon in what passed for stew, then picked up a lump of bread instead, with no butter, of course. "No kitchen," she muttered. "But my old cook would have managed, by the gods!"

Clement hacked open a lump of bread and dropped brick–hard pieces into the watery stew to soften. She was weary of other people's complaints. Even in the garden, where she worked sometimes to repair the damaged beds and coax the summer flowers into bloom, her fellow gardeners could be heard whining to each other.

"No information?" asked Ellid after a while. Perhaps it had

occurred to her that Clement, also experiencing her share of difficulties, had no one to complain to.

"No information," Clement said. "No one in Watfield admits to knowing anything about the rocketeers. No one claimed the bodies. The Paladins themselves were taken by surprise; that's all I'm certain of. It took an entire day for them to muster. If they'd known about the attack beforehand, they would have mustered already."

Side by side, they forced themselves to eat the wretched stew. Ellid finally said, "Better an old enemy than a new one, eh? At least we can anticipate the Paladins most of the time. But these rocketeers, they're a different kind of people. Do you remember, when we first came here, how angry we used to get because these people didn't fight like we expected them to?"

"I was nine years old," Clement said. "But I remember my mother was pretty outraged. That was a strange time."

"In Sainna, soldiers fought soldiers. Same tactics, same style."

"Well, we're never going back to Sainna, are we? Even if the wars are over in that country, no one would be glad to see us return. After thirty years in exile we'd look like an invading force to them."

"The wars were *never* over in Sainna." Ellid lapsed into a silence, perhaps reflecting gloomily, as Clement was, on their equally untenable situation in Shaftal.

Their silence was interrupted by a gate guard sent to fetch Clement. "A group of gray-hairs want to talk to someone about the children. They want to negotiate their return, they say."

"You can't go down there, Lieutenant-General," said the gate captain. "They'll tear you apart, and it'll be on my head."

From the watch tower, Clement surveyed the surly crowd below. She saw people in neat, close-fitting clothing that advertised their leisure and prosperity. She saw laborers in long-shirts and breeches with padded knees. She saw young people flirting or playing games of dice, and she saw old people who had brought chairs to sit in. Many of the people waved strips of white cloth on which were painted messages no one on the wall could have read. Baskets of bread were being passed overhead, from hand to hand. Clement caught a whiff of it, and watched with ravenous fascination as a man took a steaming loaf and tore it into pieces to distribute to his friends.

Clement could see no children. Most of the old people appeared to have gathered close to the gate. The siege gate was still closed, and no one could see in, so the people below looked up at the towers. "Lower a ladder," Clement said.

"Lieutenant-General!" the captain protested.

She gave him a look, and he turned briskly away to shout commands. She stripped off her weapons and insignias, and, when the ladder was lowered, climbed quickly down. Someone threw a turnip at her, but with shouts and shoving the crowd seemed to get its hotheads under control. Clement set foot on stone, and turned to find herself surrounded by old people, who showed no sign of being disconcerted by her arrival in their midst. "What's your rank?" asked one, and another said, "Do you speak our language?"

"I'm told I speak it perfectly," said Clement. One of the three people closest to her looked uncomfortably familiar. A painted strip of cloth was wrapped around her neck and hung down the front of her shirt—a farmer's work shirt, extravagantly gathered at the shoulders to allow free movement of the arms. The old woman said to the others, "This is the one who took our children. She's an officer."

There was a silence. The crowd surged, but then subsided. An old man said, "It was a stupid thing to do."

"So was burning the garrison," said Clement.

"Our children had nothing to do with that!"

"I was told you wanted to negotiate," Clement said impatiently. But someone had already jabbed the man with an elbow.

The woman said, "You look famished. Would you like some bread?" She waved a hand in the air and one of the baskets of bread made a swift journey to them. Somehow, though Clement meant to refuse, she had half a loaf in her hand. One bite, she instructed herself, but could not make herself stop before three.

These were very canny people. "The children," she said to them, "Are no longer here."

"What!" they cried.

"They haven't been here for six days. Shout their names and bang your pans all you want; they can't hear you."

"Where are they?"

Clement leaned against the ladder, with one arm wrapped casually around a rung. These people might not realize it, but the soldiers above were poised to raise the ladder, with her on it. She took another bite of the excellent bread. "What will you offer?"

"Take us instead." The woman gestured at the crowd of gray heads.

It was the second time this old woman had offered herself in place of the child. And it revealed just how little she and her fellow Shaftali understood the Sainnites, for it had not even occurred to them that the children might be more than mere hostages. Clement replied, "I'll trade for the rocketeers. One child for useful information. One child for every rocketeer, delivered to us alive."

"They are children!" said one of the people in disbelief. "They are not weights on a scale. They are children!"

"They are weights on a scale as far as we are concerned. Is that all you have to tell me?"

The woman said with unconcealed frustration, "We can't just deliver these people to you! We don't even know who they were! One market day, they were in the crowd: strangers, loudmouths with strange ideas. A few days later, your garrison was attacked. That's all anyone knows."

"Oh, I doubt it," Clement said. "Well, I appreciate you making this effort to meet with me." The impatient man uttered a sardonic snort and was jabbed with an elbow again. "If anyone wants to talk again, you can ask for me by name—it's Clement."

She started up the ladder, but paused to add over her shoulder, "Maybe you'd better clear the gate. We don't really want to shoot you, but we will if we must."

The mob began banging their pans again, and continued

long after Clement had safety reached the tower. The remains of her loaf was distributed to the guard, one bite at a time, as long as it lasted. Clement wished she had managed to bring up the entire basket.

Whatever impression Clement had made on the townsfolk, there was no particular result. The crowd at the gate did not dissipate. Everyone in the city now seemed to be wearing those printed strips of cloth. No one came to the gate asking to talk to her. Perhaps no one actually knew anything useful about the garrison's attackers, but it seemed more likely that no one was willing to be publicly identified as a traitor.

A message from Purnal, who commanded the children's garrison, eventually arrived. It confirmed the safe delivery of the children, then lapsed into one of his lengthy vituperations, full of dire predictions of what would become of the Sainnites now they had become baby thieves. "What idiot dreamed up this bizarre plan?" he wrote. "Did anyone even try to think of what might result?" She only read one page of his jagged, angry handwriting, and then threw the entire missive into the fire. Cadmar had always done the same with anything that came from Purnal, while commenting that Purnal's brains were in his leg—the one that had been cut off.

Chapter Nine

All that remained of the spring's plague was a flea in a bottle, which Zanja chanced upon one day, in the bottom of a clothes chest, underneath a pile of winter clothing that she was layering with strewing herbs to keep away the moths. Hard red wax sealed the cork, but the flea hopped vigorously in its prison. Karis never mentioned the flea, and Zanja never asked about it.

Winter snow had barricaded the household, but now the scattered neighbors regularly came calling, and the road that could be glimpsed from the apple orchard had become a busy thoroughfare. Karis worked long days at the forge with two local youths who served as her casual apprentices. Emil and Norina wandered Shaftal, J'han remained deep in the south with the Juras. Medric read books and wrote letters all night, and slept during the day. Leeba spent entire mornings or afternoons with her friends. It was quiet.

Early in the summer, Zanja, Karis and Leeba traveled to a fair in the nearby town. A company of players performed one drama after another, shouting their lines over the hubbub of hucksters, jugglers, musicians, and peddlers. Leeba spent her pennies on exotic candies that she immediately gobbled up, and ran wild with a giddy mob of her friends. In the tavern, people who rarely traveled to town lined up to stand drinks for Karis and ask for advice, having brought with them the evidence of their difficulties: withered leaves, unsprouted seeds, underweight babies, the mummified remains of aborted livestock, fistfuls of soil, vials of water, examples of weeds that they could not eradicate. As Karis listened, considered, talked, and politely took an occasional small sip from her constantly refilled cup, Zanja ingratiated herself into a group of traveling merchants who had left their stalls to the care of their underlings and had come in to escape the heat.

"Now that's a rare sight," one of them commented. "An earth witch consulting at the fair like old times."

"She's a local secret," Zanja said, though it was not exactly true any more. It had taken a couple of years for Karis to become known in the region as an earth witch, but now the word continued to spread. Some of the people here today had journeyed a good distance to seek her advice. Yet, though Karis was certainly the only earth witch in Shaftal, and though rumors of the lost G'deon had subsided but not been forgotten, it apparently had not yet occurred to any Shaftali to put the two together. The Sainnites might have instantly recognized Karis as a threat, but to the Shaftali she simply was one of them.

"Aren't you drinking?" asked a merchant.

"I'm cursed by a dislike for ale, and there's no cider to be had at this time of year."

"Ah, it's a curse indeed! In this hot weather!"

Zanja said, "I'm curious about what happened in Watfield. I don't suppose you've heard anything?"

"We've just come from there."

"That's a long journey!"

"But this fair is on the way to the big ones in the north . . ."

The complications of a traveling merchant's schedule were already well known to Zanja, but she pretended to listen.

"So what happened in Watfield?" she was finally able to ask.

"Well, you know that it was a sneak attack, in dead of night. And the attackers used some kind of device that flew through the air and exploded with fire. And they say the fire couldn't be put out . . ."

As Zanja listened, she remembered the first time those devilish devices had been used on a Sainnite garrison: the hissing of the lucifer, the rockets' garish and explosive flight. Her hand had lit the fuses. Though she smiled wryly at the memory, setting a garrison afire was not something she felt inclined to do again.

Later, she went out into the dusty yard, which was occupied by several donkeys, some chickens, and a few sickly sheep awaiting Karis's examination. A raven flew down from the rooftop and reported on Leeba's activities. Zanja's daughter had skinned a knee, been yelled at by a merchant, and was now watching a puppet show.

Zanja said, "Give Emil a message for me."

"Emil is free to speak to you," the raven said. "He asks if you have learned anything about the attack on Watfield."

"It certainly was a rocket attack, and it sounds to me like the rockets carried Annis's Fire. Annis didn't like Willis, but I suppose he might have flattered her into giving him the recipe. If it was Willis and his people who attacked Watfield, what is he trying to accomplish?"

"He's captured the imagination of the people. He's made it even easier to get recruits to his cause." The raven paused. "I believe that Willis and his company are responsible for several other incidents this summer. They are moving quickly from place to place, not following a predictable pattern. They haven't attempted something like what they did in Watfield, but everything they do seems too provocative to be laid at the door of local Paladins."

"That stupid man is going to take over Shaftal! And in the name of a G'deon he wouldn't like if he ever met her!"

"Actually," said the raven in Emil's moderate way, "his dream-G'deon suits his needs much better than the real one would."

"His dream is more impressive, certainly," said Zanja, thinking of Karis in the tavern, peering at the roots of a stunted plant that had been carried three days there for her inspection.

"Superficially, yes. But when people just want their immediate hurts to be soothed, they don't look too closely at the cure that's being offered." The raven added, "Now the Sainnites have retaliated by snatching a cartload of young children."

"Gods of the sky! The Sainnites are exacting their revenge on children?"

Zanja had been squatting in the dust to talk with the raven, but now she rose up sharply to survey the fair, which filled several flat fields on the edge of town. She was looking among the stalls and tents and strolling people for a glimpse of a dirty, bloody-kneed, sugar-smeared little girl, who by now was probably loudly talking back to the puppets, much to the puppeteer's dismay. Zanja did not see Leeba, of course, but she spotted the black bird that was keeping watch on her from the top of a distant tree. Zanja said to Emil, "The Sainnites are doing everything possible to destroy themselves. They might as well be collaborating in their own demise."

Zanja's raven lifted off abruptly as a laughing group approached the tavern. She felt an impulse to shout at them for their intrusive merriment. And now the tavern door opened, and Karis came out with the shepherd to take a look at his sheep. She had to hunch down to fit through the doorway, and then, as she stepped out, the hot sunlight seemed to set her cropped hair afire. The laughing people stopped dead at the sight of the giant, lips parted with surprise. Then, apparently misinterpreting the hard line of Karis's mouth and the glitter of her eyes, they rather anxiously crowded together. But Zanja went to her, and said, "Karis, you're worn out."

The shepherd turned to Karis, guilt-stricken. "I thought you looked a bit thin. You've been ill?"

"I'll look at your sheep," said Karis to him. "And then I'm going home."

She squatted down among the silly animals, who were too weak to react with their usual blind panic. The laughing people observed Karis in puzzlement, then bewilderment, and finally disappointment. A woman of her remarkable size, they seemed to think, should have given them more of a show.

Midsummer, and the sixth anniversary of the massacre of Zanja's people approached like a storm whose rumbling thunder and flickering lightning might be heard for hours before the rain finally fell. Once, Karis came in looking for something to eat and found Zanja lying with her aching head pressed to the cool stones of an unlit hearth. Karis picked her up and fiercely said, "Call for me when this happens!"

She sat in a chair, with Zanja huddled in her lap like a child. Karis's hands firmly pressed the pain out of Zanja's head; it dissipated like water, leaving her empty. Afterwards, Zanja felt sick with loneliness. She looked up, and Karis was staring bleakly away. "What have I done?" Zanja asked.

"You've survived what no one should have to survive," said Karis distantly.

"What have I done to make you so angry with me?"

Karis looked down at her then. "Is that really what you think?" She put a hand to Zanja's face again, a gentle touch despite her work-rough, callused skin. "I feel you pulling away from me with all your strength," she said. "But at the same time you're shouting at me to hold on. And with all my strength I am holding onto you, though I know that I have to let go."

"Unbinding-and-Binding," Zanja said in dull amazement.

"Is that a glyph?" Karis asked.

She set Zanja on her feet, and stood up. Zanja looked up to see her, and a residual dizziness from the headache nearly toppled her. Karis, with an arm around her, asked, "Can you explain to me what I've said? Because I don't understand what it means."

Zanja said, "I understand that if one of us must fall, it must be me."

In the silence, Zanja could hear a distant sound, a child's voice piping a shrill song as she came home across the fields.

As if in reply to Zanja's statement, Karis said, "That's Leeba. And Emil is on his way home. Is there nothing to eat in this house?"

Emil arrived home two days later and dropped his heavy load of books with a sigh.

"You need a donkey," Zanja commented, and poured him a cup of the tea that he always drank, no matter how hot the day.

"Oh, people are always giving me rides." In the parlor, he sat by a propped-open window, in one of the big, battered chairs that Karis was always intending to repair. Karis's hammer rang rhythmically, steadily, down at the forge, a sound that carried astonishingly far and was her only, more than sufficient, advertisement. Emil took a swallow of his tea and sighed. "I've been missing your tea." He glanced at her face and added hastily, "After a particularly messy fight, when the knees are wobbly from a close brush with death, there's nothing quite so fortifying."

She wanted to be angry at someone, but apparently it was not to be him. She found herself smiling instead, though her face was reluctant and out of the habit.

"My raven thinks you are on the verge of killing someone," Emil said.

"I might, if you continue to compliment my housekeeping."

"The house," said Emil somberly, "is keeping you."

Zanja sat on the cool stones of the hearth, folding up her limbs into a neat packet as she had learned to do when she was Leeba's age, a child as wild and gleeful as she, but required to learn quickly how to keep from using up more than her share of allotted space in the crowded clanhouse. In silence, pummeled by memories of her proud, extinguished people, she watched Emil drink his tea. A yellow butterfly fluttered confusedly into the room, then followed the afternoon sunlight out again.

"Does your head hurt?" Emil asked.

"Not right now." Zanja put a hand to her skull, where among the interwoven braids there grew some cross-grained hairs in an old scar, which marked a ridge of healed bone in her skull. At midsummer the old wound seemed fresh, and she needed to touch the scar to be certain that it was in fact healed. "There's no reason for this pain," she said, half to herself.

"Surely memories are beyond Karis's repair work." Emil set down his teacup and gave her an inquiring look. His hair, as usual, was tied back with a thong, and somehow, though at this time of year he often slept in the woods, he had managed to keep his weathered face clean-shaven. They had briefly met when she was fifteen and he was the age she was now. Even then he had seemed a deeply balanced man. Now, every year Emil arranged his travels so he could see her through the dreadful days of midsummer, and seemed prepared to continue to do so as long as he lived.

"My brother, what do you want to ask?" Zanja's voice was husky.

"I don't suppose," he said hopefully, "that your owl god is carrying you across another boundary? For the claws of truth dig deep in you this time of year."

She looked at him, puzzled at first, then with a rising awareness that her wretchedness was making her stupid. The glyph cards were already in her hands, the pouch and cord falling to the floor. Emil's card, Solitude, or the Man on the Hill, was held between her fingertips. The light falling from the heavenly bodies pierced him with deadly arrows. "I thought I was alone," she said.

"You think that every year," he said, without resentment.

He got himself more tea, and came to stand by her as the cards fell from her fingertips: Solitude, followed by the Owl, the Pyre, and Unbinding-and-Binding. "Opposing forces trapped in stasis," he said promptly. "But the paralysis can be broken with painful insight. The way the cards have landed seems to put you and me in a position of grave responsibility, doesn't it?" He bent over, teacup teetering dangerously, to point a finger at the owl, who flew with a hapless captive dangling from her claw. "Take me across that boundary with you," he said.

"Foolhardy man!"

"Oh, yes. Absolutely."

"But I can't make the crossing."

There was a silence. He said, "Tell me what is the boundary that must be crossed."

Zanja's flare of prescience appeared to have burned itself out; no new cards found their way into her hand, and she stared at the old ones in bleak frustration. Emil set down his teacup, knelt on the floor in front of her, and took the glyph cards from her hand. "Ask the question."

"What is the boundary that must be crossed?"

He did not lay down a new card, but pointed at the Pyre, Karis standing in the flames. "That card is reversed to Life-and-Death. If she moves, she will step into death, not out of it. Has she talked to you about this?"

"In the spring, when she told me she had refused Mabin's offer, she said she couldn't accept, and she couldn't take any action, and she couldn't do nothing."

"In the *spring*?"

Zanja's people had always been very formal with each other, distant and courteous, their roles and relations rigidly prescribed. Emil had learned to mimic the extreme obliqueness with which Zanja's people addressed private matters, and she recognized that he was doing it now, inquiring without directly asking why it was that Zanja had no recent insights into her lover's motivations.

Zanja said, "We've hardly even talked since then."

"I see." Emil frowned at the cards as though he was neither concerned nor very interested in Zanja's statement. "Norina has told me Mabin believes that Karis's continuing inaction is a result of bitterness and cowardice."

Is this what's wrong? he might have asked, were he being direct. *Has your unspoken blame opened up a gulf between the two of you?*

"Yes," said Zanja. "But Mabin can only see how Karis's very existence inconveniences her plans."

Emil looked up at her, his expression utterly neutral.

Zanja upended the Pyre card so she was seeing it upside-down. "Karis is brave and forgiving," she said. And then a disorientation came over her, like a traveler feels when a lifting fog reveals she is not where she assumed. "There's nothing Karis can do that won't lead to disaster, so for years she has engaged in the courage of inaction. But now that Willis claims to be acting on her behalf, to continue to do nothing is also becoming impossible."

She felt that what she had said was true, but it was also incomplete. "But why hasn't she just said so?"

Emil said, with mild reproof, "When a rock falls, do we ask it to explain itself? Earth logic is inarticulate. We know it by what it does." He leaned forward now, picked up the Pyre card, and held it before Zanja's eyes, upside-down. "What is Karis *doing*?"

The answer now seemed obvious. "She's waiting in agony for action to become possible."

Emil said grimly, "Well, that's why you and I are responsible. Making action possible is fire bloods' business."

Over the glyph card he met her stricken stare. Then, without speaking, he put down the Pyre and picked up Unbinding-and-Binding. He held it up, reversed. "What must we do to make action possible?"

There was a swirling in the room, like an unfelt wind. Nothing stirred, and yet it was not still. Zanja's voice spoke, flat and distant. "Cut me free so I can fall."

"If you are cut free, then you can cross the boundary?" He pointed at the upside-down owl.

The woman, arms and legs spread wide, was flying. The owl, wings dangling, clung desperately: a helpless passenger. "Will must precede insight," Zanja's voice said.

He picked up the card and looked at it himself, upside-down. His expressive eyebrows lifted in surprise. "Must we act without knowing what we're doing, or why?"

"We *must*! Action must become possible! Disaster must not be my fault again!"

It was death, that was the smell. And the smoke of the village burning. Zanja, stumbling among the bodies of the massacred *katrim*. The dawn mist glimmered now with the rising sun. Her foot crushed an outstretched hand, stuck in bloody mud. A buzzing sound of converging blowflies. Over the roar of flames, a baby cried for a rescue that would never come.

"What is the connection between the past and the present?" Emil asked.

His even voice revealed only his carefully moderated curiosity. But his arms were gripped around her, and he rocked with her, and Zanja's throat felt like she had been breathing smoke, or screaming. Glyph cards were scattered around and crushed between them. "What," she said.

"Why do you feel that our present moment is similar to that day six years ago?"

"I feel our doom. I am doing my duty too dutifully."

"Is Karis like the elders, in your mind? Refusing to exercise power to save her people?"

Emil's steady questions, Zanja realized, were forcing her

forward, out of the grip of memory, into the present moment, into the relief of considering her past from the distance of the present.

"Is it your duty to Karis that you are doing too dutifully?"

She lifted her head from his shoulder, and he released his tight embrace, though he did not entirely let go of her. "I've become trapped along with her."

"Well then, if will precedes insight, what do you think you should do?"

"I have to leave."

He sat back. "I'll just unpack these books I've managed to collect, and maybe say a word or two to Medric. Shall I talk to Karis also?"

"No. I will." She took a breath. "I must."

He helped her up, and steadied her until the dizziness passed. Then, she walked out of the house alone, into the heartless dazzle of the hot afternoon.

Their comfortable though much neglected house was surrounded by fallow fields, where wildflowers bloomed in a tangled riot, and at night the light-bugs swarmed. The outbuildings were falling down, but the apple orchard, hoed, pruned, and picked by industrious neighbors, provided an orderly front to their otherwise disorderly household. Zanja walked through the orchard in a daze, taking her sense of direction from the clangor of iron on iron, and so reached the forge, where Karis and the two local youths she was teaching to be smiths stepped back and forth between hammer and flame in an intricate, violent dance. Karis wore a sleeveless linen shirt under her leather apron. The muscles of her powerful right arm shone with sweat as she swung the hammer. Three deafening blows and the iron bent itself to her will. The apprentices exchanged awestruck glances. She tossed the drawknife she was making into a bucket of water, and the bucket boiled over.

She hung her apron on a hook and came to Zanja. She took her by the shoulders. Sweat dipped from the tips of the hair that twisted on her forehead. Her skin was copper, her eyes agate, her hair a burnished bronze. And her hands on Zanja's shoulders were like two mountains about to grind each other into rubble.

Zanja could not speak. Her will was lost. When her love for Karis came over her like this, there was no room in her for anything else.

Karis said, "Are you going?"

Her ravens must have been listening at the window. Was she angry at what she had overheard? Bewildered? Or merely resigned? Zanja could not read her. And to reply to her question was impossible. But Karis must have received an answer that somehow radiated from Zanja's skin into her sensitive hands.

Karis kissed her: a sweat-salty, sun-hot kiss. Then she lifted her hands and stepped back.

She had let go.

Chapter Ten

Zanja was standing in a room. It smelled of leather, and oil, and dust. The windows all were ajar, letting in light but no breeze. The glare of sunlight suggested it was afternoon. Zanja was looking at a cluttered shoemaker's bench. Beside it on a shelf stood a neat row of finished shoes—summer shoes, not the high, heavy boots of winter. Of course it *was* summer. Zanja could hear a blurry murmur of voices overhead and the creak of a floorboard under someone's restless weight. One of the voices sounded rather irritated.

She heard a scrape of leather soles on the wooden floor and turned to find Emil beside her.

"I haven't been much of a companion, have I?" she said.

"You've recited some good poetry," he said. "Your translit-erations of Koles. They're really quite brilliant. I hope you've written them down."

"How long have I been in this daze?"

"It's now three days past midsummer."

Zanja's shoulders, and the soles of her feet, were sore. These sensations brought memories of walking, of sitting blank and wakeful by a campfire, of a dark but spectacular vista where a distant lake glimmered and a dog barked, far away. Emil had sat awake with her one night, and she had staved off memories of death by talking about the lives of her lost people.

"Where are we now?" she asked.

Before Emil could explain, the shoemaker came down the narrow stairs: a thin, graying woman, hands stained with dye, who squinted a bit at them and seemed none too pleased to find them still waiting. "My mother asks you to come upstairs," she said disapprovingly.

"Thank you very much," said Emil. "Would you mind if we leave our gear down here?"

"Just put it out of the way," the shoemaker said ungraciously.

Emil led the way up the stairs. Zanja said to his back, "It has something to do with books? Books lost in a fire?"

"Just listen," he said. "And mind your manners."

In the plain upstairs parlor, a wasted old woman sat by a bright window with a letter—Emil's letter of introduction—in her lap. Her arms and face were patched and twisted by ugly, long-healed burn scars. Her breath rasped in her chest. But her gaze was bright and curious as her visitors came in. "Emil Paladin? I believe I remember you."

Emil bowed over her hand. "Madam Librarian, I definitely remember you. You are the one who insisted I put on silk gloves."

"You were to see the Mackapee manuscript. And students never remember to wash their hands before coming to the library. But you never saw the manuscript, did you?"

"I was never a student, either. I'm amazed that you remember me!"

"Those last days of the library, I remember every single moment. What happened to you, after the Fall of the House of Lilterwess?"

"I commanded a Paladin company for fifteen years. And now I am a bit of a librarian myself."

"Oh, are you a collector of lost books? How many do you have?"

"Many thousands. And one of them is the Mackapee manuscript."

She gazed at him in amazement, which slowly became delight. "The manuscript survived?"

"It seems to be unharmed. I'm working with a seer, so I've found books in some odd places, where people hid them from the Sainnites and then forgot about them. Many of the books are damaged, and I've been asking people if they know anyone who could teach me to repair them. Your name was suggested to me, finally."

The librarian said, "You're as earnest and eager as ever, Commander. Despite your gray hair."

"I'm still young enough to be a student, I hope."

Emil was at his most affable, exercising the graces and courtesies that Zanja had tried to emulate, though she could not imitate his sincerity. He produced books from his satchel, some in paperboard boxes, others wrapped in cotton cloth and tied with twine. The librarian opened them like gifts and tutted over the water-stained, chewed, and crumpled pages as though the books were children come to harm. "This is no quick lesson," she said, and then added matter-of-factly, "I'm dying, you know."

"Yes, I do know," Emil said. "Your knowledge should not die with you. If you agree to teach me, we'll take lodging in town."

For the first time, the librarian noticed Zanja, standing unobtrusively by the stairs, and Emil introduced her as a reader of glyphic poetry, which proved a certain method to win a book lover's admiration. Certainly, the librarian also wondered how a tribal woman came to have such an arcane and unlikely pursuit, but did not ask, and so Zanja did not have to make up an explanation for a thing she could not even explain to herself. "Would you like to see *my* books?" the librarian asked Emil.

"Would those be the ones that you threw by the armload out the windows of the burning library?"

The librarian rose without answering and led them to a staircase. They had scarcely begun to climb the narrow stairs when Zanja smelled old paper and leather bindings, the same scent that pervaded Medric's book-lined attic. The old librarian hauled herself up one step at a time, and behind her Emil held himself alert as though he thought she'd fall and he would have to catch her. At the rear, Zanja breathed in the scent of the books, and breathed out a few lines from Koles:

"A scent, faint and far away, ephemeral
As though somewhere a flower bloomed
As though someday it might bear seed."

Ahead of her, Emil paused and looked over his shoulder at her. "There's something up here? Besides just a wonderful collection of books?"

Zanja's soul, which had seemed only tenuously connected to her body, snapped sharply into place, like a dislocated bone popping into alignment. "Something that we need," she said.

At the top of the stairs, the old woman lifted a blind, and in the beam of light swimming dust gleamed like gold. Above Zanja, Emil exclaimed, "Blessed day!" And then Zanja was herself stepping up into an attic crammed with books, and the old woman stood grinning like a child with a wonderful secret. Books upon books: two, three layers deep on cobbled-together shelves that leaned tiredly sideways and surely would have fallen over if not for the companion shelves leaning on them in the opposite direction. Emil turned ecstatically from one book to the next. "Is that a copy of *Songs?* And is that *A History of a Coastal Town?* And a *complete* set of the plays of Barness?"

"Two complete sets," said the librarian smugly. "There's another behind that one."

They would be at it for hours. For Emil, the only pleasure greater than that of reading was the pleasure of talking about books, whether he had read them or not. The attic was narrow, and so crowded with books that there was scarcely room for the three of them. Zanja worked her way to the far end, where a comfortable chair was wedged by the second window, and she squatted down before the lowest shelf. In the shadows and dust that gathered here—for the sick old woman could no longer keep such a mess of books clean—Zanja could not hope to see the titles without removing each book and holding it up to the window. But perhaps the books' titles or contents were of no importance. She ran her fingertips across the spines, and then slid her hand through the front row of books to touch those tucked behind. Would touch be enough? When intuition gave her a target, she did not usually have to separate it out from a clutter of virtually identical objects. To Emil, all of these books would be important. To Zanja, only one of them was, but she did not know which one.

They remained in the attic until the light began to dim, and by then Zanja had worn herself with aimless searching. She and Emil ate fried fish and potatoes at a tavern, and rented some rooms that were located over a busy wheelwright's shop. One room had a battered table and a couple of banged-up chairs. Zanja sat, feeling unutterably weary. Emil opened the windows, and in a moment two ravens landed, and he fed them the greasy remains of the fish and potatoes.

One of the ravens said, "Medric is on his way to join you."

Emil stepped back in surprise. "Medric is *traveling*?"

"Karis is alone?" Zanja added.

Without answering, the ravens squabbled over the fish like ordinary birds. Emil sat at the table with Zanja. "They'll answer our questions when they're done eating. Does your head hurt?"

"I think I'm past that now. I feel like I've awakened exhausted from a night of bad dreams."

"You haven't actually been sleeping much, that I've noticed. What were you looking for in that attic?"

"A book, I think. I *know* it's there."

"Well, you'll never hear me say that books aren't important, but how can one book be so important that it brings our recluse out of his attic?"

"You think he's coming to help me find it?"

"The ravens will tell us. But yes, that's what I suspect."

Zanja put her head down on the table. "How did we wind up in this town? Did you follow an impulse of insight, or were you planning to come here anyway?"

"The second," he said. "But you know, an insight can arrive long ahead of its usefulness. Maybe it was prescience that made me start looking a year ago for an education in book repair." He stood up and put a hand on her shoulder. "Go to bed."

"Medric shouldn't travel alone," Zanja said. "Someone will think he's a madman and lock him up."

Emil smiled. "Now you sound like yourself again. Go to bed."

"Karis shouldn't be alone either," Zanja said.

"She's impervious, unassailable, and unbelievably competent. I certainly don't see why she can't be left alone. And she's got Leeba."

Zanja stood up. And then she noticed that the ravens were gone. Though Emil leaned out the window and called them to come back, they didn't respond.

"Well, that's odd," he said.

The next morning, Zanja set out to find Medric and brought him into town some days later. He baffled and charmed the old librarian in her sitting room, then climbed the stairs to the attic. Zanja, armed with a broom and feather duster, promised the librarian that she would shelve each book exactly as she found it, and followed Medric's light footsteps up into the darkness. By the time she raised the blind in the attic, he was already ensconced in the chair, with three books in his lap.

As the morning passed, Zanja sometimes heard the murmur of voices downstairs, where the librarian supervised as Emil painstakingly put back together the torn pages of a book he would later re-bind. Zanja emptied and cleaned one shelf of books at a time. Occasionally, Medric sneezed from the dust, but otherwise he seemed oblivious to Zanja's search.

Zanja had dusted the last book and was sweeping the floor when Medric, cross-legged in the armchair, looked up from his reading. "You missed some." He pointed vaguely underneath the chair.

Zanja leaned against the balustrade, exasperated. "You're worried about the dust under the chair? Sweep it yourself."

"Dust? Sweep? What are you talking about?" Medric managed to shift the chair so that Zanja could see that underneath it lay book boxes, stored flat, with warnings written on each one with a wide-nibbed pen: "Be *Very* Careful!"

She took one up, carefully, and opened it. A few tiny pieces of burned paper floated out. Inside lay the charred remains of a book.

"It's dead," said Medric sadly. "Maybe she hoped to save a few of its words. Are all the books dead in their coffins?"

Sitting together on the floor, they opened the boxes one by one. All the books were burned, some practically to ashes. They had looked in half the boxes when Zanja reached for one, and felt such heat sear her palm that she jerked her hand away.

"Ah!" said Medric, nodding vigorously. "*That* one."

"Do books have memories? I think it remembers the fire."

"It must still be alive, then, don't you think?" Medric lifted up the box, very gently, and opened its lid. Within lay the burned remains of a large book, titled *Encyclopedia of Livestock*. "Zanja, what have you found? An amazing thing!"

"Amazingly dull, maybe," said Zanja in dismay.

"Oh, I don't think so. Let us see what it has to tell me." Medric delicately put his hand to the smoke-stained, half-burned cover.

Eventually, Zanja went downstairs and found the librarian asleep in her chair and Emil busy washing a paste brush. The shoemaker's hammer had fallen silent; perhaps she had gone shopping in the cool evening. This soon after the solstice, the sun would not set for hours, but the shadows in the street below were long and black, and a cool breeze relieved the heat of the stuffy parlor. Emil looked up from his bowl of cloudy water.

Zanja said quietly, to not disturb the old woman, "You'd better come upstairs."

In the attic, Medric still sat upright with his hand upon the *Encyclopedia of Livestock*. His eyes moved wildly, focusing and re-focusing on sights only he could see. His face moved also: Zanja read in rapid succession fear, horror, humor, and a sudden surprise. Earlier, Medric had uttered a small cry, but now his lips moved in an inaudible conversation.

Emil said in a low voice, "He must not be disturbed." He sat in the chair to wait, and Zanja squatted by the stairway to listen for the shoemaker or the librarian. But the small house remained silent. Medric began to chuckle, and then a few tears slid down his face, and then he blinked and fumbled for his spectacles, took them off, and rubbed the crease in his nose. "Is that you, Emil? Is Zanja still here?"

She stood up out of the shadows.

Medric closed the book box but held it tightly in both hands. He looked pale and distressed, not at all like a man who has foreseen a hopeful future. But all he said was, "We need to keep this book."

After supper, in their rooms above the wheelwright, Zanja lay upon the bed with her boots on so that Emil and Medric could sit in the two chairs and continue holding hands, as they had done during dinner. Lovers long separated deserved some time alone, and she was thinking of how she would insist on sleeping on the floor in the other room, which wasn't much more than a garret. She might point out that she had not gotten so accustomed to sleeping in beds that she couldn't be comfortable on the floor.

Medric, who had scarcely spoken all evening, said to her suddenly, "Do you remember Raven's joke?"

Enlightenment was imminent, but Zanja found herself reluctant to ask for it. She said, with some effort, "Is Raven's joke finally ended? Will something finally change?"

"I don't know why I'm dreaming your stories," said Medric complainingly.

Looking at him, she thought she saw a man as reluctant to answer questions as she was to ask them. She said, "Delay won't make whatever you've seen less terrible, Master Seer."

"I know. And don't call me that. There's another story in which Raven steals and eats pieces of soul. I think I've heard you tell it."

"I remember it," said Emil.

Medric said, "What would it mean if you said of someone that Raven had eaten her soul?"

Zanja sat up. The blank shock of her midsummer madness felt like it was threatening to return. She thought wildly of the silent, distant, unresponsive ravens that had tracked her travels, of her and Emil's peculiar card reading the day she left home, of Karis angrily—or resolutely—letting her go. There was a pattern here. "You dreamed of my death," she said.

Medric took off his spectacles and set them down on the tabletop, as though he never wanted to see anything clearly again.

Emil said in his steadiest voice, "There are so many kinds of death. Raven's digestion could be a kind of transformation, couldn't it? What did you dream, Medric?"

Medric said in a strained voice, "I dreamed that you cut Zanja's heart out, and fed it to the Raven."

"And then?" said Emil.

"The Raven shit out an owl, and the owl flew to a Sainnite garrison, with its feathers on fire."

"And then?"

"The owl told the Sainnites a story, and as they listened, the garrison burned down around them, and then they themselves were burned to ashes."

"And then?"

Medric said nothing. Zanja asked, "What kind of fire was it? Transformation? Or destruction?"

"I hope it's transformation," Medric said.

In the long silence that followed, Zanja felt that strangeness come upon her, like the strangeness of a fever, a distance that is almost delirium. Had not a seer once predicted that the Sainnite people would meet their demise at the hands of an Ashawala'i warrior? And had Zanja not wondered, since her life was first spared six years ago, what she had survived for? But surely, she protested silently, it was not for simple revenge, a revenge she did not even want any longer.

She looked closely at Medric then, wondering whether he was thinking much the same thing. Was it irony or justice that one Sainnite seer's visions had led to the destruction of Zanja's people, and a second's would lead to the destruction of his own people? And was Medric considering now, as she was, whether the cost would be worth the result?

The room grew dark. None of them thought to light the lamp, and though the windows all were open, eventually the only light came from bright stars and a crescent moon. Zanja remembered: when she, her clan brother Ransel, and a half dozen other *katrim* were all that remained alive, they had deliberately lit their campfire on a steep peak that overhung the demoralized Sainnites below, so that the enemy would be unable to forget for even a moment that unrelenting death still stalked them. The surviving *katrim* had left the bodies of their massacred people to molder in the Asha Valley, a prosperous tribe of some eight hundred, all dead, and since then most of their fellow survivors had been killed. Now they had planned a trap that could kill or maim a great many of the enemy, but to spring the trap, one more would have to die.

They had chosen the one by lot, and when Zanja finally won the toss she was relieved: relieved at the end of the dreadful game, relieved that she no longer would spend the days and nights fearful that Ransel's crazed bravado would get him killed. It was ridiculous, really: they all were destined to die, and only desire for more revenge had kept them from choosing suicide. Yet, more than anything Zanja feared that Ransel might be hurt unto death, and it might become her duty to give him a quick and merciful ending. Of all the dreadful prospects that had haunted her in those nightmare days, that had been the most awful.

She had been chosen by lot to die, and yet Ransel was dead now, while she still lived. She had crossed the boundary into a new life, but she had never entirely forgotten that the gods had first selected her for death.

She said to her brothers huddled together in the darkness, "Will precedes insight. If we are to see beyond my death, to understand how, or why, or what it is for, we first have to accept that I *will* die."

She saw a movement in the shadows: Emil shaking his head in refusal, though for fifteen years his friends had gone to their deaths at his command. "I am to kill you with my own hand, for the mere hope that someday I'll understand why? No, I won't do such a thing."

Zanja said, "Somehow, it will make positive action possible. But, Emil, if I am to die—"

"No," he said.

"You're the only one—"

"Do not ask me!"

"—the only one I trust to do it properly."

There was a sound of wings flapping. Somewhere nearby, the ravens roosted in the darkness. Or were they listening, silently—and did Karis sit awake, alone, by an open window in their sprawling house, also listening?

Zanja got up from the bed and took up her still unpacked traveling gear: a blanket to lie on or to cover herself with should the nights turn cool; matches; a few essential tools; spare socks; a dagger at her hip; a knife in her boot, and the glyph cards in their pouch dangling from her belt.

Medric had put on his spectacles, and now they were gleaming in the faint moonlight. "You're leaving?"

"I can't endure to be with anyone. And Emil can't endure to be with me."

"Of course not," said Medric. "Well, you'll know when it's time to come back to us. Do you want some money? Karis gave me a great handful of it."

Zanja accepted a few coins to make him feel better and kissed him good-bye. She said nothing to Emil. She went down the stairs and out into the quiet night. The moon was obscured now by the rooftops, but she could tell by the glow of light in which direction it lay. She followed, and behind and above her there was the whisper of ravens' wings.

Chapter Eleven

For twenty days, Zanja lived off the land or worked for meals, for farmers always welcomed more hands at this time of year. As she drew close to the borderland, that hazy edge where Shaftal ended and the western wilderness began, she met a man as wild and solitary as she, who volunteered to cook the rabbit she had snared with the mushrooms and wild vegetables he had gathered, and soon served her one of the best meals she'd ever eaten. They were in the woods, had come across each other by chance, and parted with scarcely a word having been exchanged; but nothing seemed strange to Zanja anymore, and the wandering cook never asked her a single question, so perhaps nothing seemed strange to him, either.

Eventually, Zanja walked all night, and at dawn entered again into the outskirts of the old librarian's town. She found the rooms above the wheelwright's shop to be vacant. She jogged down cobbled streets to the librarian's house. A loaded freight wagon stood at the door, with four big horses in the traces, munching from feed bags. A hired driver leaned on one of the wheels with a half-eaten bun in his hand. "You must be the one we're waiting for," he said.

She got into the wagon, which was packed with crates that smelled of old paper and leather: the librarian's rescued books. She was making herself a rough bed among the crates when Emil and Medric, summoned by the driver's call, came out of the house with the shoemaker trailing behind them. Her eyes were puffy with weeping.

Emil leaned over the edge of the wagon and offered Zanja a bun.

"When did the librarian die?" Zanja asked. The bun was warm. She clasped it between her hands.

"The day before yesterday. She was telling me how to remove a water stain. She fell silent, and I realized she had stopped breathing. Her daughter practically begged us to take the books. And that thing there—" He gestured at a large crate whose position directly over the wheels suggested it was particularly heavy. "That's a printing press, would you believe! We've got paper, too, and those chests are full of type. It was all hidden away in the cellar."

"That old woman possessed some dangerous weapons," Zanja said.

"Well, it certainly will cost us our lives if the Sainnites catch us with this load." Emil said these words without concern; their prescience, and the raven escort, made it unlikely they would be surprised by soldiers or any other danger.

"Have you decided to kill me?" Zanja asked.

He folded his arms on the edge of the wagon. The sun was rising, and he squinted in its light. "Have you decided to die?" he replied.

"Decided? Well, I accept that I must accept my death."

"You've gotten as particular about words as Medric and I." He turned his head; Medric was talking animatedly to the shoemaker, but she listened to him with an expression of blank bewilderment. Emil turned back to Zanja and said, "I accept that I must become able to kill you. But somehow we both must become able to actually decide."

"That's a problem for the gods," said Zanja.

"Hmm. What will I do, then, since I have no gods? Shaftali supposedly worship the land itself. And if Shaftal is what's sacred to me, then that makes Karis—" Astonishingly, he seemed unable to think of the right word, and looked as baffled as the shoemaker. "Well, Karis is certainly not going to help me decide to kill you! Just the opposite, I expect."

"And yet we're going home."

"We are." He sighed. "What else can we do? Deceive her?

Hide from her?" He glanced up at the ravens, three of them, that stalked along the rooftops. "It's tempting, actually. But it's both immoral and impossible."

Medric, finished with the poor shoemaker, came down the steps with the burned book tucked under his arm. "Will you talk all day?" he said with mock peevishness, and climbed into the wagon. He turned to Zanja and added, "Who was that man who cooked dinner for you in the woods?"

"What? Gods of the sky, Medric!"

"I know I'm a surprising sort of fellow," said Medric. "But I should think you'd be used to me by now."

"I don't even know his name," said Zanja. "But I've never in my life eaten such a meal! Should I have asked him to come with me?"

"Oh, no. He needs to find his own way. Did he seem like a Sainnite to you?"

"Not at all."

"Well! He's a rare man, then, if he could fool even you. I look forward to meeting him, some day."

They journeyed home, past fields crowded with hay cutters, near ponds where naked, nut-brown children took their last swims in the last warm days of the year, through the rising dust that glittered like gold shavings in the blinding sunlight. For entertainment, the three of them wildly re-interpreted poems they had memorized, and the driver, mystified at first, soon took to declaiming poetry of his own. Medric spent the better part of a day giddily proposing arcane interpretations of the driver's explicit lyrics, and Emil laughed until he wept. They came home like drunks from the fair to an empty house and a cold forge and tomatoes rotting on the vine in a garden long since gone to weeds.

"Gods of hell," said Medric in Sainnese. He stood on the doorstep, flabbergasted, pulling tangled hair out of his face and tying it at the nape of his neck with a greasy blue ribbon. He pushed his spectacles into a better position, but appeared dissatisfied and took them off to clean them on his shirt.

Zanja searched the house, and when she came out, Emil was walking up the hill from the orchard, where he had gone to try

to get the ravens to talk to him. The driver of the wagon, who
had finished untying the ropes that secured the load, leaned
nonchalantly on the wheel.

"Those ravens are nothing but brainless carrion eaters!"
shouted Emil.

Zanja called back, "Her toolbox is gone, and Leeba's rabbit.
She left the moneybox in the middle of the kitchen table.
Everything is covered with dust."

"Gods of hell!" Medric said in bewilderment. "She's run
away!"

The word had spread that their house was occupied again, and
yet another neighbor had come by to inquire worriedly about
Karis. Zanja would have been rude and Medric unsettling, so
Emil went out to stand in the yard and attempt to explain her
absence. He came in looking angry and impatient, and said,
"He wants me to reassure him that she's coming back, that his
good fortune at living in the purview of an earth witch will
never end. I wish I had the luxury of his petty worries."

The three of them had been reading the cards when the anxious neighbor interrupted them. A three-person reading was
not for the faint-hearted, for they slowed each other down to
the point of tedium with their questions and answers, and with
the difficult task of reconciling the multitude of contradictory
insights that occurred to them with every new card. Medric
was recording the twists and turns of their grueling work, and
when he shattered a pen had managed to splatter himself, the
room, and most of the cards with ink. In Emil's absence he had
trimmed a new pen and, after reviewing his notes, had started
a fresh page. He scribbled on, ridiculously ink-speckled,
undisturbed by Emil's grumpiness. Zanja offered Emil the
bowl of raw, overripe vegetables that she had rescued from the
neglected garden. He sat down, took a bite of a rather yellow
piece of cucumber, spit it out again, and studied the scattered
cards in silence. After a while, he started rearranging them,
studying the new pattern, and rearranging them again.

The two of them were at their most maddening, but Zanja

was fortunate to be so wrung out that she welcomed even the respite of watching them trap themselves in their own ruminations. She slipped into an exhausted sleep, and when she woke up, Emil was examining Medric's paper by the light of the window, and Medric was standing over the table, studying Emil's arrangement of the cards. She had no idea how much time had passed.

"Huh!" Medric exclaimed.

"Ah!" Emil said at the same time.

They looked bemusedly at each other across the room.

Zanja rubbed her gritty, tear-raw eyes. "Wise men, explain to me my fate."

Emil said, "With all the questions we've asked, we really are asking just three questions: Why must you die? How should this death be accomplished? And what might be the future result if we are successful?"

Zanja glanced at the tabletop. The cards were arranged in three clusters, and each cluster was an answer: an answer that was a poem no less complex or resistant to reading than the poetry of Koles. Though the two men could just as easily have each played the opposite role, Emil had defined the poetic arrangements, and, she assumed, Medric had transliterated them. Zanja said, "To translate the glyphs that answer these questions, one must be analytical, practical, and visionary by turns, just as the questions are."

Medric gave a loud laugh. "While we slaved away, you saw the answers in your sleep, didn't you?"

"I feel like my head has been broken. When that happened the first time, I wanted to sleep all the time. But the Sainnites could not withstand the intelligence of my dreams." Zanja got up rather stiffly to take a close look at the cards. She did not feel intelligent, but the cards' meaning seemed clear as light, distinct as a voice speaking loudly in an empty room. "Why must I die? Here lies the owl, myself, beset by the past, by the Laughing Man, by war and truth, by unhealed wounds. I cannot fly under that weight, and only death can lift it from me."

Emil said, "How should your death be accomplished? There I am, of course, the Man on the Hill, who will send you on a journey to the underworld. The Pyre belongs there, but it's shared with the next pile, so I put the flame card there, to signify transformation as well as insight, and the raven card, which we say is the carrier of truth and you say is death. Your soul only will be consumed; your vacant body will survive, to be filled again somehow by your god. My duty is to empty you; and the card that signifies ceremonials suggests I am to enact your death through ritual."

Medric said, seriously for once, "Call it by another name, define it as we like, it is still death, and not merely a metaphor. As for the future . . ." Medric took the owl from the first pile and moved it to the last. "Death-becomes-Life: for Karis, who will step through a door; for the Sainnites, who will be subject to the flame. Past-Becomes-Future: the old G'deon, I think this means. Harald, who first refused to destroy us Sainnites when it would have been easy to do so. The three of us always assumed it was to keep Shaftali from becoming destroyers, but here we have a card of preservation, which suggests that for all the evil the Sainnites have done, something about us is worthwhile. But the three of us have not named that thing, have we?"

"I have two names," said Emil. "One is Medric, one is Karis. Oh, I mustn't forget that cook in the woods. And many more Sainnites whose names I don't yet know."

In the silence, they could hear the ravens making a racket in the apple orchard, not warning of another neighbor's approach, but uttering the harsh shouts of raucous welcome. Emil leaned half his body out the window, shading his eyes from the glare of sun. "I think there's five ravens now. Yes, I see Norina and J'han together coming up the hill. He's looking more than a little footsore, as if he never paused to rest during his entire trip from south to north. And Norina is as I'd expect her to be." He drew his body back into the room.

"Emil . . . !" Zanja stopped herself, embarrassed that she sounded so beseeching.

But he said, "Medric and I will attempt to explain all this to them."

Medric seemed inclined to object, but Emil gave him a look

so grim that Medric followed him reluctantly out, glancing back at Zanja with an expression of comical terror.

Long before Emil thought to shout at the ravens to send for Norina and J'han, the ravens must have told them to come home and orchestrated their meeting along the way as well. Through the window, Zanja watched as Emil spoke, J'han wept, and Norina raged. She listened as they came into the house and, in the kitchen, Emil built up the fire and hung the teakettle. She went into the kitchen when it seemed the leading edge of the storm was past, but she was not surprised when Norina gave her a look she rather would have avoided, and commented, "So now you have finally found an excuse for suicide."

Zanja said flatly, "I do not want to die."

Apparently convinced and at a loss, Norina sat silently on a stool. Zanja had to turn away to escape that disconcerting, unrelenting gaze. Medric abstractedly wiped out the dusty teacups, and J'han looked bleakly around himself, seeking the daughter whose absence left the house achingly silent. His heavy pack, loaded with medicines and instruments of surgery, squatted in the corner, but J'han seemed unable to sit down.

Norina said quietly, "J'han, Karis will not keep Leeba from you."

"But she *is* keeping me from her!" J'han accepted a cup of tea from Emil, but did not seem to know what to do with it.

"You promised Leeba you'd be home by late summer, and she knows the seasons now, so she will not give Karis a moment's peace." Norina accepted a cup, sipped cautiously, and added to him, "The less you have to do with this fire blood business, the better. Perhaps you should leave right away, and ask that the ravens show you the way to Leeba. And be insistent."

"Name of Shaftal," said Emil, "the poor man is exhausted—"

"If Karis is angry, let's make certain there's one person she can't be angry with. J'han, you think these fire bloods all have lost their minds?"

He looked surprised, for he was incapable of being so judgmental. But then he said, "Yes. All three of them at once. All right, I'll go." He swallowed his tea, and Emil went to get him some money. J'han fetched clean clothes and kissed them all good-bye, Zanja twice, and was going out the door when he paused and said, "But what will I tell Karis if I find her? I am utterly confounded."

"Oh!" Medric got hastily to his feet and fetched the book box from the parlor. Its pointed warnings to be careful with the contents were obscured by the twine Medric had used to secure it for its journey. "Just give this to her, and tell her to read it."

"What is it?"

"A book, of course. It will tell her what she needs to know. You'll see."

Standing in the doorway, Zanja watched J'han, bowed under his heavy load, limp down the track to the apple orchard, where the apples were starting to become visible as they blushed red. She could hear, distantly, the swinging chant of the people cutting hay, who made a noise all day long so as to know where each other was without having to look. The sky was soft, hazy with warmth. The rich land moved languidly toward harvest.

In the orchard, J'han paused to shout at the ravens in their tree. Apparently hearing no answer, he continued down the road. He was out of sight when one of the ravens lifted up to follow him.

Zanja went back into the kitchen. Emil, frowning absently, sipped his tea. Medric, now that he had started to dust the dishes, was methodically emptying the cupboard. Norina, still on her stool, made a concentrated study of the blank wall.

It was possible, Zanja realized suddenly, that Norina might not ever see husband or daughter again. As though Zanja had spoken her thoughts out loud—and she might as well have, for the Truthken would know them soon—Norina turned to her and raised an eyebrow. Zanja said, "Don't *you* think that we've lost our minds?"

"The three of you have always seemed mad to me." Norina

added dryly, "It's kind of you to pity me, Zanja. But it's also a waste of energy. Unlike you, I know exactly what I'm doing and why."

"But you're supporting us and not opposing us?"

Norina smiled, very slightly. "How do you know I'm not opposing you?" she said.

Chapter Twelve

Before the Sainnites introduced smoke addiction to Shaftal, the land had surely not been entirely free of ne'er-do-wells. Yet, examining the wretched woman who had rowed herself in through the water gate in a leaky old boat, Clement felt the vague guilt she always felt in the presence of a smoke user. The people who know such things had informed Clement of the shocking amount a smoke user must pay nowadays for the drug, and Clement lay out on the table enough money to give her guest a week without worry. The half-starved woman's fingers twitched eagerly.

"Tell me what you know," Clement said.

The woman leaned forward, and Clement simultaneously leaned away from her stink. "They said the G'deon was coming," the woman said earnestly.

"I've been hearing that story for years," Clement said. "If there were a G'deon, then why would she linger so long? If she bears the power of Shaftal in her flesh, then why hasn't she laid her hands on me, or on you, and done whatever it is G'deons do? Kill, heal, whatever." Clement put her hand out to gather up the coins. "You're wasting my time."

"One of them saw her. Talked to her."

Clement held up a single small coin, pinched between her fingertips. "One of them? What is this group?"

"Death-and-Life, they call themselves." The woman watched avidly as Clement lay the coin onto the table and pushed it towards her. A swift snatch, and the coin was gone.

Another coin: "And who is this one the G'deon spoke to?"

"Their leader, of course!" Seeing that Clement would not relinquish the coin, the woman added reluctantly, "His name is Willis."

"Willis? What kind of name is that?"

The woman tightened her lips until Clement handed her a coin and held up another. "A South Hill name, I hear."

"What does he look like?"

"Brown hair, muscular."

"Like everyone in Shaftal. You never saw him, did you?"

"These were just people in the streets! How was I to know if I saw him or not? They gave us food, but only if we ate it while they watched. No money. The bastards."

"No money," Clement echoed, closing the coin in her fist.

"They say he was a vagabond," said the woman desperately. "A vagabond from South Hill. And then he had a vision. How many people like that are there in the world? The South Hillers look after their own!"

Clement grunted and let her have the coin. She would send an inquiry to South Hill, which was too far away for a casual journey, and see if the name Willis was known to the garrison there. Perhaps she might even get a decent description. "What did this supposed G'deon say to Willis?"

"Ha! A lot of nonsense, I guess. That she was coming, of course. That she had chosen him to announce her coming and to mobilize her people. That there would be war, and you Sainnites would all die at her hand."

"At her hand? How?"

"Well, not from pleasure!" The woman leered at her in a dreadful display of gums and occasional teeth. "By fire," she said, "and plague, and floods. By mountains falling on your heads and trees crushing you under their weight. By freezing wind and heavy snow and—of course—by bloody battles."

Sweating in her filthy uniform, Clement felt a chill. Wasn't this in fact how Shaftal was killing them, quietly, steadily, irresistibly? She said, "Such things happen naturally in this bloody, bitter, hostile land."

"Is that a question?" the woman asked. "You expect an answer?"

Clement contemptuously tossed the coin to her. "Yes, do tell me why I should be afraid of this supposed G'deon's supposed threat."

The smoke user said, "Because the supposed G'deon can make these things happen *only* to you."

"I've heard enough nonsense," said Clement. "This soldier will show you out."

But after the smoke user had gone, her stink remained. Clement had left the windows in Cadmar's quarters closed to retain the cool of morning, but now she flung them open, and looked out over the wrecked garrison. As she watched, the crazy, tilted remains of a building collapsed in a cloud of ashes and dirt. Two months after the fire, debris was still being cleared, even as, here and there, a few buildings gradually rose, the construction fraught with error and delay. Ellid's re-building strategy was dictated by the rapid changes of Shaftal's seasons. On the foundations of the burned buildings, new timber frames were constructed, and on those went the roofs, so that the walls and windows could be built during the rain of autumn and even the snow of winter.

By freezing winds and heavy snow we'll die, thought Clement, remembering the smoke-user's hollow, ravaged voice. To this drug-addicted informant, there had been no reason to make a distinction between the acts of an individual, this supposed G'deon, and the acts of nature. Gilly had more than once called the abilities passed from G'deon to successor as the power of Shaftal, and what was Shaftal's power, if not the very powers the smoke user listed, of fire and plague and generally rotten weather? Powers of irresistible destruction, whether slow or sudden. Looking out at the evidence of the burned garrison, remembering the horrors of that night, Clement saw the full scope of her own lingering despair.

The summer was already two-thirds passed. At the main gate, a crowd of witnesses maintained their vigil, but their numbers were few enough now that the siege gate had been opened, and it was usually possible for a guarded wagon, or a company of soldiers, to pass in and out. Clement went out a postern gate, though, alone on horseback. The bored gate guard, an old man whose job it was to ring the bell for help if the iron-banded gate happened to be assaulted, had no choice but to let Clement through. No doubt her exit would be reported to Ellid, who later would berate Clement as much as she dared. Clement went out into a lavender twilight that suffused the narrow streets of Watfield with an unearthly blend of vivid light and purple shadow. Late shoppers, hurrying home with baskets of bread and eggs, pressed themselves to walls decorated with blooming vines to let her pass. Drinkers in taverns, who escaped the outdoors into the cooling streets, looked at her askance and, scowling, nudged their neighbors.

By the time Clement reached Alrin's pristine townhouse, the shadows had nearly overcome the light. In the spotless parlor, a painted screen concealed the cold fireplace, and the discreetly drawn summer curtains billowed delicately in the evening breeze. Here Alrin sat with her feet on a stool, dressed in clothing as light and loose as her billowing curtains. Her gravid belly, her rich breasts, these were discreetly displayed by the light cloth. She offered her hand, apologizing that she did not rise. Weak-kneed, Clement bowed over her cool, delicately scented fingers, and said in a rough voice, "I trust that you are well."

"I miss your company, of course."

"Of course," said Clement, trying not to sound skeptical. With the garrison tight as a lockbox and every last soldier working dawn to dusk on rebuilding, Alrin's business must have suffered terribly. Clement did not quite know what to make of the message, passed on verbally through the gate guards, inviting her blandly to supper. Was Alrin resorting to unseemly recruitment? Yet Clement had come, and had even, with some effort, taken something resembling a bath, and put on a uniform that wasn't as filthy as the others.

Alrin, never awkward, created topics of conversation from thin air. Over hot buttered bread and deliciously vinegared vegetables, she pretended interest convincingly as Clement obliged her with an account of the garrison attack. Over fowl in aspic and jellied fruits as lovely to look at as they were to taste, Alrin entertainingly described a disastrously bad concert she had recently attended. Over peaches and cake they both praised the fine weather and expressed hopes that it would be a late autumn. Clement turned down brandy, accepted tea, and sat sipping it by the window, stunned by such a quantity of tasty food after so many months of deprivation. Alrin asked her for the fourth time if she had eaten enough, and if she didn't want a few biscuits or a nice piece of cheese.

Clement said, "If I ate any more I'd fall unconscious. It's very kind of you to rescue me for a few hours—but the commander will go into a panic if I don't return soon."

The courtesan smoothed the cloth over her pregnant belly. Clement, who had only observed pregnancy from a distance, caught herself examining Alrin's round, taut abdomen with fascination. Alrin said complacently, "My last child."

Clement glanced up at her face. "How do you know?" she asked. She had heard that Shaftali people knew some methods for preventing pregnancy besides the obvious one practiced by the Sainnites, of simply forbidding sexual congress between men and women. Clement herself felt no particular desire to do what men and women do with each other, but soldiers of both sexes would bless her if she could learn the Shaftali secret.

Unfortunately, Alrin's answer was unrevealing. "You haven't heard that I'm leaving Watfield in the spring? Marga wants to move south, where the winters aren't so hard. So I'm going into the window and bottle business, purchasing a glassworks."

"I hadn't heard," said Clement. "Windows and bottles?" she added, trying not to sound overly doubtful.

Alrin said gravely, "I do understand business."

"Of course you do. You'll be missed. I wish you well."

"Thank you. Marga and I will be very preoccupied with running the enterprise, we expect. This child—it's unfortunate, but we can't possibly raise it. It will go to its father, as is proper."

Quite belatedly, Clement realized, as Marga came in to clear the table, that the stout woman was not Alrin's housekeeper, but her wife.

"If the father is interested," said Alrin, as Marga left with a loaded tray.

Clement, feeling dreadfully embarrassed, poured both of them more tea to save Alrin the trouble of standing up, and also to give herself a chance to recover her own composure. "I heard there were several interested parties," she said.

"Oh, well," said Alrin vaguely. "Sometimes fate intervenes." She accepted the teacup with a gracious smile. "It is presumptuous of me to even suggest you might help me a little. But I valued our friendship, Clem—"

Clement, though she was commenting to herself on Alrin's acting ability, felt a brief surge of desire.

"—and I dare hope you might sometimes think of me fondly," continued Alrin. With the teacup at her lips, she gave Clement a steady, suggestive look.

Clement said, "All officers are lonely. You gave me something I wanted, and I did appreciate it. Is there something I can do for you?" Of course there would be—Alrin had not invited her to supper out of compassion because the people in the garrison had nothing but slop to eat.

"A great man like the general must want a legacy," Alrin said.

"Cadmar?" said Clement. "Good gods!" And she began to laugh, and could not stop herself. "I beg your pardon," she managed to gasp at last. "This child is his, then?"

"It might well be," said Alrin stiffly. "As you know perfectly well."

Clement wiped her eyes. "I'll mention it to him. But I can tell you now that you'd better find another candidate." She set down her teacup and stood up. "I'm sorry I offended you. Thank you again for the delicious meal."

"Must you go?" said Alrin. She offered her hand for Clement to clasp. "*Must* you?" she said again, pointedly.

But Clement's flush of desire had evaporated. She bid Alrin farewell. She'd never see her again, probably, and she certainly would not even mention this absurd conversation to Cadmar when he returned. But it would be great fun to recount to Gilly.

Five days later, a bugle signal at the main gate announced Cadmar's return to Watfield. Clement was in the middle of dividing, replanting, and top dressing her mother's flower bulbs. She went down to the main gate with horse manure caked on her knees and her pockets bulging with bulbs. There was a scuffle outside the gate as soldiers forced back the crowd to allow a clear passage for Cadmar, who glared with fierce dignity from the back of his magnificent, nervous horse. Once or twice, Clement spotted Gilly, gray and drawn, mounted on a sturdy brown nag. Both he and his horse looked rather bored, though they were tangled in a knot of escorting soldiers who were busy with their clubs. She had missed that ugly man!

When they were in, and the soldiers had gotten the gate shut, then the soldiers on the walls remembered belatedly to cheer the general's arrival, though the angry shouts of the crowd outside the gate were louder, and less demoralized. Ellid had arrived, and stepped forward to make the official greeting. Cadmar dismounted and clasped the garrison commander's hand with every appearance of geniality. But Clement heard him say, "Shoot the rabble."

"General," said Clement, stepping forward hastily. "We've tolerated these people's presence—better a few people at the gate than a roused city. And the weather will drive them away soon enough."

"Tolerate?" Cadmar's gaze was without comprehension. "Are you a farmer now, Lieutenant-General?" He wrinkled his nose at the manure stink she carried with her.

"I beg your pardon, General. You'll find your quarters ready for you. And the stable has been rebuilt, so your horse will also be comfortable."

Looking past his shoulder, she caught Ellid's gaze. The commander looked rather pale, but at Clement's glance she gave a slight nod. Clement soothed Cadmar until he allowed that he was tired, and let himself be convinced to go to his quarters and be looked after by his long-suffering aides. When he was gone, Clement said to Ellid, "Give the citizens fair warning first, and then shoot over their heads. They'll run out of shooting range, at least, and then you can send the guard out to disperse them."

Clement turned and found that Gilly had been helped from

his horse and was leaning unsteadily on his cane, observing her with a rather red-eyed, dubious expression. She offered him her arm, and he leaned on her heavily. "The *horse* will be comfortable?" he rasped, apparently in the throes of a summer cold.

Clement said, "Actually, the horses are uncomfortably crowded because the stable is now the barracks for the soldiers displaced by Cadmar's arrival. We've cleared the soldiers out of your room, too, and I think I'd better put you to bed. You're uglier than ever," she added affectionately.

"You're crabbier," said Gilly hoarsely. "For a moment I thought you were going to clout him."

"What does he think, that I've saved a clean uniform to wear for his arrival? The laundry hasn't been rebuilt, and I gave Ellid half my clothing, since hers was burned."

"You've been free of Cadmar for two months. You've got nothing to complain about."

They moved down the road, Gilly leaning heavily on her arm, at more of a shuffle than a walk. The horses were led past them in a clatter of shod hooves on cobblestone. Behind them, Clement could hear the gate captain shouting orders. "I wouldn't clout Cadmar," Clement said. "His fists are twice the size of mine."

Gilly chuckled, then coughed wretchedly.

Gunshots. Clement flinched. Fearful cries. She said loudly, "What is written on those pieces of cloth those people wrap themselves with? Did you notice?"

"It was names."

Someone was screaming. Apparently, injuries had not been entirely avoided. "Gods of hell," Clement muttered.

"Some veteran you are," said Gilly dryly.

"Why don't they give up and get busy breeding more children? It doesn't take any particular effort!"

Gilly looked at her. "It's not children they want," he grated. "It's those particular children. No, never mind—you'll never understand it."

She took him to his room and put him to bed. She told him about Alrin's attempt to sell her child to Cadmar, but she could not remember why it had ever seemed funny.

Chapter Thirteen

In those days before autumn mud, Norina Truthken observed some remarkable things, and commented on them to nobody. She was famous for her acerbic tongue and quick temper: brutal weapons in the control of a subtle mind that no one underestimated more than once. In those days, she found herself exercising that subtlety without the weaponry, and though she saw much worth commenting on and even criticizing, she merely watched in silence.

Dust gathered in their half-abandoned house; what vegetables had survived in the neglected garden went ungathered; their storerooms that should have been filling up for the long winter lay empty. Wherever Karis had gone, she had taken the household concerns with her, and had a neighbor visited their home he would have concluded that they were soon to become burdens on their community.

Karis also remained silent: present in her ravens, but speechless. She had removed herself beyond Norina's ability to know her truths, yet that very act of removal signified to Norina a truth that the fire bloods could not perceive. They saw rejection and refusal, and perhaps even Karis herself thought that her absence meant anger. Fire bloods see in the heat of passion and imagination, and air bloods see coldly, clearly. Sometimes that dispassion was a distinct advantage.

Emil wrestled with himself in a way that was painful to watch. As commander of South Hill Company he had regularly sent friends to their deaths, but he and Zanja had an intimacy that could not be described as simple friendship, and to kill her with his own hand would kill him as well. This Norina saw, and as she watched him work his slow way to acceptance of this unacceptable, mad plan, she knew that in the end to fulfill his role would literally break his heart. Yet Norina held her tongue.

Medric, as always, was more enigmatic. Flippant and sorrowful by turns, he read his books of history frantically, looking for a fact or story that would trigger his insight and give him the broad vision that might explain their actions to themselves. So seers always spend their lives, seeking a perfect understanding that inevitably eludes them; some finally fall into madness, while others realize at last that their purpose lies not in the unachievable goal, but in the seeking of it. Medric was terribly young, still in his mid-twenties, and perhaps he was too young to bear such a personal burden for the hopes of his friends. He grew haggard from forgetting to eat and sleep, and Emil and Zanja were too preoccupied to look after him. Norina started bringing him bowls of porridge and supervising while he ate, though he complained about her miserable cooking. She watched him flounder like a fish caught in the jaws of destiny, and wondered whether he would change his shape before he was swallowed. She made no comment, though.

Zanja *was* changing, and this was the most remarkable thing Norina found to watch. If ever Norina, in all her skeptical life, had been tempted to believe in divine intervention, it was during those weeks of harvest as she watched Zanja's metamorphosis. Zanja, oblivious to the changing season, appeared to be writing a book. Norina glanced at her work one day, and found that it was a collection of Leeba's favorite stories, mixed in with other stories that Norina had never heard: more complex stories, stories that Leeba would love in a few months, or a year, or several years. One of these was an exceedingly strange tale of a woman who murdered herself to save her daughter's life, and how her daughter never forgave her for it. Norina could imagine reading that story to Leeba one day, though she could not imagine how the world around them might have changed by then.

Except for her work on the book for Leeba, Zanja seemed—not aimless, for she was too quiet for that—but distant, waiting. Examining her, Norina saw a mindless preoccupation, like a caterpillar starting to weave a silken coffin around itself, or a bear getting ready to bury itself in a winter's grave. But that peaceful purposefulness was always threatened by a pain as intense as Emil's. Zanja called herself a crosser of boundaries: her gods had named her so. And every boundary crossing, she said, was a death. So she was accustomed to dying, and knew how to go about it. But she who had endured such terrible losses in her life could not endure any more, and so she kept pretending to herself that when she died, her lover, her child, and her dearest friends would not be lost to her. It was an extraordinary act of self-deception: the kind of magic that fire bloods excel at. Norina was there when that self-deception failed, and Zanja began to weep.

She wept for days. And then she took the dagger Karis had forged for her, and laid it on the bed she and Karis had shared all these years, and she roughly bound the pages of her book with a leather seam and set the book aside, and, as the apple harvest began, she started to go out walking, from before sunrise to past sunset. Every night, when Norina saw her at supper, she saw a woman who had become a little less familiar. And still Norina did not talk about what she saw, to Zanja or to anyone.

A letter came from J'han, much dirtied by its hand-to-hand journey, that told of births attended, bones mended, and lives ended, and finished with a sentence that his raven had begun to talk to him, occasionally. Norina wondered if she would ever see him, or her daughter, again. So even she lived through the harvest season in a state of loss, but she was never bewildered by it. She had never hesitated to sacrifice passion to principle; she was an air blood and she knew no more rational way to live. So, like Zanja, she was uniquely qualified for the task that lay before her.

Even as Zanja began the process of transforming herself, Medric and Emil began to discuss, painfully at first but with increasing fascination, how to make that transformation permanent. Fire logic is the logic of insight, of seeing in symbols and stories and events more meanings than an entirely sane person could see. To turn that seeing into an act of magic was rarely done, and there were no rules for how to do it. As the two scholars talked, their plans inevitably became convoluted. To enact in ritual a symbolic understanding was complicated. Soon, as Norina expected, they asked her to take a role in the ritual, and so she was able to start making plans of her own.

Zanja said that it must not happen at home, and so it must be done outside, and since they could not do fire magic without a fire, that meant it must happen before the rains began. Because the ravens no longer even offered weather reports, Norina kept an eye on the behavior of the local earth talents. Earth witches were rare, but every farmhold had people with earth talent, who, like J'han, had earned the reputation of knowing how to do things right, whose mundane advice about building and planting was often sought and always followed. When Norina noticed that the work of harvest had become frenetic, the four of them could delay their terrible act no longer.

The last day of Zanja's life began with brilliant sunshine: a light that blinded them as they walked eastward, for the sun no longer rose quickly as it had during summer, and instead hovered along the horizon for half the morning. The four of them set forth in the dazzle of sunrise and stark, sweeping shadows that twisted away from the sideways lift of the sun. They were hailed from an apple orchard where battered baskets of red and green apples clustered under the yellowing trees, awaiting the wagon that would take them to the cider mill. Their pockets were filled with apples by the friendly, busy farmers, and later, a girl ran down from a dairy to give them a wedge of cheese and ask about the weather. Emil sighed under the burden of neighborliness, but Zanja crunched an apple as she walked and took the slender, beautiful blade out of her boot to cut them all pieces of cheese. She was as calm and remote as Norina had ever seen her and beneath the unruffled surface of her visage lay the drowned corpse of her vital mind.

Medric interrupted his anxious gabble to ask abruptly, "Where are the ravens?"

"Absent," said Emil briskly, not even bothering to scan the sky or the tops of the picked apple trees they now passed. The sound of hammers making last-minute repairs on a leaky roof was loud against the whining of the crickets.

Karis was making herself as remote in her way as Zanja was in hers, and both for the same reason. Only Norina called it heroism, and only to herself. To disturb the frail fabric of the fire bloods' illusions would have been disastrous.

Emil showed them to the high place that he had in mind, where ancient oaks spread a vast canopy, and there was a wide, comforting vista: a long horizon, a brilliant stretch of sky. The busy, distant cider mill could be seen, tucked into the curve of a brightly shining stream. They distracted themselves with gathering wood, but once the fire was lit, distractions were no longer necessary—the momentum of the ritual took control of them.

Zanja obediently followed Norina into the shelter of a grove of saplings. There, among the lobed leaves edged with autumn's bronze, she looked somberly upward, into the verdant shadows of one of the ancient trees. Norina followed her gaze, and thought she saw the hunched shape of a waiting owl. "Salos'a?" she asked, and Zanja gave a nod: the god that had made her a crosser of boundaries had come for her, to escort her soul across its final border. Norina looked narrowly at the waiting owl; it looked like an ordinary bird to her.

Norina said, "Your belongings connect you to this world, so you must give everything you've brought with you to be burned in the fire, including your clothing. And your hair."

Along with the pieces of her clothing, Zanja silently handed Norina the little knife from her boot, and the battered pack of glyph cards that she carried in a pouch hung from her belt. Her fingers struggled with buttons as her gaze kept returning to the shadowy owl; she picked ineffectually at a knot; Norina finally knelt to undo her bootstraps for her. Zanja stood quiet among the leaves that twitched a bit in a passing breeze. Now, stripped of her Shaftali clothing, she had never looked so alien: thin and wild as a ferret, her dark skin covered with a patchwork of scars, with some of her warrior's braids coming undone and her coarse black hair brushing the backs of her thighs. Norina gave her clothing that Emil had acquired somewhere: a rough, woolen tunic and baggy trousers, simple shoes, and leggings of goatskin with the hair still attached. But then Norina had to dress her, for Zanja simply stood like an addle-pate, with the clothing falling from her hands.

Norina had done much planning, but that planning proved all but unnecessary. It was easy to hide Zanja's discarded cards and knife in the leggings as she tied them around Zanja's calves, and it was just as easy to tie a red tassel onto one of the braids and then tuck it down into the loose neck of the tunic. And it was easy to turn her back on Zanja, and fill the empty card pouch with oak leaves, and lay onto the tangle of discarded clothes the knife Norina always carried, a fraternal but not identical twin to Zanja's, though Emil and Medric would not know the difference. In a lifetime shaped by truth and lies, rarely had Norina's deceptions been so simple.

Norina gathered up Zanja's clothing and the substitute belongings, and took the hand of the vacant alien who for a while had been her bitter rival and for a long time had been her friend, and led her out to the fire where Emil and Medric were waiting.

Earlier, Norina had noted the muffled sound of Emil weeping, but now he was again the battle-hardened soldier. Norina sat Zanja down beside the fire and, rather agitatedly, Medric began to speak of Zanja's life: he spoke of her birth as though he had been there, and of how the old men and women of her clan had noticed her, and how Salos'a had claimed her, and how she had traveled Shaftal with her first mentor, and how she served the Sainnites as a stablehand one summer, to learn their language. Then Emil spoke of how she had begun to fear for her people's safety, but her warnings had gone unheeded, and he spoke in detail of the night her people were massacred, which he called Zanja's first death. He and Medric took turns speaking of the revenge the surviving warriors wreaked on the Sainnites; of Zanja's second death, when she was paralyzed in an avalanche, the third death in a Sainnite prison, and of Karis's abrupt, timely, and utterly unexpected intervention. They spoke of the single summer during which Zanja had, directly or indirectly, intentionally or inadvertently, disrupted and changed the direction of all their lives: the summer when Medric deserted the Sainnites, Emil resigned from the Paladins, Norina shifted her alliances, Mabin kidnapped and nearly killed Karis, Karis broke her addiction to smoke, their family was formed and their love affairs began.

The last five years had been more quiet, and Emil was able to speak of them quickly: so, after hours of talking, they finished telling the story of Zanja's extraordinary, appallingly eventful thirty-five years.

The men were hoarse with talking and with breathing smoke. Zanja had listened, if such passivity could be called listening, in blank speechlessness. Now Norina rose up from her long, weary watch and built up the fire. Medric gathered himself up and said, clearly and firmly, "And now, Zanja na' Tarwein, your life has ended, as all lives end, and with love and sorrow your family now consigns your body to the pyre and your spirit to the care of the gods."

Norina put Zanja's good boots onto the fire, and followed them with the rest of Zanja's clothing, and, finally, the worn leather pouch stuffed with leaves—Emil, who had given Zanja the glyph cards, wretchedly watched it burn—and Norina's own knife, which she knew would later emerge from the ashes unscathed. Then, with a pair of scissors she had brought with her, Norina began cutting off and burning Zanja's hair. One handful at a time, she lay the slender braids onto the flames, where they flared and became ash all in a moment. But one braid remained, hidden for now.

It was an execution. Zanja's hair had never been cut, not since the day of her birth, and it was her life that flared upon the fire and turned to ash. Norina did it briskly. When she had finished, Zanja's hair hung not quite to her shoulders, and the tight braids unplaited raggedly. Even the shape of her face seemed changed.

Norina said softly, "It is done." She looked up at Emil, hoping she would find him resolute. One last act remained, and Medric had dreamed that Emil would commit that act alone. Emil rose up stiffly, and shouldered his satchel and bedroll. His battered old dagger, which he often did not bother to carry, hung on his hip.

"Come with me," he said to Zanja.

She obediently rose up, and followed him.

Part 3

The
Walk-Around

※ ※ ※ ※ ※ ※ ※ ※ ※ ※ ※ ※ ※ ※ ※ ※ ※

In the middle of the country, there is a valley so big it takes six days to walk across it, and that valley is a wasteland. The people of the region say that once the valley was a fertile farmland, and this is the story they tell to explain how it became a wasteland. In the middle of that valley there used to be a forest known as the Walk-Around, because everyone with any sense walked around it, even though that added two days to the journey and forced them to ford the river twice, and in the spring the river was too deep to cross at all. What with waiting for the flood to ease and various other difficulties, that six-day journey might take twenty, if your luck was bad. But it was worse luck still to walk through the forest.

Sometimes a stranger or fool might walk into the forest and come right out on the other side, whistling a merry tune and talking about how nice it was in there, with the coolness and the gentle springs and the birds so tame they practically hopped onto the spit to be cooked for dinner, and the nuts in neat piles just waiting for a passer-by to pick them up and eat them. And sometimes the traveler would never be seen again. And sometimes an enterprising farmer might plow a field going right up to the forest's edge, and plant corn and watch it sprout, only to go out one day and find the field, the farm, the cattle, and even the family gone, and nothing but forest to be seen, and then the house collapsing into the ground. That's the kind of forest it was, and that's why people kept away from it.

One day a stranger arrived in the village that was closest to the forest, though some days it was closer than others, and said that he was going to the town on the far side of the forest. And the people there warned him, as they warned everybody, to stay away from the forest because nobody ever knew what the forest was going to do. But this stranger called them a name I can't repeat here, and said boldly that he had never yet met the forest that could defeat him. For he could walk up to a deer in his stocking feet and put a knife into its heart, and he could tell north from south by the way the grass lay on the ground, and he could start a fire in wet wood, and he even could predict bad weather a week in advance, though he wouldn't say how. He even, he swore, was unaffected by the bites of poisonous snakes, and at that point everyone knew he was a fool and said to him, "Go into the forest, then, for it's obvious that even your mother won't miss you."

So the bold man went into the forest, and he took his direction from the grass, and he snared the wild birds and ate the nuts and drank the cold water and had a cozy campfire, and the next day he started planning how he would come whistling out of the woods and send a message back to those faint-hearts out in the village, telling them what cowards they were. But the shadows grew long, and the crickets started to sing and he never reached the edge of the forest. The next day it was the same, and the day after that, though every day the forest seemed a bit darker and the birds were scarcer and the nuts were fewer, until the bold man began to starve, because all his boldness couldn't fill the woods with plenty.

But still he walked, for what else could he do, until one day he came to a clearing that was a perfect circle, and in its center lay a perfectly round pool, and there at last the bold man saw that the grass lay first in one direction and then another, so that it made a perfect spiral, and that perfect pool was the spiral's center. And drinking from the pool was a big black sow with tusks like knives and hair like wire and hooves like iron. And she looked up at that bold man and didn't even blink.

Now that bold man wasn't so bold anymore, for he knew that the forest had tricked him into walking in circles these many days. But he certainly was hungry. So he picked up his spear and he charged that pig, because he was thinking that a nice pork dinner would be a fine thing after all his miseries, and mighty well deserved. But that black sow, she stood her ground and tossed him in the air like a bull, goring him with her tusks so that when he landed he was bleeding from a great gash in his leg. But he managed to hold on to his spear, so when the big pig charged him, he braced the spear on the ground and held it so the sow would impale herself on it. But that sow was a smart one, and she dodged the spear and took a swipe at the bold man's other leg, and opened up his thigh from knee to hip. Now he knew that he was dead, for he would never find the way out of the forest when he couldn't even walk, so he put his arms around that sow and held on tight, and she dragged him around and around that clearing, until at last he managed to take his spear, which he had hung on to all the while, and jab it between her ribs and into her heart. And then he fainted dead away.

As he lay senseless in the trampled, bloody grass, the forest began to step away from him. The clearing became a big, round field and then gaps appeared between the trees, and by the time he opened his eyes, he lay in open land, with no hint of a forest at all, except for a distant shadow retreating up a hillside.

So the bold man dragged himself to the farm that lay just over the next hill, and when he was no longer in danger of bleeding to death, he bragged that he had killed the sow at the heart of the forest, and they would never be troubled by the Walk-Around again. From now on, people could walk directly from one place to another, and so the bold man supposed he was a hero. And all the people supposed he was one too, until they looked out the windows and saw that the grass had shriveled up and the rivers had gone dry, and stones as big as horses were lifting up out of the soil. So the people all went running to the place where the bold man said he had killed the sow, but the black sow had turned to black stone, and it was too late to revive her.

So that is how the Walk-Around Waste was created, and now anyone who wants to cross that way had better bring plenty of food and water with them, for from one end of the valley to the other nothing grows, and no water flows.

❈❈❈❈❈❈❈❈❈❈❈❈❈❈❈

Chapter Fourteen

When a Truthken examines a fire blood, it is crucial to hold in mind the fire bloods' inability to separate symbol and reality. In ritual, for example, the content of gesture becomes concrete, and through ritual the desires, dreams, or nightmares of the fire blood are made true. Here, in this blending of symbol and reality, lies the source of the elemental madness so common among the fire folk. Here also is the Truthken's challenge, for fire bloods' lies may rapidly become truths to them. To perceive the difference of falsehood from truth may become impossible.

—The Way of the Truthken

In a wood where the leaves seemed composed of concentrated sunlight, tree branches shattered radiating cracks across the gold, and darkness broke in. There a traveling man took his companion by the shoulders, and turned her to him. She gazed into his face, but did not see him; he saw into her eyes, but did not know her.

It had been raining since midnight: a heavy, cold rain cursed by farmers who had hoped to make one last cutting of hay. Now, the rain had ended, and the woods lay silent but for the peaceful drip of water and the slow floating down of leaves like embers in a dark fireplace.

The man wore a midlands longshirt and canvas breeches; greased boots and leggings caked with heavy mud; a blanket and satchel slung crossways from shoulder to waist; and from his belt all the dangling pouches, bags, and implements of a wanderer who carries his house with him. His long gray hair was bound at the neck; his expression was complex beyond reading. The woman had nothing, not even an expression on her face.

The man said, "I ask your forgiveness." He kissed her, and she jerked like a wild creature away from his touch. Then he struck her face with a closed fist, and she staggered. He struck her in the stomach, and she fell to her knees. As he beat her, the woman's plain tunic became blotted with blood; she seemed to faint. He wiped his face with his sleeve and took a ragged breath, but, as though he dared not pause for long, drew his dagger and stabbed her.

Afterwards, he took her by the shoulders and dragged her through wet leaves and mud to drop her in the ditch by the side of the road. He stood over her, calm but old, with a hand lifted vaguely to his chest. Her eyes fluttered open; she looked at him as though he were one small piece of a monstrous, excruciating puzzle.

The man turned his head, for he could hear the faint jingle of a horse's harness. He re-balanced the burdens he carried and walked away, into the wet woods, into the darkness that flowed out of the trees as, behind the lowering clouds, the sun stumbled and fell below the horizon.

Chapter Fifteen

That day, the whole of Shaftal had lain under a cloud. The arrival of autumn mud season had taken Garland by surprise. He had nowhere to go. He dared not ask for shelter in the decrepit farmhouses that he passed, for the rains had caught him in the hostile western edge of the midlands, with its tapped out soil and bitter recent history. He could expect no friendliness here, and certainly no generosity.

He walked the entire day, through intermittent downpours, until the weight of water made his poor burdens so heavy he was tempted to simply drop them in the road. After the day ended the cold would come, which he could stave off only with wet blankets and wet, threadbare clothing; for although his matches were probably dry in their tin, he would find no fuel dry enough to burn, not even if he used his own hair for tinder.

The road had begun to rise in the afternoon. Without regrets, he had left the hostile farmlands, with their suspiciously peering residents, and climbed into forbidding, rocky country. Oak trees gave way to pine, and as sunset approached, the road petered out, and he awoke from his daze of cold and loneliness and wondered if he might die that night.

For a moment, overwhelmed by futility and aimlessness and the vacancy left behind when he abandoned his hopes, he thought he did not care. Then, he heard the ring of a woodcutter's ax, and he thought longingly of how wood means fire, and fire means a hearth, and a hearth means a house. He stepped into the woods. Soon, he was walking among no mere saplings, but trees much further around than he could clasp in two hands. What kind of people would he find, living beyond a road that had been overgrown for so many years?

The sound had seemed close, but as twilight gave way to deep, drizzling shadows, the sound of the ax mocked him, luring him further from the now distant road, without letting him get closer to the sound. The Shaftali are a people of many stories that they hold up like shields against the boredom of winter, and Garland had heard his share of them, including a number that told of malevolent forces that inhabited the forest and tried to lure solitary travelers from their chosen roads. He asked himself if he was afraid, but was too tired to attempt an answer.

The trees that had closed in around him suddenly flung him out of their company. He stumbled to his knees among slim saplings. The road had not reappeared, but now he was in a clearing, looking at a steep crag looming against a starless sky darkening to black. Between him and the crag stood a humble stone house, and between him and the house, the woodcutter worked in a circle of lantern light.

The woodcutter bent and straightened, graceful as a dancer, but with a moment of brisk violence at the end of each easy stroke. The split kindling leapt up, sometimes bright and sometimes black, and flew, and fell. Garland got up from his sprawl, but dared not step forward. The woodcutter seemed gigantic, a construction of powerful muscle that gleamed wet in the light. The wood split with a single stroke; only the sharp crack told him it was wood, hard and dry for burning. He saw beauty, art, and a fearsome anger, and stood suspended between that terrifying sight and the woods, and wondered if the malevolence of myth might be safer than the bright power at work before him. And yet he gasped as the ax entered the log, and slid through it, and transformed it.

Abruptly, the woodcutter turned, and he saw it was a woman, shirtless, bleeding in the breast where a flying splinter must have struck her. She said, "Help me to pick up the wood—quickly. It's going to rain again."

Her hoarse, homely voice galvanized him. He hurried forward, to toss his knapsack onto the porch and wander about the yard, seeking the far-flung pieces and dumping them under the porch roof by the armload. He and the woman met at the steps, she carrying the lantern and putting her other arm through a shirt sleeve, he with one last load of wood. They ducked into shelter as the sky opened up and the deluge began.

"Quietly," she said, opening the door. "Don't wake the child."

Surely bandits have no children, Garland thought, but he could not imagine what else she might be. He followed her into a kitchen, where a few coals glowed upon the hearth and dirt lay thick on a creaking floor. She hung the lantern on a hook, and he got a good look at her: a large, tangle-haired woman in clothing as worn out as his own, with big hands, and palms as black as soot. A blacksmith?

He put some wood onto the fire, and went back to get his sodden gear from the porch. A huge table was the kitchen's only furniture, but the walls had plenty of hooks, on which he hung his belongings to dry. The woman sat on the hearth: silent, monolithic. He lit a candle stub and with it in hand, located a storeroom, surprising clean and practically empty, and came back with some lard and a canister of flour. He hung a battered, soot-crusted teakettle from the crane and swung it over the fire, and by the time the water boiled he had patted out the biscuits and dropped them into the rusty hearth oven to bake.

While the tea was steeping and the biscuits baking, he put together a pot of beans with onions so sharp he cried as he chopped them, and some bacon ends that he licked first to make sure they were not rancid. He hunted through the storeroom again, and found, all crowded on one shelf, a pat of fresh butter, a big chunk of honeycomb in a cloth-covered bowl, and a bucket of russet apples. He imagined the big woman walking up the mountain from the closest farm, with the bucket of apples in one hand, the butter in the other, and an ax on her back, setting the supplies down on a stump so she could chop down a bee-tree, and then . . . Garland thought for a moment. She had run out of hands. The child would be with her, he concluded, and she was old enough to be trusted to carry the butter. So the woman had carried a bucket of honey the rest of the way up the hill.

The woman still sat unmoving on the hearth. Her face, revealed by firelight, was drawn and stark. She turned her head slowly as Garland lifted out the biscuits from the oven that sat in the coals. He buttered them generously, dripped them with honey, and gave her a tin plate full, with a tin cup of tea, and sat on the hearth himself, and watched her from the corner of his eye.

With the first bite, she uttered a small sound of surprise. She closely examined the biscuit, and then him. She stuck a finger in her mouth to suck off the honey, and then she truly began to eat: seriously, attentively. He refilled her cup and gave her the last three biscuits, but she gave one of them back to him. When the plates were empty and wiped clean, and the woodcutter-blacksmith clasped her third cup of tea within her big hands like an egg stolen from a bird's nest, she said in a quiet, rasping voice, "I don't suppose you are looking for a place to stay."

Garland cleared his throat. He had not spoken, he realized, for several days. "It's only biscuits."

"Evidence enough," she said, as though they were old friends, having an oblique but cordial argument.

"I can stay a few days," he said cautiously.

"It will rain for three more days. You can help clean and secure the house, if you will. And then the roads will be firm enough for you to travel on, to wherever you are going. It will rain again, of course, after that." Her tone of voice asked no questions.

He said politely, cautiously, "It seems you are not well prepared for winter."

"Not yet. But the roof is tight, the woodshed full, the chimney sound."

"The storeroom, though . . ."

"When the roads firm up, I'll visit a market town nearby. If you come with me, I'll buy you whatever you want."

The silence descended again: his astonished, hers preoccupied. But she seemed less vacant now; the biscuits were doing their work, which gave him to understand that she had been terribly hungry. That drawn, shadowed face of hers suggested she also had not slept well in some time. The beans began to boil. He gave them a stir, then raked the coals away, to slow the pot. "That will be tomorrow's supper," he said. "For tonight, have you got eggs?"

"I did. Leeba dropped them, though."

"Leeba is your child?" He paused. "My name is Garland."

"Karis. They tell me that my name means 'Lost.'" She seemed ironic and skeptical, but Garland thought she did seem, if not lost, then certainly bewildered.

"Well, but you have talent," he said. "You've done all this, repaired the house and cut the wood."

She raised an eyebrow at him. "Has *your* talent given you happiness?"

He said honestly, "Happiness never lasts longer than a meal."

"It lasts so long as that?"

He looked at her, not knowing what to think or say. The plate of biscuits he had already given her was all he had to offer. But she was big, and hardworking, and probably still hungry. Another plateful of biscuits, or even two, would not be too much. He went to the table, measured flour and leavening, and once again began cutting in the lard.

Karis was heavy spirited, but not difficult to live with. Her daughter took some getting used to, though: active, loud, insistent, demanding every bit of Karis's attention and at least once a day working herself into such a temper that Karis exiled her to a distant room. Since Karis was working outside in the rain much of the time, Garland often supervised this difficult child, who did not, at first, seem to particularly like him or to want him around. Then he made jam buns, and Leeba warmed up to him considerably.

Karis worked: steadily, restlessly, and oftentimes wearily. In the cold rain and mud, she stood out in the overgrown road and wielded her ax, mowing down the trees like grass before a scythe. Garland was content to clean the house, which had been abandoned long enough for bats to live in the attic, squirrels to inhabit the chimney, and rats to make the cellar their kingdom. Somehow, Karis had already shooed out the squatters, but they had left a mess that took some stomach to clean up. The rest was merely dirt and dust, vast quantities of it that Garland swept up with a twig broom Karis had made the first morning, along with a dust pan she fashioned from a tin plate found rusting in the cellar.

He showered off the filth each night, standing in the cold rain with a bar of yellow soap. Then, suddenly, the rain stopped in the night, and in the morning they walked down the track Karis had cut through the trees. The road had firmed up as she predicted, though the ditches were full and Karis made Leeba ride on her shoulders to keep her out of the muck.

"There's the ravens," Leeba said suddenly, pointing into the distance. "Tell them to come here. I want to ask them a question."

Karis said, "They're looking for food. What do you want to know?"

"I want to know why are there three? There's yours, and mine. But—" She looked sideways at Garland. "Does he have a raven?"

Karis said, in a voice like a saw cutting wood, "Zanja's raven is with us now. Do you remember what I told you? That she is dead?"

"I don't want her to be dead," Leeba protested.

Garland, outside the edges of this strange, obscure conversation, did not ask for an explanation. If Karis had to start explaining herself, then so would he have to. He was thinking he might be able to manage through the winter with these two, in their stone house that every day became cozier, though it still had no furniture. He did not want to risk his comfort by telling half truths that might make him a vagabond again.

"I don't *want* her to be dead," Leeba said again. Garland thought he saw the same pain convulse in her that Karis kept checked within herself. "I want J'han," she added. "Is he dead too?"

"No," Karis said, vaguely and distantly.

"Is summer over? My daddy promised to come home!" As they drew closer to the market town, the road became quite busy as people gathered for what would more than likely be the last market day of the year. These people who had seemed to Garland so distant and suspicious, greeted each other jovially, though they avoided even looking at Karis and Garland. Karis commented, "We've settled in an unfriendly place, but money might win them over."

When they reached the town, she casually handed Garland a bag of coins. "I'll hire us a wagon, so have everything you buy delivered to the livery stable, and we'll sort it out there." She added lightly, "Don't be overly economical. If you run out of money, tell a raven, and I'll bring you some more."

Garland gave a bemused laugh. Leeba said, "If you talk to a raven, tell him I want my daddy to come home."

"Yes, of course," said Garland. He did not understand children particularly, and did not himself remember believing that birds could talk, but he supposed this game to be harmless.

"Get yourself some new clothes," Karis commanded, as they parted ways. "I won't have you shivering in your bare threads all winter. New shoes, too. Promise!"

They parted, and Garland turned to watch Karis walk towards the livery stable, with the girl trotting beside her, one arm stretched up as far as it would go, so she could clasp two of the big woman's big fingers. Leeba was asking why the roofs were shaped with upturned edges, and then she pointed out that a woman was carrying four live chickens upside-down by the feet, and then Garland could not hear her penetrating voice any more.

It did not seem to even have occurred to Karis that, once she gave Garland her money, he no longer needed her stone house, her grim company, or her noisy child. He could live through winter in a rented room, in some large town, developing respectability and familiarity, eventually winning a permanent position in a prosperous inn, perhaps, and so end his wandering days.

But he followed the crowds to the market, and began methodically spending the money. Soon, he was too wrapped up in calculating sensible quantities of supplies, consulting the list he had constructed in his head over the last three days, and bargaining fiercely with the unfriendly merchants to feel any particular regret. He emerged from a clothiers in the late afternoon, with a few coins still jangling in his new pockets—the first new clothing he'd had since he lost his temper with the general five years ago and made himself a wanderer—and glanced up to see the source of a dry flapping sound. There on the edge of the roof stood a great raven, black as the heart of a stormcloud, looking at him inquiringly through one eye and then the other. Garland glanced around himself. He was practically alone on the street, for it was the time that most people go home to start cooking their suppers. He said out loud, feeling foolish, "I'm not quite out of money, but I think the shopping's done. And Leeba wants her daddy to come home."

The raven said, "Karis is waiting for you."

Surely the raven had not actually spoken. Certainly, it had not. Garland continued to repeat this assurance to himself, as the raven lifted its wings and flew nonchalantly down the road, to perch on another rooftop and glance back—impatiently? "I'm losing my mind," Garland muttered. "Soon the pots will start reciting recipes to me." He picked up his basket, which was laden with tins of tea and spices, a couple of pair of woolen stockings, a half dozen wooden spoons, a rolling pin, and a few other things, and started down the road. The raven flew ahead of him, never out of sight, looking back at Garland with unsettling intelligence, until they had reached the edge of town. Two other ravens waited on the roof of the supperhouse where he and Karis were to meet, and they greeted the third with raucous, hoarse cries. Were they now talking to each other? It almost seemed they were. Garland set his basket at his feet; he could not make himself go one step further.

A fourth raven arrived, and the others shouted their greetings. Garland turned, slowly, reluctantly, to look in the direction from which the fourth black bird had arrived. He saw a wandering man, shabby in the way that wanderers get, carrying a big, heavy pack such as peddlers carry. The man was

standing still in the middle of the road, like Garland, looking at
the ravens on the rooftop. His eyes were bright with tears. Garland heard the supperhouse door creak open. He heard Leeba
cry, "Daddy!" She ran past Garland, shrieking joyfully, and
jumped into the peddler's arms.

Karis came out to stand at the top of the supperhouse steps,
with her big hands tucked into her belt. The peddler danced in
the street, turning and turning with his daughter clasped to his
chest, kissing her head in rhythm with her enthusiastic out-
pouring of words: "I kept asking and asking the ravens where
you were, but they wouldn't *tell* me. And Karis is going to
make me a bed out of sticks! Daddy, is Zanja dead? I don't
want her to be dead."

"Me neither."

"Karis cries."

"So do I. Do you?" Eventually, the peddler set his daughter
down. He and Karis looked at each other.

Karis turned abruptly away from his gaze and said, "Garland, I've ordered a meal already."

Garland said, "I just came to give you these things. And to
say good-bye."

The peddler had glanced at him in some surprise. Leeba explained, "That's Garland. He makes jam buns."

"And I got you a present, Leeba," said Garland.

Karis said quietly to him, "At least come in and eat something, and let us settle our accounts."

Garland had no choice then, for Leeba had grabbed him by
the trouser leg and was dragging him insistently towards Karis,
dragging her father as well by the hand. "Come *on*. You're so
slow. I want my present!"

The man Garland had taken for a peddler said to him, "I'm
J'han."

Garland gave a nod. "Karis's husband."

"Well, not exactly."

They were in the supperhouse then, and J'han's pack was
tucked out of the way, and Leeba insisted on sitting in his lap,
while continuing to demand Garland's present. Garland dug it
out of the basket: a brightly painted wooden lizard purchased

from the same wood carver who had made the spoons and rolling pin. Soon Leeba's rabbit had come out of her pocket to make the lizard's acquaintance, and they appeared to be destined to be fast friends.

Karis, even more grim and red-eyed than usual, sliced and passed the bread. Garland gave her an accounting, and laid on the table all the money that was left. She added more coins and pushed it back to him. "For your work these four days."

"You've sheltered me and given me clothing."

"Please, take it. It can't be easy, to be a Sainnite in this land, without friends or family. I can always make more money."

With nerveless fingers, Garland took the coins. He glanced at J'han, who must have heard her words but kept right on buttering his bread. Garland said, "Five years I've been wandering, and no one's even guessed . . ."

"Earth bloods don't guess," said Karis.

Tearing his bread in half to share it with Leeba, J'han said, half to himself, "We know what we know."

In the silence that followed, Garland, who had been poised to stand and flee, felt himself grow slowly heavier in his chair. A young man swathed in an apron brought roasted potatoes, onions, and pork, and a small pumpkin with a spoon in it so they could scrape the flesh out of the skin. When he was gone, Karis said, "My mother was a Juras woman and my father a Sainnite. But no one doubts that I'm Shaftali, so why should I call you something else? We are no different from each other, really."

J'han said, easily, "In fact, anatomically the three of us are identical. Leeba, lizards don't eat bread and butter. It makes them sick."

Leeba said, "Medric is a Sainnite, isn't he? Karis, when will Medric come? I want to show him my lizard."

"Ask the ravens," Karis said.

Leeba looked sullen. "The ravens won't talk to me any more!"

J'han was gazing at Karis, though, with an expression that Garland could not interpret. He seemed a gentle man, and perhaps he knew how to help Karis. To have him in their household might be a great relief. And it would be easier to cook for four.

Garland cut himself a bite of the roast, which was overcooked, and ate a potato, which was bland, and restrained himself from grumbling about people who call themselves cooks. But Karis, her mouth full, said seriously, "You could have cooked this meal ten times better."

"Roasted potatoes should have rosemary. I'll make some tomorrow, and you'll see."

"I'll build you a bed tomorrow," she answered after a while. "I've got enough nails, now."

J'han said to Leeba, "Tell me about our new house."

Chapter Sixteen

With a half dozen nails pressed between her lips, Karis looked quite menacing, but her hands covered Garland's so gently, he could scarcely feel the scratching of her rough palms as she used his hands like intelligent tools to bend and shape the supple twig, and then hold it in position while she tacked it in place. She had carried in the twigs through the morning's downpour, from the brush pile she had formed while clearing the road. Now Karis had constructed three chairs out of the twigs, one child-sized, and had nearly finished a fourth. She had yet to break or split a single twig. Leeba had made a chair, too, imitating Karis with substantial help from J'han. The stuffed rabbit now sat beside Leeba on its own chair. "Rabbit is planning," Leeba said.

"Planning what?" asked J'han, who was methodically unloading his pack onto the kitchen table. Garland had sanded and oiled the table that morning, and now felt as if he could roll out his pastry on it without shame. When J'han had politely asked permission before putting his pack on the table, it had pleased Garland immoderately.

"Planning important things," Leeba said.

J'han nodded gravely. "Well, tell your rabbit that great things happen through the accumulation of small acts."

"Rabbit *knows* that."

"Sometimes I forget how smart your rabbit is."

Garland took note of what had emerged from J'han's pack. It was a series of miniature chests that interlocked on top of each other. J'han had the usual traveling gear as well: rain cloak, match tin, candle lantern. But Garland, who had met plenty of travelers in his five years, had never met one who carried furniture on his back. "What are those?" he asked J'han, as Karis took control of his hands again. "They look heavy."

"You'd be surprised how light they are. Karis made them of wood sliced thin as veneer. But the contents are awfully heavy. This one is an apothecary's shop. This one a medicine chest. And this one a surgeon's cabinet."

Garland said, "I thought you were a peddler."

"That's because I'm trying to look like one. But—see here?" He pulled back his hair to show Garland his earlobe. Across the dimming kitchen, Garland could see nothing unusual, but J'han explained, "A scar. From the earring. I trained at Kisha University."

The university was gone now, long since burned to the ground by Sainnites. Karis spit out her nails to say, "You'd have three earrings now, if history had been different."

Garland knew enough to know it was a compliment. It also was the kindest thing Karis had said to anyone since Garland met her. He felt obliged to stammer out an apology for the Sainnite destruction of the university, but J'han hushed him. "We're more interested in how to flesh out a new future on the bones of the past," he said. "There it is," he added, and took one last box out of his pack.

"What's that?" Leeba leapt up. "A present?"

"Not a present for you. It's a book for Karis, from Medric."

With her mouth in a thin line, Karis finished tacking down the twig, and told Garland to take a rest. He went to the hearth to stir his pot and add more wood to the fire, then rather hesitantly asked J'han if he would pull the tooth that ached so it kept him awake at night.

"Of course," said J'han. "Or maybe I could repair it."

"Can I watch?" asked Leeba.

But Garland felt Karis's hand on his shoulder, and turned, and she quietly said, "Hold still," and cupped his jaw in her coarse, gentle hand. Just like that, Garland's tooth stopped hurting.

"You're taking my business," J'han complained mildly.

Karis turned away from Garland. "What did Medric say?"

Garland tentatively rubbed his jaw, then surreptitiously stuck a finger into his mouth to probe his sore tooth. It gave him not a twinge.

"To read the book," J'han said.

Karis made a sound, halfway between a snort and a sigh. "Let's finish that chair."

But Leeba protested, "I want to know what's in the box! Show me!"

"It's Karis's present."

"Can I look at it, Karis?"

"I don't care." Karis knelt again beside the chair.

Garland went back to help her, still probing his tooth with his tongue, and thinking rather dazedly that he had yet to discover one thing that Karis could not do.

Assaulted now by Leeba's shrill impatience, J'han cut the box's bindings, and then spelled out for Leeba the letters written on the cover. "It says, 'Be Very Careful.' But I haven't been at all careful, I'm afraid." He opened the box, and Leeba said in disgust, "It's a box of ashes!"

"Oh, dear. Karis, I'm afraid even you can't fix this. Bring it to her, Leeba."

Being very careful, Leeba brought the open box to Karis, who took it from her, glanced at the bits of burned paper that filled it to the rim, and dropped it on the floor without ever taking the nails from her mouth. Leeba, apparently impervious to Karis's ill temper, got down on her knees, crying in excitement, "Look, it's not all ashes!" She began blowing enthusiastically into the box. The frail remains of the printed pages floated upward on her breath, then, as they landed on the floor, disintegrated into dust. Leeba's puffing uncovered the solid remains of the book. With the bound edge still intact, and the other edges burned into a curve, it looked like a half moon. On the charred, curling edges of the leather cover, the title, stamped into the leather and once burnished with gold, was faintly visible. Once, the book had been quite large, for even in its drastically reduced state it was big enough, and must have been a heavy weight on J'han's back.

"Can I open it?" Leeba asked, already reaching for the cover.

Karis, bending a twig, did not even glance at her. J'han said, "Be very careful."

"I *am*."

As Leeba opened the book and turned the pages, Garland glimpsed a densely printed page, and a carefully rendered etching of a pig with all the cuts of meat marked. It was reassuringly commonplace. Leeba turned the pages: more pigs, cows, sheep, oxen, horses. The fragile paper shattered as Leeba turned the pages.

Karis bent, trimmed, and began to secure the twig that finished the chair. Soon, they all could sit down, though it appeared they would have nothing to sleep on for another night, not even Leeba's lizard, who had been promised a lizard-sized bed.

"The other book isn't burned at all," said Leeba. "The baby book."

"What?" J'han came over to look. "Well. How about that!"

Garland, his hands still holding the last twig, looked over and saw that a hole had been carved out inside the massive volume. Tucked inside it lay a book so small that, despite the big book's burning, its own edges remained unscathed. Its red cover shone brightly, unfaded, as though it had never seen the light.

"Can I take it out?" Leeba plucked the child out of its womb. "I can't open it! Daddy, you try."

J'han took it from her. "Maybe its pages are pasted shut. Why would someone go through so much trouble . . . ?"

"Karis!" Leeba said. "Fix it!"

Karis spat out her nails into the nail bag, and set her hammer on the floor. "We're done," she said to Garland. "Did Medric tell you the little book was there?" she asked J'han.

"No."

"He's a sneaky little rat of a man," she said.

Leeba giggled.

Karis held out her hand for the baby book.

Silence descended. Even Leeba, who was quiet only when she slept, stared at Karis, open-mouthed, as Karis pressed the book between her palms. Her hands were so big, and the book so small, that only its red edges could be seen. The fire uttered a sudden pop, and spit embers across the stone hearth. Karis opened her palms as though they were the book's covers, and the book opened with them: sweetly, obediently, its pages rustling like starched sheets being unfolded.

"Oh!" sighed Leeba.

The way I am with cooking, thought Garland, *Karis is with the whole world.*

He glanced at J'han, who sat down in one of the chairs.

Karis said in a low voice, "Earth magic had sealed this book." She bent her head over the handwritten page, seemed to read a few words, and then, abruptly, slapped the book shut. Her face looked rather pale.

Leeba came out of her fascinated paralysis. "What is it? I want to see!"

"I think it is a letter."

"A letter in a book?" Leeba paused, her lively mind apparently stalled for a moment by the challenge of deciding which of many questions to ask. "Who wrote it?"

"Harald G'deon."

"Of course," said J'han. "Who else?" He wiped his eyes on his sleeve.

"Who's that?" asked Leeba.

"He was an important man, who created me and then abandoned me. Just like my father did, actually. I never knew him."

Leeba crawled into her own father's embrace. She had not let him out of her sight for a moment since his abrupt appearance the other day. Secure now, she asked, "Is the letter written to you?"

"I'm the only one who could have opened it." Karis looked down at her closed palms. "But he must have written it before he got sick—before he sent Dinal to find me in Lalali."

Garland had been slow to understand. Hearing the names of the last leaders of Shaftal spoken casually as part of a fragmented account of Karis's history, he thought at first that the discussion was a joke, and then that Karis and J'han were both just a little mad.

Then he remembered the fanatics he had served dinner to last winter, and their leader, Willis, who believed in a story and a vision of a lost G'deon.

Karis had put the little book inside her vest and was packing up her tools. In the book was a letter written to her by the last G'deon of Shaftal, long before his wife Dinal set out to find Karis in Lalali and Harald G'deon lay hands on Karis and vested her with the power of Shaftal.

Karis glanced at Garland, and seemed to find the expression on his face too strange to endure. She took up one of the chairs and carried it with her into the adjoining parlor, which did not even have a fire in its fireplace yet. She returned for a candle and left again, and shut the parlor door. J'han said to Leeba, "Leave Karis alone."

"I *know*." Leeba settled herself more snugly into his shoulder. "Are you going to pull Garland's tooth now?"

"Karis fixed it already."

Leeba sighed with exasperation. "She's always *fixing* things!"

"She's the Lost G'deon?" Garland said. His voice came out of his throat harsh and strange, as though he had swallowed a glass of spirits too fast.

J'han said gently, "Doesn't she seem lost to you?"

Garland sat down. The twig chair uttered a squeak as though it were surprised.

"She doesn't seem like a G'deon to you," said J'han.

Leeba was neither talking nor wiggling, which meant she was about to fall asleep. She gazed at Garland curiously, though, as if she wanted to know what he thought.

Garland said, "She's always fixing things."

Leeba grinned at him.

Garland added, "The Sainnites thought the G'deon was a war leader. A man of fearsome power."

J'han said, "Medric, our seer, has concluded that every G'deon has been well and truly terrified of his or her own power. I don't guess that's the kind of fearsome power you mean, though."

"I never thought of it that way." Garland swallowed, feeling the room, the world, shift around him like a house rebuilding itself into a completely different shape. "What can she do?"

"It's hard to know, until she actually does it. I've seen her do some amazing things. She puts things together, basically— but she could just as easily be taking them apart. And she knows it."

"But she doesn't?"

"Fortunately," J'han said, kissing his sleepy daughter's head, "Karis is disinclined to destruction."

It's a strange and unpleasant sensation to know my life is almost over. For forty of my sixty years, I have been thinking as a farmer does, not just of the next crop, but five, ten growing seasons into the future, always asking myself, If I do this now, what will be the result then? But now, when I think that way, my thinking collapses. I will not be there to repair any errors I might make now. And it makes me afraid to think at all, afraid to take any action at all. Can I tell you this, a secret I try to keep even from Dinal (though, really, it is hopeless)? Can I write to you as though you were my friend? Or are you so angry with me that to tell you my secrets will only seem an insult, a presumption, like a drunk in a tavern who whispers to you exactly how he pleasures his lover?

Despite herself, Karis uttered a laugh.

Well, really, what choice have you? You can close this book and walk away, but you will eventually read it. No . . . I am guessing. I have no way to know you. I assume you will be like all earth bloods, but how can I be certain? Perhaps your disastrous childhood in Lalali (you see, I do know something about you) will leave you bent, lightning-struck, irreparable. Perhaps it is a bitter, foolish, short-sighted woman who reads these words. Perhaps I have vested the power of Shaftal in a broken container.

Here Karis did shut the book sharply, and stared into the cold fireplace, breathing hard. Faint voices murmured in the kitchen. Rain sighed, and then pounded on tightly latched shutters. The repaired roof held. Karis opened the book again.

But I do not think so. You see, I am afraid, and yet I am not. It is too late for me to save you. You will have to save yourself. But I know, or I believe, that it's better that way. By the day you read this book, you will be healed. You will no longer rage at me for doing to you what I am going to do. And you will have found a companion, a fire blood, who in turn will find this book for you, wherever Dinal hides it, just as she would find it for me, had it been hidden for me by a G'deon of the past. Some things, I believe, will not change. And so I believe in you, as Rakel G'deon believed in me, when he threw that great weight of power into me. Like stones, it was. And then I awoke from my faint to find him dead. Though everything and everyone may seem to fail you, Shaftal will not, and you will be made strong.

So. I will write to you, to a G'deon whose name I cannot know, whose present pain and power suddenly evidenced itself to me mere days ago. I write to you on the day that the healers informed me that the strange weakness I feel from time to time is a herald of my death. I will live a half year, they say, maybe a bit longer, since we G'deons can be so tenacious. (Really, we are famous for it. But perhaps, in your time, such things will have been forgotten.) I write to you, for you and I will never speak because, in order to protect you, I must leave you in that midden heap where you were born. I write to you and I am not certain why. Because I pity you? Because my many, many guilts have grown impossible to live with any longer? No, I don't think so. I think it's that I love you, though you don't even exist yet, though you are just an idea. I love you, and from your distant difficult future, I can almost feel you looking backwards to comfort me. "Harald," you say to me, "I am Shaftal! All will be well!" And that's the truth that rises up in me that I want to say back to you. All will be well. I am an old man facing his death, writing a letter to a stranger. I have no reason to lie to you. I tell you what I know even as I doubt it: All will be well.

Karis raised her eyes from the book and wiped her face carefully. When the tears did not stop, she lay back her head and sat quietly, simply waiting. Tears fell as though from someone else's eyes. She kept wiping them, as though she feared that they would fall onto the book and blur the ink. In time, they stopped.

Dinal has just come in. She was away, tending to Paladin business, and I had not sent for her, because I have never had to send for her before. She said, "What are you thinking, to write in the dark? Your eyes will fall out of your head." I had not even noticed that the sun had set. She lit a lamp for me, and I saw by its light that she knew. No doubt she has already talked to the healers. I never have to tell her anything important. Always, she already knows. I say things to her anyway, because it lifts the weight. "I am dying," I said to her. "I'm writing a letter."

She said, "Well, it must be an important letter."

And then we held onto each other for a while. The wood feeds the fire. The fire transforms the wood. That is our love. But you know this, don't you?

Karis said out loud, "I can't endure this!" She closed the book, stood up, and paced the empty room, which Garland had scrubbed clean. The candle, which she had stuck onto a projecting stone of the wall, fluttered with her passing. Her heavy, hobnailed boots scraped the floor. The book lay on the chair seat. She looked at it from across the room. Her eyes were red, her face stark. She said to it, as though replying to its long dead author, "Did you ever knowingly send Dinal to her death? Do you know what that's like?" And then she stopped, as though she had heard the answer to her question and it was not the answer she expected. Her angry shoulders slumped. She returned reluctantly to her chair.

Now Dinal has gone, to tell our children. Half our life together she has spent on horseback, running my errands, while I usually remain in or near the House of Lilterwess. Half the year I am in the gardens, weeding the carrots and cutting great armloads of flowers to decorate the dining room tables. Young people coming to the House of Lilterwess for the first time to be novices in one or another order, bump into me in the hall-way and don't even excuse themselves. They are too preoccupied with hoping for a glimpse of the G'deon. There I am, in my work clothes, with my hair untrimmed and dirt under my fingernails, carrying a big basket of cabbages to the kitchen. This is why we don't trust children's judgment! When adults look down their noses at me, those are the people that don't rise in their Orders. Not because I am affronted, but because they still have the judgment of children, and need to grow up before they are given more power. Alas, there are too many such people here lately, besotted with their own self-importance, strutting about in their fur cloaks and whispering with Mabin about war. Where have they all come from?

Shaftal answers: they are the spawn of the Sainnites: not the children of their bodies, of course, but the people that are created each time the Sainnites commit one of their atrocities. Anger, pain, lust for revenge, shock and horror, that is what shapes these people. That is what shaped the Sainnites as well, in that land they escaped from. In turn they shape others to be like them, and soon our land will be a land, not of Shaftali, but of Shaftali whose desire to defeat the Sainnites has turned them into Sainnites.

You know this, my dear. Or, if you do not know it, if you yourself proved incapable of reversing the bitter shape into which the Sainnites forced you, you do not know, and all is lost. Shaftal does not speak to you. Or, if it does, you do not hear. You are reading this little book, thinking to yourself what an ass I am, what a fool, for going about that fine house covered with dirt, when I could be washed in milk and dressed in, oh, I don't know, a silk-embroidered topcoat. Perhaps you are wearing one yourself as you read this! Certainly, with the abilities you have, you could live a rich and comfortable life. Sainnites may well be bowing down before you as the Sainnites now want us to bow to them. Oh, what are these dark thoughts!

They are the thoughts of a man who knows he must let go and trust another to do the work that he has done so joyfully (so stubbornly, Mabin would say. So obstinately. So blindly). I *admit, I am proud of my steadfastness. But you are the child of a bitter land, a land in a future I fear, and perhaps steadfastness will be an unknown thing to you. Indeed, why should you be so strong when no one has stood by you? I shudder to think what has already happened to you. I quail at the thought of what has yet to happen, what I know must happen, what I dare not prevent, though certainly I can. Oh, my dear! I am so sorry!*

And so I have circled back again to the thoughts that I began with: I am afraid. I must trust, and hope, in the land. The future no longer belongs to me, but to you. And you curse me, do you not?

Karis put her head in her hands. "No," she murmured, after a long while. "No, not any more."

Mabin has just been visiting. Of course, Dinal told her the news on her way out to saddle her horse. (My wife is an old woman! She will ride all night, like a nineteen-year-old. Her vigor is the benefit of loving an earth witch, she says. But I wonder what will happen to her after I die. Will she age all at once? Will she lay down her weapons and start doting on her grandchildren, maybe learn to sew? I cannot imagine it.) Mabin had made herself look very grave, so I said to her with a heartiness as false as her sorrow, "Death is a fulfillment! A closing of the circle!" And she gave me the look I deserved, which forced me to laugh at her. "Come now," I said, having put her all out of countenance. "We have always been honest about our mutual dislike. Why are you pretending that the news of my death makes you sad?"

She replied in that arid way of hers, "I suppose I thought I might convince you to think of Shaftal's future."

It is so typical of her, to assume that only she is capable of genuine concern about our land's condition! To think that only she is disinterested, only she can see the dangers that beset us. I wanted to say to her that the one good thing about dying was that I need not endure her disapproval any more, but I am not entirely without diplomacy, and I held my tongue.

"Where is the heir to Shaftal?" she asked.

How could I tell her that it's better for my heir to remain a whore in Lalali than it is for her to be twisted by the angers and power struggles of this House? (I imagine, now that the House no longer stands—yes, this far into the future I think I can see—that it will be remembered fondly. But in these last few years it has been a terrible, whispering place, full of plots and angry sideways looks. And I am not particularly sorry to know it will be destroyed.) Mabin disapproves of me. How badly will she treat you? How long would it take her to turn all her forces against you? I told her a blatant lie, glad there were no Truthkens in the room. "There is no heir."

She looked at me, aghast. "Are you not relieved?" I asked her. "Doesn't it give you joy to know that at last you will have no impediments to your military aspirations?"

It took some time for her to recover. (It is cruel and small-minded of me to torture her like this, but she has earned her suffering.) At least she replied more honestly then. "An army with the power of a G'deon behind it could not be defeated. But, without a G'deon . . . How many Paladins are there? Seven hundred? Against how many thousand Sainnites?"

"Ten," I said, to see her jump with shock. "Or so," I added. "No, it will not be a pretty battle. Good luck to you. Fight well!"

"You're doing this to spite me!" she said. "You will send all of Shaftal into ruin just to ruin one woman that you hate! What kind of man are you?"

I said then, to admonish her, "I am the G'deon of Shaftal." But she will not, shall not, cannot understand what that means. She walked out in anger. So, she is to become blatantly impolite, now that my days are numbered! She is a grasping, power-hungry woman, but that I might forgive if she had a little imagination. Unfortunately, all that air in her blood has left no room for the fire. I am sorry to be bequeathing you such a enemy. For a long time, I fear, her power will exceed yours, and I have a horror of what she might do to you. Oh, my dear.

Now the healer is coming down the hall to admonish me for taking no supper, and as soon as he sees me, sitting here with *the pen in my hand, he will bid me rest, as well. Yes, here he is, saying exactly as I predicted. I will lay down my pen for now. These healers, they are gentle enough, but in their hearts they are all despots.*

Karis had been laughing, and seemed to realize it only then, as she looked up from the book as though to give Harald privacy to sleep. From the kitchen, she heard Leeba's peevish voice and the metallic clang of a ladle, banging on a tin plate. Hesitantly, she smiled at these sounds.

Morning now. Visitors were crowding the hallway when I awoke, so the healer has set watchdogs at either end of the hall, to turn visitors away. I will gladly ignore their appeals and their anxieties. If they are so weak as to be swayed by Mabin's panic, then they deserve to suffer the results. How irritable I have gotten! Well, it is but my sense that my energies are failing, and that these people would deplete them even more, snapping up my reassurances like a pack of hounds their meat, and then baying desperately for more. Is this how I will be remembered, as a man who shut his doors against a frightened people? Well, what does it matter how I am remembered?

Before I began writing again, I read what I wrote last night, and I feel it has no value. I realize now that I have written to you, not to give you something, but to reassure myself, to make myself believe in you. I realize that I have nothing to give you—or rather, that by the time you read this, you will long ago have been given the most precious thing I have. But you will receive it like an assault; you will feel as though I have destroyed you; you may never forgive me for something that to you will seem a random, desperate, and ill-considered act. So perhaps I do have something else to give you, after all; the knowledge, simply, that I am thinking of you with kindness. When your great talent awakened in you, that was when hope awakened in me. When I realized what you are, I wept, yes. Your body will always remember the abuses it has endured. Sainnites and Shaftali alike may make you a pariah because of your "tainted" blood. But to one old man, who halfway knows you, who can only guess your future, you are a hope, a love, a call-

*ing to be steadfast to the end. Because of you, I can let the dogs
howl. My certainty in you gives my life, and especially my
death, coherence.*

So I am writing, after all, to thank you.

The writer had filled up the book. There was no more to be
read. Karis closed it and sat with it held between her hands.
The house grew silent, except for the rain. The candle burned
low and dripped a long strand of yellow wax down the wall.
Karis stood up finally, and went to lift a window sash, and
open the shutters. Four wretched, sodden black birds flew in,
quarreling with each other, and found perches on her chair.
"That's a new chair. Try to aim your crap on the floor," she told
them. "Poor Garland! Maybe I should scrub the floor before he
sees it. But he'll be up before me, humming to his bread
dough."

One of the ravens said, "He'll forgive us."

"Give us something to eat," said another. "The starvation
season has begun."

She went into the dark kitchen and came back with the scrap
bucket. "Garland has started saving food for you."

The ravens set to emptying the bucket. They made quite a
mess. Karis watched them, with the book out of danger in her
hands. When they were finished and settled again on the chair
to preen their feathers, one of them looked at her and said,
"Well? What?"

"Tell your brothers in the Midlands to fly to Medric's window. He's awake, probably packing his books. I imagine he already knows what the raven will say to him, but say it anyway.
Tell him to pack up the house and come to me, with Emil and
Norina. Tell him we have work to do."

✦ ✦ ✦ ✦ ✦ ✦ ✦ ✦ ✦ ✦ ✦ ✦ ✦ ✦ ✦ ✦

Chapter Seventeen

In a ditch where water and mud were chilled by their anticipation of winter, the battered woman lay bleeding. The darkness had come all at once, and she had shut her eyes against it. The last light of the stumbling sun flickered out. Her outstretched hand lay limp, with the churned-up ruts of the road beyond reach.

Now the wagon came, hauled through the mud by weary horses, driven by a man who had repeatedly been forced to get out and put a shoulder to the wagon to get its wheels unstuck. That they traveled on this wet day was his passenger's fault: that detour east to Hannisport, those three days in the dockside fabric shops. Yet she berated him for the slow progress, the constant risk the rain posed her load of silks. Watfield was still hours away, and soon the driver would have to light the lamps. He could hear water running, but the ditches were already black, their contents obscure.

The horses shied sharply. The passenger cried, "Stop!"

A pregnant woman who had to relieve herself at every turn of the road ought not to travel at all, thought the driver. Now the wheels would sink in and it would take more horses than he had to get them loose again.

The woman had seen something, though: an open hand, the gray smear of a face. She picked her way fastidiously through the mud, and stood looking down at the woman who lay in mud and running water like another shadow. She looked again, to make certain that what she saw was there.

"What?" said the driver wearily.

"I've never seen the like," said the pregnant woman. "A border woman, I think. She may be dead. But we can't just leave her here."

"I'll light the lantern," the driver said. "A border woman? There's no tribes around here."

With impatient displeasure, the woman observed the mud staining her shoe. The driver came over with a lantern. "Look how her eye is swelling up! Someone was angry with her, that's certain." He looked around himself, worried that the border woman's attacker might still be lurking in the dark. There was nothing in the woods but trees, though.

"Look how bloody she is," the pregnant woman said. "She must be dead."

She had made it apparent that she would not touch the woman sprawled in the ditch. Sighing, the driver gave her the lantern, and knelt in the mud. Seeing no buttons, he tore open the front of the border woman's blood-soaked tunic. He spread the edges of the wound in her breast, and said sharply, "Don't look if you're squeamish. But hold the lantern steady. No, she's not hurt to death that I can see. Just fainted, probably."

The pregnant woman said, exasperated, "We'll have to take her to the next farmhouse. And she's all mud! She'll wreck the silk!"

They got her into the wagon, wrapped in a blanket to prevent her from staining anything. The horses smelled blood and tried to hurry away, but the smell followed them. The driver peered anxiously into shadows. The passenger kept a sharp eye out for the lights of a farmstead, but perhaps the winter shutters were already closed everywhere, for the darkness was unrelieved even by stars. She finally said in frustration, "We'll take her to Watfield, then. My wife will know what to do with her." Then she sat glumly tapping her foot, wishing she had not noticed that hand reaching toward her out of the darkness. Or that she had looked away.

Chapter Eighteen

The note, written in Shaftalese, remained obscure even after Gilly read it out loud to Clement: "Please visit as quickly as you can. You will not regret it." The note was signed, not by Alrin, but by Marga.

"You look flabbergasted," Gilly said, clearly enjoying the sight.

"Come to Alrin's house with me," said Clement.

"What for? It's raining!"

"It's dinnertime, isn't it? Or teatime?" Clement raised her eyebrows at him.

"Of course I'll go with you," he said hastily.

She sent an aide to put together an escort and sent another with an explanatory message to Cadmar. That day they had gotten more bad news about a nasty attack on tax-collecting soldiers in the east—some ten from the same garrison, all hunted down and slaughtered, one by one. Now Cadmar was working off a bad temper in the training ring, which was fortunate. Given his foul mood, he almost certainly would forbid both of them to go anywhere.

But the people of Watfield had finally gotten distracted from their pot-banging by the urgency of autumn work, and Clement's instincts told her it was reasonably safe for her to go out on the streets. "You just want me along to keep you out of that woman's bed," grumbled Gilly.

"I do feel like I'd do almost anything for clean sheets," Clement replied.

Getting Gilly onto his horse was a painful process, but he looked around himself with lively curiosity as, surrounded by soldiers, they rode out the gate and into the city. "What are all these people doing in town? It's pouring rain!"

Even as he spoke, the sky opened up with a deluge, and so did hundreds of umbrellas: strange, heavy contraptions of wooden spines and waxed leather that spooked the horses. The farmers that crammed the main road were so intent on business that they hardly looked twice at the company of soldiers pushing through the crowd. Parcel-laden adolescents followed their elders dutifully in and out of shops, and frequently paused to look around for familiar faces and to loudly greet the friends they were able to spot on the far end of the street, or even across the square.

Gilly pulled the hood of his oilskin cape over his head, muttering, "An umbrella would be a fine thing."

"Your horse would have a fit," said Clement.

"Not this horse."

The short journey was lengthened by the crowds, and Clement's trousers were soaked through by the time they reached the quiet side street, and the respectable townhouse where summer flowers still bravely bloomed at either side of the front steps. The curtains all were drawn, but Clement saw light glimmer in the parlor window, and it was only a moment's wait for Marga to open the door. She looked beyond Gilly and Clement at the soldiers and horses standing miserably in the road. "You can bring them into the kitchen to dry out and have a bit of cake," she said.

Clement called an order to the sergeant, who did not conceal his pleasure. She said to Marga as she and Gilly stepped in the door, "This is Gilly, the general's secretary. Why have you asked me here?"

"I'd like you to meet my brother," Marga said. "He's in the parlor. I'll leave you alone, if you don't mind helping yourself to tea." Her words were polite enough, but her tone suggested she had no intention of going anywhere near the parlor no matter what Clement said.

"Meet her brother?" said Gilly doubtfully, in Shaftalese.

"Cake," said Clement, handing over her wet cape for Marga to hang up in the hall.

"Oh, *cake*," said Gilly sarcastically as he followed her toward the parlor. "Well, if he's waiting in there to shoot you, at least you'll shield me from injury. And maybe I'll have time while he's reloading to shout that I'm a helpless cripple. And maybe he'll slice me a piece of cake."

Clement stepped through the door with her hand on her saber. The emaciated man who huddled miserably by the fire looked up at her entry, but certainly seemed unlikely to attack her.

"I can tell you what you want to know," he said. "But first I want my Davi back."

He sat silent while Clement got Gilly settled in a comfortable chair. It had been a long time, Clement judged, since Gilly had even been able to sit in comfort—somehow, she must get him an upholstered chair. She brought him a steaming cup of tea and a great slice of the splendid cake that had been sitting untouched on the side table. "What are you trying to do to me?" Gilly moaned.

"Eat slowly," Clement said. "Or I'll make you eat another piece. We've got to stay here long enough for all those soldiers in the kitchen to get their bit of cake."

She turned to the miserable man by the fire and asked if she could serve him some tea. He looked startled, and then disgusted. Nearly five months had passed since Clement took his daughter from his arms, but the sight of the tough old woman at the garrison gates with the child's name wrapped around her chest had reminded Clement of that family nearly every day. She particularly remembered the way this man had tried to soothe his screaming daughter's terror.

She said, "You want your girl back before you'll talk to me? What exactly have you got that makes you think you can make such a bargain?"

The man turned to face her then. He had looked terribly ill five months ago; now he looked half dead. "One of my husbands was in the garrison that night it was burned down," he said. "And then he ran with those people for a few months. All over the land he went, having what he said were adventures. Then he was hurt and they brought him home to recover, but he died. I can't do farmwork any more, so I took care of him. He told me some things—he wouldn't have, but he wasn't in his right mind towards the end. When I've got Davi back, I'll tell you what he told me—all of it."

"I'm not setting out to fetch your girl until I know what it is you know," said Clement impatiently.

He said, "Kill me if you want. I'm dying anyway. When I told my family they couldn't stop me from coming to you, they abandoned the farm. They figured you'd come after them, I guess, to try to force me to talk. Now there's nothing you can do to me, nothing you can kill that isn't dead already. Do what you want." His tone was flat, bitter, and utterly without hope. He sagged wearily in his chair.

"Friend," said Gilly, with his mouth full of cake, "I suggest you give the lieutenant-general a little more than that. She's got to commit a whole company of soldiers to a foul-weather journey, and she's too good a commander to do that for nothing but a vague hope. Give her an idea of what you know, anyway. You can do that, can't you?"

The farmer, apparently roused out of his lethargy by the sight of Gilly's remarkable ugliness, gave him a frankly puzzled look. He wanted to ask Gilly something. It would have been a rude question, something like *what are you*, prompted as much by how Gilly spoke as it was by how he looked. But the farmer apparently could not bring himself to be so rude.

Clement sat down, and crossed her legs, and endeavored to look as if she really didn't care about the outcome of this conversation. She sipped her tea.

Eventually, the farmer turned to her. "This group that calls itself Death-and-Life, they want to do something that will rouse all of Shaftal to join them. Then they figure they can exterminate all of you by spring. I know what that thing is that they're going to do. I know when, and I know where."

Clement set down her teacup. "It's almost winter already."

"It is," the farmer said indifferently. "Maybe you'd better stop wasting your time."

She looked at Gilly. He was rapidly, regretfully, eating the remainder of his cake. "How will I recognize Davi?" Clement asked the farmer. "And how do I contact you when I have her? Through Marga?"

As they discussed the details, Clement cut another slice, wrapped it in her handkerchief—the first clean one she'd had in almost half a year—and put the cake carefully in her pocket to give Gilly later. "It will be some time before you hear from me," she told the farmer. "Fifteen, twenty days." Because she was unhappy to know that an entire farmstead had emptied itself for fear of her, she wanted to add coldly that theirs had been an absurd overreaction. But even now she was reconsidering her decision to let the farmer go unmolested, wondering if after all it might be better to hand him over to the torturers. Perhaps, she thought, his family had been wise after all.

She lay a coin on the side table for Marga to find, and left the parlor with Gilly sighing sadly at her elbow.

In the kitchen, the dozen soldiers stood or squatted around the hearth, with pieces of cake in their hands, not eating, not bickering with each other, but listening raptly to a woman who sat on a stool at the table, with a bowl of beans at her elbow. She was telling them a story, in Sainnese.

Some of the soldiers glanced at Clement pleadingly, asking her not to interrupt, so Clement let Gilly in and closed the door behind them. Marga silently offered Gilly her stool, but he gestured that he could continue to lean on his cane. The storyteller, without pausing or seeming to notice the new arrivals, continued to weave her tale, which had to do with an arrogant man, a magical forest, and a vicious wild pig. Having arrived as the tale was finished, Clement could not follow its import, but the storyteller was an extraordinary sight. Though she was dressed in a plain servant's outfit, and covered to the knee with a stained apron, her dark, angular face could not be disguised as ordinary. She had black hair, black eyes, skin of such deep brown it would disappear into shadows, a face that was all hollows and jutting angles. She had seen some action recently, for that face was marred with fading bruises.

Her tale was finished. The soldiers uttered sighs like children when the show is over, and only then remembered their uneaten cakes. The storyteller, though, seemed to be waiting for something. Some of the soldiers gave another one a nudge, and he cleared his throat and told a soldier's tale that Clement had heard many times before, usually told better. When he was finished, though, the storyteller gave a bow, as though to thank him, and her hands, which had been gesturing to illustrate her tale, returned to the drudge's work of shelling beans.

The soldiers stuffed their cake in their mouths and reached for the rain capes that were drying on hooks by the fire. But they paused and glanced at each other hopefully when Gilly grated in his unlovely voice, "I've never heard that tale before. Might I trouble you to tell another?"

The woman said, "I am a gatherer of stories, and I will trade with anyone, story for story."

Gilly seemed nonplused, but one of the soldiers said, "Iness will make the trade for you, sir. Iness knows lots of tales."

"Well," said Gilly, "Perhaps I will accept that stool after all." He perched on Marga's stool with his hands resting on his cane. Clement, standing beside him, leaned down so he could explain himself. He whispered, "Winter entertainment."

Then the kitchen door opened and Alrin, dressed in gorgeous silk, bustled in. She stopped short in surprise at the crowd. The storyteller leaned towards Gilly, as though to directly address him. "I will tell you a tale of a people who live on the sea, whose harbor is called Dreadful because so many boats have been wrecked going in and out of its narrow entrance. Within the harbor, though, the water is still as glass, and the boats must be rowed because no breath of wind ever stirs there. The people walk from boat to boat to go visiting and never set foot on land at all, except to fill their water barrels. A woman of these people was so ugly that no one could bear to look at her, and she lived by herself without even dog or cat for company. No one would fish with her, either. So no one could explain how she came home, day after day, with her hold full of newly caught fish."

Clement had heard Alrin take in her breath, and looked at her in time to see her glance with horror at Gilly, and then open her mouth as though to stop the story. But Gilly's ugly face was decorated with a delighted smile. Clement whispered to Alrin, "Leave it be."

The storyteller's tale slowly, quietly, became hilarious. She told of the various, increasingly absurd ways that the fisherwoman's kinfolk, jealous of the ugly woman's wealth and success, tried to trick her into revealing her fishing secret. Then, they began to offer bribes, and finally offered her the one thing she did not have, and could not get for herself: a loving husband. But first she demanded that her potential husband prove his love (here the tale became as salacious as any soldier might wish) and, to his surprise, the potential husband managed to do this. And so, in the end, it was revealed that the ugly woman was sticking her face into the water, and the fish, fleeing the sight, were swimming directly into her nets.

The kitchen had echoed with laughter, and even Alrin wiped her eyes and exclaimed, "Well! Who would have thought!"

Iness, the soldier, told his own tale, but with a certain self-deprecating air, for he was a mere amateur and Alrin's servant clearly was a master.

In the crush of the hallway, as the soldiers wrapped themselves in capes and pressed out the narrow door, Gilly, Alrin, and Clement were trapped together into a corner. Alrin said rather anxiously, "I had no idea she spoke Sainnese. Or that she was a storyteller. She's just a tribal woman who'd been set upon . . . I found her by the roadside."

Gilly said, "What is her name?"

Alrin hesitated. "I don't know. She seems a bit addled."

"Really! But she tells a good tale. Perhaps we might hire her to tell tales in the garrison on these long winter nights."

Out in the rain again, once Gilly had been hoisted into the saddle and had wrapped himself thoroughly against the wet, he said ironically, "Now what do you suppose got your courtesan so flustered, eh? I'd have thought she'd have nerves steady as my horse's."

"Perhaps she feared the servant's tale had offended you. People are always assuming you to be short-tempered."

"Like that ugly woman's fish, they flee my ugly face! Ha!" He chuckled to himself all the way to the garrison.

Chapter Nineteen

It was snowing: a light snow, like powered sugar sifting down from the shimmering dawn sky. It glittered, casting a dazzling haze like dust, or mist. Shivering and sleepy, Garland picked up the milk can that Karis had hauled up the mountain the night before and left out on the porch all night, and felt that its contents were frozen solid. The four ravens muttered restlessly on the protected perches Karis had built for them, then one came flapping out and asked, "Will you feed us?"

"Be patient. I'm baking you some cornbread."

The raven flew up to the railing. "Here, here, here, here, here!" he called. Black shadows flapped in the shimmering mist of snow, and three more ravens landed on the rail in an icy spray of slush. So many ravens! Garland stepped backwards into Karis, who was just coming out the door with her head buried in an enormous knitted jerkin.

Her tousled, sleep-flushed face emerged. Her eyes, which had been stark, now glittered at him with something resembling humor. "You don't have to cook breakfast for the birds."

"But they're people."

"Created people? They're so alike, even I can't tell them apart."

"They talk," Garland said. "So they're people."

Karis jammed a cap onto her head, pulled on a sheepskin jerkin, and took some heavy knitted gloves out of the pocket. "Well, you'll also have ten human people for breakfast. Six of them have been on the road all night, running before the storm.

They're at the foot of the mountain now, with three heavy wagons and a lot of exhausted horses, and a very slippery road ahead of them. Raven, go tell them I am coming to help."

The raven that had asked about breakfast leapt off the railing into the snow.

"Will you take these three raven-people inside to get dry?" Karis said to Garland. She looked ruefully at the moth holes in her gloves which left large portions of her fingers exposed. "I hope they brought the rest of my clothes."

As Karis set forth after the bird, into the snow, Garland offered his arm to the nearest sodden raven. "I'll take you in to sit by the fire."

The raven stepped from the railing to his forearm, and thanked him politely.

The day after Karis had finished the beds, she had made mortar out of sand and slaked lime, and with scavenged bricks had built into the kitchen chimney the sweetest oven Garland had ever baked a pie in. By the time harnesses could be heard jingling in the yard, two pans of cornbread were cooling for the ravens, and the oven was full again, this time with eight loaves of bread that puffed up in the heat quite satisfactorily. Applesauce bubbled in the pot on the fire, and a pan of pork sausages kept warm on the hearth. Garland heard the front door open, and swung the teakettle over the hot part of the fire. He did not have enough plates or cups to go around, but few travelers show up without their own tableware.

A cold draft washed in, and Garland heard the grunts and curses of weary people moving heavy objects. A slim young man came blundering down the hall to the kitchen doorway, where he paused vaguely, blinking snow from his lashes and polishing his spectacles on the front of his rather dirty shirt. "I'm all snow," he complained. "There you are," he added, as he perched his still-dirty spectacles on his nose. "My brother!" He clasped Garland's hand in his own very cold one. "So happy to meet you!" he said in Sainnese. "I get so lonely for my own language, don't you? Even though I don't miss those bloody, boring soldiers the slightest bit."

Apparently oblivious to Garland's stunned surprise, he unpeeled from himself several layers of dripping jerkins, still talking.

"That's my books they're swearing at. The damned things are no end of trouble. And of course, they're going all the way up to the attic." The young man paused to peer closely at Garland through his smeared lenses. "Thank you for feeding her."

"Are you Medric?"

"For feeding Zanja," said the very peculiar young man.

"The one who's dead?" Garland felt quite bewildered now.

"In the woods, late in the summer. A rabbit stew."

Garland remembered a silent, remarkable, solitary, well-armed woman who had walked through the pathless woods as though she had been traveling there since the beginning of time. She had not been of Shaftal; she had, it seemed to him, not even been of that world. Wholly preoccupied with some massive mystery, she seemed to scarcely notice Garland. But when, along with the stew, Garland had cooked pan bread for her, with wild herbs in it, she had come out of her preoccupation to say to him, "This is the best meal I ever tasted."

"It wasn't just a rabbit stew. There was bread . . ."

"Well, I don't know *all* the particulars."

"That was Karis's wife?"

"Her tormentor," said Medric. "Her champion. Her poet. Her captive."

It appeared he could indefinitely continue with this contradictory list, but he was distracted by the arrival of two more people: a gray man, who looked like the breath had been knocked out of him, supported by the most terrifying woman Garland had ever set eyes on.

Medric hurried to grab both the man's hands in his. "What happened?"

The frightening woman, having settled the gray man on a stool, said, "They dropped a box of books. He tried to catch it, of course."

"You can't be killed by the books! After all you've done for them!"

The gray man, despite his obvious pain, managed to laugh.

"Maybe we'd better find J'han," said the woman.

With a worried glance at the baking bread, Garland fled the kitchen in a panic. In the hall, extremely muscular people, Karis among them, were heaving crates towards the stairs. In the back bedroom, Garland found J'han, already awakened by the racket and mostly dressed. "There's a man in the kitchen who's having trouble breathing," Garland said.

"Bring that box, will you?" J'han sprinted down the hall in his stocking feet.

Leeba slept in her little twig bed, with the lizard nearby in his own bed, and the rabbit smothered under a blanket, with only a torn, cotton-leaking foot showing. Garland shut the door quietly: the longer Leeba was not underfoot, the better.

"Get out the foxglove—it's labeled," said J'han, the moment Garland entered the kitchen. "Emil, lie down on the floor so your heart won't have to work as hard. Is that water heating on the fire?"

"The pain is passing," said the gray man.

"Sorrow is killing you," grumbled J'han. "For that I have no cure."

Garland said, "J'han, I can't read."

The terrifying woman turned her gaze on him. Garland set J'han's chest of medicines rather hastily on the table, and tried to think of an excuse to run out of the room again. Was the cornbread cool enough to feed to the ravens?

Medric opened the box, and plucked out one of the tin canisters, and showed Garland the handwritten label. "Foxglove," he read. "Poison. Say, isn't it time that Leeba learn her letters?" He added to Garland in Sainnese, "Take deep breaths, brother. It will pass."

The terrifying woman said in a cool voice that slashed Garland's ears like a razor, "I am Norina Truthken. Who are you?"

Medric clasped Garland's hand. "The truth," he prompted him. His hand was still cold from the snow, and soft, a scholar's hand, but there was a strength in it, too.

"Garland. A Sainnite. A cook."

The terrifying woman said, "I'll stay out of your kitchen."

"What?"

The woman laid a hand on J'han's shoulder and the healer, shockingly, pressed his cheek against it. And then she went out, and even from the back seemed dangerous. As soon as the door was closed, Garland's panic fled.

"She has a strong effect on people," said J'han. "But I guess we've all gotten immune to it."

Medric brought J'han the canister, but J'han waved him away. The gray man raised a face as gaunt and stark as Karis had looked when Garland first met her. But there was a kindness in him, and Garland immediately began to think of what to feed him. Tea, he thought. This man needs tea, and a lot of good, hot bread, perhaps an entire loaf. Then some real food. "Surely that pot's about to boil," he said, and opened the tea tin.

The gray man said, "Ah, Medric, my dear, once again you were right."

"Emil," said Medric reprovingly, "I'm always right."

"Right about what?" asked J'han, his fingers still pressed to the pulse in Emil's wrist.

"About Garland. Medric dreamed him into our kitchen."

All eight loaves of bread were eaten, and Garland also cooked two more pans of sausage before the cold-sharpened appetites were satisfied. Karis, carrying a sausage that was wrapped in a thick slice of bread, had gone down the mountain again, this time to fetch grain and hay from a distant farm for the exhausted draft horses. By the time she returned, the three drivers had fallen asleep by the parlor fire. Leeba had awakened to sit in Emil's lap for a while, as he recounted the highlights of their journey. Then she had played with Medric, a game that seemed to have no clear rules and involved a great deal of running around. Garland had started more bread dough and a pot of beans, and was rolling out the crust for a meat pie when Karis finally came in. Ice shattered from her jerkin as she pulled it off to hang near the hearth. Her moth-eaten gloves must have dissolved, for her unprotected hands were white with cold. Garland gave her a cup of hot tea to hold.

No one spoke. Norina and J'han appeared from the bedroom where they had been unpacking a crate, but Norina leaned on the door frame and did not come into the kitchen. Emil rested in a twig chair brought in from the parlor, his face pale with exhaustion, though he had turned down Garland's offer of his own bed. All of them had been waiting for Karis, but now that she was here no one spoke. After she had drunk her tea, Garland gave her the half loaf of bread and the sausages that he had hidden away for her, and she uttered a sigh of gratitude. Garland said, "You've done three days' work this morning, and no doubt you'll spend the afternoon making chairs and beds." For these travelers, despite their extraordinary quantity of baggage, had not transported a stick of furniture with them.

Karis said, "Well, carpentry is easy work. Wood is so willing."

Garland pulled up a stool to the table, and gave her the butter and the butter knife.

She sat down and buttered her bread with intense concentration as everyone, even Norina, lounging in the doorway, watched her. Garland had given Leeba some pastry dough and the rolling pin and it appeared that her poor lizard was becoming a lizard pie.

"But there's other work," Karis said, mouth full. "Like healing Emil's—" she glanced inquiringly at J'han.

"Heart," he said.

Emil said, "I do not ask for healing. What I need is your forgiveness."

Karis set down her bread. "You'll accept both," she said, "or you'll get neither."

Emil said flatly, "Karis, I don't forgive myself."

With the small knife that usually dangled, along with a number of other small tools, from her belt, Karis had speared a sausage. But she eyed the sausage without interest, put it back on her plate, then stood up and went to Emil, and, with an abrupt, heavy movement knelt at his feet.

He looked at her blankly. She lowered her head to rest on his knee. His hand lifted as of its own will, to stroke the wild tangle of her hair. She said, her voice muffled, "Did Zanja think I wanted her dead? Because I did not stop her?"

Norina said from the doorway, "What did you hope she would think?"

Karis raised her head. "That I was trying to be worthy, maybe."

She sat back on her heels. Garland could see only the back of Karis's head, her exceptionally square shoulders, her arms at her sides with her hands apparently resting on her thighs. But whatever Emil saw in her face brought the life back into his. "You let her go?" he said, amazed. "Karis? *You let her go?*"

"Not very gracefully." Norina's tone was cool, but when Karis glanced at her, Garland thought he understood a little of how rare and difficult—and satisfying—it might be to win a Truthken's approval.

"You knew?" cried Medric at Norina, outraged. "You let us think Karis was angry? And you knew all along that she was—"

"—merely devastated," Norina said.

Karis said quietly, "You know I loved her. And I let her die. What kind of person would do that?"

Garland, attempting to fill the pie crust with meat and vegetables without looking at his hands, saw a quiet descend on all of them.

"A remarkable person might," Emil answered Karis finally. "A G'deon might." He brought his hands up and began undoing the polished horn buttons of his heavy shirt. "Let me serve you a little longer, Karis."

She said harshly, "How much longer do you think you can endure it?"

"As long as it's interesting," suggested Medric.

"As long as Shaftal requires it," said J'han.

"As long as *you* can endure it," Emil said to Karis, smiling now.

"A very long time then," said Norina dryly. They all looked at her, and she added, "Well, look at the evidence! She can endure anything, for any length of time."

Emil's unbuttoned shirt revealed that he had experienced his share of violence, and that he was fortunate for the armor of his ribs, which had turned aside more than one Sainnite saber. Karis put her hand to his scarred chest. Leeba, apparently not as oblivious as she had seemed, abandoned her rolling pin to run to Emil and lean on his knee. "Is your heart broken? Does it hurt?"

He put an arm around her. "Yes, dear one."

"Karis will fix it," she declared.

"It's fixed," said Karis, sitting back.

"Our child is growing up in some very strange circumstances," said J'han worriedly.

Karis got heavily to her feet, and scooped Leeba up. "Are we having lizard pie for supper? That's a very *rare* dish, isn't it, Garland?"

"Extremely," he said. "Fortunately, for those of us who haven't acquired a taste for lizard we have a more commonplace sort of pie also. But you," he added, "should eat your breakfast, or you'll never get any pie."

"He's very bossy, don't you think?" said Karis to Leeba. But she set her giggling daughter down, and made quick work of the bread and sausage that she had before been unable to eat. Now maybe she finally would be able to gain some weight, Garland thought. As he was putting his meat pie in the oven and helping Leeba to put her lizard pie in as well—into the other oven, which was not very hot—it occurred to him that the most important people in Shaftal were gathered here in his kitchen.

He turned around and looked at them: sturdy J'han, who had brought Norina a cup of tea and was leaning companionably against the opposite doorjamb as she sipped it; Medric, who had somehow gotten into the chair with Emil, done up his buttons for him, and kissed him a couple of times with unrestrained affection; Karis, uncombed and unkempt, looking a bit unhappy that she had eaten all there was to eat, glancing up now at the two unlikely couples with the stunned sorrow of the newly widowed.

"How about an apple or two," Garland suggested.

She looked at him, and he feared she might complain again about his pushiness. "Two," she said.

When he came out of the store room shining the apples on his apron, she said, "Well, now you have an idea of what you've gotten yourself into."

"I've gotten myself into a kitchen," he said, endeavoring to sound as if the rest of it was of no importance to him.

The Truthken in the doorway uttered a snort. Startled, he looked at her—he had almost forgotten her intimidating presence. Had he said an untruth? Perhaps he had.

Medric said, "What did you think of the book, Karis? *The Encyclopedia of Livestock?*" He was grinning like a madman.

"It was Zanja who found it, wasn't it?"

"She didn't exactly know what she had found."

Karis bit into an apple and held it in her teeth so her hand was free to take the little book out of her vest. She handed it to Medric, took the apple out of her mouth, and said with her mouth full, "There's an old man in it, with a basket full of cabbages."

"Oh, now at last I'll dream of him!" Medric began leafing eagerly through the book.

"I found it," Leeba said belatedly. "The baby book—I found it inside the big one."

Emil had looked puzzled, but only for a moment. With one finger he stopped Medric's enthusiastic page turning. "Mabin," he said, and read for a while. Then, he uttered a sharp laugh. He looked up and explained to Norina, "Harald wrote it. To Karis."

"Ah," she said. "A misunderstood man attempts to explain himself to his greatest victim. I always wondered why he hadn't."

Karis said, "Victim?"

"Things do change quickly," said Norina. "Sometimes it's difficult to keep track of what's actually true. Karis, I know something that will surprise you."

Karis sat down on the stool, with an apple in each hand, and looked at her. The men in the chair looked up simultaneously from reading, like startled birds.

Norina said, "Zanja na'Tarwein isn't actually dead."

There was a shocked silence.

"Physically—" began Emil.

"Metaphorically—" Medric started.

They both fell silent as Karis said in her hoarse, hushed voice, "Nori, what did you *do*?"

"There were some deceptions," the Truthken said.

Medric shut the little book. "Gods of bloody hell!"

Emil said in a shocked voice, "With my own hand . . . !"

"I *saw* her die!" said Medric.

"Fire logic," said Norina dismissively.

Obviously untroubled by the outraged chorus, she gazed steadily at Karis. Karis said in her strained, raw voice, "You are the most underhanded, disagreeable, uncanny, hardhearted person in the world."

"Do you know this for a fact?" said Norina curiously.

"You might be loyal, also," said Karis grudgingly.

"These idiotic fire bloods, *they* know I'm sworn to serve you. You only—not their insane visions."

"I take offense!"

Norina glanced at Medric, and he lapsed into a restless muttering that struck Garland as a kind of play-acting. The odd man might actually have been amazed rather than angry—and if he was, then Norina's expression of faint amusement made a kind of sense. But not one word in this obscure conversation seemed sensible to Garland, and these people, who had seemed so kind to each other, so remarkable, now seemed only very strange. The strangest thing of all was their apparent ability to understand each other.

Norina wasn't even looking at Garland directly. But she apparently knew his thoughts anyway and said, "Master cook, we've learned to cooperate with and tolerate each other, so now we're surprised to remember that our logics are incompatible. You understand, the elements shape how we think? They also determine what we can see. Air logic enabled me to see something that Zanja, Medric, and Emil could not."

"You might have seen something," Medric burst out, "But you had no *vision*."

"Oh, no," said Norina coolly. "Zanja thinks she's dead."

Norina stopped, for J'han had sharply kicked her foot. She glanced at him, then glanced at Leeba, who was raptly watching the action in the oven. Norina continued, rather obscurely, "So whatever you fire bloods thought to accomplish by doing what you did can still be accomplished."

"Madam Truthken!" said Karis fiercely. "What did you *do*?"

J'han held up a hand to silence them, and went to squat by the oven with Leeba. He began talking with her about fire, lizards, and pies. Norina began to speak. She gave a quiet, precise, detailed, emotionless account of Zanja's death. J'han and Leeba sang together a child's song about the odd things that might be baked in a pie. They made up a verse about lizards. Norina concluded, "So Zanja thinks she's dead, just as you thought she was dead. But those who deceive themselves, as she did, always know the actual truth, though often they do not know they know it, unless someone says it to them."

Medric muttered, "And I thought *I* was obscure."

Karis had covered her face. Garland thought he might see tears when her big hands lowered, but instead he saw something he did not expect: impatience. "Can we get her back?" she said. Then, more sharply, "Master seer! Is it possible?"

Medric said, "It's extremely unlikely. Don't call me that."

Karis clenched her big hands, fingers interlocked. Fascinated, Garland watched her biceps swell. "How do we make it certain?"

"Ow!" Medric had been upset from his cozy berth and dumped summarily to the floor.

The gray man, who had come in seeming so frail, was on his feet, facing Karis, saying as ferociously as she, "Send your ravens, then! Tell her that her death was a farce! Bring her back to the certainty of a world in which change is impossible!"

There was a silence. Karis unclenched her hands. "No, I think not," she said.

Emil said, more gently, "If you didn't fail her when you were in despair, perhaps you won't betray her out of hope either."

"I need to do nothing?" she said unhappily. "Even more?"

Emil took two steps to her, and clasped her big hands in his. "With all your heart," he said earnestly.

"How much longer?" she said desperately.

"Until Long Night," said Medric, still sprawled on the floor. He sat up then, looking as surprised as Karis did. "Long Night? I have to write a book by then!"

Emil turned to him, still clasping Karis's hands. "Better make it a pamphlet," he said.

❄❄❄❄❄❄❄❄❄❄❄❄❄❄❄❄

Chapter Twenty

Two days into the six-day journey to the children's garrison, the first snow fell: heavy, wet flakes that turned the roads again into quagmires, and forced Clement and her mounted escort of seven to spend a day and a night holed up in an abandoned barn. On the seventh day, when Clement should have already reached her destination and begun the journey home, it snowed again: real snow this time. The soldiers cursed, the horses stumbled and slid; in the tiny village that was the only settlement they could find, the people sullenly vacated an entire house for the soldiers, stabled their horses with the cows and sheep, and showed up at the door with placating offerings of cooked food.

In the cozy room she had commandeered, Clement cracked open a shutter and observed the villagers below, who went watchfully about their business as the snow continued to steadily fall. At this rate, it would soon be knee deep. She had been a fool for relying upon the reprieve in weather that usually comes between autumn mud and winter snow. Now, she was stranded, with eight horses too valuable to abandon. She watched angrily, enviously, as a villager strode briskly across the snow in snow shoes, pulling a sledge laden with firewood, atop which perched a laughing young child in a red coat.

And we sneer at them for going afoot, thought Clement. *How hard is it to learn the virtues of traveling light? Apparently, too hard for us.*

* * *

That poor village was the last before the wilderness. The road petered down to a mere path, snow-veiled, invisible except for blazes on the trees. Horses and dismounted soldiers alike went floundering through the woods. The sun appeared for a few hours and the snow began to melt, which increased the journey's misery. After sunset the snowmelt froze to ice, and the wind picked up. Eyes burning, tears freezing, Clement hoarsely reassured her company that there *was* a shelter.

But when the soldiers at the head of the line shouted back that they had found it, Clement's relief was short-lived. The shelter had an unmended roof, walls of rough-sawn planks with airy gaps between them, and a circle of stones for a hearth, with a hole in the roof above, that had allowed this hearth to be filled up with snow. For the horses there was corn and hay—that was a relief—but in place of firewood there was a half-barrel of cider. Whoever ran the supplies up and down the mountain during the warm season had apparently valued some comforts over others.

They got what warmth could be had from huddling together as the wind whistled through every knot and crack. They ate their rations cold, and Clement, to much approbation, allowed them each two cups of surprisingly potent ice-cold cider. Later, a few sleepers snored, but most of them sat awake like her, too cold to sleep, drearily awaiting dawn.

They spent the next day in a bitter, steep climb, up a path that the wind had now blocked with snow drifts. The soldiers cursed whenever they had breath to spare; the weary horses sometimes balked and had to be dragged or beaten. The sun used the snow as a reflector to blind them.

"Is that it?" someone asked.

Watery-eyed, Clement stared up through a haze of light. There, at the top of the mountain, at the end of the path, in splendid isolation, stood the children's garrison.

Someone, a hazy shadow, took a noisy sniff. "Woodsmoke!"

The company uttered a ragged cheer, and even the horses blundered forward with somewhat more enthusiasm. In the shadow of the building now, Clement's scoured eyes could see more clearly, but the building still looked very strange. What had the sun done to her eyes? She rubbed them, and looked again. "The bloody thing is round! I thought I was losing my mind!"

It really was no garrison at all. A fortress, maybe, with narrow, out-of-reach windows and an unfriendly, arched entrance big enough for a small wagon to pass through, but barred quite decisively by a padlocked iron gate, through which the snow had drifted.

Clement peered between the bars. The dim passageway plunged into silent darkness. "Oh, hell," said one of the exhausted soldiers who crowded up around her to take a look. "There's no one here."

"Quiet as a tomb," said another gloomily.

"Not for long," said Clement. She reached between the bars, and took hold of the frayed bell rope.

The clangor of the bell was jarring. The horses jumped, the soldiers cursed some more. Clement jerked the rope until her arm ached, and finally there emerged quite cautiously from the gloom a boy in heavy clothing that was much too big for him, wide-eyed and clutching a knob-headed cane as though it were a drawn sword. "Uh . . . ?" he said inquiringly. Insignias sloppily tacked onto his cap identified him as a lieutenant.

"Urgent business," said Clement briskly.

He cleared his throat nervously. "Your orders?"

"I write the bloody orders!"

His gaze traveled to the insignias on her own hat, and he belatedly and confusedly saluted. "Lieutenant . . . ?"

"Lieutenant-General. Let us in, sir!"

"I haven't got the key."

From the darkness of the passageway grated another voice. "Gods' sake, boy, you're a soldier! Stop wailing like a baby and open the gate." The boy-lieutenant scurried to meet the approaching old man, who limped on a wooden leg with the support of a cane. He gave the boy a big, rusted key, and stood leaning on his cane as the boy fiddled it into the snow-clogged lock.

"Lieutenant-General," said the old man.

"Commander Purnal?" asked Clement.

The man uttered a bitter laugh. "Been a while since anyone called me 'commander' to my face. Well, it's about time Cadmar sent you here! How many people you got with you? Six?"

"Seven. And eight horses. I hope you've got a stable and fodder."

"What do you think we do with the donkeys that haul supplies for us, eh? What's taking you so long, boy?"

The padlock opened with a sullen groan. The gate squawked open. Purnal turned away and started thumping down the passage, shouting backward over his shoulder, "Send a couple of your soldiers to the kitchen and the rest of you follow me to the infirmary. Boy, you get the stabling crew together. Some real horses for once. Good practice for them. Anyone gets kicked and I'll hold you personally responsible. Come on!" he bellowed, his voice much magnified now by the echoing passageway. "We've got some sick kids here!"

"Gods of hell," muttered Clement.

The exhausted soldiers were looking at her beseechingly.

"You two." She selected them at random. "See the horses are cared for, find your way to the kitchen, and make yourselves useful. The rest of you come with me. Not one more complaint!"

The arched passageway eventually emptied itself into a big, circular yard, with a center post thick as a tree in its exact middle, from which beams radiated out to support the massive roof. The horses milled anxiously in the shadows, then settled down, probably recognizing the familiar shape of an exercise ring, though this one was large enough to easily turn a wagon around in. To the left, a big double door likely led to the stables. Ahead, a more human-sized gate hung ajar, giving access to the corridor that encircled the ring behind a sturdy half wall.

"This way," said Clement. She could see little, but she could hear Purnal's peg leg and cane, thumping down the hallway.

The soldiers, muttering so quietly she could hear no words or distinguish one complainer from the next, followed.

They did not catch up to Purnal until he had nearly reached the end of the hall and they were, Clement judged, near the outer wall of the building again, on the far side of the entrance gate. "You've got some kind of winter illness here?" she asked, haunted now by a memory of the dreadful illness that had mowed the Sainnites down that spring. "How bad is it?"

"About as bad as usual. The older kids haven't gotten sick yet. When that happens, my whole operation falls apart. So the adults are in the sick room and the kids are running the garrison. Good training for them. What are you doing here?"

Clement began to answer, but Purnal jerked open a door, and the stink of feces and vomit all but knocked her over. "Good gods!" she cried, gagging.

"You'll get used to it," he said.

They lay in darkness, like moles. No discernible warmth came from the smoldering hearthfire at one end of the big room. The sick children lay with nothing but thin straw pallets between themselves and the cold stone floor. Three exhausted men and women did what they could to care for them, but that was not much, since all of the caretakers were one-armed. In the dim, stinking room, to the accompaniment of an incessant, dreary whine of hopeless misery, some forty kids were puking and excreting themselves to death.

"No worse than usual?" Clement said to Purnal, once he had given her the grim tour.

"I've seen a hundred kids in this room. And the rest of them trailing about like wraiths. Five years you've been lieutenant-general—don't you read the reports?"

Clement said hastily, "Every garrison is understaffed right now."

"Because there ain't no one growing up to replace us old and broken ones," said Purnal. "And whose fault is that, eh? I got fifteen cripples looking after near two hundred kids. And as soon as the few survivors are old enough to be some use, you take them away and get them killed. Go ahead and demote me!" he added viciously. "It'd be a bloody mercy!"

"You won't be that lucky today," said Clement. "We'll need some lamps."

"Can't have lamps around kids. They'll burn themselves up quicker than you can stop 'em."

"Candles, then. And fresh linens."

"You'll have fresh linens after you've washed and dried them."

"Broth, or weak tea?"

"That's what your soldiers are in the kitchen for."

"Warm water and soap," said Clement evenly.

"You'll find them in the laundry. But you'll have to light the fires first, I expect."

"After we've chopped the firewood," said Clement. "No, that's not a question, I understand the situation. Now you listen to me, sir. My soldiers are worn out. They'll work until the night bell, and then they're getting some rest."

"Hell," said Purnal, "what's it take to make you lose your temper?"

"Plenty of people have tried and failed," Clement said, but she was talking to his back. He stumped away, calling to the three sick-nurses that they should get some sleep while they had the chance.

Clement washed and force-fed children, emptied basins and packed fresh straw into stinking pallets until she couldn't stand it any more. Then she took a turn at the wood chopping, and after that went to stir boiling cauldrons of laundry until the cold had been chased from her bones. Back she went to the sick room, where a soldier told her that two of the kids had been discovered to be dead.

Night had long since fallen, but there had been no night bell. She took up a basin of warm water and set to work again: she was so tired that every time she stood up from where she

squatted or knelt on the floor, she practically fell over. Some of
the kids who had been whining earlier had gotten quieter. Perhaps they too were dying.

Someone was calling her. Dim candle in hand, she made her
way between prone bodies to the door, where a boy-sergeant
executed a crisp, startling salute. "Lieutenant-General?"

"What is it?"

"Compliments of the commander! Would you care to join
him for supper!"

In the sick room, two of Clement's soldiers continued their
dreary rounds. "My people have not been relieved."

"Yes, ma'am! The night watch is at supper! They will come
to the infirmary shortly! The rest of your people are eating
with the senior officers! Then they will be shown to quarters!"

Feeling quite overwhelmed by the boy-sergeant's energy,
Clement set down her basin and candle on the table. The boy,
alert and over-sprung, did not put even one toe over the threshold of the sickroom.

Clement's uniform was wet and filthy, but her change of
clothing had disappeared with the horses. In any case, she
doubted she could eat, after such a wretched afternoon. She
said to the boy-sergeant, "I do need to *talk* to Purnal."

He took this as an urgent command and set a military pace
until she told him to slow down. They passed the open door of
the refectory, where a crowd of children sat in size order at the
trestle tables, watched over by youthful goons with knob-
headed canes in their hands. They went out to the circular corridor, where it was as cold as the outdoors and Clement
wondered suddenly what had happened to her coat. Then they
followed another hallway to an open door, where firelight
flickered. A table was set by the fireplace, preventing Clement
from getting close enough to those inviting flames. Purnal
stumped out from his bedroom. "Well, sit down. I hope the
food's still warm."

She sat, but it felt like a collapse. She wolfed down the stew
the boy-sergeant ladled into her bowl, and the bread he sliced
onto her plate, and when he offered more, she ate that too.
When the boy had cleared away the dishes, poured hot ale, and

served a wedge of cheese and a bowl of apples, Purnal dismissed him.

"Cheese!" said Clement, cutting herself a slice.

Purnal gestured vaguely. "There's a dairy."

The cheese was astonishingly good with a slice of apple. No wine, though, and the ale was typically bitter. She said politely, "Your young soldiers are well disciplined. I'm quite impressed."

"They want to learn their jobs so they can get out of here, the silly fools."

Clement sighed, but Purnal had restrained himself during the meal, so she supposed she should be grateful.

He said, "What happened to Kelin, eh? She was a good girl! And I wrote to you personally!"

Clement cut another slice of cheese. "And I personally commanded her to stay out of action. But when the sky started exploding, I guess she got to thinking she could be a hero. I chased her halfway across the garrison, trying to stop her. So don't you rage at *me*."

He let her enjoy the cheese in peace, after that. And then he said, grudgingly, "I teach these kids to shoot a gun and swing a sword, but I can't teach them any sense. She was a good kid," he said again. "Smart, even-tempered. Officer material."

Clement eyed him in some surprise—had he been drinking? But then she felt the sting of tears—Gods, she must be tired! She hid her face by swallowing some ale. Kelin: she had managed to avoid thinking of her for months. She cleared her throat and changed the subject. "I'm here to find one of those kids I sent you from Watfield."

Purnal took a deep, preparatory breath and uttered a roar. "A scandal! You sent me a wagonload of *babies*. Half of them couldn't even do up their own *buttons*. What was I to do with them, eh? Use them for target practice?"

She cut him off. "I'll take one of them back."

"Good luck. A lot of them are dead."

It had been a dreadful journey already, and Clement had no idea how she'd manage to get back to Watfield. To do it empty-handed, to wait for Death-and-Life to do whatever they planned, to watch the Sainnites collapse into their own hollow center . . . "Gods," she said wearily, and put her face in her hands. "All for lack of one little girl? A weight in the scale, indeed!"

"Eh?" Purnal looked at her blankly.

"Do you think I traveled here on holiday? You will produce the child, or give me an accounting of what became of her."

"Or what, eh? You'll hack off my other leg? You'll exile me to some gods-forsaken corner of some wretched land and order me to turn babies into soldiers?"

"How about if I blame you personally for the destruction of your people in Shaftal?"

He uttered a phlegmy snort, but followed it with a shout to the boy-sergeant in the hallway.

"Sir?" the boy stuck his head in.

"One of the Watfield children, a girl named—"

"Davi," said Clement.

"Is she still alive?"

"I don't know, sir!"

"Well, go ask your fellow officers. And then ask the clerk to check the death records. Report back to me in the dormitories." He added to Clement, as the eager sergeant raced away, "The longer it takes to find her, the longer you and your company will remain. Don't think I haven't thought of that."

"Apparently, you think your garrison's interests are the only ones that matter."

"Take some advice from an old man," he suggested. "Stop trying to shame the shameless. Let's go look for your girl."

In the youngest children's dormitory, a dozen older children were putting the younger ones to bed. They were able to point out the Watfield children, who huddled together in shared beds. Clement spoke to them in Shaftalese, and soon regretted it, for they cried out for their parents, siblings, and homes. She had thought they would have forgotten them by now. None of them was Davi.

The boy-sergeant caught up with them in the hallway, and

reported that there was no Davi in the death records. When Clement asked how accurate the records were, Purnal shrugged. "If we never knew her name, we couldn't record it, could we?"

"I've only seen fifteen of the Watfield children. Where are the others?"

"Sick or dead. You know where the sick ones are."

"You'd better hope she's still alive, commander, or I'll have you digging up the graves next."

"We burn 'em," he said. "Sorry."

Clement returned to the sick room. There, it smelled just as bad as before, but at least it was quieter. A bitter chill was setting in, and she stopped first to add fuel to the fire, for what good it did. The signal of a candle flame led her to a one-armed soldier who bathed with cold water a child delirious with fever. He told her he had not noticed a child like Davi, but then who had time to pay attention?

She found a candle of her own, and started the dreary business of working her way down the rows of pallets, turning back blankets and pulling up nightshirts. If she had to leave this place empty-handed, she would at least be absolutely certain that the child was indeed lost.

After the Battle of Lilterwess, Clement had assisted in the gruesome job of identifying the dead. The Sainnite corpses had been lined up on the hillside, while beyond them the soldiers methodically took the ancient building apart, stone by stone. It was the height of summer, and the flies swarmed, and the rooks noisily invited their friends and neighbors to the feast. Sometimes, Clement identified a soldier by clothing or gear, because the face was gone. Sometimes she stripped a corpse, seeking clues in flesh, in scars, in gender. Friends and lovers were thus revealed.

There was great celebration, that day, and the Sainnites called themselves conquerors. Twenty years later, Clement knelt in a cold, stinking room and searched the bodies of parentless children, and knew herself a fool in an army of fools.

The night was old when she found a very small girl with a mole on her knee. The illness had gone into the girl's lungs, the sick-nurses said, and she would not survive to morning. "She will," Clement said, gathering up the child, blanket and all. "I won't have my labors be for nothing."

The one-armed veterans, who surely thought that the labor of their lives had long since come to nothing, rolled their eyes at each other, and refrained from comment.

Chapter Twenty-One

"Clement is no longer in Watfield," said Gilly to Alrin, as she politely quizzed him at the door about why he had refused to be shown to the parlor. "The general needs me at his side, and so regrettably I have no time for tea. The woman is here? In the kitchen?"

He stumped down the hall, refusing to even let her take his snow-dusted coat. Alrin bobbed ineffectually in his wake, saying, "I'm truly sorry for putting you through such trouble. But her answer to your note asking her to tell stories in the garrison was so . . . complicated! I urged her to give you a plain reply, but—well, she's got some peculiar ways."

She added, surprisingly, "Clement is traveling? The snow can be heavy, even so early in winter."

"She is a soldier," growled Gilly.

He opened the kitchen door to find the storyteller standing in the exact center of the room, utterly still. Her clothing shimmered in the flickering light: silk, a deep red vest over a rich purple blouse, and trousers black and glossy as her hair.

"Don't you look fine!" Alrin sounded more nervous than complimentary. "Those deep colors, they suit you!"

The storyteller turned her head as though to seek the object of Alrin's admiration somewhere behind her, and Gilly noticed for the first time that, though her hair was chin length, a single slim braid hung down the center of her back, black as a burn, with a coal-red tassel dangling from its tip. It was no more strange than the rest of her: peculiar but not frivolous. Alrin certainly had known how to dress her.

Gilly said to her, "It's foolish and dangerous to dicker with Sainnites over price. All we're paying for is a few tales."

The woman turned, and slowly said, "What does it mean, to be the General's Lucky Man?"

Alrin made an anxious sound. "Oh, sir, you see! She's not right—she'll say something to offend."

Gilly said to the border woman, "I'll explain that to you, if you tell me why no one knows your name. A trade, tale for tale." She nodded her assent. "Well, then. The Sainnites say there's a certain allotment of suffering that the gods set aside for each one of us. Some few are given all their life's curses at once, when they are still in the womb. They are born monsters, but they are lucky, for all their allotted ill fortune has been used up already. Powerful people have monsters beside them, as barriers against the ill will of the gods. So, I am Cadmar's Lucky Man."

As though she did not quite trust her finery, the storyteller sat cautiously on a kitchen stool. She said, "A curse has taken away my name, and made me a gatherer of stories. The witches of my people took my weapons, and cut my hair, and burned all my belongings, and destroyed my name, and with my name they destroyed my memories. I know this is what happened, but I don't remember it. Now, I am just a storyteller, and have been for many years."

"Without memory the stories are all you have?"

She said quietly, "You want to be my friend, Lucky Man, because I am as monstrous as you are. Beware, or I will make you into a story."

Gilly said, "Make it a good one."

She gazed at him, unsmiling, her eyes hidden, as always, in shadow. "I am a collector of tales," she said. "And I will *trade* story for story."

"No pay?" He glanced at Alrin. "Is *this* what you couldn't tell me?"

Alrin sighed mightily. "Surely you see that I couldn't let her work at the garrison for no pay—she would be no use to me, but I'd still be paying her expenses. Why would I do that for a complete stranger?"

"We'll pay for her room and board. She can find a place in a boarding house, if you don't want her here."

"Oh, I'm willing for her to stay."

"It's settled, then."

Alrin said worriedly, "But she says whatever she likes! She has neither manners nor fear!"

"That's not your problem, is it?" He turned to the storyteller. "I will arrange for the soldiers to tell you their stories, as many stories as you tell them. Is it agreed?"

"It is," she said indifferently.

"An escort will bring you to the garrison this evening. You can eat with us if you like, but I don't recommend it."

"I will eat with you."

"Well, it is arranged." Gilly lifted his cane, and thunked it to the floor again. "What was this punishment for?" he asked.

"Perhaps I murdered my wife."

He looked at her, and she looked back at him, neither sad nor ashamed, nor even interested. "I'll see you tonight," he said, and left.

By evening, the snow covered the world like a flour paste, ankle-deep and ungodly slippery. Though men of unsteady gait should stay safely by the hearth on such nights, Gilly borrowed Cadmar's aide, and leaned on him, and on his cane, and on whatever railings were convenient, and so managed to journey to the refectory without falling too disastrously. But it was the journey back to his rooms again that Gilly dreaded, for by then the snow would have hardened to slick ice. Too soon, the winter would lock him indoors, and the pain brought on by cold would cripple him truly, and in the darkness of winter he would wonder what his life was good for. It happened every year.

In the refectory, which, fortunately, had been rebuilt before the snow began to fall, they were just hauling in the cauldrons on wheeled tables, with one person pulling and one person pushing and a third person holding down the lid to keep the contents from spilling out. The soldiers stood drearily with their tin plates in their hands and held them out to the cooks in the hopeless manner of people who can no longer be disappointed. They were given as much stew as they wanted and fist-sized lumps of bread that were sure to be as hard as stones. Gilly had lived since boyhood on such fare, and when the aide brought him a serving, he broke his bread into the stew and ate what he had been given. The table at which he sat was slowly, discreetly emptying as its occupants spotted friends and casually went to sit with them. The big room became intolerably noisy; conversations between neighbors were conducted in shouts.

But the incredible racket faltered abruptly. Gilly raised his gaze from the splintered tabletop. The storyteller had arrived. The soldier who had escorted her was hanging the woman's fine wool cloak from a peg, and then, proprietarily, he showed her to Gilly's table. The soldiers turned and stared at her so frankly Gilly feared she'd take offense. But she did not seem to notice.

"The soldiers avoid you," she commented as she sat beside Gilly on the bench.

"Like fish fleeing into a net."

"And does that fearfulness make you rich? Or get you a good husband?"

"It merely makes me feared."

She said somberly, "Your life is all wrong, then."

The soldiers had let the storyteller's escort cut into the front of the line. To pay for his privilege, though, he apparently gave those nearby an explanation of her presence, and Gilly watched the news spread like a wave across the room, and out the door. Gilly's table quickly began to fill again; the soldiers, trying hard to behave with civility, introduced themselves and their friends to the storyteller, and asked eager questions that the storyteller, with no apparent effort, replied to without answering. They resorted to volunteering information: that the stew she was now eating was better than they had eaten for some time, but still was pretty bad; that the big, meaty beans in it were fallow beans, so-called because they were grown in fallow fields; that the kitchen had been re-built at last, which explained the improvement in the food. She looked up from her nearly empty bowl and said, "You know the difference, don't you, between information and stories?" She glanced at Gilly, and it seemed she was curious and not intending to be mocking.

"You will be paid," he gruffly said. "These soldiers here are just intrigued by you, and making idle conversation as best they can. We never see anything new here."

She stood up, then, and stepped up onto the bench, and from there to the tabletop. She did not need to call for quiet; the only sound came from the soldiers, summoned by fleet-footed rumor, who struggled to get in the crowded doorway. She said in a loud, clear voice, "I am a gatherer, a carrier, a teller of tales. I have come to trade with you, tale for tale. Once, when I was walking through the southland, along the edge of a lake, I found an old man, who sat on a stone by the water and wept with sorrow. 'Old man,' I said . . ."

Sitting directly below her, Gilly could clearly see the thin scars that criss-crossed her hands. She shaped the old man in the air, with words and gestures telling how he was haunted by the ghosts of three women, each of whom blamed him for her untimely death. She stood balanced, poised, with her weight on her toes like a dancer. The tassel at the end of her braid bounced lightly, softly, communicating the rise and fall of the story, and then signaling its ending.

The soldiers pounded the tabletops and roared appreciation. And then her hands smoothed the air like a magician soothing a troubled ocean, and the voices fell silent. "I am sure you have heard of Haprin," she said. "But do you know that Haprin has a spring that bubbles out of the ground so hot, you can boil eggs in it? And yet no one goes near that spring, not even in dead of winter, because it is a place of bad luck. Long ago, when Shaftal was a young and wild land . . ."

The refectory became so jammed with soldiers that no one could reach the food line any more, and the listeners passed plates of hot stew hand to hand, across the room, and even out the door. In the rapt silence that followed her sixth story—a love story, this time, with a satisfying ending—the night bell could be heard to ring. She glanced down at Gilly, and Gilly got stiffly to his feet. "Will you return tomorrow, storyteller?"

"You owe me six stories," she said, speaking to the crowded room.

One of the captains, whom Gilly had spoken with that afternoon, promptly said, "My company will pay." He named a place and time for her to meet with them the next day. She bowed, and descended, and though Gilly had to hold his ears against the din of acclaim, she did not seem to hear it.

"I'll accompany you to the gate!" he shouted.

Once outside, he regretted his offer, for the footing was worse than he had expected. She held out her arm, though, saying, "It's hobnail season already."

"Hobnail boots are too heavy for me," said Gilly. When he leaned on her, she was steady as stone, despite her light build. And that strength spoke to him again of the past she claimed she could not remember. He said, "Your body betrays that you are a knife fighter."

"I have a warrior's scars," she confirmed. "Sometimes, I feel how muscle and bone remembers a long training. But I have been weaponless a long time, I think." She added, after a moment, "Do you suspect me, Lucky Man? Do you think I am trying to disguise myself? I can't disguise a self I do not know."

"Only when I noticed your scarred hands did it occur to me to doubt your tale, peculiar though it is."

She said, with just a trace of humor, "Oh, a storyteller can be most dangerous. Your caution is very sensible. Since I don't care who hears my tales, or who tells them in return, simply send me away!"

"I am sure you don't care. I think you are truly indifferent about everything."

"The people who remember are the ones who live passionately. They believe they have something to protect or a future to anticipate. I am not that kind. What kind are you, Lucky Man?"

He could not answer her, and the rest of the journey to the gate, they walked in silence. The clouds were breaking up, and a brisk wind began to blow. As the storyteller went out the gate, the wind blew back her cloak, and in the faint light of the gate lamps, her red silk shimmered like flame.

Chapter Twenty-Two

"Lieutenant-General? May I have a word with you?"

Clement had found one comfortable chair in the garrison, and had it put by the fireplace in her own spartan quarters. There she sat, with a washed uniform hanging nearby to dry in the heat of the brisk fire. She had slept in that chair no few nights, but now it was Davi who slept, curled in Clement's lap, with her thumb in her mouth.

"Come in," she said to the sergeant at the door. "But be quiet."

"It looks like snow again," he said in a low voice. "Unbelievable weather."

"It was this bad when we first came here, thirty-five years ago. It's been this bad every year since then."

"Well." The sergeant was a relatively young man, probably Shaftali-born. The habit of complaining about the weather was endemic, though, even among those who had never known anything else.

"Come closer to the fire," she suggested. "What's on your mind?"

"Ten days we've been here. The sick kids are getting better, and you've found that one you wanted. The company's wondering when we'll head back to Watfield."

"Do they *want* to make that journey?"

"If they have to do it," he said honestly, "they'd rather now than later."

"Well, I'm thinking they'll be trapped here all winter. I know it's not what they expected."

The sergeant looked more relieved than apprehensive. "I don't know that they'd mind. Conditions in Watfield are pretty bad."

"It's dirty work here, too."

He shrugged. "We've got fresh food, warm beds at night—"

"Luxury!"

He gave a grin. They'd gotten comfortable with each other over the days; working elbow-deep together at one or another disgusting task had been a great leveler.

"I won't tell the folks in Watfield how comfortable you are," she promised. "So they won't harass you about it, come spring."

His jaw went slack with surprise. "But you—"

"Ssh!"

He lowered his voice. "How will *you* get there? And surely not alone!"

"Not quite. I'll have Davi with me."

"You *can't* make the journey unattended." His voice was strained by the depth of feeling he struggled to convey without volume.

"You may be right, but I've got to try."

"But how?"

"There's only one way, Sergeant. By pretending to be Shaftali."

He shut his jaw with a snap. "Huh!" he finally said. "But you look pretty military."

"If I have to, I'll pretend to be a Paladin."

"You think you can?"

"You think it would occur to anyone that the Sainnite lieutenant-general would travel alone, on foot, in winter, with a sick child? I'd think they'd find it more believable that I'm one of them, even if I do seem strange. It doesn't matter, anyway. I've got to try."

"If the Paladins should capture you . . ."

"I'll be dead." She gave a shrug, and Davi mumbled a complaint. She stroked a hand down the child's head to soothe her, and that seemed to work. "Cadmar would be angry about it, I suppose. But I can be replaced. And no one will blame *you,* considering how far I outrank you."

"But still," he said.

"You've told me your objection. You've done your duty. Anything else you want to talk about?"

He left, apparently more wretched than when he had arrived.

Davi awoke. Clement persuaded her to eat some of the sweet cake they were feeding all the convalescent children. She put her head onto Davi's chest and listened to her breathe. The rattling sound had not returned, though Davi continued pale and weak. How soon, Clement wondered, did she dare take this hollow-eyed child out into the wind?

"Do you want more cake?"

Davi solemnly shook her head.

"I need to go hunt for something in the stable. Do you want to come along?"

Davi's nod was no surprise. The child had gotten to the point that she could tolerate being out of physical contact with Clement, but if Clement went out of her sight she became hysterical. Clement was getting used to carrying Davi everywhere with her, balanced on her hip, and the soldiers had gotten used to seeing her and didn't stare any more. Clement could swear the child was getting heavier, but at least she was no longer completely passive, did some of the work of holding on, and could even use a chamberpot on her own.

"You've turned me into a beast of burden," Clement complained as she carried the bundled child to the stable.

Davi looked at her blankly. Her eyes reminded Clement of some soldiers—casualties, sometimes without a visible wound. But Davi was slowly improving, and lately had even said some words and had been coaxed to smile. In the stable, several older children, crowded into a big stall with a demonstration horse, were being instructed in hoof care. The horses were exceptionally popular; there had been interventions to keep them from being overfed by the doting children. Clement set Davi in a pile of clean straw. "I'll be over there. Just call me if you want me."

Davi huddled passively in the straw. Clement felt that stark gaze on her back as she began her hunt through the junk that filled what had once been the tack room. She kept in Davi's sight, as if she were a helpful target and Davi the archer.

This odd, round building had once been a kind of school for Paladins, when Paladins were known as deadly philosophers, rather than as farmers who took up weapons in place of hoes. A sturdy building, with fireplaces and small windows, it was intended for year-round occupation. Surely it had once contained the kind of equipment Clement hoped to find, particularly since the Paladins had abandoned their domiciles in haste to attack the Sainnites after the Fall, leaving much behind.

Clement heaved aside a tangle of oddments and broken objects that should have been thrown out. Rats fled, squeaking outraged protests. She choked in dust and wished for a lantern. A generation's worth of dirt and debris lay moldering here, and much of it had settled on her by the time she discovered the treasure trove: A rack of skis, their bindings rotted away; snowshoes, their webbings gone but the frames still intact; and a sledge. She could not restrain a whoop of triumph. A sledge!

She dragged it out. Davi crawled out of her nest to inspect it, and some of the other children abandoned their lesson to take a look. They soon lost interest, but Davi solemnly mounted the contraption and sat down. She pointed at the rotted remains of the harness. "How will you pull it, Clemmie?"

"I saw some old horse harness in there." Clement went back to the junk and extricated some stiff leather, the buckles rusted, but nothing that some sand and grease could not fix.

"It's too big," Davi objected.

"Well, I am a soldier, which means I can make anything out of anything. Soldiers die if they can't adapt, you know."

Davi nodded somberly.

"You can help me clean the sledge. It'll be a cold trip, but you'll have blankets."

"Will we stay in people's houses?" Davi apparently had

some experience with this kind of travel already, perhaps from seeing visitors at her family's farmstead.

"Yes. You mustn't tell anyone I'm a soldier, though. It's a secret."

Davi shook her head vigorously.

"If you eat more, and rest, in a few days we'll leave. I'll take you home."

"Home?" She looked confused.

"I'll take you home because you're a weight in the scale. Because your father is willing to be hated and persecuted just to have you back again. Why, I don't know."

"Mmm." Davi gave a tentative, confused smile.

"Are you getting cold? I can take this harness to my room and start working on it. I want you to eat more cake to make you strong."

Davi held up her arms for Clement to pick her up.

Another five days had passed before Clement took Davi and the loaded sledge out the gate. The runners had been sanded and sharpened, the snowshoes re-webbed, the harness adapted, and Davi had a straw-stuffed mattress to sleep on and an oil-cloth cover to keep out the snow. Both of them wore the heaviest, warmest clothing that could be found, non-issue right down to the skin. Uneasy though she felt without weapons, Clement had left even them behind.

Her soldiers stood speechless; even Purnal seemed amazed. But the children, who knew an adventure when they saw one, cheered the travelers out the gate.

Clement had never worn snowshoes before, but managed to avoid tripping over her own feet until the watchers could no longer see her. That first day, she fell down regularly. That first night, she lay with Davi on the sledge, sleeping in short bits until, awakened by cold, she got up to put more wood on the fire and to turn her drying clothing. The child slept undisturbed in a solid, wool-clad lump, with a wool cap tied under her chin. When the snow began to glow faintly, reflecting a distant dawn, and the stars that populated the frozen sky began to wink out, Clement dressed in clothing that was almost dry and halfway warm, loaded up the sledge, strapped herself in the harness, and set forth once again.

That day, she finally mastered the snow-shoer's leg-swinging waddle. The sledge seemed almost weightless as she guided it down the hillside, and even when they reached the flat, she was amazed at her own speed. Davi rode behind her, complaining once of thirst, but subsiding when Clement explained that the water had frozen solid in its jug. But Clement became aware of her own thirst now. Dry-mouthed, she could not swallow the sweetened oatcakes in her pockets. Snow-blind, she could not see the passing countryside. A tugging at the harness brought her out of her daze.

Davi pointed, it seemed, into the sky, which was, Clement noted giddily, a gorgeous color: winter twilight. Across it lay the faintest smear of smoke.

"Ah!" Clement turned them down the hillside, where she could not see a wagon track, and in a last burst of blind energy got them practically to the farmhouse door before she fell for the first time that day, and was too tired to get up.

"Haven't got your snow legs yet?" A farmer in woolen clothing redolent, though not unpleasantly, with cow manure, hauled her to her feet and undid the harness buckles. "I saw you coming," she added. "So we've put the kettle on. Snow took you by surprise?"

"Not really," Clement gasped. "I planned to travel home before autumn mud. But the child took sick."

"Bad luck." An angular woman Clement's age or older, she made light work of lifting the sledge to the shelter of the porch, while Clement stood in dumb tiredness with Davi in her arms. She had concocted a much more elaborate explanatory tale for herself, but the farmer didn't ask for it. The farmer said, "We've got an empty bed. Two of the children married out this year. Twins. Went to the same household so they could still be in the same family. Come in, come in."

In the kitchen, a half dozen people looked up from chopping

vegetables to chorus a distracted welcome. The angular farmer collected a tea tray and led the way to an equally crowded parlor. Clement sank into an empty chair and was plied with hot tea and generously buttered bread as Davi drank a mug of hot milk, sitting in her lap. The angular farmer waved away Clement's thanks, saying obliquely, "It's been a good year. Good milk, healthy calves."

And if it hadn't been a good year, Clement wondered vaguely, what would the farmer say instead? That there was always enough to go around, or that what is given comes back eventually? Davi got down from her lap and joined some other children on the floor, who moved over to let her watch their game. The angular farmer, Mariseth, Seth to her friends, refilled Clement's teacup, cut her some cheese, and sat knee-to-knee with her. Clement recognized the cheese, which was even better here, where it had been made. The fear in her slowly came undone, like an old, stiff knot. Seth's knee was warmer than the heat from the fire as she recounted bits and pieces of information that might interest a traveler, and Clement asked questions, expressed surprise, uttered an occasional cautious comment. There was not much she needed to do; the farmer's incurious friendliness was like a path she needed only follow.

During the raucous supper, some twenty-two people ate willy-nilly, sitting or standing wherever there was space, all talking at once about cows and cheese and distant news from far-off places. Seth had status here, Clement noted, a lieutenant in her way, risen to that unacknowledged position over many years. Davi circled back to Clement's lap again, and ate obediently from her spoon. "I didn't tell!" she whispered.

"Good girl." Clement fed her some cheese, but Davi didn't like it, and the farmer offered a bowl of curds instead, which Davi emptied happily. Then the child fell asleep, and Seth, who had not been out of conversation distance all evening, commented, "A smart girl you've got there. But serious for her age. What is she, three?"

Clement nodded vaguely. "I wonder if I should have given

her longer to recover from her illness. But I needed to go home."

"She's a bit too pale and quiet. But maybe she's a quiet kid? Those thinkers often are, like you."

"Me?" Clement gave a laugh.

"Thinking hurts, doesn't it? Too much, maybe. I'll show you where you'll sleep."

In a bare cubby of a room, heated by a stove tiny as a kettle, someone had brought the contents of the sledge and hung everything that was damp to dry. With the farmer there, Clement had cause to be grateful for her recent sick nursing, for she undressed Davi and put her to bed without any obvious display of inexperience. Seth lit a little lamp that she put on a high shelf, out of child's reach. She set out a chamber pot, and folded Davi's clothes. Clement felt a rising warmth, as though that muscular leg still pressed hers.

Seth said, "You're not so tired as you looked when you first arrived."

"It was food and drink I needed. Tomorrow, I'll have Davi hug the water jug to keep it from freezing."

"Oh, we'll send you on your way with a foot warmer full of coals. That'll do the job, and keep your girl from getting chilled if the wind starts to blow. Some of that cheese, too, since you liked it so much. How about a nip?" she added.

Clement followed Seth down the hall to her own room, where apparently she slept in grand solitude beneath brightly colored scrap quilts, beside a small stove that she swiftly lit and stoked, then poured Clement a little cup of brandy from a long husbanded bottle. Clement sipped very cautiously, thinking to preserve at least some of her fleeting wits. "I feel a bit like a cow you're herding," she said.

Seth gave a wide, startling grin. "If you were a cow, I could force you into the barn."

"Oh, I'll let you herd me in. But why—?"

Seth sat beside her on the settle, thigh to thigh. "You've seen some things worth seeing, and I like the way it's marked you. But you don't want me asking."

Clement thought, *this woman is too smart to be a cowherd!* And she knew she ought to be afraid, or at least more cautious than she was. She said, "While you were having a good year I've been having an awful one. I want to forget. To pretend, maybe, that my life isn't mine."

The farmer said, "No questions, then. So . . ." She gestured, palm up, as though requesting the gods to fill her empty hand. "What? What do we do?"

Clement kissed her. That worked very well, so she kissed her again. After that came an extremely pleasant and quite long-lasting and stunningly satisfying confusion.

Clement dreamed a very strange dream in which she was a cowherd, but the cattle paid her no heed, and kept wandering away and getting eaten by wolves. When there were no beasts left, she stood alone in an empty field under an empty sky, with nothing to do but ponder her own incompetence. "Your girl's calling you," the angular farmer said blurrily. So Clement awoke from emptiness to surprise: a cozy bed, a warm shoulder against her cheek, the lingering memory of an extremely memorable night.

Davi's voice came very faintly down the hall.

"It's dawn," Clement mumbled. "Well, almost dawn. I think I'll get on my way. Long journey ahead."

"Stay," said the farmer quietly.

Clement swallowed surprise. "I don't know a thing about cows."

"Not much to know. You'll come to hate milking and mucking as much as we do. It doesn't take long!"

"Davi's father—"

"I'd say he's not much of a husband. Neglectful."

Clement let that sink in. Had she acted neglected? She had indeed. "A good father, though," she said.

"But what have *you* got to go home to? Stay the winter. Send him a letter. My family won't mind."

Seth's hands were good, and for a little while Clement didn't try to escape them. Davi subsided, back into sleep. But eventually, Clement got out from under the warm quilts, put on her clothes, and got underway. The angular farmer stood on the porch and watched her leave, but when Clement looked back, she was gone, to the cow barn, no doubt, to start the milking, or to the dairy, to check on the cheese.

These things happen, Clement told herself.

Bittersweet regret followed her all the way to Watfield. Nine days later, blistered and frost-bitten, she unwound her muffler in the middle of a blinding snowstorm so the gate captain could recognize her face. Later still, with Davi big-eyed and frightened in her arms, she endured the wrath of Cadmar. She had been gone twice as long as she had promised, and had taken untoward risks, and had abandoned her soldiers. She admitted all that, and did not argue with his anger. Still later, with Davi asleep in Clement's bed, she sat with Gilly while his nighttime pain draught was taking hold, and told him about the blinding white days, the one bewildering storm that did its best to kill her, the nights in cold barns on straw beds with only pauper's bread to eat, the nights of sharing hearty meals at family tables and sleeping in a bed hospitably vacated for her and Davi. And she told him about Seth.

Gilly did not laugh at her. After a long silence, he said, "If you become Shaftali—"

"What?"

"Oh, don't be dishonest with me. If you become Shaftali, I couldn't endure my life. And with both of us gone, Cadmar would fall like a house without a center beam, and maybe the Sainnites would fall with him."

Clement said, after a stunned silence, "My face is known. I'm the notorious baby thief of Watfield. I can never escape that. I never even thought to try."

"Stop playing these dangerous games, then. Be what you are."

The next day, Clement was back in uniform. Her hair was trimmed, her buttons polished, her feet, though they ached with frostbite, were jammed into her newly blacked boots. Davi found her attire fearsome, and cried. She refused to eat her porridge, fought the bath, huddled under the blankets in Clement's bed, and was generally defiant and exasperating. "I want to go home!" she whined. "You promised!"

"I see you're feeling much better. Well enough to accuse a lieutenant-general of being a liar. You've got a lot of courage, little girl, but not much sense."

Davi glared at her: sturdy, angry, not much intimidated. "You promised!"

Unable to leave Davi unattended, Clement had paper and ink delivered to her room, and she tried to work on the task Cadmar had set her, but even without the distracting child it would have been impossible. He had refused to accept the closure of any garrison and demanded alternatives. She wrote an extremely irritable list of impractical and intolerable solutions:

1. Go back to the homeland and recruit a few thousand mercenaries to join us in exile.
2. People the garrisons with straw dummies.
3. Command each soldier to kidnap and personally raise two children, while also fulfilling all other duties.
4. Take a thousand Shaftali women prisoner, impregnate them all, and force them to raise the resulting children as Sainnites.
5. Require the female soldiers, myself among them to bear and raise children. (Though I am too old, probably.)

She snorted. She didn't have to look beyond the child glowering at her from the bed to see why her people were childless. What would she do, if Davi were hers? After a year of pregnancy and a year of nursing, two years off the battlefield, if she survived childbirth and did not suffer any of the terrible injuries birthing women were subject to, would she then carry Davi on her back into war? Or leave the child behind to be inevitably orphaned? And who would raise her then?

"Lieutenant-General?" A hesitant tap on her door. "Davi?"

Davi came out from under the covers, big-eyed. "You should have trusted me," said Clement sourly, and went to open the door.

The steady, quiet father of this sturdy girl came in, pushed past Clement, and snatched up the child. "Oh, blessed day! Davi! You're so thin! Oh, my sweet girl!"

Davi clung to him, and cried, and then declared that she had been very brave, though she had been in a scary place, and that Clemmie—she had forgotten that she hated her, apparently—had taken her home across the snow.

"So much adventure for such a little girl." The man gave Clement a look and added dryly, "I thought you Sainnites were cowards about snow."

"Your information had better be worth what I've been through." Strange that it hadn't occurred to her until now to wonder if this man were telling the truth. But the Shaftali were an honest people, a quality that was, according to Gilly, embedded in the culture by the once ubiquitous Truthkens. In most of her dealings with the Shaftali, when they agreed to speak at all, they spoke the truth.

Davi's father had brushed most of the snow from his clothing. His skis and ski poles were slung across his back, and an empty sling for Davi to ride home in. He set all this gear down and sat reluctantly, with Davi clinging to his neck.

"These people, Death-and-Life," he said. "They're going to rescue the children. But they aren't going to send the Watfield children home, not right away, because they think you Sainnites would blame their families, and the people of Watfield have suffered too much already, so maybe Davi would have been safe anyway. But I'd never see her again. And I couldn't bear it."

"I didn't tell anybody Clemmie was a soldier," announced Davi. "And I didn't cry."

Her father said, "All your mothers and fathers will be so proud of you."

Clement, while gathering up Davi's warm clothing, had noticed a loose button and sat down to sew it on. The man gave her a surprised look, and she glared at him, saying, "I suppose you feel required to explain to me now how badly you feel, but I wish you wouldn't. Tell me: nobody knows where the Watfield children are. So how are they to be rescued?"

"Not just the Watfield children. All of them."

She looked up again from her stitching, genuinely surprised now, and even more dismayed.

The farmer said, "I suppose you thought it was a secret that you've got a garrison full of children. But those people knew you Sainnites had to be keeping your children somewhere! And your children aren't in the garrisons, because no one's ever seen one, and a child's not easy to hide. So the rebels have been looking around, and asking questions, and they've found your secret place, and they know the Watfield children are there. They wouldn't say exactly where that place was, though. I guess they feared the Watfield parents might go there and wreck their surprise. And I *would* have gone, too, if I had known. In fact, my husband wasn't supposed to tell anything at all, even to his family, but he did because he was so sick. And my husband was sure those Death-and-Life people knew exactly where the children were."

"They planned to steal our children? All of them?"

"To *liberate* them. Because they're all Shaftali children, they say. You Sainnites don't bear children, so every last child you've got is a stolen child. But that's not true, is it?"

"It's not true," she said, outraged.

He seemed relieved. Bad enough that he was allowing nearly forty of his neighbor's children to remain imprisoned while his was rescued. No wonder his family had abandoned their farmstead rather than endure the public shame! And no wonder he clutched his girl so tightly now that she protested, and then complained that she was hungry.

"She wouldn't eat her porridge," Clement explained. "She wanted milk, but we don't have any."

"Have you been fussy, love?" The man produced a neat packet of oat cakes from his pocket, and Davi was as contented with these as Clement had ever seen her. "You haven't fed her right," he said.

"She's been very sick. I nursed her back—she would have

died otherwise. So don't complain." Clement bit the thread and tested the button. "When are these kids to be 'liberated'? And how?"

"On Long Night. The people of Death-and-Life figure that by midwinter, the children will be so isolated by weather that when the initial battle is over, they'll have a couple of months to haul the kids away to their new homes, at households scattered all over Shaftal. A surprise attack, at night, sure to succeed. The children aren't well guarded, they believe. And Long Night's an important holiday to us, you know."

Clement said nothing, but she did not doubt that with enough attackers the plan he described would probably succeed. The only weapons at the children's garrison were carried by the seven soldiers she had abandoned there. Unless one counted the practice weapons the children used.

"That's all I know," the man said. "Shaftal forgive me! Can I go?"

"Tell no one what you've told me."

"You think I would? I'm a traitor to my people, now."

"Maybe you might try to clear your conscience by alerting Death-and-Life that their secret ambush isn't a secret anymore."

The man said stiffly, thoroughly offended now, "Those people? You think I owe them something? There's nothing to admire in them, no more than there is in you." He stood up with some effort, and said to Davi, "Let's get you into your jacket and hat. It's time to go."

Clement helped bundle her up. "What's going to happen to her, come spring?" She did not want to say in front of Davi that her father was dying, but he knew what she referred to.

"I've got a plan. I don't have to tell you what it is."

As Clement tied Davi's cap strings, Davi blinked at her. "Aren't you coming, Clemmie?"

"No." She couldn't manage to say more.

"But Daddy," Davi protested, as her father picked her up again, "why isn't Clemmie coming?"

"She isn't in our family," he said. And they were gone.

❀❀❀❀❀❀❀❀❀❀❀❀❀❀❀❀

Part 4
❧

What's Inside
The Buffalo

❀❀❀❀❀❀❀❀❀❀❀❀❀❀❀❀

"You are slow and stupid," the grass-lion said to his friend the buffalo one day. They always shared the shade on hot summer days and were lying together, the buffalo chewing her cud and the grass-lion licking the blood from his paws. "I wonder sometimes why I don't just eat you."

The buffalo looked up at her friend and coughed up another lump of cud. "Who would dig the water hole for you?" she said.

Looking at the buffalo, the grass-lion decided she was disgusting. Her fur was clotted with the dried mud she rolled in to keep off the flies. Grass mush dripped from her mouth. Her eyes were big and watery and contented. "I can dig," the grass-lion said. "I can dig better than you can."

"Well then, who would eat the grass to exactly the right height for stalking rabbits?" said the buffalo.

Looking at the buffalo, the grass-lion decided she was ugly. Her horns sat up on her head like an ugly hat. Her fur hung to her knees like dead grass. Her hooves looked like gray turds that when broken open have maggots inside them. "I can stalk rabbits in grass of any height," he said.

"Well then, who will sing to the stars with you, to please the ears of the gods?" said the buffalo.

The grass-lion looked at the buffalo and decided she was ridiculous. Her legs were short and her body fat. Her mouth was wide and her tail had a puff of hair on its tip. It was difficult to imagine that anything she did could please the gods.

"My voice is so much sweeter than yours," said the lion. "Maybe the gods would like me better without you bellowing beside me."

"Well then," said the buffalo. "If you don't want to be my friend that's fine with me. But I have to warn you that if you try to eat me, it's me who will eat you in the end." And she got up and walked away.

So now the grass-lion had to dig his own water hole and chase the rabbits in high grass and sing all by himself and all this made him angry. And he watched the silver buffalo from afar and thought about how much meat was on her bones, and how it would keep him fat and contented for many days. And finally he was in such a fever of anger and bloodlust that he went sneaking up on the buffalo in the tall grass, and jumped onto her back, and dug his claws in.

Now, the buffalo set to work trying to get that lion off her back. She jumped and twisted and kicked, but she couldn't dislodge the lion, who kept ripping away with his claws until he had opened up her back like a shirt. Suddenly the buffalo's skin fell off, and out of the buffalo hide stepped a man. He shook his head as if he were waking up from a long sleep, and then he took a look at the lion, who certainly was feeling somewhat surprised. "Oh, it's you, trying to eat me," the man said. "Well, I have to warn you that it's me who will eat you in the end."

The lion was annoyed at the man's arrogance. "We'll see who eats and who is eaten," he cried, and jumped onto the man's back and dug in with his claws.

The man didn't like having the lion on his back any more than the silver buffalo had. He yelled and he rolled on the ground and he tried to hit the lion with a rock, but the lion hung on, ripping with his claws, until the man's skin had opened up like a shirt.

Suddenly, his skin fell away, and out stepped a big yellow hare. That hare yawned and scratched her chin, and then she noticed the lion standing there, so surprised he didn't even try to lift a paw and grab her. "Oh, it's you trying to eat me," she said. "Well, I have to warn you that it's me who will eat you in the end." And then the hare took off, kicking her yellow feet in the air, taking great bounds over the high grass. The lion chased her, of course, all up and down the length of the grassy plain, from the ocean in the east to the mountains in the west, from the forest in the north to the wasteland in the south. At last, the hare was so tired she fell down gasping, and the lion fell down right on top of her, with his red tongue hanging out of his mouth. "I've got you now," he gasped, and ripped with his claws until the hare's back opened up like a shirt.

Inside the hare's skin was a pool of darkness, and then that pool began to move, to uncoil, and out slid a fat black snake with a flickering tongue. The lion lay exhausted, panting and weak from the long chase, looking into the hard black eyes of the black snake. "You warned me that you would eat me in the end," said the grass-lion.

"Oh yes, I almost forgot," said the snake. And he opened his mouth, bigger and bigger, until his mouth was as big as the lion, and he swallowed the lion whole.

And that's why the grass-lions never hunt the buffalo.

Chapter Twenty-Three

The sun rises and falls like a ball tossed from a hand, and Zanja na' Tarwein walks steadily across barren mountaintops. The owl floats ahead of her, a feather-down guide lit faintly by a sun that is always in twilight. As long as she can see, Zanja follows the owl. When it is dark, she squats down wherever she is, and takes a handful of twigs and dried grass that she has managed to gather among the rocks, and with it builds a fire no bigger than the palm of her hand.

Over her shoulder she has carried all day a fire-blackened tin pot with a length of rope tied to its handles for a shoulder strap. She also carries a wooden box that once was decorated with pastoral scenes, but from which most of the paint now has been scraped off. Although in her day's journeys she sees nothing but stones, when she stops walking she can always find a pool of water within a few steps of her fire: a pool just big enough to fill her pot. And as the water heats, she takes out of the wooden box a porcelain tea set and a tin of tea that is neither full nor empty. By the time the twigs burn to ashes, the water boils. She steeps a pot of tea and drinks it while looking at the stars.

These stars are unfamiliar: not unremembered, but entirely different from night to night. Yet the landscape across which she travels by day remains the same: rocky mountaintops that give her no glimpse at all of what lies beyond them. Nothing distinguishes this landscape. She cannot even be certain that the sun rises in the same place every dawn. She is following the owl, who is leading the way to the Land of the Dead.

By the time the teapot is empty, it is sunrise. She packs the tea set and slings her burdens over her shoulders. She spots the owl, flying in the distance. Again, she follows.

The day's bread was in the oven. With the storm shutters open, Garland could watch the tentative dawn of early winter: its stark, crisp shadows, black on white, the rising glimmer of the snow. He could see the ravens on the porch rail, impatient for their cornbread, bickering like children over perches in the sun. Garland had awakened to a kitchen hung with snow-shoes—Karis, apparently unable to sleep again, had done her insomniac's work here.

The kitchen door clicked open and he turned, surprised. Medric, who he last had seen wrapped in Emil's arms in the attic room the three of them shared, stumbled in: only half dressed, spectacles askew, fingers still ink-stained from the previous night's work on his manuscript. "Brrr!" He squinted at the pale light reflecting in from the snow.

"It's called a sunrise," said Garland. "What are you doing up so early? After Karis was awake all night? Trading places with her?"

"Gods! No!" Medric shuddered. "It was a dream."

Medric didn't drink tea or spirits and didn't eat butter or sugar or meat or cheese, and so was a thin wisp of a man who felt the cold quite keenly. Garland distractedly considered what to feed him at what was for Medric a wretched hour. Hot milk. "I suppose you don't take honey?"

Medric shook his head mournfully. "I'd like to stay sane. Or not get any madder than I am."

"Honey causes madness?" Every day in this household was another amazement. Garland warmed the milk, determined to do it slowly so the milk would sweeten on its own.

Medric rubbed his eyes, mumbled crankily, and then burst out, "You know her!"

"Who?"

"The one I dreamed of. I never met her, so *you* must have, in Watfield. Otherwise, I couldn't have dreamed of her."

"A soldier? I knew them all, five years ago. What did this dream woman like to eat?"

Garland had asked his question flippantly, but Medric replied promptly, "Cheese, with an apple and a glass of wine."

"And a couple of butter biscuits, I hope."

Medric shrugged. Clearly, he was a man who saw no reason to think about food.

"With tastes like that, she's probably an officer." Garland stirred the milk steadily, peacefully, letting his memories rise: sergeants, captains, lieutenants, commanders. The higher the position, the older the person who held it, generally. "How old? Thirty? Fifty?"

Medric grumbled something, pulling himself out of his daze. "She's energetic, not so beat up as most veterans get. But she's not young. A lucky fighter."

Garland was remembering his last day in Watfield garrison. Summoned to the general's quarters, he found himself confronted by a very angry, very large man who gestured dismissively at the untouched plate on his table: beef in gravy with mushrooms and vegetables covered by a crisp pastry. Garland had been worrying all evening that he had used too much rosemary in the gravy, which is a mistake impossible to recover from, and surely that was what the general wanted to complain about. "Do you call this soldier's fare?" the general had roared when Garland came in.

Garland could vividly recall what at the time he had scarcely noticed: that the other plates on the table were scraped clean, that the woman who sat at Cadmar's right had looked sharply away when the general uttered his unimaginable, unacceptable command that from now on Garland was to cook badly. What had she been hiding from Garland—or from Cadmar—when she looked so swiftly away? Embarrassment? Contempt? Garland wanted to describe her to Medric now, but he could not think of what distinguished her in appearance from any other Sainnite. There were some things the soldiers had said about her, though, and he repeated them, struggling to remember. "She learned the names and history of every single person in her command. If they went hungry or cold or wet, so did she. She always hauled her own load."

"I think I like her," Medric said. "Whoever she is."

"The lieutenant-general, Clement."

"The *lieutenant-general*?" Medric sat upright, blinking. "She *hauls her own load*?"

"I'm just telling you what I heard when she first arrived." Garland tasted the foaming milk. Not sweet yet.

"I understand the general is a bloody fool," said Medric.

"That certainly is true."

"Then how did he get himself a competent lieutenant?"

"She'd been his lieutenant an awfully long time. Every promotion for him was a promotion for her."

"It was *torture* for her." Medric's spectacles were reflecting the fire again. Garland felt a shudder. Karis might exercise her talent invisibly, or at least in a way that almost seemed ordinary, but this peculiar man could not pull off that trick. "They came over on the boat together, from Sainna," he said. "She was a child. She thought he was a perfect soldier. She learned better—but she couldn't escape him. He remained her superior. His rise controlled hers. But, finally, she managed to escape him and for a few years they both were commanders, equals. And then the old general died."

Medric was only half articulating. In the twilight region between sleep and wakefulness, he opened his mouth and through speaking understood what he had no business knowing.

Medric opened his eyes. "Am I making your skin crawl yet?"

"Yes," Garland said, and let out his breath. "The milk is ready, I think."

"You're being very helpful, you know."

"Helpful for what? Why do you want to understand her like this?"

"To intrude on her, you mean? Oh, don't deny it—I know it seems unsavory. But how else are we to win this war, except by knowing the enemy better than they know us?"

Garland poured two mugs of milk, gave one to Medric, and then flavored his own with honey and spices, the scent of which made Medric look distinctly rueful. "The enemy," Garland repeated. "You mean our fathers' people."

"Oh, I'm a traitor no matter who I mean by 'enemy,'" said Medric lightly. "And so are you. You might let me have just a tiny bit of that cinnamon."

Garland grated some cinnamon into Medric's milk. The young seer's eyes closed as he breathed in the smell. He said, still sniffing, "No one in this house has ever asked me to be un-principled, though. And they won't ask it of you, either."

"Unless I'm asked to murder Karis's wife," said Garland recklessly.

Medric's spectacles had steamed up as he held his nose over the mug. He took them off, rubbed his eyes, and said with terrible sadness, "Emil and I—we are always exactly parallel to each other, and we couldn't step on each other's toes if we tried. But Karis and Zanja, they had to fight their way into that dance of theirs. Gods—it was exciting to watch." He put his spectacles back on, found them still steamy, and irritably took them off again. "I won't deny that Zanja's murder was barbarous, heartless, and cruel," he said. "But don't call it unprincipled. Norina loved her for her discipline. I loved her quickness. Emil, well, he just loved her. Killing Zanja was a triumph of principle over passion. It may have been the most principled act of my life. I certainly hope I'm never asked to do such a thing again."

After a moment, Medric added gloomily, "I'm better at being silly in Shaftalese." He sipped his milk, and raised his eyebrows in surprise. "How did you do that?

"It just takes patience."

"I'll never be able to do it, then."

They sat a long time without talking. The smell of baking bread began to suffuse the kitchen. The ravens on the rail outside cried hoarse curses at each other. Medric said, "This milk is making me sleepy."

"It's supposed to. What *was* the dream that woke you up?"

"I dreamed that the lieutenant-general was making love with a Shaftali cow farmer."

"Huh!" said Garland after a long silence. "Are you sure?"

"I may be an addle-pate, but when a couple of people take off their clothes and tangle in a bed like that, it's difficult to mistake what it is they're doing."

"What does your dream mean, though?"

Medric put on his spectacles, found them clear, and blinked at Garland quite sleepily. "She's loyal to her people, isn't she? Not confused, like us?" He didn't wait for an answer, but shook his head sympathetically. "She doesn't even realize what's happened to her yet."

Chapter Twenty-Four

Clement noticed Gilly on horseback at the garden's edge, watching her and Captain Herme put the reluctant soldiers through their drills—familiar drills, except that they were done in deep snow, wearing snow shoes. The soldiers floundered and lost their tempers. After Clement had dismissed them, she went to stand at Gilly's stirrup. He said, "I really do admire your persistence. But what idiocy!"

Herme's company trailed ignominiously off the field, most of them dangling their snow shoes distastefully from their hands. They would return to the work of building themselves a barracks, and no doubt they would complain about her all afternoon.

She said, "So you too believe that Sainnites are naturally unable to cope with snow? Just like Shaftali are naturally incapable of fighting?"

"No. I am a man of facts."

"Fact is, those soldiers would die rather than learn something new."

"Fact is, like anyone, they'd rather be incapable than incompetent."

"It's hard to blame them, when observers call them idiotic. Well, it doesn't matter. I need for them to learn to walk and fight on snow. And I outrank them."

"You outrank almost everyone, from sheer endurance."

"At least you have no illusions about my native abilities." She grinned up at him. The unflappable, sure-footed horse pushed her gently, and she scratched his forehead as well as could be done in heavy gloves.

Gilly added, with a trace of genuine concern, "Oh, but the soldiers do hate you today."

"Everyone hates me, lately. But not you, for some reason."

"Make me wear snow shoes and I'll hate you too."

"What *are* you doing here?"

"The storyteller's coming to hear some stories, and I'll be supervising, as usual. Come with me."

"Any particular reason?"

"None at all." Under her suspicious examination, his face remained bland as his horse's, though much uglier.

"Give me a moment to undo these bindings," she said.

Since her return to Watfield, Clement had frequently glimpsed the storyteller, whose red silk clothing could hardly be missed in a world of white snow, gray slush, and even grayer woolen uniforms. And in the bitter evening cold, while walking past the refectory, Clement had sometimes heard the storyteller's voice. Perhaps a few words, so crisply articulated they hardly seemed words at all, but notes of music, might linger in Clement's ear. More often, she heard at a distance the roar of soldier's voices, and the pounding of their hands and feet, which signaled another story told and now owed.

Walking at Gilly's stirrup, Clement commented, "I don't know that I'd want to spend so much time in that woman's company as you've been spending. See that icicle?" She pointed at an extraordinary one that dangled from the eaves of an unfinished building. "That's her. Not human at all."

Gilly gazed at the icicle. "But her stories don't make us cold," he said.

The storyteller was waiting in the guard shed, huddled with the soldiers around the brazier, watching a game of cards. The soldiers started guiltily as Clement looked in the door, and leapt to their feet in a tangle of salutes. "Lieutenant-General," said the captain. "Gilly was late, and we thought the storyteller shouldn't be left standing in the snow."

Clement said mildly, "You shouldn't have let her in." In fact, the discipline of the gate guard was not her concern, and the soldiers were probably confident that she wouldn't report them.

The storyteller greeted her with cool courtesy, and as coolly said to Gilly on his horse, "Good day, Lucky Man."

"Good day, storyteller. I trust you are well."

"I am. You owe me ten stories."

"You will be paid." Gilly added, as they started down the street, "I have a question for you. Do you ever repeat a story?"

"No, never."

"So what will you do, when you have told us all your stories?"

The storyteller walked beside Clement, sure-footed and precise on the slick paving stones that here and there emerged from ice. "It will not happen."

"Never? You know, they're taking bets on how long you can continue without repeating yourself."

The storyteller seemed unamused. "Your people's stories will run out, but mine will not."

Clement protested, "We Sainnites have a long history!"

"No histories," said Gilly. "Forbidden."

"By command? Or by the storyteller's preference?"

"I hear whatever tale people choose to tell," said the storyteller. "So long as it is new to me."

"If I told you how I got my flower bulbs," began Clement.

"No personal tales," interrupted Gilly.

"I hear whatever tale people choose to tell," said the storyteller again, in a tone so neutral that a listener might not even notice that she was contradicting Gilly.

Clement said, "But if you heard a story about flower bulbs, that isn't the kind of story you would then tell, is it?"

When at last Clement turned to see why the storyteller had not answered, she noticed first that the woman continued to find her balance on the slippery stones, as easily and unconsciously as a dancer. Then she noticed that the storyteller was not even looking at her feet, but at her. Her attentiveness and silence both were deeply unsettling.

Clement felt irresistibly compelled to speak. "This kind of

story: The fighting had been incessant, and it was the first time I had seen my mother in days. We had just heard that the enemy was coming over the wall. She came to the barracks, took me out into the garden, and we began digging. She wore a coat like this one I'm wearing, with big pockets. We filled her pockets with bulbs—all different kinds—until we couldn't cram any more in. Then she picked me up, and ran with me. I looked over her shoulder and saw the enemy coming down the road. I could hear my mother gasping for breath. I could feel the great lump of bulbs in her pocket, and I remember hoping that none of them would fall out."

She stopped. She felt Gilly's gaze, but did not want to look at him. The general's Lucky Man had been a child beggar in a ditch when she first met him. There was not much doubt that Cadmar had abused the boy, those first few years. There were many topics that Clement and Gilly never discussed with each other, including both their childhoods.

It was time for one of her listeners to ask a question, to rescue Clement from embarrassment. But Gilly was silent, and the storyteller did not appear to be capable of asking questions, or of engaging in anything resembling a normal conversation. She said, "Your mother's power came to you through those flower bulbs. Because she loved you, she rescued that power for you in the face of disaster. When I tell this story, I will tell how you rescued that power for *your* child."

Clement found she had lost her power of speech.

Gilly was gazing intently at the icicle-decorated eaves of a half-built building. He glanced at Clement, finally. To her surprise, his glance was serious, with no mockery at all. He turned to the storyteller and asked the question Clement could not. "How will she do such a thing?"

"When I tell that story," the woman said, "then we will know how."

In a crowded, dirty room, a dozen soldiers gathered, all men from the same company, who had come directly from the construction work. They had pulled bread and meat from their pockets and were eating companionably and passing a surreptitious flask as they awaited the storyteller. They leapt up in confusion when Clement entered, and settled down again at her gesture, though now the flask was nowhere to be seen. She could smell forbidden spirits, though, and a stink of dirt and sweat and slightly rancid meat. After Clement and the storyteller had helped Gilly to dismount, he had scarcely been able to walk. But now, as he sat and took a pen from behind his ear, an ink bottle from his pocket, and a roll of paper from inside his coat, he became the very model of grimy officiousness. In fact, of everyone in the room, only the storyteller was truly clean, as though even dirt could not adhere to her.

The soldiers began telling stories almost at once, their order of recitation apparently having been worked out in advance. Half listening, Clement watched the storyteller, whose attention in turn was focused on whoever spoke: an attention the likes of which Clement had never seen, not even in a predator whose life depended on such watchfulness. When one or another speaker began to falter self-consciously, the storyteller would look away, to give him some relief. Every single time, she looked into Clement's eyes instead. Clement perceived nothing in that glance: not curiosity nor self-consciousness nor weariness nor wonder. Certainly, the storyteller didn't care that Clement stared at her. In fact, she hardly even seemed to notice.

Gilly, skimming his list, interrupted one man's story, and then another, to say, "Sorry, that one's been told." For other stories, he wrote a few words down on his paper: a title, or a description, Clement supposed. After some mental ciphering, Clement concluded that the woman probably had already told, and been told, well over two hundred stories. And if the storytelling continued to winter's end, it would easily be more than a thousand. Surely the soldiers were making bets on when the stories would run dry because they had realized, however vaguely, that the storyteller was uncanny, and that she was doing something that should have been impossible. But, apparently, it had occurred to no one, except perhaps to Gilly, that extraordinary events are seldom benign.

* * *

The storyteller was in the refectory, being served an early supper so she could be refreshed and ready to perform when the meal bell was rung. Clement and Gilly stood out in the chilly street, both of them on foot now. As always, Gilly crouched over his cane like an old man, but he looked even older in winter, and in the last few years his hair had begun to go gray. Clement took off her hat and brushed a hand self-consciously across her own hair, close-clipped for the helmet she hardly ever wore anymore. Was she also going gray? She tried to think of when she had last looked into a mirror.

"That storyteller is more than strange," she said. "She is supernatural."

Gilly gave her that peculiar sideways look of his, but did not speak.

"Is she a witch?" Clement asked.

He said, "I believe she has what the Shaftali call an elemental talent, an unusual ability that gives a remarkable shape to her thinking. If she were a witch, though, she'd be turning her stories into reality."

"If Cadmar knew about this . . ."

Gilly looked grimly down at his hand gripping the cane. "The soldiers adore her. I'd hate to take her away from them for no good reason, after such a year as they've had to endure."

"I think," said Clement, "that you yourself might like her a little."

He looked sideways at her again. "A monstrous creature like her?"

They were silent until Gilly added, quietly, "She must be aware of what danger she puts herself in by entering these gates. But she seems incapable both of fear and of self-protection."

"Isn't she as much a danger to us?"

Gilly said, "You think she's a Paladin spy? With that memorable face? Dressed in extremely visible flame-red silk? Always the center of attention?"

"Well, if she was lurking about trying to be invisible, she

wouldn't have soldiers blabbing to her for hours every day with official permission."

"What one thing has she been told today that could be even remotely useful to our enemies?"

"It's not what they're telling her that matters," said Clement. "It's the *habit* of telling."

"Yes," said Gilly. "The habit of telling. And the novelty of being heard. It matters, yes. But how is it dangerous?"

Clement could not think of when she had felt so unbalanced, so utterly confounded. Gilly's steadiness, his very seriousness, only contributed to the sensation. She wanted him to make a joke of the entire afternoon. But he clung to his cane as though he feared he would fall over, frowned distantly at the icy ground, and waited for her to speak.

Surely something the storyteller had said to Gilly had unnerved him also. Perhaps, because of her, he now shared with Clement this lingering sensation that he had overlooked the possibilities of his life. But the sensation would pass, and they would still be what they were.

Clement said, "Well, we can forbid the storyteller to enter the garrison. Or we can arrest her and do to her what we do to witches. Or we can pretend like we haven't noticed a bloody thing, and let the soldiers hear her tales." She paused. "Do you think you can make certain she has no other conversations like the one she had with me today? With anyone? Including yourself?"

There was a silence. "Yes," Gilly said.

"Has Cadmar showed any interest in hearing her tales?"

"None."

"Let's make certain he doesn't." The bell was ringing. "Shall we go in?" She took his arm, and felt him lean into her.

It was the first time Clement had sat down in that room to watch the storyteller's performance. The eager soldiers struggled with each other for the best spots, but they had left a seat for Gilly, and Clement sat in the place the storyteller vacated. A soldier said, "Lieutenant-General, you've not come here before? You'll be amazed."

She turned to the soldier, and found a hard-faced, embittered veteran, who had already turned away from her to look up at the storyteller with an expression of childish anticipation. "Why?" said Clement.

"Oh, she's *good*." The veteran put a finger to her lips. "This is the best part."

What followed was a ripple of silence, and the tension of anticipation. The storyteller waited on the stage of the tabletop: poised, taut, intent. Just as Clement thought the performer had waited too long, she spoke. "I am a collector of tales, and I will trade, story for story. This is a tale of the Juras people, who are giants in an empty land, whose voices are so big they sing the light into the stars."

She told the tale of the grass-lion and the buffalo, which Clement thought was about the dangers of underestimating the enemy, or of overestimating oneself, or perhaps of being so stupid as to assume there is no more to be understood about the world. The storyteller told five more tales, and each one was a disappointment to Clement, for none of them was a tale of magical flower bulbs.

"Oh, dear," Gilly said. "Clem, I fear you are in trouble. Something very odd is happening to you."

But he added, after a while, "At least get Cadmar's permission."

Clement made certain Cadmar was in a jovial mood, which, after so many years with him was not too difficult to engineer. He laughed at her request, which she expected, and then granted it. He liked to think he was generous with his inferiors, especially in matters that were irrelevant to and not inconvenient to him.

Clement rode to Alrin's house early one cold afternoon, alone and unexpected. Marga must have been out, for the storyteller opened the door and admitted her without comment. She was not wearing her performance clothes, but Alrin's tailor certainly had been exercising his skills on her: her wool

suit was austere, not impractical, and very flattering. Clement
had been curious what possessed the courtesan to take in this
unconventional lodger, but, watching the uncanny woman go
up the stairs to announce Clement's presence, it occurred to
Clement that Alrin might simply be indulging in a passion for
exotic decoration.

"She asks you to come upstairs," said the storyteller when
she returned.

"You did tell her—?"

"Business. As you said."

Clement made her own way to Alrin's room. The courtesan
lay in bed, supported by pillows, with the lamp lit and an account book beside her. Her round belly jutted before her.
"You're not well?" Clement said.

Alrin waved a graceful hand. "Oh, it's nothing. Marga made
me see the midwife, and now I must lie abed all day. I'm sure
you wish that you might suffer so."

Clement was particularly glad that she had managed to
bring a gift, which she now unpacked from its makeshift wrappings. The pottery cup was no more than a broken discard
found outside the refectory. The cup was full of plain water and
ordinary stones, but the bulb planted in it had bravely and in-
souciantly put forth its buds, and just that morning one of the
buds had cracked open to release a pale pink flower.

Alrin exclaimed, "Oh, what a scent! How did you convince
it to bloom so early?"

"Soldier's secret." Clement set the broken cup with its perfumed contents on the nearby table. As she stood at the foot of
the bed, watching Alrin breathe in the scent again and again,
each time with fresh pleasure, she had the amazed idea that
perhaps she had accomplished one worthwhile, though extremely small, thing this year.

"What do you want from me?" Alrin finally asked.

"I would like," Clement said, "to adopt your child."

"Surely you are not serious."

"Very serious." Clement looked around, found a chair
nearby, drew it closer to the bed, and sat in it. "How much will
it take?"

."You could start by being a man," Alrin said.

This directness was new, and very strange. Perhaps, since Alrin's retirement had been thrust upon her early by this illness, she had begun to practice bluntness in preparation for her new career.

Clement said, "If I had pretended to be acting as Cadmar's intermediary, you'd give me the child, and never know the money wasn't his."

"But you didn't."

"Of course not."

They both were silent. The heady scent of the newly opened flower gradually filled the room.

Alrin finally said, "I'm stunned by this proposal."

That was when Clement knew she had a chance, for if there had been no hope, Alrin would have simply refused. Clement said, "If I were a man, how much would it take to outbid the other candidates?"

Alrin rather delicately named a sum.

Clement offered substantially more than that.

Alrin looked involuntarily at her closed account book.

Clement stood up. "Let me know when you have made up your mind. I have a journey to make in a few days, and may be gone from the garrison for some time. But Gilly will act as my agent in my absence, and he has access to my funds."

Alrin said in some surprise, "Is he your brother?"

Clement felt rather blank. But surely it should have been a simple question? She finally answered, "Gilly is what I have."

Chapter Twenty-Five

On any night, Garland might open his eyes to the glow of Medric's candle, a red blur behind the curtain that divided the attic. Medric's pen might be scratching, or he might be steadily, rhythmically turning the pages of a book, or he might be mixing a new batch of ink. Sometimes he muttered to himself, and Garland might wonder sleepily how anyone could possibly work in such cold. One night, though, Garland awakened to Medric's voice, raised in excitement, and Emil's voice, moderately responding. Garland got up, and peered cautiously through the curtain. Emil sat on the edge of the bed with a sheaf of papers on his knees. Medric, lenses aglow with candlelight, talked wildly, his long, thin fingers flickering in the cold air.

Emil spotted Garland and said wryly, "Sometimes we have nights like this. There's no point in begging him to be quiet."

"Oh, my brother!" Medric cried. "It's finished! And you can read it, too!"

Garland said groggily, "I *still* can't read." For although he had been sharing Leeba's alphabet lessons, he suspected he had quite a distance to go.

"But Emil will read it to you. He's a fine reader."

Emil tugged at the tangle of blankets. "Do get in the bed, Garland, and listen for a while. I would consider it a great favor."

The effort of getting the bedding straightened out was enough to wake Garland up completely. "Blessed day," Emil grumbled, shivering in his underclothes. "How did these blankets get to be such a mess? And Medric, why must you and I always be condemned to the one room without a fireplace?"

"It's for the books, really," said Medric. "They like it airy."

"But why must we sleep with them? A man might be forgiven for wishing he might occasionally be just a little comfortable."

"Oh, no, no, no," Medric admonished him. "Not a little, not even for a moment! Shaftal is a discomforting mistress!"

Garland got rather self-consciously under the blankets, which were extremely heavy but not at all warm, and Emil tucked a stale-smelling pillow under his head. "That was a re-markable thing you did with that fowl tonight," he said. Be-yond him, Medric bounced excitedly on his toes, apparently trying to jump out of his skin. "I have to say," continued Emil, "it's a pleasure to see Karis finally putting on that weight she lost from being sick this spring. She was looking an awful lot like a smoke addict again, and I was finding it unsettling. Pre-sent miseries are bad enough, without always being reminded of past ones."

Garland said, "Karis used to look like a smoke addict? Why?"

"Because she was one." Emil got under the blankets beside Garland, and muttered, "Well, *that* was hardly worth the effort. Do you think we have even a hope of becoming warm?"

Garland, trying and failing to imagine Karis as one of those numbed, obsessed, starved, shadow-people that in the last few years had become increasingly rare in Shaftal, replied rather vaguely, "No hope at all."

"What is the matter, Medric?" said Emil innocently.

Medric pushed the sheaf of papers at him. "I beg you! Read! In your clear, compelling, quavering—"

"—candid, cantankerous—" said Emil.

"—querulous voice!"

Smiling, Emil picked up the first page and held it at an angle to capture the candle light. "A History of My Father's People," he read. "Being an Account of the Sainnites, and How They Came to Shaftal, a Discussion of How to Understand Them, and Why They are Doomed."

He put down the sheet and rubbed his eyes. "A very specific and compelling title. Who could resist reading the book?"

Medric rubbed his hands gleefully. "I should think that no one could resist! And at this time of year, there's nothing else to do anyway, and thanks to the Sainnites, there's nothing to read."

"They can cook," interjected Garland.

"While someone reads to them."

"And fix things," said Emil.

"But someone will read to them while they work! Twenty or thirty people at once might hear a single reading. And then they'll bring it to their neighbors, who will bring it to their neighbors . . . !" Unable to contain himself, Medric leapt to his feet, with the quilt in which he was wrapped trailing him like a cloak. But the attic was filled with books—floor to ceiling—and he could only walk three paces before he ran into a pile of stacked crates. Nose to nose with the crate, he cried, "We'll print five hundred copies! And two hundred thousand people will have read it by spring mud!"

"I know better than to question your ciphering," Emil said, "But there are a few *practical* problems."

Medric snorted dismissively.

Garland said to Emil in a low voice, "Are the Sainnites really doomed?"

"Hmm." Emil leafed through the sheets, and gradually his face became nearly as gleeful as Medric's. "Look at those numbers! That's got to be giving some poor officer any number of sleepless nights. They have only a few hundred children, and it takes as many as ten to replace one dead soldier? They're doomed, all right! Medric, bring the candle, will you?" Medric sat on the bed with the candle in his hand, grinning like a maniac. In a steady, clear voice, Emil began to read, interrupted only by Medric's occasional snort or chuckle.

The people you call Sainnites would more properly be called Carolins—born into a soldier caste that happened to serve under the warlord of Sainna. My father served that warlord with honor until he was driven out of Sainna by fellow Carolins, who served different warlords and were simply following or-

ders. My father was just a young man then and it's difficult to say how accurate his version of events is, but I have talked to several other veterans and they all tell a similar story, so I believe it is true enough. They say the lord of Sainna was a greedy man whose holdings encompassed a great stretch of sea coast, including several important harbors. In Shaftal, the harbors are important to the fisherfolk who ride the high tides over the rocks that will wreck their ships at lower tides; in the harbors the fishing boats can safely unload and can take shelter from the storms that make navigation so hazardous. But in Sainna, the harbors were big and deep, accessible at any tide, with long docks that served ships two or three times the size of the largest Shaftali fishing boat. These harbors were places that people went to make their fortunes, young people hoping to sign on as sailors, merchants with money to invest, hoping to sell a boatload of something to another country at a profit, and the Lord of Sainna himself, who collected inordinate shipping taxes and regularly punished his land-bound neighbors by refusing to let them travel to the coast or to use his harbors. So the day came that three of the neighboring warlords banded together against him, having agreed in advance that they each would get one of Sainna's ports and a corridor to the sea. Their Carolin soldiers were no better fighters than those of Sainna, but the numbers were overwhelming, and they literally drove the army of Sainna into the sea. Eventually, the refugees reached Shaftal, far to the north, after a hazardous crossing of an unfriendly sea that sometimes is covered with floating ice mountains.

My father was eighteen, more than old enough to fight, a marksman of some renown already, but who was, he used to tell me, of no use at all in that last, chaotic battle where it was all hand-to-hand fighting and there was no time for loading pistols. He survived unscathed by simple luck and can scarcely remember his escape, he was so bewildered and exhausted with fighting. He had four close friends of his own age, and by the time he was climbing the ladder to board a commandeered ship, all of his friends had disappeared and he never saw them

again, nor did he know what had become of them. Of all the
griefs he bore in his short life—for he was dead at thirty-five—
it was the loss of those friends that weighed most heavily on
him, for though there are many criticisms my father's people
justly deserve, it can't be said that they aren't loyal to their
friends.

My father drew a map once, of that faraway land he hailed
from. He could not read or write, but he remembered where the
major rivers and boundaries lay, and where an army on the
move might easily travel, and what lord ruled what territory.
He had studied that map as a boy, for like all Carolins, his life
depended upon knowing where he was and where he was going. Still, he might leave on a journey through a friendly neighbor's territory and have the friend turn enemy before the
journey's end, and there was nothing he could do to save his
life then.

Lately, travel in Shaftal has also gotten hazardous, for there
are bandits and hostile farmholds where before they were un-
heard of. Still, it is difficult for a Shaftal-born person to imagine what my father's homeland was like: I have caught
glimpses of it in my dreams, an easy, sunny place of gentle
winds and fertile soil, criss-crossed by guarded boundaries
and walls to keep one lord from encroaching on another's territory. The soil is rich because of all the blood that's been
spilled in defense or attack, and some of the slights over which
these lords still battle are centuries old. I asked my father once
to explain it to me, why the people all are willing to die over
some high lord's whim, and my father was angry with me that I
did not instinctively understand the requirements of a soldier's
honor.

To understand the Carolins—the Sainnites, as they are
called here—it is necessary to understand what they mean by
honor. To discipline oneself to accept and fulfill one's station
and to do it with pride, that is honor. To do as commanded
without question or hesitation, that is honor. To want with all
your heart and soul for your people, whoever they are, to gain
ascendancy at any cost, that is honor. To dishonor oneself,

then, is to question tradition, to think for oneself, to desire differently from one's father or mother. These are the things a Carolin soldier will never do, or at least will not admit to.

I am, by Carolin standards, a dishonorable man. I suppose I should disclose this fact early, so that you might slam this book shut in disgust if that is your bent, and not waste further time on it. I am writing this book that you might understand the tragedy of my father's people, how their honor has brought them to the point of extinction in this land they once thought their refuge. And yet I am writing in my mother's tongue, Shaftalese, because it is the Shaftali people who most need to learn from this history. The worst thing they have done to you, who are my mother's people, was not to destroy your government, take your food and children, deny your traditions, or outlaw your greatest powers. The worst thing they have done is to replace your version of honor with theirs. They are making you, the Shaftali people, into Carolins. So when you read this book, read it not as a history of the enemy, but as a history of your own future: what will happen to Shaftal when the Carolins are extinct, but live on in you and your children. Rather than defeat the enemies, you must change them—or else, someday, their story will be your story.

The text continued, but Garland fell asleep. When he awoke to rising daylight, Emil and Medric were still huddled together in the bed with him, with pages of the manuscript scattered about. They seemed to be arguing their way through it, word by word, and inexplicably enjoying themselves so much that it had not occurred to them to go to sleep.

Garland stumbled downstairs to light the ovens and knead the bread dough. His hands knew their work, and he shaped his loaves in a daze of sleepy satisfaction.

Karis appeared and went outside with the scrap bucket, and soon Garland could hear the ringing of her ax. Then Medric poked his head in the kitchen door and asked, "Did you tell her?"

"Tell who what?"

"Very good." Medric disappeared, and Garland heard him go out the front door. "Karis!" he called. "Karis, Karis, Karis!"

The ax fell silent. Garland left his loaves to rise and his ovens to heat, put on his coat, and took another coat from the hook for Medric. Outside, the ravens fought over the scraps that Karis had spilled across the snow. The ax, driven into the stump, quivered in the cold glare of the sun. Karis and Medric sat together at the top of the porch steps. Her hair stuck out stiffly below her cap; her eyes were as blue and crisp as the sky. Garland put Medric's coat on him.

"I did wonder what we were hauling a printing press around for," Karis said to Medric. "But does anyone know how to use it? I doubt it."

"Oh, you're as bad as Emil," Medric said. "It doesn't *matter,* Karis. It's just a *machine.* You'll figure it out."

"Not necessarily. I never learned to cook or sew."

"Your hands are too big, and you just didn't like the idea. But you like the idea of printing a book, don't you?"

She looked at him askance. "I think you'd better get J'han to mix you a potion."

Leaning on the wall nearby, Garland began to laugh helplessly. He muffled his face in his collar.

"You think," Karis added, "that we can typeset, print, and bind five hundred books."

"Emil knows book-binding."

"But the typesetting, Medric! It takes years of training!"

"It only has to be readable, though. And we have to do it."

"Oh, well, if we *have* to . . . ," she said sarcastically.

"Good!" Apparently having become aware of the cold, Medric huddled, grinning, in his coat. "Emil and J'han between them must know practically everyone worth knowing in Shaftal. We'll get the books to their friends, and they'll give them to their friends . . ."

"We?" said Karis. "How, exactly? In dead of winter? You *are* mad."

He nodded so enthusiastically that his neck appeared pliable as a noodle. Karis gazed at him with fond exasperation. "Tell me, master seer," she said, "We need sledges to move the books, but how can I build sledges without any wood?"

He gestured expansively at the nearby trees.

"Green wood will be too heavy."

"Well, you'll think of something." He yawned so abruptly and prodigiously that Garland yawned with him in sympathy.

"And what of Long Night?" she asked.

Medric looked for a moment like he didn't know what she was talking about. "I can't see that far," he finally confessed. "Too many possibilities, too much unknown. If I knew that Zanja knows she is alive . . . or if I knew what the creature in her skin is doing . . . or if I knew anything about her, really . . ." He seemed, then, suddenly human: crestfallen, his fierce enthusiasm burnt to ashes, his wild certainties revealed as mere guesswork.

"Is it time to send a raven to Watfield?"

"No, no, I think not. Not yet. Restrain yourself."

"You're hardly the one to lecture me about restraint!"

"Hardly," he said agreeably. "By the lands, I am exhausted. I don't even know why. I'm going to bed now."

When he was gone, Karis glanced at Garland. "He doesn't know why he's tired? One conversation with him and *I'm* exhausted."

"You just need some breakfast." Garland's face, stiff with cold, felt as if it would crack.

"Will you cook eggs? Should I go down the hill and get us some?"

Garland squatted with his back against the house's sturdy stone side. "The G'deon of Shaftal wants to walk two miles in the snow to fetch her cook some eggs?"

"Yes." She stretched her long legs, and her feet reached to the bottom step. "I have no patience, Garland. Zanja liked to comment on her lack of patience, though as far as anyone could see, her patience was supernatural. She could wait with such stillness that she practically disappeared. All the while, she was silently, motionlessly, unnoticeably—exploding."

Garland couldn't see Karis's face. She was looking across the snow's aching glare. But her big, dirty hands, belying the quiet, steady tone of her voice, had clenched into fists.

Garland said, "The two of you were a bit alike, I guess."

Karis looked at him. "Let me fetch some eggs. It'll be another hour in which I won't go mad. I can stretch it out to two hours, probably, by chatting with the farmers about their livestock. When I get home, you'll feed me a lot of good food, and only then will I have to figure out what to do with the rest of the day. Maybe I'll be lucky enough that someone will break something, so I can fix it." She sighed. "The G'deon of Shaftal?" she said belatedly.

"There's a lot I don't understand about that. But these learned people insist that's what you are."

Karis said dryly, "I've heard that rumor too. But I never gave it much credence. *Do* we need eggs?"

"I'm afraid not."

"A kind man would have lied."

"One never knows when a Truthken might be listening."

She tilted her head back to look at him. The corners of her eyes were crinkled with squinting into the sun. "You mustn't like us, Garland. It's terribly dangerous. We'll catch you up in some mad scheme. We'll make you pack up your pots and abandon that sweet oven, in dead of winter, to trudge about in the teeth of various snowstorms, trying to convince a bunch of bored farmers to read a seditious book."

"Oh, I don't mind." Garland looked at her sun-brilliant eyes, her weathered skin, the twisted mess of her hair. "To have my own kitchen used to be my life's ambition," he added in some amazement. "It was not too long ago."

"Oh, for pity's sake. What has that crazy seer done to you?"

Garland tried to think of an answer. He did not think Medric was even to blame.

Karis continued, with an agitation that seemed altogether unfeigned, "We come to you with our weary spirits, our broken hearts, our extremely baffled minds, and you make us biscuits, sausage rolls, jam buns, poached eggs with that amazing sauce, seed cakes, roast fowl varnished with that delicious shiny stuff—"

"Raspberry jam glaze."

"I walk into your realm, and you hand me something to eat.

Whatever it is tastes so good that my fears and worries drop dead on the spot. I sit there with my mouth full, knowing nothing but how good it is. It isn't *food*, Garland. It's *sanity*."

Garland picked flakes of dried dough off his hands. He felt quite speechless.

"Don't change," she said.

"I'll stop cooking for you when you stop needing to eat. And I don't need a kitchen."

"Is that a promise? I'll hold you to it." She was laughing. She had no idea what she had just given him.

Garland managed to say after a while, "Can you explain something?"

"Explaining things, that's what Emil does."

"But I have trouble understanding him, he uses so many words."

She glanced back at him. "He does that to entertain Medric. Words are as good as sex to those two."

"Oh," Garland said. Then, as comprehension belatedly came to him, he exclaimed, "Oh!"

She was grinning. "But Emil can be perfectly plain spoken; just ask him. What do you want me to explain? You understand I'll do it badly?"

"Why is it so important that you don't take any action, if inaction is driving you mad?"

Garland began to wish he hadn't asked, after a while. He could see that Karis's light spirits had gotten heavy, and she was squinting across the yard again, as though she could see through the woods, down the mountain, across the rough landscape of that rocky land, all the way to Watfield. And perhaps, he realized suddenly, that was precisely what she *was* doing. It was a dazzling, unnerving possibility. She said at last, "Imagine you've got a tray of food balanced on one hand. And you need to add something really heavy to the tray."

"A steamed pudding?"

"Yes, a steamed pudding. The only place you can safely put that pudding is in the middle of the tray, right above your hand. If you get it even slightly wrong, the entire meal goes to the floor."

Garland could almost see it: the shattered plates, the splattered gravy, the flying peas, the dismayed cook, the ravenous diners startled by the disaster. "I'd be very careful where I put that pudding," he said.

"Well, I'm the pudding."

"Oh." There was a long silence. "I do need eggs after all," Garland finally said. "And I was wondering if you could—" He hastily considered his long list of chores. "If you could sharpen my knives. And don't you need to figure out how that press works? And where to get some wood for sledges?"

"So much to do," said Karis gratefully. "And I haven't even chopped the firewood yet. I'd better get busy."

❀❀❀❀❀❀❀❀❀❀❀❀❀❀❀

Chapter Twenty-Six

It was a howling night, one of those godawful storms that made Clement wonder how humankind ever managed to get a foothold in this dreadful land. She had been checking on the progress of her sledges in the carpentry shed. The armorers had finally finished the runners, which should have been simple enough to fabricate, and all that remained to be done was the harness work. Soon Clement's soldiers, who had finally developed a sullen competence with snow-shoes, would have something new to learn and complain about.

She built up the fire in her small, plain room, but unless she stood right on the hearth she couldn't feel the warmth. The night bell had long since rung, Gilly would be deep in a drugged sleep, and Clement decided she might as well go to bed. Like all soldiers, she had saved up her housekeeping tasks for winter, and could have done some mending, or put a new coat of paint on her table. But it was too cold.

There was a knock at her door and she opened it with her tunic half unbuttoned. A man with snow thick on his hood gave her a shivering salute. "Lieutenant-General, the storyteller is at the gate."

"The storyteller? What is she doing here at this hour?"

"She says you must come with her at once. Bring the money, she says."

They exchanged baffled looks.

"The storyteller can be a bit close-mouthed," said the gate

guard. "So I thought you ought to talk to her yourself. I'm sorry, though. It's a wretched night."

"Here, stand by the fire for a bit, not that it'll do you much good, since that wind is blowing directly down the chimney."

After she'd bundled up in every warm piece of clothing she had, which she was certain would still not be enough, Clement left the guard still shivering by her poor fire and went downstairs to Gilly's room. She didn't bother to pound on his door, but simply went in and shook him vigorously by the shoulder until he mumbled. "What?"

"I have to go into town."

"Clem?" He turned his head and blinked blearily at her. "That wind," he said, articulating carefully, "will flay you."

"Hell, I'm half frozen and I haven't even been outside yet. Gilly—I think Alrin's decided to accept my offer."

"Congratulations," he said dryly. "You've succeeded in completely mystifying me. And why *are* you going out? Have you explained already, when I was asleep?"

"The storyteller's been sent to fetch me, and she wasn't too forthcoming with the gate guard. But—"

"Oh, Clem!" With his face muffled in the pillow, Gilly uttered a grunt of laughter. "You're about to become a mother."

"I'm afraid so."

"Early."

"Apparently."

"Unprepared."

"Desperately."

"What do you expect me to do about it?"

"Explain my absence to Cadmar, will you? If I'm not back by morning."

"Clem," Gilly said, as she stepped away. "What are you going to do with it?"

"With what?"

"With the baby."

Gilly was just a shadow in the darkness, but she stared at him. "What do you mean?"

"When Alrin hands you her baby," Gilly said, *"What are you going to do with it?"*

She found herself incapable of reply. When she left Gilly's room, he was still laughing, and she could hardly blame him.

When Clement finally reached the gate, having first awakened the garrison clerk to get her funds out of the lockbox, the storyteller waited in shelter, huddled by the brazier alongside the lone guard in the shack. At the sight of Clement, she rose quickly, wrapped a muffler around her face, and pulled on a pair of fur-lined gloves.

They went out into the storm. Clement was still speechless, but in any case, the storm would have made conversation impossible. A miserable journey, staggering down narrow roads with the wind blasting like a river down a canyon. One step at a time, tears freezing on her lashes, face numb, feet like blocks at the end of her legs. A killing wind, flinging ice like daggers. Shutters banged, a piece of slate torn loose from a roof shattered at her feet. "Bloody hell!" The storyteller glanced at her, her eyes a smear of black, rimmed in white snow stuck to the wool that wrapped her face. They staggered on.

The wind was barred from Alrin's house, but still it roared, only somewhat muffled by latched shutters, locked doors, and heavy curtains. A single lamp flame flickered in the hall; the house seemed empty. The storyteller pulled the muffler from her face. Clement followed her to the kitchen, where together they built up the fire and then unwrapped themselves. When Clement's face had thawed enough, she asked, "How long until the child is born?"

The storyteller stomped snow from her boots. "I will ask the midwife." She left the kitchen.

A chair was drawn up to the fire, with a work basket beside it. Clement sat down, shivering, and waited. She waited a long time. Once, she thought she heard a groan or cry, but it could have been the wind. The storyteller returned. "The midwife cannot say how long it will be."

"But Alrin has borne several children."

The storyteller held her hands out to the fire; her fingers were still gray with cold. "This one is different."

She swung the kettle over the fire, and then went moving about the dark kitchen. Distracted, still thawing out, Clement stared into the fire until the kettle began to utter enthusiastic spurts of steam. Then she watched the storyteller make tea: a surprisingly fussy process of pouring small quantities of water, waiting, swirling the pot, sniffing the steam, and adding more water. The rich, grass-and-flower scent of the tea brought Clement out of her daze. "I've never seen anyone make tea like that."

The storyteller paused.

"Usually, they just pour the water and let it sit."

"This is the way I know."

"How do you know it?"

The storyteller poured some water, took another sniff, and put on the lid. She brought over the tea table, on which she had laid bread and butter, and a selection of cold foods: pickles, cheese, salt meat, jam. She poured the tea, and Clement took a sip. Whether due to the method or to the ingredients, it was delicious.

"I can't answer your question," the storyteller said. "I know many things but I don't know how I came to know them."

After a moment, Clement said, "I suppose having no memories could be a blessing."

The storyteller said nothing, as though loss and gain were no more important to her than they were to a dumb beast. She drew a stool up to the fire, and took a cup of tea.

Clement sipped her tea and waited, and the storyteller never became impatient, never looked at her questioningly, never seemed restless at all. She held the teacup in her palms of her hands and warmed her fingers with it. Her solitary, remarkably long braid lay across her wool-clad back like a mislaid piece of yarn. Her boots steamed in the heat of the hearth.

Clement said, "I haven't even considered what to do with this baby when it's born. I suppose I assumed I'd have time to . . . do whatever I am supposed to do."

The storyteller said, "You must find someone to nurse it. A woman in milk, who will raise this baby beside her own, or whose own child is dead, or has been taken from her."

"I have no idea how to find such a woman."

"The midwife will know." There was a silence, and the storyteller added, "It may be difficult."

"You mean it will cost me even more money?"

"The Shaftali people do not raise children casually."

While Clement watched in stunned silence, the storyteller sipped her tea until the cup was empty. "The child could *die*," Clement finally said. "While I'm running around looking for a young, willing woman with milk in her breasts . . ."

The storyteller nodded indifferently. "The Laughing Man is doing his work tonight."

"The Laughing Man?"

The storyteller reached into her boot and took out a pack of cards. Without looking, as though she knew the cards by feel, she took one out: a primitive woodcut of a man, laughing gleefully in the midst of a wrecked house. The storyteller's fingertip touched the red symbol stamped on one corner. "This glyph means fate, or chance. The Laughing Man's actions are so unexpected, and their effect is so profound, that his victims think it is a bitter joke. He destroys everything—even trust and hope. But there is one power that can counteract his." She took out another card: a circle of people, arm in arm. "Fellowship," she said.

Clement said, finally, as the storyteller secured the pack with a leather thong, "To own these cards is illegal. To use them, to know how to use them, to use them in front of a Sainnite officer . . . !"

Silent, serious, fearless, the storyteller tucked the cards into her boot.

The strangest aspect of this woman's madness was how sane it seemed, how utterly coherent. If Clement asked the storyteller where she got her cards, or how she learned to read them, the storyteller certainly would respond that she did not remember. But she used them, as she used everything, as a tool for storytelling. She was not a friend or a lover, a member of a tribe, of a family; she had no past and neither feared nor desired the future. She was a storyteller only, and that was what both explained her coherence and defined her madness.

The storyteller gazed at Clement: a long gaze, incurious, unblinking.

Clement said, "Don't let anyone else see those cards, or you will be a dead woman. Do I owe you a story now?"

"You told me a story already, a tale of a woman who contracted to buy a child without realizing that she also had to make a home for it."

Clement snorted. "A ridiculous tale. Who wouldn't realize—" There was a sound from upstairs, a wrenching cry of a sort Clement had heard too often in her life, but always before on a battlefield. "My mother's gods!"

She leapt to her feet, but the storyteller's voice stopped her. "Marga will not allow you into the room."

"She's dying!"

"Yes." The storyteller picked up her empty cup from the floor, and re-filled it.

The house again lay still, a silence wrapped around by howling wind. The Laughing Man leaves wreckage in his wake, inevitably, unstoppably. Clement returned eventually to the chair; there was nothing she could do.

Sometime before dawn, the storm began to lose its force. Clement was awakened by the storyteller building up the fire. She had slept in the chair, covered by a blanket, but the storyteller had perched unmoving on the stool all night. Now, she swung the kettle over flame once again, and began the ritual of making another pot of tea. Clement said, "Has something happened?"

Her reply was a faint rapping at the front door. The storyteller went to answer it, and quickly returned. "The Lucky Man is here."

"What?" Clement leapt to her feet, snatched the corner of the blanket out of the coals, and then wrapped it around herself like a shawl. She went out into the bitter chill, into a city glazed with ice, with drifts of snow piled head-high by the harsh wind. A snow plow, dragged by two massive, steaming plow-horses, worked its way slowly down the street. At Alrin's gate, which was half buried in a drift of snow, Gilly waited on horseback, attended by a red-cheeked, shivering young soldier. The storyteller came out behind Clement, with cups of tea emitting clouds of steam in the chill. She gave one to Gilly and one to his aide, then disappeared into the house again.

Clement said vaguely, "It's almost as if the storyteller knew that you were coming."

"People with talents like hers often have some prescience." Gilly gulped his tea. "Any word?"

"Not yet."

Gilly looked grim. "And Alrin has been laboring all night?"

"The storyteller implies . . ." Clement took too deep a breath, and choked on the searing air. "Gods, Gilly, what are you doing here?"

"The storyteller says what?"

"Alrin will die."

"Well." He gulped his tea again, and handed Clement first the cup, then the basket that rested before him on the saddle. "I've made inquiries. But it will not be easy to find a nurse. Meanwhile, I think I've gotten everything you need, even some milk." He spoke briskly, no doubt to cover his embarrassment.

She stared at him, speechless from gratitude and sleeplessness.

He continued, "Ask the midwife to show you how to care for the child. And offer her a commission for helping you to find a nurse. But don't offend her."

"How would I do that?" she asked humbly.

"By giving her orders as though she were a soldier."

"Gilly . . . I can't keep a baby in the garrison!"

"I'll tell Cadmar it's temporary. Now get inside." He smiled a gruesome smile, twisted as always.

"I'm in your debt, I think."

"Are you? I lost track several years ago."

She reached up, and he reached down, and briefly clasped her hand.

Back in the kitchen, the storyteller took the empty cups from her, then examined the contents of Clement's basket, and gave an approving nod. "Fellowship," she commented, and went to put the bottle of milk in the cold cupboard.

Some hours later, Marga came into the kitchen, carrying a bundle wrapped so as to reveal a solemn, old man's face and blue, unfocused eyes. Clement gave Marga the money, and Marga put the baby in her arms, like a shopkeeper handing over a sack of sugar.

"I need to speak to the midwife!" Clement said in a panic.

"She's busy," Marga said. "The storyteller will show you out." She left the kitchen, hurrying, leaving Clement with a fleeting glimpse of her harried face and fatigue-smeared eyes. The storyteller followed her out, and for some little time Clement was left alone to stare at the baby, who blinked vaguely at her, opened and closed a toothless mouth and made random movements in its bindings. Clement felt a swift, deep shifting in her heart. Everything felt askew, and yet this giddiness was not entirely due to fear.

The storyteller returned. "The midwife knows of a possible nurse. She'll speak to her tomorrow, and send her to the garrison, if she's willing."

"But I need her to show me what to do!"

The storyteller said, "She cannot leave Alrin."

Clement stood like a dumb animal, watching without seeing, as the storyteller put a few things in a basket: her silken performance clothes, a wooden comb. Then she took the baby so Clement could put on her coat. She gave the infant back, now wrapped in three small blankets from Gilly's basket, and put on her own outdoor clothing. She got the bottle of milk from the cupboard, and picked up both the baskets in one hand.

The storyteller held open the kitchen door for Clement. On the table in the front hall, where the lamp had long since burned itself out, she placed a latchkey. She opened the front door, and Clement walked out into the blinding day, where a cold sun glanced around scudding shreds of clouds, and the street was busy with people, old and young, all wielding snow shovels. The storyteller closed the door firmly.

The infant stirred in the cold and uttered a small complaining sound. The storyteller arranged a fold of blanket to shield its face, then took Clement by the arm to steady her on the snowy walk.

"You're coming with me?" asked Clement.

In a voice made rough by cold the storyteller said, "I will teach you to care for your son."

"My son?" said Clement blankly. She looked down at the bundled baby. Then, the finality with which the storyteller had shut that door sank in. "Storyteller? Marga won't tolerate you after Alrin is gone?"

"Marga will do what she wants, now."

A silence. The street had been scattered with sand, and the storyteller took her supporting hand from Clement's elbow. Clement said, "Gilly and I will take care of you, somehow."

The baby in her arms seemed suddenly much heavier. She looked at him, and realized he was asleep.

Chapter Twenty-Seven

In the dim, chilly cellar, Karis painted the blocks of type with viscous ink that Garland had cooked the day before. She took the sheet of paper from Garland, carefully checked the side that was already printed to make certain she oriented it properly, and laid it delicately on top of the plate. She screwed down the press, waited a moment, then swiftly unscrewed it and lifted off the printed sheet, to hand to Garland.

Both of them were covered with ink, their clothing stained, their fingers black, their faces smudged. Holding the sheet carefully by the edges, Garland felt so tired he could not summon up a comment, though it seemed to him an appropriate moment for ponderous statements. Karis dug her knuckles into the small of her back. "Is it right side up?"

Garland glanced at both sides of the big sheet, on which were printed eight pages of Medric's booklet. "It's right."

"We're done, then."

He carried the page up the narrow stone stairs to the kitchen, which was strung with rope on which the drying sheets hung like tablecloths on a busy tavern's laundry line. The entire household had gathered, and, as Garland came through the door, they clapped and uttered huzzahs.

Leeba, who ran giddily up and down the strung lines of paper, contributed a few shrieks. Though she had not been allowed in the cellar, she had managed to become an ink-child, more smeared than Karis, more stained than Garland. She chanted as she ran: "The last page! Of the last book! Of the last year!"

J'han captured her. "But not the last ba⎯

She squealed like a piglet. J'han, who h⎯ ⎯⎯
one of them patient and persistent enough t⎯ ⎯⎯
ting, gripped her a bit more determinedly than ⎯
got to get her to go to sleep," he said ominously.⎯

Norina took the child from him. Leeba abruptly ⎯⎯ limp
and obedient, for which Garland, although he could now tolerate being in the same room as Norina, did not blame her.
Medric took the last sheet of paper from Garland's hands, and
ceremoniously hung it from a line.

Karis had been wearing a shirt that belonged in the rag bag.
Ducking paper, she stripped it off, tossed it to the floor, and, in
her undershirt, lay face down on Garland's table. "I need a
healer," she moaned.

J'han went to her promptly, and examined her back. With
unconcealed appreciation he said, "You are a fine specimen!
Look here," he said to Garland. "You don't often see a *musculus trapezius* so developed. Even her *musculus triceps brachii*
is obvious. What an anatomy lesson she would be!"

Garland looked where J'han pointed, apparently surprising
the healer by actually showing some interest. J'han happily explained the details of Karis's construction, pulling aside her
shirt to point out the connections of muscle to bone, to explain
what each one did, and to speculate on why and how the muscles of her back had developed as they had.

"Blessed day," said Emil in a muted voice.

Garland looked around to find that Emil, with Medric folded
comfortably to his chest, was gazing at Karis's amazing back
with an astonished expression, as though it had only just occurred to him to be impressed by her. A deep man like him might
neglect to notice the surfaces of things, Garland supposed.

Karis groaned pathetically.

"I'm done lecturing," J'han assured her. His probing fingers
paused. "Spasm. I guess that hurts." He leaned all his weight into
the heels of his hands and shoved the breath out of Karis's chest.

Emil sighed. "The methods by which we divert ourselves
are rather peculiar."

"Eccentric, even," said Medric.

"Desperate," said Norina, who had gotten the abnormally passive child into the washtub.

Both men blinked at this. Emil said, "Desperate. And bookbinding is next. If you thought printing was dull . . ."

"I won't do it," Karis said, her voice strangled by the pressure on her back. "All that fussing. I need to move more."

"Deliveries after that," said Medric. "Lots of moving."

"Oh!" said Karis.

"There," said J'han in satisfaction, apparently addressing Karis's anatomy. "That was very obedient of you."

Karis took several deep breaths, but seemed disinclined to move otherwise. J'han began methodically to work on one muscle at a time, and Karis grew so limp that Garland wondered if she might simply slither off the table like a very slimy fish.

Eyes closed, she mumbled, "Emil, are you still there?"

"Still here, and still diverted. But now it's by envy. Why has J'han never done that to me? Obviously, I'm not as beautiful to look at—"

"Where are we going?" Karis asked. "Have we decided?"

"Oh, while you were down in the cellar we did take a look at Norina's maps, and we figure that we only actually need to visit some ten people—the right ten, of course, who know a lot of other people—but I've got a good idea of who the right ten people are. So we can walk right across the middle of Shaftal, west to east, with a certain amount of meandering north and south. The weather will be terrible, I suppose, but you'll help us dodge the storms. Do you want to see the map?"

"I put them away," said Norina, busy with the wash cloth. Leeba peered, rather trapped looking, from behind a mask of soap bubbles.

Garland fetched the map case, and took out a roll of several maps on heavy, sturdy paper, the most remarkable maps he had ever seen, for they appeared to be marked with every single road and path, village, hill, waterway, and stand of trees in the entire country of Shaftal. He held up the maps one by one before Karis's eyes until she reached with an ink-black finger to point at an undistinguished area. "What's here? I can't read it."

Emil took the map from Garland to bring it closer to the

lamp. "I think you were pointing at a sheep-shearing station. It's pretty far from anywhere, and surely it's not even occupied at this time of year."

J'han had switched his attentions to Karis's shoulder blades. She had shut her eyes again. She said, in a heavy, exhausted voice, "No, Emil. Mabin is there."

Mabin, Garland thought. Councilor Mabin, general of Paladins. The one with the spike in her heart.

"Do you want to visit her?" Emil's tone was neutral, but Garland noticed a sudden liveliness in his face.

"Want?" Karis said. "No, of course not."

"Ought," Emil corrected himself patiently.

"Ought," said Medric firmly.

The Truthken briskly rubbed her shivering daughter with a towel. "Karis will protect you, Garland, so don't go into a panic."

Garland realized then that panic was exactly what he felt.

"The earth will open its mouth and chew up that woman alive if she even threatens my people," said Karis. "And she'll *beg* me to let her heart stop beating."

Her tone was so hard, and so matter-of-fact, that Garland said in a small voice, "Literally?"

Emil said, "Earth logic, you know, is awfully literal. And Karis, well, she's always been a bit—" He paused, apparently to hunt down and capture the most exact term. "—Definite," he said. "When she does something, she does it. And you know she's done it. And you never forget it."

"And it can really hurt," said Medric.

Karis raised her head. She looked at Medric, and then at Emil. "You two can hardly wait," she said.

The parlor had become a makeshift bindery, lit by the household's entire collection of lamps. Norina stood in the corner, methodically folding and slashing sheets of paper. Emil sorted and ordered the pages and then, like Garland, plied a heavy needle and thread to sew the pages together. Finally, J'han and Leeba glued on the paper covers, and yesterday's ink-child had been transformed into a glue-child. After an entire morning of sewing, Garland still could not quite believe that books are held together at their centers by needle and thread. Such a homely thing! His fingers hurt, and he was glad to abandon the sewing occasionally to check his stewpot.

In the afternoon, Medric came down the stairs, and Leeba, who had gotten very bored with painting glue on paper, leaped up with a cry. "Medric! I have a surprise!" She produced with a flourish a very crooked, glue-blotted, ink-smeared book.

"Is that it?" said Medric. "My book?" He swept her up, book and all, and went twirling up and down the hallway with her in a dizzy dance, while she recounted, between shrieks of laughter, her very important role in the construction of this first book. Medric said, "I know exactly where this one is to go." He poked his head into the parlor. "Stop slaving away in the gloom! Let's give this book a proper send-off."

But first the book had to be wrapped in oilcloth and tied with twine, and the knots sealed with red wax. The resulting package was carried outside in triumph, with Medric waving it proudly, and the rest of them following in grimy procession: J'han rubbing his sticky hands ineffectually with a rag, Garland sucking a needle-pierced fingertip, Emil playing a riddle game with Leeba, Norina intent as a cat stalking a mouse. Out they went into the cold, bright day and Karis came up the slope to greet them, pulling a completed sledge. To get the wood she had dismantled every cupboard in the house, leaving Garland's kitchen in complete disarray as a result. A hammer was tucked into her belt, and her pockets bulged with pegs or nails. Planes, a brace-and-bit, saws, and mallets scattered the porch where she had been working.

"What's that?" she said, when Medric waved his package at her.

"A book," he said importantly.

"Just one?"

"The *first* one," Leeba said.

"Well, put it in the sledge. And then go make four hundred and ninety-nine more."

"You have no sense of ceremony," grumbled Medric. "Now listen! This book shall not be hauled across the snow. No weary journey 'cross hill and dale, no hostile, porridge-eating farmers to be tempted to use it to start their breakfast fires. No, that may be its brother's fate, but not this one. Not this one!" He held it up, and shook it for emphasis. "This one shall be delivered by ravens!"

"Give it to me," Karis said.

Medric came down the porch steps and handed it to her. She weighed it in the palm of her hand. "You should have written a shorter book. How far do you expect it to be carried?"

"To Watfield."

The amusement faded from her cold-flushed face. "Medric—"

Medric gave an elaborate shrug, that seemed to begin with his feet, and traveled upwards in a loose-limbed movement that made him seem on the verge of collapsing into a pile of disconnected bones.

She looked at him, eyes glinting, mouth drawn tight, Garland suspected, to keep herself from uttering words that might at best be discourteous. When she spoke at last, however, it was to say prosaically, "Fortunately, Garland has been stuffing the ravens with corn bread."

The ravens arrived as she spoke: dropping from the roof, from the treetops, from the cloud-draped sky. "What—what—what?" they cried.

Medric turned completely around, a giddy man in a maelstrom of flapping wings. "You're sending them *all*?"

"I have to, so they can carry your heavy book in relay." With a very small, very mocking bow, Karis returned to the seer the packaged book. He lifted it over his head, balanced on his fingertips. The ravens rose up again in a flapping cloud that briefly cloaked him, and then he was empty handed, and one of the departing ravens dangled the package from its claw.

"Good-bye!" Medric cried. "Good luck!" Leeba, and then the rest of them, joined him in shouting their farewells. But Karis stood silent, monolithic, with her hands jammed in her pockets, squinting in the light as she watched the ravens fly away.

Chapter Twenty-Eight

The door latched softly. Clement, who had fallen asleep with the baby in the crook of her arm and a nippled milk bottle resting precariously on her chest, slitted open her eyes to see that it was the storyteller, slipping in unhindered and unescorted, pulling the hood back from her sharp-edged face. Clement mumbled, "Is it day or night?"

"Almost suppertime."

"Where have you been?"

"I owed Alrin a story." The storyteller hung her cloak on a hook and began stripping off and folding her plain wool clothing.

"How is she doing?" said Clement with surprise.

"She's dead. Since yesterday."

The storyteller had been telling stories to a dead woman.

Clement looked down at her son, who blinked at her as though in abject amazement. She felt a sensation she could not put a name to; it seemed too unfamiliar to be called, simply, sadness.

The room was dark, the storyteller an indifferent shadow, doing up the buttons of her silken performance clothes. Clement had hardly slept in two days. And she was shaken by the enormity and suddenness of the catastrophe she had brought upon herself. Clement let a few tears fall, a luxury so long forbidden she wasn't even certain how to do it. The storyteller, if she even noticed, offered no comment.

Before the woman left for the evening's performance, though, she put a fresh bottle of milk on the windowsill to keep cold, then came over to the bed to check the baby. She had drilled Clement in feeding and diapering as determinedly as Clement had ever drilled a soldier. Clement said, "Do you approve?" Her voice was still rough with tears.

"I visited the midwife," the storyteller said. "The nurse will come tomorrow morning."

"What has taken so long?"

"She's very young. Her parents are reluctant."

Clement thought of a young woman, as young as Kelin, maybe, arguing angrily with an array of disapproving parents. "Hell," she muttered. "Will you tell Gilly that she's coming? And ask him to visit me after the night bell."

After the night bell, Gilly arrived with the storyteller and an aide who was carrying a precarious supper tray. The stew had gotten stone cold on its journey from the refectory, but at least there was some meat in it. Clement ate, and Gilly said, "Cadmar complains that he is unattended."

Clement crushed a fragment of frozen butter onto her cold bread. "He knows I'm leaving in just a couple of days. What does he want from me?"

The storyteller approached them and handed the baby to Gilly, who accepted the bundle with some surprise. She silently left the room.

"Where is she going?" Gilly held the baby awkwardly, looking unnerved.

"She'll sit on her heels in the hallway. Gazing into space."

"Peculiar."

"But it does give me some privacy. Are the soldiers now letting her wander the garrison unescorted?"

"I'll look into it. She mentioned that the nurse is finally coming tomorrow. Are you thinking that the four of you can live in this one room, in harmony?"

"Won't the nurse will take the child away?"

The baby was uttering rhythmic grunting sounds. Gilly looked down at him with a puzzled expression, as though the arrival of this small person were nearly as dismaying to him as it was to Clement. "A young woman, unmarried, no household of her own, apparently acting against her parent's wishes? She'll expect you to provide for her. She's got nowhere to take a child."

"Someone might have told me!" Clement smeared more butter onto her roll. "The storyteller could have told me, if she knew how to volunteer information." Then she mumbled, her mouth full, "I feel like I'm eating frozen sawdust."

"It goes well with that frozen mud puddle." Gilly indicated the gelid bowl of brown stew.

Reminded, Clement swallowed a few chilling spoonfuls. "Fortunately, I know you'd never point out a problem until you'd thought of a solution."

"There's a place available not two buildings away from the gate."

"Keep my own establishment?"

"I would hardly call two rooms an establishment."

The baby uttered a cry, rather experimentally, but Gilly gave a start, which in turn caused the baby to cry in earnest. Clement shoveled in a few more mouthfuls, then took the baby, and admonished him, "Listen, little soldier, we're strategizing your future, and strategy requires concentration."

"The storyteller could also live there," said Gilly, speaking loudly over the baby's wailing. "I'll help with the cost, of course. I've always wanted to be somebody's uncle."

Clement said, "I'm not sure I heard you, with that shrieking in my ear. Did you say you want to be an *uncle*?"

Grinning, Gilly stood up and leaned upon his sturdy cane. "I'll check those rooms in the morning, and if they look passable, I'll rent them on your behalf."

She opened and held the door for him. Out in the hallway, the storyteller rose up lightly from where she had been squatting with her shoulders against the wall. "Let's get some sleep if we can," Clement said to her. "Will you be all right on the stairs, uncle?"

Gilly gestured crudely and shuffled into the shadows.

* * *

When Clement first set eyes on her son's new wet nurse, she was flirting with the soldiers at the gate: a plain, thin, sullen girl, younger than Kelin had been. She unbuttoned despite the chill to display her swollen, milk-leaking breasts. "Satisfied?" she asked sharply, then added placatingly, "Madam."

"What became of your own baby?"

"He went to the father's family." Winking at the goggling soldiers, the girl did up her buttons.

No doubt that this girl would be a trial to Clement, just as she surely had been to her recently discarded parents. In the rented rooms, though, where at Gilly's instigation the plaster was being repaired and furniture was being delivered, the girl sat down beside the glowing coal stove and demonstrated that she could suckle, though the baby appeared to need some training. The storyteller squatted on her heels and watched this amateur performance with what seemed to Clement a healthy skepticism.

Clement squatted beside her. "If this were your son, would you leave him in this girl's care?"

"I cannot answer that question," the storyteller said.

Clement hired the girl only because she had no choice. That night she lay in her own room, alone, trying to convince herself that she appreciated the luxury of an uninterrupted night. At sunrise she was in the rented rooms again, holding her son beside the newly lit stove, having a quiet conversation with him while the nurse and storyteller slept.

"Acquiring a child is no different from acquiring a horse," she said to him. "For every Sainnite but me."

The baby lay in her arms, an unopened package, a blinking, sleepy stranger. "For me," Clement said, "it appears to be a shocking occasion. Perhaps as much as it is for you."

She glanced at the door that hung half ajar to let in the heat, beyond which the storyteller slept on a pallet on the floor. "You can thank the storyteller for this. Or curse her, if you like. Whatever you think she deserves."

The baby uttered a small burbling grunt.

"No, I can't make up my mind either," she said.

* * *

The day of Clement's departure for the children's garrison had arrived too soon. "Where did all those ravens come from?" said Gilly from the back of his horse, as he escorted her to the garrison gate.

Black birds swarmed above the garrison gate. As Clement watched, their flying mass compressed together, then exploded upward, uttering eerily gleeful rattling cries.

The forty gloomy soldiers who awaited Clement at the gate watched the departing birds with undisguised anxiety. "Hell," Clement muttered. Ravens were battlefield birds; Sainnites loathed and feared them. "They'll be thinking those birds are an ill omen."

Gilly was usually contemptuous of soldier superstitions, but now he looked worried.

The gate captain was approaching. Though he was one of the most dispassionate soldiers in the garrison, even he looked discomforted. He carried an unlabeled package wrapped in oilcloth, sealed with red wax, tied with twine, and smeared with bird droppings. "What is it, captain?" asked Clement sharply.

"Lieutenant-General, this thing seemed to fall from the sky."

Involuntarily, Clement looked again at the disappearing flock of ravens. One had separated from the group and now swooped down to land on the peak of a rooftop. Gilly's voice spoke harshly. "Keep your imaginings to yourself, captain!"

It was what Clement should have said to the gate captain. She turned to him belatedly and said, "Morale is going to be tricky enough without the soldiers thinking we're getting packages from ravens."

"Yes, ma'am. But what should I do with this?"

"Give it to me," Gilly said. In a low voice he added to Clement, "Go talk to your soldiers."

She stepped forward to greet Captain Herme, and with him beside her walked through the ranks of the gloomy company, greeting every soldier by name, enthusiastically touting the inevitable success and importance of their venture. By the time she had finished trying to raise their spirits, she could see Cadmar and Ellid arriving for the official departure. She hurried back to Gilly.

Looking both unhappy and unwell, he briefly held up a slim book for her to see, then hid it again in its dirty oilcloth wrappings.

"A book?" said Clement. "In Shaftalese?"

"It purports to be written by Medric."

"That's a Sainnite name," she said. Then she remembered who Medric was. "The one who claimed to be a seer? The one who disappeared from Wilton Garrison? He's written a bloody book?"

"Not just a book, Clem. It's about the Sainnites. And Medric is in fact a seer—a true seer."

"How can you be certain of such a thing?"

"Because he knows the numbers."

She stared at Gilly, dumbstruck. She knew perfectly well what numbers he meant: the secret numbers, which Gilly had ciphered only once and then had burned to ashes. The numbers that were only known to the two of them and to Cadmar.

Gilly continued, "This seer can cipher too. And he has a printing press. No doubt this book is right now being read all over Shaftal. And that seer is taunting us by sending us a copy! Because he knows there isn't a thing we can do about it!"

Clement took in a breath and let it out. "There's nothing we can do," she said. "So don't tell Cadmar."

"Clem—"

"He'll prevent me from going on this mission!"

They stared at each other, then Gilly said grimly, "And that would only compound the disaster." He tucked the grimy package inside his coat. "I'll give you a day."

"Two."

His gaze briefly focused over her shoulder, then he smiled stiffly at her, apparently trying to pretend this was a pleasant conversation. "He's coming over to us."

"Two days, Gilly. I can't be out of his reach in one."

"Right," Gilly said. "Well, I certainly look forward to hearing about all your adventures, and wish you a safe journey."

She turned around and found Cadmar and Ellid had come within hearing. "Well, General, will you wish us well?"

He did. She saluted. He saluted. Ellid saluted. The gate was opened. The soldiers marched out, snowshoes on their backs, dragging awkward sledges that would soon be gliding on snow. Clement followed them out the gate, reeling.

Ten days later, in the teeth of a howling snowstorm, her company arrived at the children's garrison. As Clement explained to Commander Purnal why she had returned, and with such a large escort, his astonishment soon turned to sarcastic appreciation. "So, your bungling has turned our garrison into a symbol! And now you're finally forced to take us seriously! Well, it's six days yet until Long Night, and there's plenty of roof repairs needing to be done in the meantime."

"We're going to remain invisible indoors. You will continue your business as though we were not here. And I'm placing those soldiers I left behind under Captain Herme's command."

"It's only what I expected of you," Purnal said bitterly, and stumped off in a temper.

An experienced Paladin commander who was planning an attack would keep a watch on his target for days beforehand, so to keep their arrival unnoticed Clement's company had avoided roads and farmlands as they neared their destination. Snow-covered streambeds had often offered the best paths as they navigated through the woods by compass and dead reckoning. One glorious day, they had followed a frozen river and had been lucky to find shelter in an empty building with its dock pulled onto the riverbank to keep the ice from destroying it. Most days, though, had been grueling, and at night they sheltered themselves in makeshift constructions of snow, branches, and tarpaulins. It took two days by the hearthfires of the children's garrison for the soldiers to thaw out. But every night, once full dark had fallen, with an audience of fascinated children they rehearsed the battle.

As she endured the empty days, Clement desperately wished she could distract herself. Her room had one small window, and often she opened the shutters and peered out at the pristine snow, sunlit or starlit. Sometimes there were children out in the snow. Watching them, Clement felt a pulling in her chest, as though some physical pieces of her had been left behind in Watfield.

With the visiting war-horses as allies, the children beat down a circular track along which they marched, or chased each other, or pulled each other on makeshift sleds. Around and around the garrison they went. So also Clement's thoughts circled around and around, but they circled a distant place and time, five years in the past: the seer Medric's most recent posting, Wilton Garrison, in South Hill, the summer after Cadmar became general.

That summer, Wilton garrison had been attacked and burned by rockets. The rockets had been invented by Annis, a Paladin woman of South Hill Company. Those same rockets had burned down Watfield.

The leader of Death-and-Life, Willis, had also come from South Hill. If he had learned from Annis how to make the rockets, he must have been a member of South Hill Company—the same company that had held firm in the face of what should have been an overwhelming force of soldiers.

Medric had been a resident of Wilton garrison when it was burned, an attack he inexplicably failed to predict, even though, according to Commander Heras, under whose command he had served, his previous predictions had been devastatingly accurate. Later that summer, he had disappeared.

Willis disappeared. Annis disappeared.

The longtime commander of South Hill Company—a formidable leader, respected even by Heras—disappeared.

Heras reported vague rumors of treachery, of a mysterious member of South Hill Company who Paladins thought was a Sainnite spy. But she also, it seemed, had disappeared.

Surely all these disappearances mean something! Wildly, desperately, Clement wore away the floorboards with her pacing. In the dead of night, in a building filled with sleeping children, she spoke aloud to her empty, solitary room: "What happened in South Hill?"

Some hours later, she asked the question again, differently: "What *began* in South Hill?"

Then it came to her: in the autumn of the same year, a gigantic woman had supposedly plunged a spike into Councilor Mabin's chest without killing her. She had done it because of a mysterious woman. And then the so-called Lost G'deon had disappeared.

Had all these people disappeared together? Would they also reappear together? Annis had reappeared—or at least her devastating rockets had. Willis had reappeared as the leader of Death-and-Life. Medric had reappeared, to blithely publish the Sainnites' most dangerous, most closely kept secret. And a mysterious woman was telling stories in Watfield garrison.

Some hours before dawn, Captain Herme sat up in startlement as Clement walked into his room. "Lieutenant-General, what is wrong?"

She wanted to say, *I am trapped ten days' hard journey from Watfield, and I am going mad.*

But instead she said apologetically, "I'm having a bad night, captain. And it's occurred to me that we've got to capture the leader of this group alive, somehow."

Herme groaned.

"I know—to kill a cage full of rats is easy. To kill all but one is practically impossible."

He groaned again, his hands rasping loudly on his unshaven cheeks. "Can I ask why?"

"I need to ask the man a question."

"But to try to keep him alive will risk our success. Is it that important?"

She wanted to say, *Perhaps it will spare us from being completely exterminated.* But instead she said, "Yes, captain, it is that important."

✳✳✳✳✳✳✳✳✳✳✳✳✳✳✳

Chapter Twenty-Nine

They were huddled around Karis, in the single room that had been afforded them by the farm family on which they had imposed themselves. Leeba, on whom the great adventure of this winter journey had quickly palled, had whined herself to sleep. The rest of them, blistered, frostbitten, and still chilled to the bone, clustered together in their underclothes. A fire burned in the fireplace, but its heat was blocked by drying boots and breeches, long shirts and wool coats. Karis was on her knees before Emil, with his frostbitten foot clasped in both her big hands. His boot, having developed a leak, was in the kitchen being repaired by the farmstead's cobbler.

"You know how still Zanja could be," said Karis.

Emil said, "If Zanja were thinking, or waiting, or listening, she could almost seem absent."

"She is like that all the time, now. Present, but absent. Visible, but invisible. Listening, and silent. I see her form, her flesh, but I don't see *her*."

Emil said, "Perhaps a part of her has replaced the whole."

J'han, who recently had come in from attending an ailing member of the household, got under the covers with Norina and Leeba. Norina asked, "What else do the ravens see? What do they see this woman doing?"

Garland, against whose back the exhausted Medric had companionably curled, watched Karis shut her eyes so she could look through the eyes of her raven. She said, "She is inside the garrison, in a building, where the raven can't see her now. But I can hear her voice." A silence, and she said, "'. . . Frost sparkled on the stones . . . The crack was wide as a hand . . . It seemed to go on forever.'"

"Apparently, tortoise-woman has just noticed that the world is splitting in two," said Emil. "The woman is telling stories to the Sainnites, as Medric dreamed she would."

Garland wrenched some of the blankets from Medric so that Emil could tuck himself in. The three of them would share the single narrow bed, a feat they had accomplished several times now, in several different beds, though each time it seemed quite impossible. Karis, too big for the rooms, the doorways, and the furniture, had no choice for a bed but the floor.

Medric, his face buried in the pillow, mumbled, "What about the book?"

"The ravens dropped the book inside the garrison gate, like you said to do," said Karis. "Zanja—or rather whoever she is now—was standing on the other side of the gate. On the garrison side, many soldiers were gathered, with sledges and snowshoes. A soldier picked up the book from the snow, looking puzzled. He gave it to a woman, who gave it to a man on horseback. A very ugly man, terribly deformed."

"That must be the general's Lucky Man," said Garland. "He uses a tincture for pain for his twisted back."

"He's a Shaftali," said Medric.

"But they say he's privy to all the general's secrets."

"Still, he's Shaftali." Medric smiled smugly, with his eyes still tightly closed, his spectacles safely put away for the night. "Did he like the book, Karis?"

"He and that woman, they had an exceptionally dismayed discussion."

"Oh, very good! And what is the woman doing now? That woman was Lieutenant-General Clement, by the way."

"She left the garrison with the soldiers. I don't know where they went."

"I think you'd better keep an eye on her," Medric said.

* * *

The work of travel was far from easy. But neither was it as grueling or frightening as Garland had feared. Some of the ravens had returned from Watfield, but their aerial scouting was no real necessity, and only rarely were Norina's maps unpacked. Because the land revealed itself to Karis, the travelers never took a wrong turn, and were never surprised by the weather, though their hosts were certainly surprised by their arrival. Day after day, the load of books grew lighter.

Leeba wore red, like most children, to make it easier to find her when she got herself buried in snow. Karis also wore red: a coat of red felt, exuberantly decorated with red tassels. She looked magnificent in it. When she first put it on, Garland thought such a coat contradicted everything he understood about her. Someone else must have bought the coat for her, someone who saw her differently from how she saw herself. Zanja, he thought.

"Yes, it was a gift from Zanja. I've never seen Karis wear it," Emil said, when Garland finally asked. "Perhaps she was afraid she'd wreck it, as she wrecks all her clothes. Did you see the spot where Norina clipped off the tassel that she tied in Zanja's hair? Oh, our Truthken was thinking like a fire blood that day!"

In his wandering years, Garland thought he had learned something about winning the trust of Shaftali farmers. A sober decorum and a distinct sense of shame at one's landless state had proven essential. But this garrulous group strolled into a farmstead like a bunch of holiday-makers: oblivious to danger, indifferent to their lack of food and shelter, radically unconventional and making no attempt to seem less so. Then Karis took out her tool box, J'han his medicine chest, and Garland his rolling pin. Leeba would make instant friends with the children, who knew a mischief-maker when they saw one, Emil and Medric coaxed the elders to talk about the past, and Norina kept out of the way with her mouth shut. The skeptical farmers were more than won over: they were astounded. This visit became an event, a progress, a performance. Whole families stayed up late and wasted precious lamp oil so they could gape a little longer at their amazing guests. Sooner or later, Emil would read part of Medric's book to them. Sooner or later, someone looked at Karis a little too long or deeply, and would suddenly find a Truthken whispering in his ear, and then there would be a pale and thoughtful silence.

Sometimes, though, the entire performance proved unnecessary. One day, with the wind coming bitter from the north, and the clouds piling up in the sky like dumplings in a stew, they reached the untidy edge of a sprawling town and slipped in under cover of an early twilight, dragging their sledges up a narrow alley from which no one had bothered to clear the snow. Leeba had lapsed into the incessant whining that was the warning that they had better stop soon. They paused at someone's back wall, which looked like all the others except that it had a few stylized glyphs carved into the stone. Medric read the glyphs for Garland while Emil let himself in the gate, waded through the snow-choked kitchen garden, and knocked on the back door. "It's the owl glyph, which can mean searching or restlessness, and the glyph that's called Peace, combined with Come-to-Rest. It's pretty unambiguous, for a glyph sign. I guess that this used to be a healer's hostel, or at least that this wall used to enclose one."

"There was one around here once," said J'han, who had plucked his irritable daughter from her sledge and was rocking her vigorously to make her be quiet.

The back door opened. Emil talked, with his hat in his hand, and then waited, and then someone flung open the door, crying, "Emil? What in the name of Shaftal . . . ?" There was much energetic embracing, and Garland caught glimpses of a stout, brightly dressed woman, who eagerly started for the back gate when Emil pointed.

"What's this?" she cried. "A circus troupe?"

Karis, Medric, and Garland all started laughing and could not seem to stop. "Come in!" the woman said. "Books, you say? Well, say no more! Goodness, look at that bright little girl. I'll bet you run your parents ragged, don't you?"

"Yes," said Leeba proudly.

"So did I, and look at how I turned out. Come in, will you? Well, I don't know what we'll do with all your gear, but we'll figure something out. Quickly, since there's a storm brewing. I guess you'll be staying a while? I hope you don't mind sleeping on the floor. Well, get busy. You look strong enough."

This last she said to Karis, who was still struggling to compose herself, wiping her eyes on the end of her muffler.

The whirl of words fell silent. Norina took a step forward, but Karis lifted a big, black-palmed hand and the Truthken stopped in her tracks. "I'm Karis."

The woman put her hand in Karis's: stunned, amazed, then suddenly in tears. She said to Emil, who had come up beside her. "I should have known she'd be with you! Where anyone with any sense would be! The one everyone is looking for, you already found her!"

"I found her before anyone started looking," said Emil. He added somberly, "You need to keep this secret. Not even your family can know. Can you do that?"

The woman turned again to Karis. "Yes. Yes, but . . ."

"I am a Truthken," Norina said, "and by your oath I bind you."

The woman replied fearlessly, "May I not ask a single question? I will go mad!"

"A shame," said Norina.

"Shaftal!" the woman breathed. "Well, what am I supposed to say?"

"Say, 'Madam Truthken, by the land I accept the binding of an oath of silence.'"

The woman said her part, obedient, ecstatic, like an actor rehearsing a play.

Hers was a family of tailors, it turned out, who were as appalled by the state of their guests' clothing as Garland was by the state of his hosts' kitchen. When they left after the storm had passed, every last one of the travelers was wearing a new suit of clothes, though their old clothes had also been so finely mended that to replace them hardly seemed necessary. And they left behind at least a hundred books, which the tailors swore would be scattered through four regions by day's end, and as far as the southern and northern borders within a week.

The travelers would soon run out of books.

* * *

The day before Long Night, they came through the hills on a sunless afternoon, a ragtag collection of wool-dressed wanderers with chillblained, blistered hands. They had tied their snow shoes atop the sledges, for the snow had crusted enough to bear even Karis's weight. Leeba had played like an otter all morning, sliding hilariously down every icy slope. She played without her regular playmate, for Medric was utterly worn out. Now, she rode in state in her sledge, blanket-wrapped in a pillowy nest.

Medric wiped his frosted spectacles for the fiftieth time. "Maybe I'm just too old to play with Leeba. Maybe it's time we had another child."

Norina said, "I hope you're volunteering to be the mother, little man. I'm sure Karis could alter your equipment."

"Never mind," said Medric hastily.

They had seen no signs of settlement since dawn, when they staggered forth from the abandoned shepherd's hut in which they had spent the night. A barren land: open, rolling, practically treeless, with boulders poking through the snow like broken teeth. Sheep country.

The wind picked up. They wrapped their faces, tied down their hats, put a second pair of gloves on their already gloved hands, and faced the wind only when they had to. There was no more laughter. Karis stopped once, pointed at Medric, and pointed at the half-empty sledge of books she hauled. He mutely took a seat in the sledge, and folded himself up against the cold, passive as a piece of luggage. Karis hauled him.

Later, she stopped again, and turned her back to the wind. They huddled around to hear her cold-slurred words. "We've been seen."

Emil tried to speak, vigorously rubbed his frozen face, and tried again. "How many?"

"Many more than us."

"Armed?"

"Yes."

"Paladins. They'll try to head us off first."

They sorted themselves out, with Emil in front now, Norina at his right, Leeba complaining in Karis's arms, Medric afoot again, hauling the empty sledge, Garland hauling the sledge of supplies and J'han the sledge of books. Garland supposed Karis carried Leeba for the child's protection—there was no place safer. But perhaps Leeba would also protect Karis, for the Paladins might go out of their way to avoid injuring a child.

Soon, a black-dressed woman swooped down the hill, flying on her skis as the ravens swooped on the wind overhead.

She blocked their way. Two pistols, certainly loaded and primed, were holstered in the belts that crossed her chest. A dagger was sheathed at her side. "You're lost," she informed them politely.

Emil pulled open his muffler.

"Emil?" she said. "Shaftal's Name!"

Garland thought, *Is there anyone in Shaftal who does not know and admire this man?*

"Greetings, Commander. Do you know Norina Truthken?"

The commander said after a moment, "By reputation."

Garland could see only a part of Norina's muffled face, but whatever Norina heard in the commander's voice appeared to have amused her greatly.

Norina said, "We're inviting ourselves to Councilor Mabin's Long Night."

Certainly the woman's duty was to deny the Councilor's presence, but that she apparently could not do with a Truthken two paces away. Her visible surprise became perplexity. "How do you know the Councilor is here?"

"Perhaps you would have one of your people carry a message to her that Karis wishes to speak to her."

"Karis?" said the commander blankly.

"You weren't there by the river five years ago," said Emil, "but surely you've heard about what happened there." He stepped aside—a small movement, but it brought the commander's attention to the large, somber woman behind him, with the wide-eyed child in her arms.

Norina said, "Karis G'deon."

When something incredible must be said in such a way that it will instantly be believed, then certainly, thought Garland, that was the time for a Truthken to speak.

"I bind you," Norina added, "to silence."

The commander's jaw shut with a click. She turned and signaled. A whole host of Paladins came flying down the hill.

They were as graceful, deadly, and powerful as any bird of prey. Impressed and terrified, Garland wrapped his arms around himself, shivering, thinking that at least if he were killed he would not feel cold anymore. Medric, swaying with weariness beside him, said in Sainnese, "If they'd had a few thousand more like that, you and I would have never been born, my brother. Think of it!"

"How can you even talk?" said Garland.

"I can always talk," said Medric. "Gods of our fathers! What a sight!"

His spectacles had frosted over again, so Garland was uncertain exactly what he saw. The past? The future? Or even both at once?

The Paladins brought their swift approach to a halt in shining sprays of snow. One, designated to carry a message, skied away nearly as swiftly as he had arrived. The others formed a polite but impenetrable escort: one took Garland's sledge, while he worried unreasonably what would become of his far-traveling rolling pin. Soon after they had begun to walk again, one firmly pressed the stumbling Medric to become a passenger again. Leeba reacted with outrage when Medric curled into her nest of pillows, but he made faces at her, and soon it became a contest. Garland realized that he, J'han, Norina, and Emil had all drawn up around Karis like ribs around a heart. Around them skied the Paladins, ice-masked, indistinguishable, wordless. If Karis stopped, they all would come to a halt. But she kept a steady, restrained pace, square-shouldered, forward-gazing, like a brave prisoner walking to her execution.

It was a long walk. At last, it brought them to a great complex of buildings near the edge of river, from which the snow had been cleared to make it a highway. As they approached, an ice skater could be seen in the distance, but he traveled so swiftly that he had passed before they arrived.

On the broad porch of the central building, an old woman, flanked by Paladins, awaited them. The sun was already setting. In the garish glare the shadows were long and black, but the old woman's face was in the light and the three gold earrings in her right ear glittered as the harsh wind swept by.

She, too, had the blank look of a prisoner awaiting the executioner.

Karis gave Leeba to J'han. As she turned her head, Garland saw the white lines of tears, frozen solid on her cheeks. She walked forward, and stopped at the bottom of the steps. The wind tore at her hair, tried to rip off her cap. She jammed her hands into her pockets, and waited, stolid.

The old woman asked, "What are you doing here?"

"Aren't you tired," Karis said, "of the pain in your heart?"

"Yes, Karis."

"Will you allow me to heal you?"

The old woman took a step forward. Then, stiffly, she knelt in the blowing snow. Her companions started forward too late to help her, then stepped back at her impatient gesture. The black-dressed Paladins were folding back their masks, uncovering their faces, staring in bewilderment at the old woman unbuttoning her coat, her jacket, her shirt, to bare her breast to the wind's deadly breath, and to reveal the dull steel of the spike embedded in her heart.

Across the glaring red field, a murmur of shock and surprise. Had these people lived with and served Councilor Mabin, never knowing that the rumor of her spiked heart was true? Karis started up the steps, peeling the gloves from one hand and then from the other. She towered over Mabin. On her knees, with her shame exposed, Mabin looked in Karis's face. She did not ask—for healing or for forgiveness. Her proud features revealed no repentance.

Karis lay one hand to the woman's breast. With her other

hand, she plucked the steel from Mabin's heart. Mabin uttered a gasp of pain, but there was no blood. Karis crushed the spike in her fist, and handed to the wind a twist of glittering dust.

Mabin caught her breath. She said, distinctly, so that everyone within hearing could understand her, "What does this act mean? Are you forgiving me, or are you merely weary of keeping me alive?"

"I will not come to the Lilterwess Council," said Karis. "I will not sit in the G'deon's chair. I will not renew the old order. I will not justify this terrible war."

Mabin stared at her, pale.

"I will not serve you," Karis said. "I will not serve your dreams. I will not be your hope. I will not be your symbol. Do you understand me?"

Mabin said, harshly, bitterly, *"Then what are you doing here?"*

"Councilor, I want you to go to the Sainnites, and offer them peace."

"I will do no such thing!"

"I'll do it without you, then."

Outraged, Mabin got to her feet, rejecting the many hands that reached out to help her up. "By what right?"

Karis looked at her. Then, she turned her back on her, and Garland could see her drawn, wind-flayed face as she looked closely at the stunned audience of Paladins. The tears frozen on her cheeks were visible to everyone. Garland discovered it was easy to track her gaze as one Paladin at a time looked into her eyes.

When Garland looked back at Karis, Norina was mounting the steps. "Be silent, Councilor," the Truthken said, and only then did Garland realize that during all that time Mabin had been directing an angry tirade at Karis's turned back.

Councilor Mabin held her tongue.

Norina said to the Paladins, "On the day Harald G'deon died, he vested this woman, Karis, with the power of Shaftal. Also, on that last day of the existence of the Lilterwess Council, they chose not to confirm Karis as G'deon. So for twenty years, in accordance with that decision, Karis has not exercised the power of Shaftal. By my vows as a Truthken, I affirm that I am telling you the truth."

Someone in the crowd of Paladins said in astonishment, "Madam Truthken, why did the council not confirm a decision already, irrevocably made?"

Norina said, "At the time, Karis was a smoke addict, which is no longer the case. At the time, she was only fifteen and had only ever lived in the whore-town of Lalali. And at the time it was unacceptable that Karis's father is a Sainnite."

The silence seemed very long. Garland realized he was shivering violently.

Someone said, "Karis, what does Shaftal ask of the Paladins?"

Karis's gaze found the speaker, an older Paladin in the middle of the crowd. She spoke, it seemed, only to him. "Lay down your arms," she said. She did not sound audacious, or even courageous, but only certain.

The entire host of Paladins tossed their pistols, daggers, and other weapons into the snow.

When Karis turned again to Mabin, the councilor remained speechless. With the brute force of implacable fact speaking for her, Karis also said nothing. Mabin, General of Paladins, last legitimate member of the old Lilterwess Council, drew her dagger and dropped it to the ground.

Chapter Thirty

On Long Night, the people of Shaftal burn candles to remind the sun to come again. But in the children's garrison there were no candles, no night-long parties to keep an eye on those candles, no festive meals of carefully balanced sweet, savory, salty, and bitter foods to guarantee a balanced year. In the children's garrison, the youthful soldiers were put to bed and barricaded into their dormitories by the disabled veterans who kept watch over them. For everyone, it would indeed be a long watch, but not a festive one.

Clement sat awake in her room, with a clock borrowed from Purnal to chime the hours. With Captain Herme she periodically inspected the preparations. They began their inspection at the top of a ladder, in the attic where six soldiers and a few children kept a crouched, dusty lookout at the cloudy windows tucked under the eaves. It was terribly cold up there, and the watchers were frequently replaced to thaw out in the warm dining hall where their fellows dozed uncomfortably in their boiled leather armor. Through the wavery glass of the attic windows, Clement might peer at a starry sky and a glowing field of snow, across which no one could have approached unseen. The inspection then continued, to the corridor that encircled the big central courtyard, where the ammunition lay ready: orderly bags of lead shot and powder tins, the little lamps by light of which reloaders could see to measure the powder. Again, Clement would check to see that nothing was visible in the darkness. They could make no mistakes.

The wait was terrible.

More terrible was the moment a child soldier pounded on the door and cried excitedly, "They're coming!"

Clement was on her feet immediately with the door slammed open, the girl's loose shirt captured in her fist, hissing, "Follow your orders, soldier! In silence!"

She let her go. The girl ran for her prescribed position without another sound. Clement stood a moment, listening, and could hear only the faint whisper of footsteps, near and far, hurrying across stone as the company got itself into position. No voices, no lights.

Gods, it was a bitter night.

Clement walked, swiftly and quietly, to the round building's center. The corridor that encircled the round central courtyard was protected by a chest-high half-wall, sturdily built to withstand any accidental crashings of horses and wagons making the three-quarter turn to enter the stables. The corridor's circle was interrupted only by the main passage through the building to the front gate. Here, both ends of the broken circle were blocked by barred doors. With the doors to the stable also barred, anyone who entered the building could take only two routes after coming into the courtyard: through the entrance to the main hall, or over the top of the half-wall.

And the invaders would have no reason to climb over the half-wall. They might look over it, but they would see no danger. Though faint starlight filtered down the long arched passageway from outside, the half-wall cast the corridor into unrelieved darkness. And there was nothing to see, in any case: the piles of lead balls, the powder horns, the spirit lamps, these were draped in dark cloth. The soldiers waited behind locked doors: on foot, their weapons sheathed for quiet, forbidden to utter a word, or shuffle their feet, or do anything other than breathe shallowly. There was nothing to see: nothing, that is, except Clement and her signal-man.

He was already in position: a light, lithe man, black-dressed, in soft, silent shoes. He had made a game of slipping through shadows these last few days, of learning to be invisible even to observers who knew he was there. But Clement's knees sometimes crackled; her leather armor might creak, and after crouching a long time in the shadows she would be too stiff to move soundlessly. If the game were given away prematurely, she would be the one to give it away.

The signal-man said in a voiceless whisper, "The watchers count thirty-two people approaching the gate. There might be more, hidden in the trees."

Clement nodded. The defenders outnumbered the attackers, and also had the added advantage of surprise. Awkward in stiff leather, she knelt on the waiting cushion and carefully picked up the loaded and primed pistol. The signal-man helped her to veil her head and body with black cloth, and then he made himself disappear. With the pistol resting on one thigh, Clement pressed herself to the half-wall where the shadows were most impenetrable, uttered a silent prayer to the god of luck, and put her eye to the peep-hole.

She could not see the roof beams; the center post at the middle of the circular courtyard was visible only because she knew it was there. The courtyard itself was mostly obscured in shadows that only faintly lightened near the arched passageway, down which the snow had reflected a trace of the starlight from outside. There was nothing to see. It was so silent that Clement could hear only the rhythmic rush of blood in her own veins. The attackers had perhaps realized by now that the padlock was too cold and rusty to be picked, and were quietly filing the metal instead.

To wait and watch, freezing cold, even colder from anxiety, skin crawling, nose itching (inevitably!) was terrible. Clement's face rasped against the wood, as loud as a cough in her hypersensitive ears. Her armor creaked with every breath. She became convinced that the black veiling was slipping off, and that the revealed polished leather shone as brightly as a lamp. Cold sweat crawled from her armpit down to her ribs, and the tickling became such a torture she could think of nothing else.

Of course, the tension and discomfort seemed unendurable. It always did.

A movement in the faint light of the arched passageway.

One person only. A man by the shape of the shoulders. What did he see? An echoing vacancy of blackness. An unguarded building where the occupants slept soundly, unsuspecting, where hearthfires warmed the rooms behind shut doors. What did he hear? The creak of Clement's armored breaths?

He came in: not overly cautious, a shadowy shape whose hobnails crunched on gravel. Relaxed, in no great hurry, he tried one of the barred doors, peered over the half wall, walked part way around the circle of the courtyard, then stepped through the entrance to the corridor. Clement could no longer see him. Would he appear in the curved corridor to her right? If he did, then he might spring the trap too soon, and this would not be the ambush she hoped for: her soldiers would be chasing the attackers through the snow instead.

He stepped back out into the courtyard. Perhaps he had walked the other direction, or had gone down the main hall, trying the doors, looking into the empty refectory. Perhaps he wondered why so many doors were locked. Or had he even noticed? He finished his casual circuit of the courtyard. He brushed by Clement's peephole. Not an arm's length away, he peered over the half-wall. He stepped back, and stood a moment. She glimpsed his teeth, his glittering eyes, as he turned into the starlight.

She let out her breath. The leather creaked. He walked away. She knew he must be Willis: he would be a leader who insists on going in first. A leader for whom image matters more than common sense. Who did not see what he did not expect to see.

She breathed. She needed the air.

More shadows in the archway. His entire attack force was quietly coming in. They formed four clusters. If it were Clement's force, and if she knew in advance that one quarter of the building was stables, one team would secure the exit and the other three would each secure a quarter. Again, she spotted her man, Willis, going confidently from team to team, clasping hands, patting shoulders, whispering assurances a bit too loudly.

He turned, smiling, to walk towards the last group, towards her.

She lurched to her feet. She sighted down the pistol. She squeezed the trigger. Gunpowder exploded, a handspan from her face. She dropped behind the shelter of the half-wall.

Chaos. The startled attackers promptly wasted their shots and time. Lead balls thunked where Clement's gunflash had been. Doors crashed open. Crouching soldiers ran past.

The soldiers in the tack room raced out to block the exit.

"To me!" cried a hoarse, shocked voice in the courtyard.

"Fire at will," said Clement quietly.

The signal-man began to pipe upon his whistle.

The positioned soldiers opened fire.

Clement could see a little now: the glow of spirit lamps being lit, the movement of the reloaders' quick hands, the rhythmic rising and ducking of the soldiers.

She put her eye again to the peep-hole. Explosive flares along the half-wall wildly lit a chaotic scene. Struggling, jerking shadows. Bodies. Shouts of anger. Shouts of terror. Screams of pain. Gunfire's echoing racket.

She could see that the invaders were no longer returning fire, which meant they had used all their shots. *Not enough discipline,* she thought. *Too late to learn it now.*

The struggle now focused on the exit passage.

Even if the invaders broke through the bottleneck of soldiers, they would find the gate chained closed again.

"Hold fire," said Clement.

The signal-man changed his tune. The guns gradually fell silent.

"Sabers only. Attack," said Clement.

And then she ran, with him cheerfully piping the signals behind her. She ran for the entry to the slaughterhouse stink of the courtyard, as the reloaders unshielded their lamps and put them atop the half wall, so the gunflash-blinded pistoliers could see to fight.

She ran, and with her saber's hilt dealt a ringing blow to the helm of a soldier who was about to strike open the neck of a fallen man. "Mine!" she screamed into the soldier's startled face. "Go forward!"

She had to trust her rivets to protect herself, and her prisoner, from accidental attack: polished, light-reflecting brass that studded the front and back of her leather armor, and marked her as a fellow soldier even in the hazy light, the rising dust, the spray of blood. The wounded man thrashed and shouted, struggling to rise. His beard was fouled with straw. His eyes . . . she could not quite endure them. The purity of his rage.

Her shot had blown out the back of his thigh. Inside the ugly wound, she saw broken bone. She wrestled him down, knelt on his back to hold him. Shouted hoarsely for a medic.

The signal-man piped on. No one responded to her shout, a single hoarse cry in a roar of shouts. People ran past her, tripping on her prisoner's sprawled limbs. "Soldier!" she shouted at each one, futilely. "Get the medic!"

Impossible to know how the battle was going, but easy to predict the outcome. A tangle of struggling, shouting shadows in the arched passageway. A dozen or more bodies, dead and dying, scattered. A few soldiers now, somewhat dazed in the aftermath, dispatching anyone who still moved.

"Medic!" Clement shouted.

Finally, a man rushed up to her, with a pale boy bearing a lantern. "Lieutenant-General? What is your hurt?"

"This prisoner. He must live."

The medic took one look. "His leg must come off, then." The boy was tottering. The medic snatched the lantern from him.

"Give me the light." The prisoner's thrashing was losing its strength, so Clement could hold the lantern reasonably steady while the medic put hands into the wound, and pinched shut a spurting artery.

"It may be too late," he commented.

The boy crumpled.

Someone was shouting for her.

"Here!" she answered. It took a few more shouts before Captain Herme found her. Meanwhile, she noticed the soldiers coming out of the arched passageway, noticed the rising silence.

"It's over," Herme said, unnecessarily.

"Get that kid out of the way, will you?"

A soldier picked up the boy and took him away. Others took control of the injured prisoner, so Clement could stand up. Something hurt. Her ribs. Willis must have gotten in a good punch. She stood by the medic. "Don't amputate yet. But get his bleeding stopped."

"There's wounded soldiers," said the sergeant.

"Unless the wounds are life threatening, they'll have to wait."

In the dining hall, the wounded gathered, limp or giddy, attended by their comrades. The medic put his cauterizing irons on the fire. The lantern-boy vomited helplessly in the corner. Clement checked the waiting soldiers, and found no life-threatening wounds. The rebels' guns had used up their shots before they had targets to shoot at; their daggers had rarely penetrated armor. Death-and-Life had been cornered, helpless, so overwhelmed they'd hardly been able to fight back.

She went out again to the courtyard. Soldiers worked in pairs to carry the bodies away.

As she walked down the arched passageway to the gate, she lifted her lantern. Blood smeared the wall and puddled the cobblestones. She stepped carefully. The smell made her stomach churn.

She went through the gate, which now hung ajar. The chain with which the soldiers had secured it dangled. The original padlock, its hasp filed open, lay tossed upon the stones. Outside, the snow was churned up, pink with blood. She followed the trail toward the sound of soldier's cursing.

"By gods, I thought I was skewered."

"Isn't that one dead yet?"

"Hell, this is dirty work!"

They fell silent at the sight of her. In solitary silence she viewed the bodies piled in the snow. A boy. A woman older than she. A man with his guts trailing. Not much blood now, just a discarded pile of flaccid gray flesh. The soldiers' pockets bulged with pilferage.

She turned away. Behind her, she heard the voices start again.

"It's fucking cold!"

"Haven't we got them all yet?"

"What did the lieutenant-general want?"

"Did you hear she's making the medic treat the prisoner first?"

She could hardly lift her feet, she was so tired. The stars shimmered coldly overhead. Her breath puffed out, obscuring her vision.

She was walking away from the garrison.

She could not stop herself.

Her boots caught in deep snow. She fell. She lay.

Her lantern had gone out.

Under guard, the prisoner lay raving, tied spread-eagle to a table. His leg, roughly splinted, smelled like charred meat. His cut-open clothing trailed from him in bloody, unraveling rags.

Clement said to the guards, "Go eat something." She pulled up a chair, and sat, and crossed her legs. She had forced herself to swallow a sweetened corncake, but her stomach still churned. "Willis," she said quietly in Shaftalese, "Stop your ranting. There's no audience anymore—just you and me."

He fell silent—with surprise?—and gave her a scouring, baleful glance. "When the G'deon comes," he said, "she will take out your heart. She will dissolve your flesh. You will beg her for death. You will beg!"

Clement said, "Yes, I'm rather afraid of that. When can we expect the G'deon to come?"

"When we prove our devotion to her! When we prove that we are willing to serve her unto death!"

"What will it take to prove this?"

He said through pale lips, "The abandonment of mercy."

Though Clement had managed to get herself back indoors, she remained weak and stunned by the horror of the massacre. Yes. The abandonment of mercy.

What mercy had the Sainnites ever granted?

She shut her eyes. She opened them to find he was looking at her. "Are my people all dead?" he asked.

"Yes, they are."

Now, his turn to shut his eyes. A furrowed face, much hardened and battered by the bitter weather of this godsforsaken place. His lips moved. Perhaps he said the names of the dead.

"Tell me about your G'deon," said Clement. "I want to know about her. What does she look like? What has she said to you? Why isn't she here with you, helping to fight your battles?"

His eyes opened, his weathered face creased into a baleful grin. "You fear the day that happens! And so you ought to! The land itself has been tainted by your presence, but she will not foul herself with Sainnite blood. She named me her champion. But do you think I am the only one? After this night, hundreds will rise up. Thousands!"

He paused to gasp for breath. Though the bleeding had been stopped, the pain must have been excruciating. Yet, despite agony and weakness, his words were chilling, terrible. The effect he had on his followers must have been profound.

Clement pulled herself together, considered what he had said, and asked quietly, "How many of your people did you hold back in the woods?"

"What difference does it make how many? They're flying down the mountain now!" He uttered a raw laugh. "Oh, no, you'll not keep this night a secret! All will be known. That we are heroes. And that you—" He glanced at her again. "You cannot silence stories. The land itself will know our names."

Like Cadmar, the man only seemed able to make speeches. He was a figure, as Cadmar had become a figure.

He lay gasping, shivering. There were no blankets here, and the warmth of the fireplace did not travel far. At the far end of the hall, where the medic was cleansing and binding the last wounds, soldiers trailed in, checked on their comrades, ate a cold corncake or two, and exchanged muted accounts of what had happened. Clement heard no bragging; even hardened soldiers would find this night's butchery difficult to be proud of.

"Willis," she said. "Tell me about South Hill."

He looked at her blankly.

"Surely, what happened there no longer matters, after so many years."

He said, shallow-breathed, "Who *are* you?"

"I'm Clement, daughter of Gabian. I want to understand what is happening to us." She leaned a bit forward, her stiff leather creaking. "There was a mysterious woman, a traitor, who came to South Hill. Tell me about what happened there, and I'll tell the medic he can give you a pain draught."

Some people when injured lose all their intelligence, but this was not one of them. He said, "She was one of yours. You know what happened."

"I am being honest with you, one commander to another. We Sainnites knew nothing of her, or of her doings. This is the truth. At least tell me her name."

"Her name? If you don't know, why should I say it?"

"Did she *have* a name?"

He gave her the scornful look one madman gives another. "Everyone has a name!"

"Did she tell stories?"

"Stories?" His tone was blank. Was he concealing something, or was there nothing to conceal?

She sat back, and it occurred to her to undo some buckles so the leather would not keep digging into her aching ribs. "Was she a border woman?" She fumbled with the buckles.

Of course, he would not answer a single question. And there was no point in torturing him for the answer. He would simply die.

"Ashawala'i," he mumbled.

His vague gaze sharpened. She realized she was staring; perhaps she had even turned pale. "Ashawala'i," he said more firmly, apparently appreciating the effect this word had on her.

Hard to say who was in charge of this interrogation, hard to say which of them had the most power. "She *claimed*," he added. "So she got herself into the company by playing on the commander's sympathy. Because you Sainnites destroyed her people."

Clement said, "So she was just *pretending* to be a survivor of the Ashawala'i people."

"She was a traitor. She admitted it. Telling secrets to a man in the garrison."

"To what man? To that seer, Medric? It was he who turned traitor against us! It must have been because of her."

The leader of Death-and-Life gave her a baffled look. "Then why did Mabin tell me to kill her?"

She stared at him, stunned and chilled. "Mabin knew of this woman?"

"It does not matter," said the man. His eyes were glazing over.

No, Clement thought, *it does not matter.* Except that the Ashawala'i had been massacred because another seer had foreseen that a member of this distant, isolated tribe would cause the destruction of the Sainnites. And the shadow-woman of South Hill and the shadow-woman of the Lost G'deon story were linked by councilor Mabin. And a raven had dropped a book out of the sky.

"Lieutenant-General, you are not injured?"

She was holding her head, she realized. The medic had come up to her, with his knives and his bone saw. The cauterizing irons were once again on the fire.

"It's been a long night," she said.

He snickered, apparently thinking she was making a pun. And then he said viciously, "Hell!"

She leapt up. The medic tore frantically at Willis's tightly bound bandages, which were suddenly sodden. Blood pooled on the tabletop, and dripped to the stone floor. But Willis lay quiet, profoundly at rest. Even his fanatical heart had stopped beating.

❀ ❀ ❀ ❀ ❀ ❀ ❀ ❀ ❀ ❀ ❀ ❀ ❀ ❀ ❀ ❀

Chapter Thirty-One

From one exterior wall to the other, nothing interrupted the open space of the big building's first floor. At both ends, hot fires crackled in stone fireplaces, but could not do more than lift the chill of so vast a space. As the whole host of Paladins came in, however, the space began to seem too small. They stripped off their winter gear, and soon a wall of pegs was hung with clothing, skis, and weapons. Garland, pushing his way through the convivial, loud-spoken groups towards the kitchen, heard scattered words of conversation that mixed together like the ingredients for a soup.

". . . when she took my hand . . ."

". . . dizzy!"

". . . what Mabin is saying to her now?"

"I never even felt like hesitating."

". . . how often do we have that confidence?"

"And I just want to know what . . ."

". . . the first day of the first year of Karis G'deon?"

Garland found the kitchen, another grand space, crowded with a half dozen sweating cooks, who upon every surface were rolling and filling pastries, on every fire were turning massive chunks of roasting meats, and on a number of auxiliary stoves were stirring big pots of strong-smelling soup. Garland had thought he was exhausted, but now his heart began to pound with excitement.

Someone grabbed him by the shoulder. "Who are you?"

"Tea for Karis?" he said. "I'm a cook," he added.

The cook, a crabby-looking woman with a wool cap on her head, pointed the way to hot water, then followed Garland suspiciously to the steaming kettle and watched as he unpacked Emil's teapot from its box and measured out the tea. Abruptly, she asked, "You're a cook? Will you help us out in here?"

"Yes, as soon as I can."

"Is it true what they're saying? That it's really her, the Lost G'deon?"

"It's true."

"What's going to happen now?"

"I don't know. Making history isn't much like following a recipe, I guess."

"Well! Maybe if she gets something to eat!"

The cook hurried off to fill a tray with lovely crisp bits of filled pastry that had just come out of the oven, exactly as Garland would have done in her position. Yet if he had asked her if she thought that good food could make people wise, she would have laughed at the idea.

Karis had picked up and returned every discarded weapon to each Paladin. By the time she was finished, the sun had nearly sunk below the horizon. Now, as Garland edged his way through the crowded shearing room, the Long Night candle was being lit: a monstrous candle, red as Karis's coat, set on a table in the middle of the room. As its wick sputtered into flame, the Paladins began to sing, a rather mysterious song full of great symbolism, that Garland vaguely remembered having heard every year. As the singers finished the last verse, the kegs were tapped, and the singing was obscured by cheers. Garland had safely transported his tea pot and tray to the door of the side room, where, he supposed, brokers and shepherds had conducted their negotiations during shearing time. Within, Karis, Emil, Norina and Medric had drawn sturdy wooden chairs up to the hearth, their sodden hats, gloves, and mufflers lay on the floor, and they held out cold-whitened hands to be toasted by the flames. Karis's frozen tears had finally thawed. Now, vivid red patches on her cheeks revealed where the wind had peeled the skin away.

Mabin was scolding her. While Karis stole away the hearts of her Paladins, Mabin had sat indoors, fuming. She had begun her rant even before Garland had taken Emil's tea set and left in search of hot water. Her angry speech continued as Garland filled and almost immediately began refilling the little teacups. ". . . have you not even one thought of justice? Thousands of Shaftali people have been killed on their own soil, defending their own land. Do you think we can simply forget those wasted lives? The great talents of my generation and of yours—hunted down, extinguished, their knowledge and understandings forever lost. Our libraries burned, our university razed . . ."

Karis took the food tray from Garland, offered it to her friends, then balanced it on her knees. By the time Mabin had finally worn her anger into silence, Karis had drunk four cups of tea and eaten most of the pastries. The Paladins, having sung several songs, apparently had now begun to dance. Their heavy boots stamped out the rhythm on the wooden planks. Belatedly, some musical instruments began to play: a squealing fiddle, and a breathy flute.

"Are you done?" Karis said to Mabin. Her voice was racked, a raw edge of sound giving rough shape to hollow silence. She turned to look at the councilor, and added, "I hope?"

Mabin pursed her thin lips. "Will you respond?"

Karis ran fingers through her hair, which melting ice had left a damply curling tangle. "No," she said.

"No?" Mabin's voice rose. "No?"

Karis sat back in the chair, which gave an alarming squawk under her weight. "My logic supersedes yours."

Mabin stared at her. Norina gave Karis an impressed glance, eyebrows raised. Emil said, "The Sainnites are weak, and we are rapidly becoming the kind of people who can do what we must do to overcome them, without any further trivial dithering over the morality of our actions. And then we'll live in a land like Sainna, where all disagreements are decided by violence and every generation wreaks vengeance on the next. Is that the justice you want?"

Mabin seemed relieved that someone, at least, was willing

to tangle with her. As though Medric, inconsequential in his shivering, red-eyed misery of cold and weariness, were not even in the room, she said with disgust, "Is that what your Sainnite seer predicts?"

Emil said, "Medric was not the first to see it. When Zanja na'Tarwein was brutalized by Sainnites and then by Paladins, she rightly wondered what real difference there was between them and us. So she was the first to see that the habitual use of brute force was changing us, including she herself, into brutes. That's a lesson you yourself managed to teach her."

"Shall we be the victims of brutes instead? Shall we let them—"

Karis said, "If you want to convince me, you'd better come up with some new arguments."

Though Karis's voice was a mere shadow, at these words Mabin fell silent.

Norina said crisply, "Karis, you don't need Mabin. Ask her to retire. Spare yourself and us the aggravation."

Karis said wryly, "When Mabin raves at me how wrong I am, that's the only time I'm certain that I'm right."

Norina said, "You don't need that certainty. You have your own, the certainty of action."

As Garland leaned over Karis's shoulder to take the teacup out of her hand and fill it up again, he noticed that her palms had been fissured by dry cold and hard work. J'han came in to report that Leeba was asleep. Garland whispered in his ear, and J'han went off to rummage in his pack, and returned to rub an unguent into Karis's battered hands. Mabin, rigid, glared into the fire. Karis appeared to be considering Norina's suggestion, but said finally, "Aggravate me all you want, Mabin. Shaftal needs its hero."

Mabin cried, "By the land—you're just like Harald!"

"Obstinate as a tree stump," said Norina coolly.

Karis said in her shredded voice, "Oh, I don't think so—a tree stump *can* be moved."

J'han, with a choked snort, dropped Karis's hand. Emil fought for composure. Medric began to snicker helplessly. Apparently immune to their stifled hilarity, Norina said, "Councilor, you know that's a truth to be ignored at your peril. Your continuing resistance will only force Karis to continue to humiliate you. I recommend another strategy, one that will make both of you less miserable."

Mabin opened her mouth as though to utter a fresh recrimination. Norina raised her eyebrows. Mabin stopped herself, and took a breath. "Karis, what does Shaftal need of me?"

Emil gave Norina a congratulatory glance. Clearly, the two of them understood the shifts and starts of this conversation far more profoundly than Garland could hope to.

Karis said, "Responsibility. For Emil."

This strangely worded request meant nothing to Garland, but Emil jerked with surprise. His fingers rose to his scarred earlobe, then he controlled the movement, and closed his mouth tightly over what Garland thought might be a strenuous objection.

Mabin said, "But Emil resigned from the Paladins."

Emil replied in a strained, muted voice, "No, I resigned my position in South Hill. I wrote in my letter to you that I could no longer serve under your command. But I did not renounce my vows."

After a moment's thought, Mabin said with rigid discipline, "I see. And you are not refusing Karis's request?"

Emil looked at Karis. Her lips were drawn tight; her jaw was set. He said unsteadily, "I know better than to refuse the will of Shaftal."

Mabin seemed to be gathering herself to rise, and Garland said, "What do you need, Councilor?"

She glanced at him, surprised. "My commander."

"And a cork," said J'han, who was again rummaging in his pack.

Garland went out and signaled the commander, who came in and talked to Mabin, then bent over Emil's huddled form and said something quietly to him, with a hand on his shoulder. Emil raised a tear-stained face to talk to her.

J'han had opened his chest of surgical instruments, and selected a sturdy needle from among the strange devices. Garland examined the contents of his pockets: a packet of salt, a nutmeg, a short length of string, a tin of matches, a wad of tinder, a sewing kit, a tin of tea, and an array of corks. He offered them all to J'han. "Which one?"

"You keep corks in your pocket?"

"Where else would I keep them? J'han, I don't understand what is happening. Why is Emil so unhappy?"

"He's being promoted," J'han said.

"And that makes him miserable? You people are *nothing* like Sainnites."

Smiling crookedly, J'han selected one of Garland's corks, and stuck the needle in it. "Emil has always wanted to be a scholar. The last few years, he's been calling himself a librarian. I never heard him express a desire to be a general. Give that to Karis, will you?" He handed Garland the needle and cork.

After Mabin's commander had stepped out, Emil said shakily to Medric, "Master seer, what is my future?"

Medric said, with strange gentleness, "You know the answer, Emil."

"Karis—!" Emil cried.

"After what you've done to *me*—!" Karis said.

Norina uttered a sharp laugh, perhaps because Karis's aggrieved tone so exactly matched Emil's.

Garland gave Karis the needle and cork, which she examined determinedly. He collected the empty teacups, and hung sodden clothing on hooks. J'han, having packed away his gear, went to Karis and appeared to be explaining to her the anatomy of ears, pointing at his own ear as an example. Emil withdrew into inexplicable suffering, and no one disturbed him.

When Mabin's commander re-entered the room, a dozen others followed her in. The Paladins were somber; the music in the big room had been silenced. The commander put three gold rings into Mabin's hand.

Emil refused the handkerchief Medric offered, and knelt before Karis. No one seemed surprised that he was weeping; some of the Paladins seemed ready to weep themselves, in sympathy.

Three times, Karis put the needle through Emil's earlobe.

Mabin put in the earrings. When she was finished, she said solemnly, "Emil, General of Paladins."

Everyone moved towards Emil: it appeared to be time to comfort him, embrace him, reassure him that he would survive.

But Emil did not rise. Karis's hand rested on his shoulder. Apparently, she was not finished with him. Emil gazed steadily, starkly, into her face.

When Karis finally spoke, her voice was scarcely audible. "Emil, will you form and serve at the head of a new Council of Shaftal?"

He replied without surprise, in a voice that did not waver, "What Shaftal requires of me I will do."

Norina said, "Emil, General of Paladins, by this vow you are bound."

Then, Karis helped him to rise, and kissed him apologetically, and passed him to Medric, who passed him to his friends, who passed him to the Paladins, and they each did what they could for him.

Garland spent Long Night as cooks do, in the kitchen. When he emerged with trays of food still crackling from the oven, he saw Emil dancing gracefully with Mabin's commander. He saw Karis laughing, with a half dozen people crowded around her. He saw Paladins dancing around the candle and kissing drunkenly in the corners. He saw Norina and J'han leaning shoulder to shoulder against a wall, fingers intertwined. Another time, he saw Norina and J'han dancing, Emil serious in the middle of an earnest crowd, and Karis crouched on a crate, delicately repairing the neck of the fiddle, with her toolbox at her feet.

Garland lost all track of the time. When he eventually found his way back to the celebration, the ovens were cold, the dishes washed, and the First Day sweet bread was rising in bowls on the hearth. In the great room, the Long Night candle was two-thirds burned. People dozed in companionable huddles by the fireplaces. The fiddler played a melancholy tune while four people, leaning on each other for balance, sang soulfully but unclearly about leaving home. Garland could find none of his companions and did not know where to look for them. He found a chair and watched the candle burn.

Eventually, he noticed Karis's toolbox, pushed out of the way against the wall. Above it was an empty peg where her coat had hung.

He put on his coat, and went outside.

The cold struck with such violence that he could not much appreciate the crystalline beauty of the starlit night. Snow cracked under his boots, and despite the hobnails his steps skittered on ice as hard as iron. The wailing singers, the howling fiddle, these sounds seemed far away as he tread around the glittering stones that composed the exterior wall of the building. The river was a road of ice, hedged on both sides by barren, bowed-over trees. The sky was light-spangled black, remote and mysterious. By habit he located a few familiar stars, and noticed the rising and setting constellations. He heard a sound of ragged breathing, and walked down the quay that stuck a stubby finger into the river here. Karis huddled there, like a boulder shoved up out of place by ice. He reached an arm around her, for she was weeping.

The cold seemed unendurable. When Karis spoke, her breath covered them in a sudden cloud, but her voice was just a crack of sound. "I've made a lot of tools in twenty years. Scarcely a household lacks one now. I feel them, gathering dust or being used. Just like with Medric's books, I know where they all are. Like stars."

Garland looked up and tried to imagine being surrounded always by such a constellation of knowledge. He wanted to ask her to come inside, to be again the one who turned tree prunings into furniture and cupboards into sledges. But the transformations of that day had been irrevocable.

She said, "I made some metal files one year. And one of those was used a while ago. It's the only one of my tools used tonight. Now, the one who used it is dead, and the file is still in her bloody pocket."

She breathed sharply in. Her muscled back gave a shudder under Garland's arm. "Now another one is dead," she said, in her shredded voice.

"What is happening? What is killing them?"

"Violence," she said heavily.

"But it's Long Night! A new year!"

She raised her head from her knees. "And it would be acceptable on any other night?"

Garland heard the scrape of hobnails on ice, and then the distant, distinct rhythm of Sainnese curses. He stood up, and shouted. Medric, his feet jammed into unlaced boots, and Emil steadying him with one hand while buttoning his own coat with the other came down the quay. Medric crouched beside Karis, shivering violently. "Hell, hell, hell! She's given them a martyr!"

Emil stood back, hands in his pockets, grim in the faint starlight. He looked up—the habitual movement of a traveler, checking his orientation, confirming with the sky that it was indeed winter, the dawn of a new year. His earrings glittered faintly in the starlight. He said obscurely, "That idiot, Willis. Inevitable."

Medric responded, "But Clement is a short-sighted, bloody fool! If she had just read the book! She had it in her hand . . ."

Karis had raised her head again. She said to Garland, "These men speak a strange language, don't they."

"I guess Willis is one of those that was killed," said Garland, "And that's a disaster. I don't know how!"

"My poor little book," said Medric. "All I did was tell the humble truth, and trust the common sense of the Shaftali people. But Willis, his is a grand, heroic tragedy. My little book can't compete. His death is what they'll heed."

Garland burst out, "You mean it's all for nothing? The writing, the printing, the hauling, the worry? It's all wasted? Because that fanatic got himself in the Sainnites' way?"

In the silence, the distant sound of celebration seemed drunken self-indulgence. If such great labors could be so casually undone, thought Garland, what was the point of effort?

Karis asked Medric in her cracked whisper, "What future do you see?"

The seer said miserably, "I can't see a bloody thing."

"What about Zanja?" Her shattered voice made it seem as if Karis had lost all hope.

But Medric looked up. The frosted lenses of his spectacles glimmered. "Maybe it's time I talked to her."

Zanja na'Tarwein filled her pot and lit her fire. The stars were coming out. She examined them as they appeared, but not a single star seemed to be in the same place as it had been the night before. She asked, "Does the pattern lie in the lack of a pattern?"

And then she knew something had changed. In all these fleeting days and patternless nights, she had never spoken out loud. Now that she had done it, she recognized the soundlessness of this barren place: she heard not even a far away bird song, or the soughing of the wind, or the crackle of the flames under her pot of water.

A footstep grated on gravel. She turned her head, and Medric squatted down beside her. "You're not easy to find," he commented.

"Are you dead, Medric?"

"Oh, no, just dreaming. You've got Emil's tea set! And that old tin pot we used to put kitchen scraps in."

The water was boiling, so Zanja made tea. As she swirled the pot, she could smell it: half grass and half flower, the scent she would always associate with Emil, since it was his favorite kind of tea. She heard her clothes rustle, felt the heat of the pot on the palms of her hands, the ache of pain in her chest.

Medric sat beside her fire in peaceful silence. She said, "You've brought sensation with you."

"Have I? Is it unpleasant?"

She poured him a cup of tea, but hesitated to hand it to him. "If you eat or drink in the Land of the Dead . . ."

"This is not the Land of the Dead." He took the tiny cup from her, and sipped. "You know, this is the first time I've tasted your tea? It *is* good."

Zanja tasted the cup she had poured for herself. The complex flavor of the tea made a fist of sharp pain clench her heart. She said, "If I'm not in the Land of the Dead—and you can visit me in a dream—have I traveled so small a distance? How long does it take for a soul's journey to end?"

"It's been four months," said Medric.

"Thousands of nights!"

"A hundred. A hundred and twenty, maybe. It's Long Night now. A few hours before sunrise. I lay down under Karis's red coat, because I thought it might help me to find you. Karis made me sleep. I suppose she's still beside me now."

"Gods!" Zanja's dropped teacup uttered a musical ring against the clapper of a sharp stone. She pressed her hands to her chest, but the pain there did not ease. "My agonies should be ended! I should have earned some peace!"

She jerked sharply away from Medric's uplifted hand.

Instead of touching her, he picked up the fallen teacup. "What does it take to break these things? After so many journeys and so many battles, the box is a wreck, but the cups and the pot, not a single chip."

She took the teacup from him, and examined it. "I can no longer read this symbol. Your comments are obscure."

"Obscure? Nothing is obscure to you." He blinked at her. "The storyteller has your insight, is that it? And so you can't see the pattern."

"What pattern?" she said desperately. "Is there one? What is this place? Why am I not dead?"

"I see that you are suspended between life and death, and can't get to either state."

Unsurprised, she said, "Forever?"

"When your body finally dies, I suppose you'll be set free. But it may seem like forever to you."

"But you severed my soul from the flesh!"

"I'm afraid Norina subverted our logic with her own. She thought she'd make a way to get you back. But you know air logic, cruel even at its most merciful."

Zanja said, bitterly, "I cannot even curse her!"

A long time they sat together. The sun, usually so quick to pop up from the horizon, was slow to rise. At last Zanja said, "I demand that Norina right her wrong."

Looking miserable, Medric dried out his teacup on the tail of his shirt.

"Medric!"

"You mean that you want her to finally kill you." He put the little cup into its spot in the box. "I'll tell her. I never thought I'd be killing you twice."

He took off his spectacles to wipe his eyes. It was terrible to see such a merry man so sad.

"I wish you would leave," she said. "And take your heartache with you."

"Would you like to have this? It's my book, the one we printed on the old librarian's press."

She accepted the oddly made book he had taken from his pocket. It had a child's gluey fingerprint on the cover.

"Will you also take this coat?"

Now that the light was finally rising, she recognized the vivid red of the coat he wore. "No!"

"But this is a cold place."

She had not known it was cold until he said so. Shivering, she said, "I need to be cold. Please go!"

He got to his feet, and walked away, into the blaze of the rising sun. He did not look back. She did not call out to him. It was a relief when he had gone.

They had gathered around Medric while he dreamed, a collection of weary travelers sharing blankets and using each other as pillows in the airy attic of a building never meant for winter habitation. Garland dozed, awoke shivering, pressed himself against the nearest body for warmth, and slept again. When voices woke him, some faint light had begun to filter in, and a distant window floated in the black, framing a couple of fading stars. Downstairs, the Long Night candle would soon be extinguished. The first day of the first year of Karis G'deon would soon dawn.

Karis still sat beside Medric with one knee drawn up and his hand clasped in hers. But he was mumbling irritably, and Emil stood over him, hauling him to a sitting position.

"It's no good," said Medric.

"You couldn't find her?" Emil said.

"She's dead?" Karis said.

Medric said. "It would be better if she were dead. Norina—"

"I'm awake," she said.

Garland was quite startled to realize that the body he clasped so tightly was the Truthken's.

She said, "Well, what?"

"We have to kill her again. Her body, this time."

"We? You mean me." Norina tucked the blankets back around Garland and J'han as she got up. "In your opinion, Medric, would killing the storyteller be a just and merciful act?"

"Zanja demands that you right your wrong. It seems a demand both for justice and for mercy."

"She asks this out of anger? Out of despair?"

"Oh, she's angry. But your interference trapped her in a dreadful place, a between place, a nothing place. We can't just leave her there."

Norina asked, with that inhuman coldness of hers, "What if the storyteller would rather live?"

There was a silence. Emil said, "I think Zanja's desires take precedence. But you might gain the storyteller's acquiescence when the time comes."

"Yes, you can probably do that," said Medric. "If she's the one with the insight, she'll understand."

Norina settled on her heels. Garland realized she was looking at Karis.

Karis spoke in a voice that had shredded to a whisper. "What do you want me to say?"

"That you won't interfere."

Karis was silent.

But as though Karis had spoken, Norina said, "You must consider this further. If I am forced to act without your consent, it will be the end of our friendship. And I feel that I have no choice in this."

I know," Karis said. "Leave me alone."

Sighing, Emil said to Medric, "Did your dream yield only bad news?"

"Zanja is trapped in a single empty moment. It is impossible for her to have any understanding that might be of use to us."

The light was rising. Garland could almost see the expression on Emil's face, as it changed from pained to startled. "Then we're asking the wrong one," he said. "We need to ask the storyteller."

Part 5

How Tortoise Woman Saved
The World

� � � � � � � � � � � � � �

Tortoise Woman's son had married some farmers to the north, and one day she decided to visit him. It was a bright, warm day, and she hummed to herself as she walked. Normally, she was a grumpy, solitary person, but on days like this even she could be in a good mood. When she stepped across a crack in the earth, thin as a grass stem, she hardly noticed it.

Returning home, though, she stopped at the crack, which was as wide as a finger now. She had seen cracks like this before, in flood plains after the water had receded, but this soil was sandy and it had not been that long since the last rain. She put her eye to the crack. It seemed to have no bottom, and the darkness was very dark indeed. But she stepped over the crack, and continued home.

The next time she walked that path, the summer was over and frost sparkled on the shadow side of the stones. When she came to the crack, it was wide as a hand, and even as she watched, she saw a rock teeter into it and disappear in the darkness. "I wonder how long this crack is," she said to herself, and walked along the crack in one direction and then in another. It seemed to go on forever. But she stepped over the crack and went on to her son's house.

"Has anyone noticed that big crack in the path?" she asked her son and his family. No one had.

When she returned home, the crack had gotten much wider. She measured it with her walking stick, and then sat down beside the path to take a nap. When she awoke, she measured it again, and although it had not gotten much wider in so little time, it was certainly wider.

She went home and said to her own family, "I am afraid the earth is splitting in half."

"You are being ridiculous," they said.

The fall mud came, and then the killing frost. One day, Tortoise Woman told her family that she was going to visit her son one more time before the snow began to fall, but it was a lie. The crack that would soon separate the world had gotten much wider.

"Perhaps the two pieces of the world might be pulled back together," she said to herself. "But if I wait until spring and bring all the people I know to see this problem, and get them to use cables and horses to pull the pieces together—by then it might be too late; it might be impossible to get from one side to the other."

Besides, her son's family had not even noticed the problem, and her own family thought she was ridiculous. Later, they would regret not having paid attention, but she could not wait for that to happen.

She lay down across the crack, with her front legs on one side and her back legs on the other, and she dug in with all her claws and began to pull. She pulled for many days and nights, and the winter snows began to fall. Her family assumed she had decided to stay with her son for the winter, and of course her son thought she was comfortably at home.

After the spring mud, though, her family went out looking for her. "There is the crack she was so worried about," they said, as they stepped over it. "It is not nearly as wide as she said it was." On the way back from their son's house, very worried about her now, they found Tortoise Woman's walking stick. They noticed the marks she had made on it to measure the width of the crack, and they laid it across the crack to measure it again. "According to these marks," they said, "this crack has gotten much narrower. That's ridiculous." And they walked away, looking for any sign of what had become of Tortoise Woman.

In fact, she was very close to them, so close that she had

heard the entire conversation. With her legs dug deeply into the earth and her head tucked in out of the weather, she had gradually been covered with mud, and looked like a big rock straddling the crack in the earth. She had been pulling the edges together all winter long, and was glad to hear that she had made progress.

Several years later, her son brought his children that way, and they did not even notice the crack, though he did wonder what had happened to it. Tortoise Woman had begun to sink into the earth, and plants had taken root on her back. Even if she had dared let go, she could not have pulled herself loose. But she knew she needed to hold on, for she was the only thing keeping the world from splitting in two.

And there she remains, to this very day.

Chapter Thirty-Two

The winter sun, a pallid and late-arriving stranger, still lingered below the rooftops as the heavy iron gate of the garrison swung open. A small, precise woman in a gray cloak, with flashes of red silk shining through like flame in charcoal, stepped out onto the crisp ice. "Good day, storyteller," said one of the soldiers who had just come on duty. "Get some sleep, eh?"

He and his fellows might have benefited from that same advice, for they were blinking wearily in the rising light. One of the others called after the storyteller, as the gate was locked, "That was a fine night!"

The storyteller walked away across the ice. As sunlight suddenly gilded the attic window of a narrow building, she pushed the hood back from her face and looked up. The sky was clear but colorless. The golden glare on the roof seemed sourceless and mysterious. Across that glare, a raven stalked, his ragged black blurring in a halo of light.

It was the first day of the new year. Already, though the iron winter stretched before them, farmers would begin to plan for the distant spring. The storyteller climbed the steps, opened the door to the silent house, and went in.

In the sparsely furnished upstairs rooms, the baby slept beside a cold stove. The storyteller soundlessly lit and built up a new fire, then she went to a dark window over which thick curtains were drawn. She opened the curtains, lifted the stiff, ice-crusted sash, and opened the shutters. Now the sun's reluctant rise cast its tentative brilliance across her features, sprinkling a golden flush on her sharp cheekbones but leaving her eyes in shadow.

In a rush of cold air, the raven landed. His ragged feathers rustled dryly as he lifted his wings and hopped from the windowsill into the room. The storyteller lowered the window sash, then turned and politely offered the raven something to eat.

"Thank you," the raven said.

She brought him a plate of bread and cheese, poured him a mug of water, and knelt on the floor near him as he gulped down the food. "It cannot be easy to find a meal in winter, even in the city," she said.

"Do you know who I am?" the raven asked.

"You are a raven who wishes to talk to me." The woman looked at him a moment, as though she knew that she should be surprised. "Do you know who I am?" she asked.

"No, I am not certain."

"I am a collector of tales. But I have never traded stories with a raven."

"I will gladly tell you a story," the raven said. "But I do not want to hear one of your stories. I want you to answer me a question."

"I can answer no questions. There is very little I understand."

"You have insight, do you not?"

"Insight? I suppose I do. But I have no memories. And insight without memory has little value."

After a long silence, to which the storyteller seemed indifferent, the raven said, "I know you are a reader of glyphs. I ask you to cast the cards for me."

The storyteller rose up lightly, checked that the baby was not too close to the rising heat of the stove, took the packet of glyph cards out of her boot, and squatted down by the raven again. "What is your question?"

"How can the Sainnites be overcome without destroying the spirit of Shaftal?"

The storyteller moved her fingers through the cards, seeming scarcely interested in the raven's question or in the cards. The room's only light came through the unshuttered window. A card fell to the floor: the Wall, also called the Obstacle, which glyph readers often interpret as an impermeable and insurmountable problem. The storyteller examined this solitary card, and then she reversed it. On the right and left of the Wall she lay out a pattern of cards. Her actions seemed swift, casual, and random, but, gradually, as she added cards and relocated those already laid down, the scattered cards began to group together and overlay each other in some complex relationships. She had dropped fifteen cards when she finally stopped, though her fingers continued to sort through the cards in her hand.

"The pattern is not complete," she finally said. "But that is all I know of it."

The raven walked around the cards, examining them. The storyteller rose up to check the infant again, and this time she moved his basket a small distance from the warming stove. Beyond a half-open door a sleeper moaned.

"Is this a pattern of present-and-future?" the raven asked. "Or is it cause-and-result?"

She returned to look at the cards. "Both, perhaps."

"What is the obstacle that must be broken through?"

"I don't know."

"Is it a place? An idea? An event? A people?"

"People," she said. "Persons. But perhaps it is just a wall."

The raven continued to ask questions about various elements of the pattern, both those elements to the left and those to the right of the overturned wall. To some questions the storyteller offered several tentative or overlapping answers. To others she could offer no answer at all.

The sleeper in the next room moaned again, and the infant became restive. The raven asked, "How much longer do you think we have?"

"Not long."

"I promised you a story," said the bird.

The storyteller said, "But I have not truly answered your question."

"You have answered—but I must work to understand that answer. Therefore, I will tell you a story without an ending. Is that a fair exchange?"

The storyteller had picked up the baby to quiet him. "It is fair."

The raven told her a story about a woman whose spirit had been irretrievably split in two. Half her spirit was exiled to wander aimlessly in a distant dream world. Half her spirit remained in her body, and could only tell stories. So those separated halves were doomed to continue, the raven said, without any alteration in their condition, as long as the woman's body lived.

The storyteller stood by the stove with the infant in her arms. She said, "If I were telling this story, it would properly end with death uniting the two halves into a whole."

After a long silence, the she added, "Ah, Raven, I understand! What a favor you have done!"

The raven said, "With your consent, I can arrange your death."

"But you are a trickster. To what am I truly consenting?"

The raven said, "I will not trick you. In twelve days time, you will be killed. If you consent."

"I do consent," the storyteller said, without hesitation and without sorrow.

The girl in the next room asked an irritable question. The storyteller went silently to open the window, one-handed, with the baby starting to wail with hunger into her shoulder. The raven flew out, and was gone in the blaze of pale sunlight.

It was the first day of the first year of Karis G'deon. She huddled on the rough, unfinished boards of the shearing-house attic, weeping. Garland had his arm stretched across her broad back. Leeba, recently awakened, huddled with her arms wrapped around Karis's bent legs, frightened into tears herself.

Emil had been the one who talked to the storyteller, through the medium of Karis and the raven, but it had been Karis who offered the storyteller her death. Now, Emil knelt beside Medric, who under Karis's direction had laid out the glyph pattern on the floor, using cards borrowed from a sleepy and confused Paladin.

Medric said unhappily, "This is worse than reading Koles."

"She was able to give us some clues of how to read it," Emil said.

"But glyphs without context . . . !"

"The reader always creates the context."

"We are not seeking a subjective truth, though. And to read these cards as though my experience of them somehow reflects a political reality is not just specious. It's dangerous."

Emil put his hand on the seer's shoulder. His three earrings glittered briefly in a beam of sunlight. "We sent her out to explore the wilderness. Now she has found a way through, but it is up to us to read the trail markings so we can follow her."

"What if we are too stupid?"

"Stupid? Oh come now, Medric!"

To Garland, this discussion was incomprehensible. He understood, rather vaguely, that Emil had thought it reasonable to let a casting of cards determine Shaftal's future. He understood now that Medric, who would be responsible for interpreting those cards, thought that to read them reliably was impossible. But Medric's explanation for his reluctance made no sense, and neither did Emil's steady assurance that it could be done. What if Emil were as mad in his way as Medric was in his? Surely, Norina would not allow lunacy to continue. Garland glanced hopefully at her.

Norina stood with her arms folded, her back against a post that supported the center beam. She watched Medric fret over the incomprehensible glyphs. Her face was inscrutable.

When Norina killed the storyteller, it would be with that very expression on her face: passionless, impersonal. She was as mad as the rest of them.

Karis's desperate, shuddering sobs had fallen silent. One of her clenched hands unfolded, to stroke Leeba's head. J'han, who embraced Karis on the other side, dug out a preposterously clean handkerchief for her to use. Leeba made a fretful sound, and Karis said hoarsely to her, "I'm sorry I'm scaring you. But I'm just sad."

"You're always sad," Leeba said.

Karis let her limbs unfold to take the child into her embrace. "I'm sorry. But you make me glad, you know."

Emil said, "Karis, can you talk to me about politics?"

Karis, bowed over Leeba, did not respond.

Emil persisted. "I think I must call an assembly, and it will take two months at least to gather people together. I have the Paladins now to act as messengers, but I assume we won't be bringing them to Watfield with us—"

"You're going to visit the center of Sainnite power without any Paladins?" said Mabin, who had joined them earlier. "Well, this is certain to be a short-lived government."

Karis looked up then. "That battle last night was the last. There will be no more bloodshed in Shaftal."

Mabin looked blank, and Garland felt that blankness also. No bloodshed? How?

Norina said, "Under the law, the G'deon's declarations are to be understood as fact."

"Her words only sound like hope to me!" said Mabin.

Norina straightened from her post. "Break the law at your peril, Mabin." Her tone was cold.

"Fact?" said Karis in a small voice.

"You speak for the land," said Norina to Karis, as though that explained everything. "You'll get accustomed to it."

Not by accident, Norina's foot sharply nudged Mabin's. The councilor said, "If Karis says we don't need an army to defeat an army, then she must be correct." She looked like she had taken a mouthful of putrid fish and was trying to determine how to spit it out.

"For war cannot make peace." Emil gestured at the cards on the floor. "And I see no war there. Do you, Medric?"

Medric said irritably, "This is *not* a predictive casting. It's an *advisory* casting." He sat back on his heels. "War, defeat, victory, none of these are *advised*."

Abruptly, mysteriously, Garland understood all of them. Medric, who examined possibilities, could conclude that war might continue, despite the storyteller's advice. Except Karis had said that it wouldn't. And Mabin clearly thought that peace without victory would be impossible, and Norina might well have agreed with her, except that the law required her to agree with Karis, no matter what. So she agreed with her.

Karis said flatly, "The war is over." A statement of fact.

Karis's advisors all nodded distractedly: fire logic's uncertainty was resolved; air logic shifted its entire rationale to match a new principle; earth logic remained inarguable. Emil, apparently the quickest to readjust his thinking—a dancer, that man, always poised on his toes—said, "Well, Medric will grumble over the cards, however long it takes. You and I, Karis, we need to decide what I am to do, if I am not re-establishing the old government."

Karis shut her eyes. Emil began to say something apologetic, but a gesture from Norina silenced him. Garland, still embracing Karis, thought she might be analyzing the distribution of weight on that loaded food tray she had once described. Her desperate sorrow was not past—and would never be, perhaps. But Karis said sturdily, "Call an assembly, Emil, and name everyone who attends it a councilor of Shaftal."

Emil blinked. "No Council of Thirteen? No Lilterwess Council?"

"The Lilterwess Council is to be formed by the G'deon," said Norina. "But if she chooses not to form one, and to transfer their power directly to the assembly, that does not contradict any law."

"It contradicts tradition—" began Mabin, and got herself kicked again. Apparently, she was to endure a painful retraining, but Garland could not manage to feel sorry for her.

Karis said, "Master seer, what do you think?"

Medric looked up from his glyph puzzle. For once, he did not protest the formal way she had addressed him. And his spectacles seemed perfectly clear. "You are choosing the right way. Now leave me alone."

Emil asked Mabin, Norina, and J'han to help him decide who to invite to the assembly, and how to compose the important letter that would coincidentally announce to all the people of Shaftal that, after twenty years of chaos, they had a G'deon again. Apparently, Emil would then recruit the entire company of Paladins to simultaneously write dictated copies of the letter, which the Paladins would hand-deliver to the recipients. Garland cried, "Do you mean to tell me that every single Paladin carries pen and ink?"

Emil blandly produced a pen and a packet of ink from his waistcoat's inside pocket. Mabin kept hers inside her black jacket, in a buttoned pocket that seemed designed for no other purpose. "I don't believe it," Garland muttered in Sainnese.

As Emil took his contingent towards the stairs, he said over his shoulder, "Garland, I know you'll make Karis eat, but get her to rest also, will you?"

When they were gone, Karis commented, "Apparently, you're the one who gets the impossible task, Garland."

"I beg to differ," muttered Medric.

Karis kissed Leeba's head again. "Listen, Leeba! They're singing the First-Day song! Let's go down and watch them put out the candle."

✼ ✼ ✼ ✼ ✼ ✼ ✼ ✼ ✼ ✼ ✼ ✼ ✼ ✼ ✼

Chapter Thirty-Three

The second day of the new year ended prematurely as the weary sun was engulfed by advancing clouds. In the brief twilight the stars appeared to cast away their light with frantic haste before the clouds smothered them. By this frail, rapidly failing illumination, Clement led the company of soldiers down the hill, into the gently sloped grazeland of a river valley blanketed by faintly glimmering snow. The soldiers' snow shoes crunched; they walked in a fog breathed out by their weary fellows.

Because Clement's thoughts were in turmoil, she had given her company no rest that day. The morning's chatter had long since given way to plodding silence. In the dark valley stood a cluster of buildings: an established, successful farmstead that boasted a huge red cow barn.

A big shaggy dog came out from underneath a porch to bark a sharp alarm, and in a moment the door opened to spill its light. An angular woman with a lantern in her hand examined the company of soldiers bearing down on her, quieted the dog with a command, then turned and spoke into the doorway.

By the time the soldiers had all reached the bottom of the slope, a dozen of the cow farmers had come out onto the porch. Clement stepped into the light.

The level look that the angular farmer gave Clement was a puzzlement. Seth turned and spoke to her family, words Clement could not hear, and then she came down the steps. She said, "Your people can sleep in the barn, in the milking room. There's a stove, and fuel. Take straw to make beds. You *do* know the difference between straw and hay? And light no open flames, of course." She added, "We'll bring down some bread and cheese, or we can cook a hot meal if you want to wait for it."

Clement heard words come out of her mouth: "No, all I ask is shelter and permission to draw from your well."

"There's a pump in the milking room."

Both of them were performing parts. This performance was necessary. But the old illness came over Clement, a self-loathing that for two days had continually risen like nausea, only to recede in response to the counter-pressure of panic. The self-loathing was familiar; it arrived after every battle, and lingered longer every time. The panic, that was new.

Clement spoke some words that were not necessary or part of a performance. "My people will do no harm to your family or your family's livelihood. I promise you."

Seth's right eyebrow raised, very slightly. "This is a rare assurance." This neutral comment revealed something in Seth that Clement could not clearly see or make sense of. It was not what it should have been: not anger, nor resentment, nor hatred.

There was no reason why even a modicum of trust should exist between them, and Clement was wasting her time looking for it.

Clement's company was conveying impatience by shuffling their feet, gasping loudly at the cold, and rocking their weight noisily in the snow. Clement said over her shoulder, "Captain Herme, take the company to that big barn, but don't go in until I get there."

When she could hear the company's sledges starting to move behind her, she said to Seth, "We'll be gone when you come down for the morning milking, and you won't know we were there."

"More promises?" Seth took a step forward. "Is Clem your true name?"

"Lieutenant-General Clement."

Both Seth's eyebrows lifted now, but still there was no visible revulsion.

Clement said, "I apologize for deceiving you."

"Oh, I imagine that you thought honesty was impossible," said Seth.

"I should have chosen not to pretend my way into your bed."

A corner of the cow farmer's mouth curled. "Make amends, then," she said. "Come to my bed again—without pretense, this time."

The sound of the soldiers' snow shoes had become distant. The farmers had begun to go back inside the house, though some lingered to keep an eye on Seth. Clement noticed these things. She also noticed how the cold was seeping upward from her feet, how weariness crushed her earthward, how sounds echoed in the crisp air. But Seth's words seemed beyond understanding.

"My fire is lit," Seth said. "My family will let you come in. There is no lock on any door. You only have to find your way to me."

"It is impossible," said Clement.

"It seems simple to me."

Clement heard crunching footsteps. Captain Herme, having complied with Clement's command, apparently had now taken it upon himself to make sure of her safety. Fortunately, he did not understand Shaftalese. Clement said to Seth, "You've asked for an end to pretense. But if I came to you, pretense would be unavoidable. The pretense that we are not enemies."

Seth said quietly, "You and your people are strangers. I and my people are offering hospitality, according to the traditions of Shaftal. We—I—choose to offer it. Now what will you choose, Clem?"

"Lieutenant-General?" said Herme tentatively.

She said to him, "Yes, I'm coming." In Shaftalese, she said to Seth, "There *is* no choice."

"There is," Seth said. "I am giving you the choice."

But Clement had already forced herself to turn and walk away.

* * *

Over thirty years ago, when Clement was first judged mature and skilled enough to go into battle, duty had become the fence that delimited the territory of her life. When she led her rested soldiers up the slope in the morning, leaving the milking room as pristine as it had been when they arrived, that was duty. When she did not raise a hand in farewell to the woman who stood watching from the porch, that was duty. That her heart rebelled was, and always had been, irrelevant.

Ten more nights, at ten more farms, Clement requested shelter for her company. Shelter was freely given, food was generously cooked and served. Clement continued to demand that the soldiers behave courteously, and that they accept this food and shelter as a gift and not a right. The soldiers gradually shifted from resentment to amazement. Clement herself was surprised by the cautious, awkward, but inexplicably friendly conversations initiated with her by their involuntary hosts.

"Is it true your people are refugees?" asked one old man.

"How can you survive without a family?" inquired a shy young woman.

A middle-aged woman with gnarled, work-hardened hands declared, "If you soldiers can make flowers bloom you can grow vegetables." And when Clement and her soldiers were leaving, the woman tucked some packets of vegetable seeds into Clement's pocket and urged her to plant them.

"What has come over these people!" exclaimed Herme.

Clement was unnerved. When and how had the Shaftali people become so well-informed? How did the woman know that soldiers grow flowers, for example? The members of Clement's company, who could not understand these conversations, were mystified enough by the hospitality, but Clement felt that a monstrous disaster loomed just beyond the limits of her ability to see and understand it.

Even though the company slept warm and ate well, it was no easy journey. Clement participated in the rotation of hauling the sledges and sitting the night watch. When a storm blew in, or the wind turned particularly cold, or the trees took it upon themselves to dump loads of snow onto their heads, she cursed the hostile landscape as viciously and sincerely as the rest of them. When they were tired, or fighting their way up a hill, or wanting courage for crossing a frozen river, she joined with them in singing to raise their spirits or keep the pace—a breathless, harsh, and tuneless chorus, perhaps, but sometimes even she felt carried by the sound of it. She sat with them on straw or stone, and ate whatever they ate, and slept wherever they were sleeping, and by the third night of their return journey had acquired two bedfellows. "Should you sleep cold just because you've been promoted?" the soldier asked, when she and her partner hauled their blankets over to Clement's solitary bed, in a very drafty barn.

"You've been good to us," her partner explained vaguely.

"It's a cold night."

"And there's that wind."

"By the gods," said Clement, with all sincerity, "I could use a warm night's sleep."

After that, every last one of the soldiers in the company, including Herme, seemed to forget who Clement was. They shouted at her when necessary, and did not take their cold hands from their pockets to salute, and even called her by name. She pretended to be oblivious to this deterioration in discipline.

The entire company recovered abruptly from their sloppiness when they entered Watfield. "I'll pull that sledge, Lieutenant-General," one of her companions said, and she was gently, irresistibly forced into the proper position for a commanding officer, the center of the column. "Well, Captain," she said regretfully to the man she had been calling Herme for the last eight days. "I guess the journey's over."

"Yes, Lieutenant-General."

"I'd like to thank the company myself when we're inside the gate. And I'll ask Commander Ellid to give the company a few day's rest before you return to regular duty."

"Thank you, Lieutenant-General. The company will certainly appreciate that."

It was a gray day, and the bright colors of the city's latched shutters and doors were further muted by a haze of chimney smoke. They walked between ridges of snow that walled either side of the road, and the sledge runners clacked rhythmically on exposed cobblestones. The garrison gate lay ahead. Clement could hear a distant cheer as the gate guards spotted them, and then a bugle pealed the news of their arrival. Suddenly the entire company walked in step, lined up, straight-backed.

By some unlikely piece of luck, Gilly was already waiting at the gate. Clement could see him, hunched like a crow on his exceptionally steady horse, exactly as he had been when she left. Had he been as haunted by anxiety as she had been, this last month?

Now they were passing the building that housed Clement's small, peculiar family. The door opened; the girl-nurse came out onto the stoop with the heavily-bundled baby in her arms.

Clement had broken formation and climbed the stairs before it even occurred to her that now the entire company had no choice but to come to a disorderly and rather confused halt. She took her son in her arms. He seemed to be asleep. The small weight of his body simultaneously relieved and oppressed her. She kissed his forehead softly so as to not awaken him.

The girl-nurse looked pale. "Is my son well?" Clement asked. "Has Gilly looked after you?"

"Of course," the girl said, looking flustered.

"Come into the garrison with me. Captain Herme—"

Clement gave the baby back to the girl, and the captain stepped forward to help her down the stairs. Now the door opened again, and the storyteller came out, carrying a basket, with her heavy cloak loosely wrapped around her shoulders.

Clement thought, *Now it begins.*

She said, "Storyteller, are you on your way into the garrison? You might as well come with us."

The storyteller's dark, narrow, sculpted face was beyond reading. Yet it seemed to Clement that the woman knew she had no choice but to comply. The storyteller followed the girl-nurse down the steps, and silently accepted the soldiers' greetings. The company continued its progress, and was admitted with the usual fanfare into the garrison, as Gilly watched, his ugly face drawn and unsmiling.

Clement made a laudatory speech and dismissed the weary

company. As the soldiers sorted out their gear and began to disperse, Clement took the gate captain aside. "Captain, I want you to take the storyteller into custody and keep her under guard in the gaol. Do it as quietly as you can. I don't think she will resist."

"Yes, Lieutenant-General. May I ask—?"

"No, I can't explain."

He gave her a stiff salute, signaled his company, and with several soldiers behind him approached the storyteller. She spoke a couple of words, and handed the captain her basket. Then she turned and walked off with the soldiers. It was a very quiet arrest, but the girl-nurse noticed and understood. Uttering a small moan, wild-eyed, she clutched the baby to her breast. What reason had she to fear she might be next?

Gilly's stolid horse breathed out a puff of fog as Clement went to him, and took his proffered hand in a pretense of greeting.

"What are you doing?" he asked in a low voice.

"I believe the storyteller's tribe is Ashawala'i, the tribe that would destroy us, a seer once said."

Gilly said after a moment, "Seer's visions are explanatory or tentative, not necessarily predictive. Even if she is a survivor of that unfortunate tribe . . ."

"She also may be the Lost G'deon's lover."

Gilly sharply turned his head to look after the departing woman and her respectful escort.

Clement said, "She might be fully capable of destroying us."

"With a G'deon's power behind her? Most certainly." Gilly's gaze became unfocused. Then he blinked, and said, "Clem, look up at the roof."

Clement did. Two ravens stood together near the roof's edge. One of them watched the departing storyteller. The other looked directly into Clement's eyes.

"They can behave like natural birds when they choose to," said Gilly. "At the moment, apparently, they don't so choose. How long has that one been following you?"

"I don't know." Clement felt very cold.

"The other one follows the storyteller." As Gilly spoke, the raven lifted up and flew over the rooftops, towards the gaol. "I think it would be safe to say that nothing you have done since the ravens first appeared a month ago, has gone unnoticed. If the storyteller is the Lost G'deon's lover, then there seems little doubt whose supernatural agents these birds are."

The remaining raven continued to gaze at Clement, an unearthly, unblinking stare. Clement, her face stiff with cold, said with difficulty, "Until this moment, I thought I was just guessing."

"How will imprisoning the storyteller prevent our destruction? Isn't it possible you might bring destruction upon us?"

"Don't you think I have driven myself mad with that question already?"

"You *look* mad," he said, with a frail shadow of his old sarcasm.

A soldier approached with the storyteller's basket, which was crammed with the baby's supplies. "She said to give you this, Lieutenant-General."

Gilly said, "You're taking your son back inside the walls?"

"Put the basket with my gear," Clement told the soldier. "Gilly, how did you know I would arrive today?"

"The storyteller told me. Not just the day, but the hour as well."

"Apparently, she expected to be arrested. Why didn't she flee?"

There was a long, strange silence. "Well, here's Cadmar," Gilly said, as though that were some kind of answer.

Cadmar strode down the road briskly, with Ellid practically trotting behind to keep up. Clement said, "I'll deal with him. I'll meet you in your room, in about an hour. Will you get that girl and my son settled in my quarters?"

Gilly leaned over stiffly, to clasp her hand again. "What will happen to us?" he asked. Fortunately, he did not seem to expect an answer.

Cadmar was only interested in the success of Clement's mission, and since all the attackers of the children's garrison had been killed, with no Sainnite casualties, he considered it a success. Clement explained very precisely why and how this success could prove to be a disaster, but Cadmar would not hear of it. With Willis dead, he said, the movement he had inspired would surely falter. Cadmar also dismissed the importance of Medric's book. "This Medric himself admits he is a traitor to his own people—and he obviously is a madman. Get Gilly to read some of it to you and you'll see what I mean."

It was without much hope that Clement explained to Cadmar why she had arrested the storyteller. By the time she was done, Cadmar appeared to doubt her stability. "There is no G'deon!" He went on to explain why, as though she were a particularly simple child who could not seem to learn anything. "This mission has been a trial," he finally said patronizingly, and, dismissing her, told her to get some rest.

Clement had expected nothing else from him. As long as she had known Cadmar, what he could not understand or imagine he had always declared impossible. She went to her quarters to change into a fresh uniform, to reassure the nearly hysterical girl-nurse, and to pick up her sleeping son. "I'll watch him for a while. Why don't you take a nap? You look tired."

The girl's bleak stare followed Clement out the door.

In Gilly's room, the fire had been built up and a lamp had been lit, and now he sat in a sturdy chair near the fireplace, waiting for her. "Well, I have to find some kind of proof that even Cadmar will accept," said Clement wearily as she sat down beside her old friend. "He treated me like an addle-pate, of course."

"Of course," said Gilly. "And if not for those ravens, I'd agree with the general. This is another puzzlement, Clem: you wonder why the storyteller did not try to flee; I wonder why the ravens want us to realize they are watching us."

"Or why Medric wanted us to know the contents of his book."

"Or why a woman whose power can shift the very foundations of the land has done nothing at all for twenty years."

"Well, as far as Cadmar is concerned, that inaction proves that she doesn't exist."

Gilly said quietly, "Cadmar can only imagine her as a general, like him. And you and I also have fallen into that error, up until now. But if we now imagine that this woman's inaction has been intentional, then, suddenly, we must reconsider everything. When the old general sent a battalion to eliminate an entire people from the face of the earth, did he never once think that his actions might well be causing the very fate he intervened to prevent? Surely this Ashawala'i woman, this storyteller, has pursued our destruction for nearly six years *because* of what we did to her people."

"Yes," Clement said. She had considered this possibility so often that it had finally lost its ability to dismay her.

For a long time, the two of them sat side-by-side by the crackling flames as though they had nothing of importance to do. Clement, who for nearly a month had worried about the son she had abandoned to the care of a callow girl, allowed herself a little while to think of him. He did not seem much bigger; but would he be livelier now? Would he recognize her at all, or would he mistake the one who fed him for his mother?

Gilly had asked earlier what would happen to them. And now Clement wondered what would happen to her son, should the Lost G'deon exercise her destructive power as Willis claimed she would.

She said musingly, "My mother saved me and her flowers . . . but after all, she was merely running away from soldiers much like her, and she knew that a ship was waiting, and the tide was turning. All she had to do was reach the boat before the people chasing her did."

Gilly said, "Well, your problem is much more complicated. If you can confirm the storyteller's identity, will that prove the Lost G'deon's existence?"

Clement said sadly, "The storyteller will soon explain everything. She will not be able to help herself."

"Don't torture her," Gilly said.

She looked at him—her monstrous friend, whose sympathy for this monstrous woman would only be more acute, now that he had an inkling of what her life had been like. She said, "One woman's life gives us the lives of six thousand soldiers."

"Exactly," grated Gilly. "Her life, not her death. And after all she has survived, you won't be able to frighten her with mere pain, not unless you torture her beyond recovery."

"I must prove something, somehow!"

"Fine. Torture the storyteller, get your proof, win Cadmar's approval . . . and what have you really gained? You've hardened the G'deon's determination, and you've thrown away an extremely valuable hostage. I'm starting to think you *are* addle-pated."

"No, I'm cornered."

"At this moment, it is only your thinking that is cornered."

"Bloody hell, Gilly! Get me out of the corner, then!"

"Is it possible you will not—cannot—respond defensively to this threat? This seer, Medric, seems to think it's possible." Gilly stood up stiffly, and went to the lamp table to leaf through the crudely constructed little book that lay there.

Watching him, Clement felt a darkness descend on her. What if Medric's book had been a weapon? And that weapon had reached its target: not her, not Cadmar, but the Shaftali man who advised them both? What if Medric had won Gilly's heart?

Gilly found a page he had marked, and began to read out loud. Clement could hardly pay attention. But the words were rhythmic, the sentences clear. Dismayed as she was, Clement began to listen.

"'What has always distinguished the Shaftali people is their hospitality. The great historians have written of it repeatedly: of the effort the Shaftali people go through, to treat every stranger as a member of the family. They say, perhaps rightly, that this tradition has an element of self interest, for to feed and shelter the homeless wanderer prevents crime and theft. But in fact this custom goes much deeper than self-interest.

"'The Land of Shaftal is unforgiving, a place of harsh winters and brief summers, where sometimes only luck might decide the difference between death and survival. In such a brutal land, it seems the people should also become brutal. That once was the case, long ago, in the time of the first G'deon, Mack-apee. But as Mackapee sat in his isolated cave by a peat fire, watching over his sheep, he imagined Shaftal as a community based on mercy. Kindness and generosity, he wrote, can never be earned and will never be deserved. Hospitality is not an act of justice, but of mercy—a mercy beneficial to everyone, by making it possible to depend on and trust each other.

"'But now, Shaftal has again become a merciless place. I do believe the Sainnites more than deserve the destruction that even now bears down upon them. But the Shaftali people will one day regret that they allowed their land to be transformed by rage.'"

He interrupted himself. "Why are you looking so desperate?"

"Those farmers," she said.

"Which farmers?"

"All of them! Seth, the woman with the vegetable seeds, the man who knew the Sainnites are refugees."

"That is in the book."

"That we don't have families?"

"In the book."

"Hell! I knew there was something ominous about those people's behavior! They all had read the book!"

Clement had left Gilly in the dark, she realized, but in a moment he had achieved his own understanding and was saying, "They offered you hospitality, I gather. And you find it reasonable to conclude that the hospitality was actually threatening. Does it not occur to you that if Medric is with the Lost G'deon, and published this book with her consent, perhaps with her participation—"

"You *want* to believe this man is sincere. And you want to believe that what he wrote, the G'deon agrees with."

He looked at her a long time before he looked away and said regretfully, "I do want to."

"But in fact they have much to gain by making us believe they don't intend to destroy us. If we lower our defenses—"

"No, a G'deon is not a general! She does not think this way."

"Whatever she is, that doesn't change what I am. When my people landed here on the shores of Shaftal, perhaps we *could* have thrown ourselves on the mercy of the Shaftali people. But we made ourselves criminals instead! How will we escape that culpability, Gilly?"

Gilly shut the book and lay it down. For some time, he stood beside the bright flame of the lamp, with his ugly head bowed over the table. At last, he said quietly, "You were just a child, Clem. It was your elders, including your mother, who made the choices that made you a criminal. And now you have a son. What will you choose for him?"

The crackling of the fire seemed awfully loud. The scraping of Gilly's cane on the floor made Clement flinch. She looked down at her sleeping son and felt the depth of what she had done to herself when she allowed him to be put in her arms. How could she bequeath to this baby the violence and ostracism that shaped her life? How could she not bequeath it to him?

He lay very still. It seemed odd that he had not awakened yet. She opened the blanket to feel his chilly, flaccid hand.

"Gilly, stop blocking the lamplight!" Gilly hastily stepped back from the table.

She turned the baby so the light shone full on his face. The violet shadows that bruised his eyelids seemed stark and terrible. She had seen children who were sick unto death. She knew what it looked like.

Gilly came over to her. He looked into the baby's face. He put an arm across her shoulders. Of all the clumsy, graceless actions Clement had seen him do over the years, this was by far the most awkward.

She pressed her face against his arm, which was all knotted with the muscle it took to support his ungainly body's weight on the cane. "I'll send for the midwife right away," he said. "Listen," he added desperately, perhaps fearful that Clement would weep. "If you're a criminal, so am I. And I'll gladly share your fate with you, if I can die your friend."

❀ ❀ ❀ ❀ ❀ ❀ ❀ ❀ ❀ ❀ ❀ ❀ ❀

Chapter Thirty-Four

Sometimes a babe just fails, the midwife said. The nurse's milk is plentiful, but milk does no good if the child won't suck. He was born early, and his mother died—such infants commonly don't survive. The midwife gave Clement a cool glance. She seemed to think Clement should have expected this outcome.

Clement sent the midwife home.

The baby remained with his nurse in Clement's quarters. Though Clement pursued business that was too urgent to wait, she forced herself to keep returning to make certain the frightened girl attempted to make the baby take the breast. Each time Clement returned, she took up her son, and held him, and watched the nearly indistinguishable movement of his breathing. Each time, she learned a new lesson in excruciating helplessness.

She could endure anything but hopeless waiting. That her urgency drove her out again into the bitter night seemed almost fortunate.

In the refectory, she talked to the night watch as those soldiers came on duty, and then to the much larger day watch as they came in for their evening meal. She found some soldiers who had been posted in South Hill, and in nearby Reece before that. They remembered the seer, Medric, quite vividly: a ridiculous, voluble little man, nearly blind without his spectacles, hopelessly bad at combat, and, reportedly, a drunk. Yet under his guidance the Sainnites in Reece had decimated the Paladins, and at first it had seemed they could do the same to the Paladins in South Hill. The informants agreed on the man's practical incompetence, and doubted he could have survived as a deserter. It did not occur to them that such a man might get himself some powerful friends.

The ringing of the night bell customarily would have ended Clement's inquiries for the day, but if she delayed until the dawn bell, Ellid would inevitably hear of her activities, and just as inevitably would ask Cadmar why Clement's inquiries had not proceeded by the usual slow but methodical transfer from commander to captain to soldiers. Then Cadmar would certainly stop her investigation and might well relieve her of duty, for she was acting without orders.

Clement burst into barracks, roused the sleepers, dealt with the affronted company captains, and dismayed the soldiers with her urgent questions. By halfway to morning, Clement had spoken to all four hundred soldiers in combat companies, and also to the armorers, the cobblers, and the stable crew. It was in the stable that she finally found a man, the stable captain, who had participated in the attack on the Ashawala'i. A bow-legged man Clement's age or older, he had been burned while rescuing horses from last summer's fire, and after all these months the injury still kept him awake nights. In the back room of the newly built stable, he stoked the fire in the stove and set on top of it a rusty pot of what appeared to be treacle, though he claimed it was tea. He appeared to view Clement's unprecedented visit as the opportunity for a leisurely chat to while away the night, and he was less than pleased when, upon learning that his duties had prevented him from attending any of the storyteller's performances, she insisted that he immediately put on his coat and come to the gaol with her.

The night had gotten bitter cold. The deserted roadways, transformed to narrow passageways by the piled-up snow, offered a very slippery argument for the value of hobnailed boots. It was the kind of cold that silences speech, but Clement persisted with questions that the captain answered with chilled brevity.

He had witnessed the attack on the Ashawala'i from a distance. The Sainnites' approach had been noticed in time for the tribal warriors to set up a defense, but the war horses had galloped right over them, and had herded the fleeing villagers into the second prong of a two-pronged attack. What followed was a bloody slaughter.

"So that was it?" Clement asked. "The Ashawala'i were all killed?"

"We certainly wished that were true. Some ten, twelve days it took us to get out of the mountains, and sometimes we feared not one of us would get out alive. They burned our supply wagons, drove our pack animals over a cliff, and shot a dozen pickets. That was just the first day."

"How many survivors were there, do you think?"

"We didn't know. We hardly saw them."

"What did the people of this tribe look like?"

"Like racers: deep chests, light build, strong legs. It's hard to even breathe in them mountains. And if you're not grinding your way up a heartbreaking slope, you're trying to keep from falling down one. Those people, they could run all day up and down those vicious ridges, and then they would sneak into our camp at night, and cut throats so quietly no one would even notice until fifteen or twenty soldiers were dead. It got so no one dared sleep."

"They were fearsome, then. But what was their appearance?"

"Dark skin. Black hair: straight, coarse, long as a horse's tail. Eyes the color of their skin. Their faces were sharp and narrow. Long, braided hair—dozens of braids, all knotted together."

There was a silence while in her mind Clement compared this description to the storyteller, and found no difference but in the length of her hair—excepting that solitary braid.

The stable captain said, "You're not thinking this storyteller is the one that was captured alive? Because I can tell you now, she's not."

"One of these warriors was captured alive?" she said in amazement.

"She lured us into a canyon, and then her companions dumped a mountain of rocks onto our heads. We pulled her out

of the rocks, and it turned out she spoke Sainnese, so the commander thought she might be some use, and didn't kill her."

"Good gods, she spoke Sainnese? Would you recognize her,
do you think?"

"I tell you, it's not her. This warrior we captured, her back
was broken. She was paralyzed—when they chopped off some
of her toes she didn't even flinch. And her skull was cracked,
too, a kick from a war horse, probably. The medic figured
she'd die any moment, but she was still alive when we reached
the garrison. I don't know what became of her, but she sure
isn't walking on her own two feet!"

They had reached the gaol. As they went through the ritual
of recognition and admittance, Clement's exhausted thoughts
were overcome by a dreadful image of a woman warrior like
herself—maimed, broken, tormented by memories of a massacre—and yet alive. Then, Clement and the stable captain
stood at the barred door of the gaol cell. Within, the storyteller
sat awake, huddled in her cloak, gazing blankly into darkness.
Clement held up the lantern so its light could enter through the
grate. The stable captain peered in. He stumbled back. He gave
Clement a look of terrified disbelief. "It's her."

In Clement's bed the girl-nurse slept, puffy-eyed and tangle-
haired, in a mess of blankets that testified to a terrible restlessness. She must have realized the child was sick, and was
terrified even before she saw the storyteller arrested. But she
had found a temporary peace now, and Clement left her alone.
The baby, closely wrapped in his basket near the fire, was still
cold, still limp, still unresponsive, but still breathing. She
talked to him softly and bid him farewell. An eventful, possibly dreadful day lay before her, and she doubted she would
manage to see him alive again.

She left him in his basket, and went to Gilly's room. Perhaps
two hours remained before Cadmar would have reason to angrily summon her, and even the sight of Gilly's sleeping face,
gray and drawn with pain, could not make her wait to awaken

him. She shook him. He opened his eyes, squinting in the lantern light. "You look like hell," he mumbled.

She sat heavily in the chair by his bed. "I'll help you to get up. I don't even know where to look for your aide at this hour."

"Give me some time to wake up, or I'll just fall over. How is the baby?"

"I doubt he'll survive the morning."

He sighed.

"Gilly, what do you know about earth magic? How does it work? What can it do?"

"Earth magic?" Gilly rubbed his face with one hand. "It is physical—a physical power with a physical existence. It inhabits the flesh of the earth bloods, and it flows out of them through physical contact. Whatever earth witches do, they do it with their hands."

"Are earth bloods healers?"

"Yes, people with earth talent might be healers, farmers, stone masons, artisans of any type."

"Could an earth witch heal a broken back that had caused paralysis?"

Gilly's painful effort of sitting up was excruciating to watch. He finally said, "I doubt it. I don't know what the limits are, but surely something so dramatic would be talked about."

"Could a G'deon?"

"A G'deon?" Gilly considered. "Yes, it seems possible."

Clement said, "Well then, the proof of the Lost G'deon's existence, and the proof of the storyteller's identity may all be written down, in a document that even Cadmar can read."

"What document?" said Gilly with great surprise.

"The storyteller's body: her skin, her bones, her scars."

Gilly rubbed his furrowed face again. "You must be awfully frightened, Clem," he said. "Terror brings out your genius."

The storyteller waited, as she always waited, in silence and stillness, without impatience or fear. Gilly entered the cell behind Clement and sat heavily on the stone bench.

The walls of the cell were shiny with ice. A barred window, as big as a hand, let in a little gray light. When the wind picked up, it blew in a cloud of fresh snow. A few flakes decorated the storyteller's shoulder.

Clement said, "Take off your clothes."

The storyteller commented, "This is a strange conclusion."

Gilly said sharply. "What do you mean?"

In the silence that followed, the storyteller stood up and undressed. Under cloak and jacket she wore her close-fitted suit of heavy gray wool. Under that there was silk, and linen, and under that nothing. Her skin, even the skin that was never exposed to sun, was brown, almost black. She had a light build, a deep chest, and powerful legs. It was not at all difficult to imagine her running lightly up and down the vicious ridges of the high mountains, or sneaking into a heavily guarded camp to cut the throats of sleeping soldiers.

Clement lay her hand on the woman's bare shoulder. She felt a shudder, but the storyteller only seemed to be shivering from cold. Clement put a hand to the woman's coarse, stiff hair. She dug her fingers to the skull, and her fingertips encountered the hard ridge of a healed fracture. She felt how the woman's hair tangled there, where it grew out crooked from a ragged scar. "How long has it been since your head was broken?" Clement asked.

"My head was broken?" the storyteller asked.

Surely this flat curiosity was feigned? Exasperated, Clement said sharply, "Turn around so I can see your back."

The storyteller turned impassively.

"Good gods! Gilly, hold up the lantern!"

The storyteller's back was a shocking patchwork: a disease, or a terrible burn, had left large pale patches in her skin. But when Clement touched the pale skin, she found it soft, healthy, unweathered as a child's. What could cause such a thing?

Gilly said, "Lying a long time on the back in an unclean bed can cause the flesh to be eaten away, I've heard." He was speaking with difficulty; the lantern trembled in his hand.

Clement said, "Did that happen to you, storyteller?"

The storyteller said nothing.

"Hold still." Clement pressed her fingers down the length of the woman's backbone. When she found the lumpy mass of a healed bone in the woman's lower back, she felt no surprise, only relief. She knelt, taking the lantern from Gilly to illuminate the woman's bare feet. Some of her toes were brown, others were pink. And then, as Clement raised her face, she found right in front of her nose the distinct, round scar of a gunshot wound in the side of the storyteller's thigh.

"You must have taken that gunshot when you were in South Hill," Clement said. "When you were a Paladin. But a wound like this would have putrefied. It wouldn't be a clean scar like this—in fact, you should have lost your leg entirely."

The storyteller looked down at her. "What a story my skin is telling you."

"I read here that you are longtime enemy of my people, an Ashawala'i warrior whose back was broken six years ago."

"Katrim," she said.

"What?"

"You believe I am an enemy of your people, a Paladin, and a *katrim*?"

"I believe you are the last survivor of the Ashawala'i. I believe your injuries were healed by the Lost G'deon."

The storyteller said, "May I get dressed?"

"Oh, for gods' sake! What possible purpose can your pretense of forgetfulness serve?"

"I do not pretend." Without permission, the storyteller began dressing.

Clement sat next to Gilly and put her head in her hands. Her relief had given way to crushing exhaustion. Like a wanderer lost in a dark night, she could see no further than her next random step. After a night's desperate work, she could prove that the Lost G'deon existed. And now she had no idea what to do with that knowledge. "Gilly, help me."

Gilly said, "I have always believed the storyteller to be telling the truth as she understood it. Storyteller, will you tell us what is your purpose in Watfield?"

"I am collecting stories," the storyteller said.

"It occurs to me that a fire blood could probably make a great deal of sense of us, just by hearing our stories."

The storyteller looked up from doing her buttons. "A fire blood can make sense of anything. Perhaps I could also, were I more than half a person."

"You are half a person?" said Gilly blankly.

"That is what the raven told me."

Clement lifted her head from her hands. "Gods of hell!" she breathed.

"You've been talking to a raven?" said Gilly casually. "What did you talk about?"

"You must ask the raven, Lucky Man. I do not owe you a story."

Clement was nonplused, but Gilly apparently had overcome the lingering mental dullness caused by his pain draught, for he promptly said, "But you do owe a story to Clement, now she has read to you the story in your skin."

Prompted by a jab of Gilly's elbow, Clement said politely, "I would very much like to hear this tale."

The storyteller covered her once-mutilated feet with heavy wool socks. Then, she reached into her left boot and took out her packet of glyph cards. "The raven told me that I am part of a whole, and that the remainder of my self is lost. In return for this story, he asked me to cast the cards, to answer a question. The question was, *How can the Sainnites be overcome without destroying the spirit of Shaftal?* This is how I answered him."

As she lay fifteen glyph cards on the bench in a complicated arrangement, Gilly said in a low voice, "To read the glyphs with any depth requires long study—and I thought this arcane knowledge was lost entirely. How a tribal woman learned it is difficult to imagine."

Apparently finished laying out the cards, the storyteller put on boots, jacket, and cloak. She pulled the hood over her head, and sat on the bench with her knees tucked to her chest and her cloak wrapped around herself against the cold. The illustrated people on the glyph cards variously spoke, shouted, screamed, or wondered—but they were all speechless, and the odd situations the cards depicted seemed meaningless. Gilly said, "Ask her to explain, Clem."

Clement said, "Explain these cards to me, as you explained them to the raven."

"I could not explain the pattern to the raven, and I cannot explain it to you."

"You cast the cards without understanding them?" said Gilly in dismay. "What good do you suppose it did the raven?"

The storyteller said, "The raven did not seem disappointed."

The dawn bell began to ring. Its crisp sound could be heard clearly in the small cell. The storyteller said, "This is the twelfth day of the new year. Now I am done telling stories."

And, though Clement and Gilly both asked increasingly frustrated questions, the storyteller remained as implacably and unreadably speechless as her cards.

Chapter Thirty-Five

In one of four rented rooms, in the center of a table, there lay a small, bloodstained file. A raven had filched it from a dead woman's pocket and had brought it to Karis, who had carried it in her own pocket for the last five days of their grueling journey to Watfield. Next to the file lay Emil's pocket watch, ticking merrily, oblivious to its exile from the little room where Emil and Medric studied, questioned, and argued over a pattern of glyph cards laid out on the floor. The twelfth day of the first year of Karis G'deon had dawned—and Karis sat at the table with her head in her hands, still waiting for her two wise men to tell her what to do.

Nearly six years had passed since Garland left Watfield to become a wandering exile. Last night he had returned, hauling a sledge packed with blankets and cooking gear, surrounded by a dozen companions, including Councilor Mabin and six of her Paladins, plus one bored and irritable little girl, and a raven too tired to fly. To find shelter at that late hour for such a number of travelers had proven quite difficult. Garland had heard the midnight bell ring in the garrison as they finally built up the fires in their rented rooms.

Just past midnight, Norina had sat beside Karis at this very table. "It is time for the storyteller to die."

Karis said, "The Sainnites imprisoned her this afternoon. She's safely out of your reach."

Norina had silently studied her, until Karis hid her face in her hands and told her to leave her alone.

Norina said to Garland, "Has Karis slept at all since Long Night?"

"She's slept a little, some nights."

"She has a sturdy constitution, but she can't continue like this."

Karis said, "Leave the nagging to your husband—he does it better. And go away."

Norina had complied, but not for long. The Paladins, sent out to locate some specific townsfolk, began to return with them: more of Emil's numerous friends, Mabin's agents, members of the local Paladin company—all confused by this abrupt summons from their beds, and inclined to react with amazed tears when they were introduced to Karis. She endured their adulation with a certain graceless patience. Mabin and Norina talked with these people all night, and Emil's incomprehensible work with the glyph cards was frequently interrupted as he was asked to greet newcomers, or to answer questions.

Soon after dawn, when the city elders arrived, Garland went out to purchase a nearby baker's bread as it came out of the oven. But Karis could not eat anything. Now, the two of them sat alone, waiting.

Clement and Gilly arrived in Cadmar's quarters a few moments behind Commander Ellid. They walked in on her complaint about not having been forewarned of Clement's actions, but Cadmar was still too dumbfounded at what he was hearing to have yet become angry.

Clement attempted to explain herself.

Ellid, who knew nothing of the political matters that concerned Clement, lapsed into a bewildered silence, which she broke only once to comment, "Well, perhaps there was some justification."

But Cadmar scarcely seemed able to hear what Clement was saying. "I told you to rest!"

"Yes, general."

"And instead you took it upon yourself—"

Gilly said, "General, in this one case, perhaps . . ."

Cadmar roared, "I will not overlook it!"

In the past, Clement's frequent disagreements with Cadmar had always been resolved by a combination of persuasion and manipulation in which Clement and Gilly had usually collaborated. Clement knew better than to oppose Cadmar directly: Cadmar loved to fight and delighted in displaying his superiority, and she could not possibly win against him. Now, the flood of Cadmar's rage washed over her, and she could only endure the shouting, seething at the waste of time.

At last, she was able to say, "I apologize, general."

But to Clement's surprise, Ellid said, "General, if I may speak, it does seem that what Clement has learned is quite urgent."

Cadmar glared at her, then turned a suspicious look on Gilly, who managed to be preoccupied with trimming a pen. Cadmar said reluctantly, "Tell me again what you've learned, Lieutenant-General."

Clement told him again. When she finished, he was staring at her with such disbelief that her heart sank. She had thought she was prepared to battle him into comprehension, but her will simply failed her.

She said hopelessly, "Whether I'm right or not, general, we must have some kind of plan—"

At that moment a shame-faced soldier came in, carrying a glittering knife that was cautiously wrapped in a piece of leather. Gilly had taken custody of the storyteller's glyph cards, and Clement had told the soldiers on guard there to search the storyteller, and to block the cell window to prevent any further conversations with ravens. The soldier gave Clement the knife he had found on the storyteller's person, saying, "Careful, Lieutenant-General. It's got a wicked edge on it."

As the soldier left the room, Cadmar, still in a temper, began vehemently stating the various reasons why it was impossible to develop a strategy without any solid information about the enemy's plans. Of course he was correct; but that their task was impossible did not alter the fact that they needed to do it. It would be easiest if Cadmar could argue himself into accepting that fact, so Clement pretended to listen to him, while with feigned abstraction she unwrapped and examined the little knife.

It was the most beautifully crafted blade she had ever set eyes on. The metal shone like polished silver, and though its surface was smooth as glass Clement could see wavery lines, like ripples in sand on a beach, as though the molten metal had been folded and hammered flat, over and over. Clement was no expert in metal-craft, but the skill displayed here seemed, simply, beyond possibility.

Clement stepped over to Gilly and showed the knife to him. He stared, and muttered, "No mastermark? A metalsmith of such skill, working in secret?"

Cadmar paused in his argument to glare at them. Clement had not taken off her coat, so she dropped the blade into her pocket. And then she noticed a stinging in her fingertip, and a swelling bead of blood. She could have sworn she had not even touched the blade's edge.

One of the Paladins had brought in a plate of hot dumplings for Karis, but the plate remained untouched. Garland picked up Emil's teapot and re-filled Karis's cup: a bit of porcelain the size and weight of an empty egg shell.

Karis gave a flinch. "How hard is it to avoid cutting yourself?"

"What?" Garland said.

"Zanja's knife. Every time someone touches it, it draws blood." Karis poked the raven-scavenged file with her fingertip. "Even an act so innocent as making a knife, or a file, isn't innocent at all. Blood is shed. People die."

The file, rolling away before her fingertip, struck Emil's watch with a metallic ring.

"And yet I must act," said Karis heavily.

The door opened. Mabin, apparently immune to weariness, came briskly in. "How long does it take to read a handful of symbols?" Karis did not even look at her.

The old councilor sat down, and looked at the ticking watch. "When do we run out of time?"

Karis said, "When I go mad."

"A little *before* that, I hope." Mabin picked up the file and rubbed its rough surface lightly with her fingertips. She said, "Karis, it's not your fault: they could have cut through the padlock with any file."

Karis turned to her. She said in some astonishment, "Are you trying to be kind to me?"

Cadmar seemed to think he was making a speech. "Over twenty years have passed since our people in a decisive victory became the rulers of Shaftal. At great risk we destroyed every last one of these so-called witches—fire bloods, dirt bloods, and all the rest of them. There's been not a hint, not a whisper, of magic as long as I can remember!"

Clement watched him pace and gesture. No doubt he was imagining the shouts of praise and bursts of applause that would greet his resonant words. Willis was dead, and Cadmar was not particularly clever, but she could think of no other important difference between the two leaders.

Gilly sat on his stool, gray-faced with pain. His hooded gaze was hard, bitter, and even contemptuous. He had been a desperate street beggar once, and Cadmar had ridden past on a fine horse, and noticed him, and given him a ride, a meal, a place to shelter from the cold. For such minimal kindness, a crippled child might sell his soul and not be blamed for it. Clement could not so easily excuse herself.

She said abruptly, "General, I've neither slept nor eaten since yesterday."

Cadmar glanced at her, then at Gilly who had not yet been able to take his morning tincture, then at Ellid, whose breakfast was probably congealing in her quarters as her lieutenants wondered what had become of her. "Come back in half an hour, all of you," said Cadmar. "And I want to hear what you imagine might be done to avert this supposed threat."

Dismissed, Clement started for the stairs. She heard Gilly's door close quietly, and then the distant slam of the outer door behind Ellid. But Clement remained at the foot of the stairs.

She could not take the first step up that long climb to her quarters, where the hysterical girl watched over the dying infant. She simply could not do it.

She finally walked back down the hall to the outdoor door. The soldier on duty opened it with a smart salute, and politely advised her that since it was bitter cold she had better button her coat.

She did so, standing at the top of the steps, squinting in the pallid light. The rising sun could be spotted between rooftops. The road was empty, the construction work halted by cold, everyone not on guard duty huddled indoors. She went down onto the ice, which made secret, crunching sounds under her boots.

After a few steps, she could not continue. She could not see. She stood in the blank, cold light of day where anyone could have observed her, with tears scalding her cheeks.

Something black flapped across her vision. Wiping her eyes on her sleeve, she said harshly, "Tell the G'deon I'm a weakling. I don't care."

The raven gazed at her through one eye, and then the other. The bird's lack of expression and attentive energy seemed to invite her to further explain herself. Clement said, "My son is five weeks old. He doesn't even have a name. And he is dying."

The raven maintained its illusion of interest.

Clement tried to imagine what the bird might want from her. And then, she reached very cautiously into her pocket for the storyteller's knife, found a bit of string in another pocket, and used it to bind the leather around the blade. She lay it on the snow, and stepped back.

The raven walked to the slim packet, hooked a claw into the loop of the string, and lifted off. In a long, gradual climb, the bird swam through bitter air to the rooftops, over the rooftops, over the garrison wall, and out of sight above the city, with the storyteller's blade dangling from his claw.

Gods of my mother, thought Clement. *The G'deon is already here.*

* * *

Karis raised her head sharply from where it rested in the support of her palm.

Garland lifted his head from his arms. He had, though it seemed impossible, been dozing.

Karis said fiercely, "I need some milk!"

"If you'll eat one of those dumplings, I'll go get some," said Garland.

Karis picked up a dumpling and took a bite. She raised an eyebrow at him.

"Chew," he said. "Swallow. All right, I am going."

Clement was the last to re-enter Cadmar's room. She had a hot roll in her hand and a half dozen more crammed into her pockets. She gave one to Gilly, who had washed and shaved, but did not seem much improved. His gaze asked her a question she could not interpret. She offered one to Ellid, who appeared only more worried, now that she had taken some time to think.

Cadmar said sarcastically, "Well, Clement, what do you think we should do? Shall we send out our soldiers? To where? To attack what?"

Clement said, "We don't have to go out looking for the Lost G'deon. She'll come in person to rescue the storyteller, as she did before when the storyteller was Mabin's prisoner. And she's going to do it soon, for she's already in Watfield."

Gilly gave her a startled look. "If the G'deon—the supposed G'deon—is in the city . . . and she wants to be sure of the storyteller's safety—and you've made it impossible for that bird to keep an eye on her—"

"She'll be at the gate at any moment," Clement finished for him.

Ellid grunted with dismay, but Cadmar's face lit up.

Clement said, "What will we trade the storyteller for?"

Cadmar said, "If a woman claiming to be the G'deon shows up at our gate, do you really think I'll *bargain* with her?"

Clement sat in a chair, tore open a roll, and made herself take a bite. Even fresh from the oven, the bread was dry and tasteless.

. Cadmar said, "You thought it would be so complicated. But all we have to do is kill her."

Frowning worriedly, Ellid looked at Clement. Although Ellid was an inadvertent ally, unused to this alliance, she already seemed to have learned that it was Clement's job to contradict Cadmar.

But what could Clement say to him? Her son was dying, Kelin was dead, those children in the garrison would never see their homes again. Why was her heart still torn like this? Why not kill the G'deon? Why did she want to make an argument she herself did not believe?

She said nothing. In silence, she ate her roll.

When Garland returned, the room was cold with a recent draft, and Karis was forcing shut the window sash. The plate of dumplings was empty. Garland said accusingly, "You fed your meal to the ravens?"

Karis held up a glittering blade.

"The knife? How did the raven get it?"

Her smile was tight, and her eyes were a bit strange: focused, but also intensely preoccupied. Garland gave her the small bottle of milk he had purchased. She put it into the inside pocket of her long woolen doublet, lay the glittering little blade in her toolbox on the floor, and picked up Emil's watch. She crossed the room, opened a door, and tossed in the watch. There was a startled exclamation. Emil came out with the watch in his hand, having apparently managed to catch it before it met its demise. He said, "Are we out of time? Or merely out of patience?"

"I'm going to the garrison now," Karis said.

He blinked at her, rubbed his eyes, and blinked at her again.

Wild-eyed and gaunt with weariness, Medric came out of the room. Glancing in, Garland saw the glyph cards arranged carefully on the floor. Karis said to Medric, "Tell me how you read the storyteller's glyph pattern."

"So our torture is finally to end? Well, what shall we decide this pattern means, Emil?"

Emil looked very unhappy. "If we could have some semblance of certainty!"

"Pretend that you're certain," said Karis.

"We believe we need to kill someone, and we are only guessing who. Wouldn't you rather we could be positive?"

There was a silence, but not a particularly long one. Karis said, "I have with me a very small assassin. Who shall I kill?"

Clement finally brought herself to say reasonably, "If the woman *is* the G'deon, she may not be easy to kill. Isn't that right, Gilly?"

"Not easy," said Gilly morosely. "And certainly we would not be wise to try."

Cadmar said, "But we are *soldiers* and I don't see why this storyteller's scars convince you of anything other than that she's had a dangerous and lucky life."

"A recovery from paralysis," said Clement. "Regrown body parts."

Cadmar snorted. "Impossible."

"Well, general, that's exactly my point." Doomed to keep repeating the arguments that Cadmar would not ever become able to hear. Clement said, "This Lost G'deon may be able to do *anything*!"

"But we don't know that."

"If we let her demonstrate her power so that we become certain, then it will be too late to negotiate," she said impatiently.

"What would you have me do?" His voice, gaining volume again, had also gained an edge of sarcasm. "The first woman who tells me she's the G'deon, should I bow to her and give her the keys to the garrison?"

Clement cried recklessly, "General, if she is the G'deon, you'll wish you had!"

Cadmar loomed over her, his face flushed red with anger.

Fists clenched, Clement forced her voice to plead rather than shout. "Talk to her first," she said. "General, just talk to her first."

"General!" The gate captain looked in the door. His expression was one of bafflement.

Cadmar's big hand clenched Clement's shoulder painfully. "What is happening at the gate?"

"General, three people are asking to speak to you. One is that cook who deserted some years ago."

Of course it would be the cook, thought Clement wildly.

"He says one of the people with him is Councilor Mabin. And the other he introduces as the G'deon of Shaftal."

Cadmar's not inconsiderable strength was crushing Clement into her chair. "What do they want?"

"The cook says they are here to make peace."

Cadmar snorted. "Captain, have someone fetch Gilly's horse. Tell those people that I am coming. Do they have weapons?"

"I don't see any, General, but I haven't searched them—they're still outside the gate, of course."

"Don't let them in. And Captain, let your soldiers be prepared for action."

"We are always prepared," said the captain stiffly.

As he left, Cadmar explained to Gilly, "I need you to translate."

He was going to talk to the Lost G'deon.

Perhaps, thought Clement, *we might yet survive.*

It's a little late to be wishing I'd never heard the sound of Karis's ax that day, Garland thought, as he stood beside Karis at the garrison gate. Or he should have left these odd people the day the raven first talked to him, when Karis gave him money and told him to go his way. But he had fallen in with them instead, and now here he stood, with a half dozen guns and crossbows trained on him by the armored guards in the towers.

"Ridiculous!" said Mabin, stiff and impatient at Karis's other side. "How much weaponry do they think it takes to kill three unarmed people? Have they no skill, or art?"

She was comparing them to the stylish Paladins, Garland supposed. Certainly, these armored killers seemed no more subtle than an angry bear or a deadly avalanche. But he could not imagine why Mabin found this fact surprising or worth commenting on. Perhaps, he thought, she was covering up her fear. He did not find this reassuring.

Since announcing she was going to the garrison, Karis had hardly spoken at all. Now she waited silently, with a gloved hand gripping one of the gate's iron bars, as if she were about to utter a disparaging comment on its workmanship. She gripped the iron a bit too hard, though. Garland could see the tense muscles swelling under her coat's heavy wool.

The dozen guards inside the gate, who bristled with guns, blades, and other weapons, and stood in a formation that seemed poised to go barging through the gate, snapped themselves into rigid attention. "The general is coming," said Garland shakily.

Karis looked at him and then, very lightly, lay her left hand reassuringly on his shoulder. "The war is over, Garland."

"I don't think these soldiers have heard that news."

"A big man, isn't he?" commented Mabin skeptically as General Cadmar strode into view, with several soldiers trailing him, and his crippled Lucky Man riding behind on horseback. "Which one is his lieutenant?"

"That hungry woman," Garland said.

Mabin peered through the gate at the rigid, hollow-eyed, weary woman, who kept a few reluctant paces behind her superior. "Hungry," she agreed. "And worried. Very worried."

By contrast, the general, though he kept his face schooled to an expression of grim severity, showed no sign of having suffered lately. "He is complacent at his good fortune," said Mabin, with no little sarcasm. "He can hardly wait to see us die."

Karis's hand had tightened on Garland's shoulder. He glanced at her worriedly, for his frail courage was entirely propped up by hers. She was breathing too fast, her face was pale, her expression startled and dismayed. She stared at Cadmar.

"Karis?" said Garland.

Mabin glanced at Karis. "What is it?"

Karis pressed her lips together and gave a slight shake to her head. The general was approaching, his people holding a few paces back. Lieutenant-General Clement was staring at Karis now, seeming to share her mysterious startlement. Baffled, Garland turned his attention to the general who so many years ago had demanded that Garland cook badly. His glance passed over Garland without any sign of recognition. "General Mabin," Cadmar greeted his old adversary.

Mabin looked distinctly disgusted.

Garland said in Sainnese, "General, this is Karis, the G'deon of Shaftal."

The bottom half of the gate was solid iron, but, like Karis, the general was so tall that the metal shielded less than half his body. The iron bars divided his upper body into vertical segments: gray uniform under a heavy coat of wool-lined leather, a furrowed face that may once have been handsome. Karis's thicket of hair curled manically while his was straight and thinning, but his hair may have once been bronze like hers. Karis had his broad shoulders. He had her big hands. They stood eye to eye, and those eyes were blue, an eye color scarcely ever seen in Shaftal outside the southern grasslands.

"Gods of hell!" breathed Garland in disbelief.

Cadmar glanced blankly at him.

In Shaftalese, Garland said to Mabin, "He is her father."

"Well, what do you have to say?" said Cadmar impatiently in Sainnese.

Mabin said, "Tell the general he'll wish he'd been less careless with his sperm!"

Karis said, very quietly, "What difference does it make? Just tell him why we're here, Garland."

What *difference* does it make? Garland looked back at Cadmar. How could this dolt not see what stood before him? Cadmar had carelessly, indifferently, obliviously spawned his own salvation, the bloody fool! All he had to do was recognize what a great and terrible thing he had done!

But Garland, dizzy with wanting to shout at the man, desperately holding back the horror that lay behind his anger, forced himself to say, "General Cadmar, Karis G'deon and General Mabin are here to make peace with the Sainnite people."

Looking amused, Cadmar gestured to the crippled man, who rode his horse up to the gate. The Lucky Man gave Karis a sharp, inquiring glance: the look of an intelligent man who desperately wished for the answers to the questions he could not ask. But, in stiff Shaftalese, he said, "Madam, the general wishes to know your terms."

"Karis," she corrected him. "Gilly, *will* he make peace? On any terms? Or is he just playing with us?"

The ugly man looked like he wanted nothing more than to honestly answer her question. But he was on the Sainnite side of the gate's iron bars, and that fact meant he had long ago traded his freedom for security. He said to Cadmar, in Sainnese, "She asks if you are sincerely interested in making peace on any terms."

"Will the Paladins lay down their arms?" asked Cadmar loudly.

Garland translated.

"What is this, a duel of questions?" said Mabin. "Is giving a straight answer a sign of weakness?"

"I'm afraid it is," said Garland.

Karis said, "Lucky Man, tell him that when the Paladins no longer need weapons, they will lay them down. Will the Sainnites lay down their arms?"

"Will the Shaftali people acknowledge the Sainnites as their rulers?" Cadmar countered.

Karis looked into his hard, mocking eyes. "Do you truly believe that people can be ruled?" she asked in amazement.

While the Lucky Man translated, Garland heard Mabin say, "This is just a game to him, Karis."

"I need to be certain that it's hopeless!" Karis said.

The general seemed to find Karis's most recent question disconcerting, or perhaps merely irritating. "You offer me nothing!" he said. "Why should I make peace?"

"I am offering you something: a choice. I will make peace with you, General Cadmar. Or I will make peace without you."

Mabin, who had been nonplused when Karis gave her the identical choice, seemed much amused by Cadmar's bewilderment. Then, the general uttered a harsh, mocking laugh, and gestured—at the pistols and crossbows overhead, at the bristling soldiers that surrounded him. "*You* threaten *me*?"

"Surely the person who needs no weapons is far stronger than the one who does," said Mabin. Perhaps it was a Paladin maxim. Garland was not certain who Mabin meant to address, but the Lucky Man translated her words, and Cadmar no longer seemed amused.

Karis said, "I will not give you this choice again. Will you make peace?"

Cadmar said, "You give me no reason to choose!"

Karis said to Mabin, rather blankly, "How could I possibly *give* him a reason?" Then Karis glanced deliberately at the tired, desperately attentive woman who stood several paces away, but well within hearing. "Reasons are created by the reasoner!"

The lieutenant-general looked jolted, and half opened her mouth as if to protest that a soldier, whose job is to obey orders only, certainly has no use for reasoning.

The Lucky Man's translation was distracted and awkward. Cadmar glared impatiently at him.

Mabin was saying to Karis, "If the general is incapable of making his own reasons, he's incapable of making peace. Is that what you're thinking?" Karis nodded. "That's a pretty piece of air logic," Mabin said dryly.

"It's hopeless. By any logic."

The Lucky Man had not missed this interchange. As he summarized it in Sainnese, he tried to soften it. But the general turned on Karis. "Incapable? Because I choose not to bow my head to a rabble of dirt-grubbing peasants? Because—"

Garland, beginning to translate, noticed distractedly that Karis's often-mended glove had worn through again in the palm. Her soot-black skin showed through in patches framed by frayed red yarn as she lifted her left hand from his shoulder, took hold of the thick iron bar, and bent it neatly aside like a green twig. She reached through the gate, and took hold of

Cadmar by the collar. The heavy wool of his uniform ripped like paper.

The general's big hands pounded helplessly at hers. His shout became a gurgle.

The lieutenant-general cried sharply, "Hold!"

The silence and stillness that reigned there at the gate was a wonder. The fascinated, horrified soldiers stood rigid as stone, unable to shoot lest they injure or kill the general by accident. Then, Lieutenant-General Clement stepped forward. "Clement!" cried the gate captain. The Lucky Man grabbed for her shoulder, but missed. She heedlessly put herself within reach of Karis's other hand, and said, "Let him go. Please. I beg you."

Karis said, just as calmly, "Only a fool picks a fight with a blacksmith."

Another maxim, thought Garland wildly. This one was probably from Meartown, where fistfights were said to be rare.

The lieutenant-general put her hand on the arm that was strangling Cadmar to death. She said reasonably, "Your strength came from him, though."

"He left me to become a smoke-addicted child whore in Lalali. What strength I have certainly did not come from him."

Cadmar struggled again in Karis's grip. She tightened the garrote of his collar, and he stopped, his eyes starting to glaze.

Garland looked at the lieutenant-general. She seemed only distantly aware of Cadmar's desperate, humiliating position. She seemed to be thinking of something else—something painful enough to make the soldier's mask slip off her face. She said, "My people have forgotten how to take responsibility for a child, Cadmar among them. It is true."

Karis gazed at her steadily, patiently, as though she were waiting for a wild bird to make up its mind to alight on her finger.

Clement said, "But do you want to be the kind of person who would murder her father because of his carelessness?"

"I will not murder your general for that particular carelessness," Karis said quietly. "His personal failings are no longer important."

Garland knew what Karis really meant, but Clement looked expectantly at her, as though she thought she had won something.

With her right hand, which had not let go of the gate, Karis bent another iron bar casually out of the way. The lieutenant-general, either very brave or very well-disciplined, did not flinch or draw back out of reach. Karis reached into her doublet and then put her hand through the bars of the gate. She offered Clement the bottle of milk. "This is your son's life," she said. "Give it to him, Clement."

Clement's ungloved hands were numb with cold, but the bottle was warm from the G'deon's breast. Clement closed her hand around the bottle and then she jammed it into her pocket.

She had been precisely, deliberately, irresistibly coerced, and she knew it.

The G'deon said, very gently, "I'm sorry for what I'm about to do to you." She released her hold on Cadmar's throat. He stumbled back, gasping for breath, then opened his mouth in a raw shout of rage.

Karis gazed somberly at him through the twisted bars of the gate. The iron lay between his fist and her.

Clement had stepped forward to steady him, but that courtesy only brought her within range. *I should have known better,* she thought, just before his massive fist smashed into her face.

When Clement's vision cleared, she found herself sprawled on ice and cobblestones. There was a lot of shouting. She was dragged aside like a sack of turnips. Something clattered lightly on the stones. She reached for it, but could not quite seem to grab hold of it. It was farther than she thought, then closer. Finally, she grasped it, and examined it with puzzlement.

A piece of a shattered crossbow bolt.

She lifted her head and peered at the guard tower. Her vision swam—but those dismayed shouts concerned her.

"Lieutenant-General, keep your head down!"

It was very forward, and very thoughtful, of the soldier to shout at her like that. She ignored her, and with some effort got

herself on her elbows, knees, and finally to her feet, in a sick-
eningly spinning world.

The soldier caught her before she fell again.

"I have got to talk to the general," she slurred.

"Not wise," the soldier said. "Give it a moment. You're addled from the blow."

"Wise?" She looked at her in confusion.

"Gods of hell," said the soldier. "Why can't they get the gate
unlocked?"

Clement looked at the gate. The captain fought the key in
the resisting lock. He shouted an order at the towers. Clement
looked up—when would the sky stop that nauseating spin? In
the towers, armored soldiers picked up a ladder. It fell apart in
their hands. Rungs clattered onto stone. Side supports broke
into pieces.

The whole world seemed to be coming apart. Perhaps the
guns also lay in pieces. Not a shot had been fired.

Clement wrenched herself out of the stunned soldier's grip.
Cadmar and Gilly had taken shelter against the wall on the
other side of the gate. She stumbled across—were the stones
actually heaving under her feet?

"Cadmar!" she cried.

He turned. His throat was already bruising purple. His face
was red. He had the weird, blank gaze of a berserker.

She shouted at him. "Call after the G'deon! Tell her you've
changed your mind! Tell her you will make peace!"

The soldier had been right: she was addled. And she was too
slow to turn away from his fist. Her nose gave a sickening
crack. She went down in snow. She could not pay attention to
much of anything for a while. Then, she realized she was suf-
focating on snow and blood, and began choking and coughing,
and then she could breathe.

Her face was a pain so vivid that it cleared all the clutter of
fear straight out of her mind.

She felt her pocket. The bottle of milk had not broken. She
rested her battered face gently in the soothing, scarlet-stained
snow, and waited for the chaos to end and the bleeding to stop.

Chapter Thirty-Six

The soldiers and their shattered weapons were trapped behind walls they could not climb and a gate they could not open. Garland strolled away with Karis's hand again on his shoulder, and Mabin snickering to herself at Karis's other side.

Emil stepped out of the alley from which he had been watching, and showed them the way down a maze of back roads. They were not escorted by the visible and remarkable Paladins, but by a half dozen ordinary, if somewhat self-important, townsfolk. These people looked sidelong at Karis, who plodded like a plow horse coming home from the fields.

Near someone's back garden, Norina paced up and down by a covered delivery wagon. She uttered an exclamation at the sight of Karis's face. "What happened?"

Karis crawled into the delivery wagon and folded herself up in a corner. Norina gave Emil a significant glance, and followed her in.

"What went wrong?" Emil asked tiredly.

Mabin leaned her head close to his, for the gathered people had anxiously drawn forward. "General Cadmar is Karis's father."

Emil glanced sharply at Garland, who nodded a confirmation. "Did she kill him?" Emil asked. "Or not?"

Garland thought that if Karis had killed Cadmar it would have devastated her. And if she hadn't, it still would have devastated her. In the shadows of the van, Karis's face seemed like a pale mask. Norina had clasped one of her hands, and was talking to her urgently, with her mouth close to her ear.

"She *seemed* resolved," Mabin said uncertainly.

"She killed him," Garland said.

Emil glanced at him again, inquiringly. Garland held up his hands as Karis had when she put them both through the gate. "This is your son's life," he quoted Karis, gesturing towards the right. Then, he gestured towards the left, holding an invisible Cadmar by the throat, speechless.

"This is my father's death," said Emil.

Garland put his hands down, feeling extremely self-conscious. Mabin was giving him a very surprised look, but Emil clasped Garland's elbow and said, "I knew you were the right one to send in with her."

They got in the wagon and closed the doors, and were taken on a jolting journey across rough cobblestones. Garland supposed that Norina's fierce whisper continued to fling itself at Karis's obdurate silence, but all he could hear was the rumble of the wheels. When the wagon stopped and the door opened, the light revealed a sight Garland had never imagined possible: Karis in a huddle, with her face buried in Norina's shoulder, Norina's hand stroking the mad tangle of her hair.

Yet another contingent of awestruck citizens had met the wagon at the back of a dry goods shop. Emil firmly pushed the crowd back, and Karis crawled heavily out of the wagon. White-faced, stark-eyed, she began to remove a ragged glove so she could properly greet this new group of strangers, but Emil said firmly, "Karis, you've done enough. Who's in charge here? Take us where we're going, please."

Walking next to Karis, Garland took part of her weight—not a light burden. Karis asked Norina, "Where's Leeba?"

"Is there something wrong with your ravens? Emil!"

Emil extricated himself from an intense conversation with Mabin. Norina said to him, "We've got to find the ravens somehow, and get them into shelter. And does anyone know exactly where Leeba is?"

"She's with my children, ice skating," a nearby woman said. "The pond is over there—see those treetops?"

Emil said, "Send someone to bring Leeba to Karis. And J'han also—he's with her."

"I'll go myself." The woman left.

Emil picked another member of their escort, apparently at random, who found himself in a very peculiar conversation with the G'deon of Shaftal as she attempted to tell him where the ravens were by describing what the birds could see. They walked down a narrow passageway between buildings, and Karis was saying, "It seems like a big garden, with a fountain in the middle."

"Is there a red and green house nearby, with a tower? And a lightning rod with a blue glass ball in it?" Apparently, Emil had managed to pick the exact person in their group who knew every minuscule detail of his town's landscape.

Karis stumbled on a loose cobblestone. Up ahead, there stood an extremely dilapidated house, with a Paladin standing guard at the sagging back gate. They appeared to have arrived at their next destination.

The baby's girl-nurse still huddled in the bed, but she was awake, and wide-eyed with fear. "Lieutenant-General, I'm sorry—I didn't know—" The baby lay in his basket, blanket-wrapped, though the stupid girl had let the fire practically burn out. The girl's terrified babbling continued, but Clement paid her no heed. She picked up her son and sat down by the cold hearth.

A couple of confused soldiers had helped Clement to her quarters, and now stood uncertainly in the doorway. Clement broke the wax seal on the milk bottle, stuck in her finger, and let a drop of milk fall from her fingertip to the baby's mouth.

She waited. His mouth moved. She dipped her finger again, and put it into her son's mouth, and felt the slight movement of his lips and tongue as he sucked.

A drop of blood fell from her nose to his blanket. As she tilted her head so the blood would run down her throat, she noticed the wide-eyed soldiers. "Escort this girl out of the garrison."

"I'm not sure we can."

"If they haven't got the gate open yet, lower her over the wall with a rope. Tell her to go home to her parents."

"Yes, Lieutenant-General."

The other soldier said sympathetically, "The general's got a heavy fist, eh? I'll find a medic for you."

They left, dragging the sobbing girl, who probably thought she was going to be killed. Clement fed her son from her fingertip. Later, she paused to build up the fire and to boil a clean bottle. She returned to find the baby blinking at her from his basket.

She said, "Well, I've ruined my career for you."

His mouth opened; he sucked her finger hungrily.

She said, more to herself than to him, "So the child creates the parent, eh? Backwards though it seems?" She added, "Listen, little guy. I have to tell you some surprising news: you aren't going to be a soldier."

As they entered the run-down, back-alley house with a roof that seemed certain to leak and a garden that was piled with frozen ordure, Garland could hear a muted commotion of cleaning, of furniture being brought in and the rapid, confident banging of several carpenters' hammers. They entered a big, crowded kitchen, and Garland was immediately irritated to see how far advanced the cooking had gotten without his help. A survey of the first-floor rooms revealed that all the bedrooms were in the midst of a frenzy of cleaning, so he told Norina to bring Karis into the parlor. As Garland put together a plate of bread and cold meat and got a pot of tea steeping, J'han arrived with Leeba, followed by a woman carrying two exhausted ravens. In the parlor, Karis held Leeba on her lap, and listened, as though she had no other concerns, to her daughter's excited account of alphabet lessons, ice skating, and playing with a pet ferret. J'han had gotten Karis's boots off and was affectionately admonishing her for getting her feet wet.

Garland sat on the stool beside Karis and piled a little mound of cold ham onto a small, slim square of black bread, dabbed it with mustard, and decorated it with transparent sweet pickles. This he rather summarily slipped into Karis's mouth. Leeba found the operation hilarious and demanded that she be allowed to help. Karis ate passively and obediently from her daughter's hand. For the first time, Garland could see the lingering ghost of Karis the smoke addict, who had gotten in the habit of cooperating with the people who worked to make her survive a drug that eventually killed everyone who used it. It was a terrible insight.

Garland felt Norina's discomforting gaze on him, as he piled up more ham for Leeba to feed to Karis. "Careful—don't let it fall apart," he said, as the little girl snatched it from him.

"Karis doesn't *like* pickles," Leeba announced when a pickle slice fell to the floor.

"She does so. You're the one who doesn't like pickles."

"The *ravens* don't even like pickles," Leeba persisted, as Emil came in with another raven. "Open up!" she said severely to her mother, and jammed the food into her mouth.

Garland glanced at Norina finally. The Truthken had done something to Karis—had grabbed hold of her somehow and pulled her back from a cliff she was about to fall over. Now the danger was past, and Norina looked cool and distant as ever, and the hand she rested on Karis's shoulder was merely reminding her that she was there.

"Emil, that pot on the table should be ready to pour," Garland said.

Emil had put his raven on the back of a chair. "Bless you," he said sincerely and began pouring tea. "Do you want some, Karis?"

"No tea," J'han said. "By Shaftal, she's going to sleep."

Karis wiped mustard from her lip. "I am? How?"

"Feet first." J'han had one of Karis's big, callused feet in his hands. He reached for the oil that he had set on the hearth to melt and proceeded with a demonstration.

Karis sank visibly into her chair. "The Sainnites—" she began.

Mabin, who had just come in, said, "Karis, give some credit to your people. If Sainnites start tearing things apart, we'll take care of it. You don't actually have to solve every single problem with your own hands."

As Emil gave Mabin a confused look, Norina uttered a sharp laugh. "Are you supplanting me as Karis's scold? I doubt she can endure two of us, but I'd be glad to find a new occupation."

"No, thank you. It seems a pointless job."

Emil went to lean wearily by the fireplace. "Karis, I'm told the Sainnites managed to get two parties of soldiers over the wall, but that the soldiers seem very skittish and are only going through the motions of hunting for us. Every person in Watfield is keeping an eye on them. Believe me, it is safe for you to sleep."

Karis had shut her eyes. Whatever J'han was doing to her foot seemed irresistible. "I suppose," she said. "Since they're got no weapons."

Emil straightened sharply, and had to steady his teacup in its saucer. "None at all?"

Karis murmured, "J'han, I concede. Your power is greater than mine."

J'han said, "Leeba, let Karis lie down on the floor. You can help her take a nap, if you want to."

"Even the edged weapons?" said Emil, as Leeba crawled off Karis's lap.

"Dull beyond repair," said Karis. "Even the kitchen knives."

Garland stood up. "I'll get some blankets and a pillow."

But he paused at the door, distressed suddenly by the memory of that tired and hungry soldier, the lieutenant-general, reeling back from the general's vicious blow. "Emil?"

Emil was sipping spilled tea out of his saucer. He gave Garland a glance of a sort that had never been directed at him before: not merely inquiring, but respectful. It was unnerving.

"Do you *want* to make the Sainnites completely desperate?" Garland asked.

"No, no, not at all. I want them reasonable."

"Without kitchen knives, they'll have nothing to eat but porridge. That's going to make them desperate."

Emil gazed at him thoughtfully, obviously waiting for a suggestion.

"Let's feed them a decent meal," Garland said.

Mabin uttered a snort of disbelief. "Five hundred soldiers?"

Emil, leaning on the wall again, crossed one booted foot over the other. "Oh, Garland can do it," he said.

A tap at the door awoke Clement, and she was surprised to find that the room had grown dark, the fire had burned to coals, and her infant son slept in her arms, in the tangled mess the girl-nurse had made of the blankets on the bed. The medic had come by to set her broken nose. The pain had been awful, but somehow she had fallen into a doze despite it.

The door opened. "Clem? Can I come in?" It was Gilly.

"Has the garrison fallen apart yet?" Clement asked indifferently. She got up, and helped her old friend to a chair, and put the baby in his arms. The baby squinted at Gilly, yawned, and uttered a mild complaint.

Gilly blinked down at the infant, and smiled reluctantly. "This G'deon exercises a cruel generosity, eh? She gives you your heart's desire so you can destroy yourself with it. But you're so glad you don't even care that you're dead."

"She apologized," Clement said wryly. She lit a lamp, looked around rather hopelessly for something to eat, and was briefly distracted by the sight of her face in the little mirror tacked to the wall.

"You're even uglier than me at the moment," Gilly said.

"I see that."

"I always feared Cadmar would smash your face in someday."

"It was inevitable, really."

"Have you heard? The postern gates and the water gate can't be opened. The weapons can't be repaired. Not a blade in the garrison will hold an edge. We've got nothing to defend ourselves with but our bare hands."

Clement couldn't bring herself to be concerned. She sat heavily beside him, her face throbbing. "So what will Cadmar do? Surrender, or let us be massacred?"

"Hell, I don't know. The man's been in a temper all afternoon. Maybe he's trying to shout the G'deon to death. Do you think she's actually his daughter? She seems too astute, frankly."

The baby yelped. "Are you hungry again, Gabian?" Clement picked up the bottle that she had left to keep warm on the hearth. Gilly handed her the baby.

"A good name," he commented. "Your mother's, I believe."

Gabian sucked the bottle energetically, gazing into Clement's face, apparently indifferent to her swollen nose and black eye.

"Has Cadmar had you write my demotion orders yet?" Clement asked.

"Not yet. But you don't actually care, do you?"

Clement looked at her bent, worried, desperately unhappy friend, and felt a wrenching helplessness. "Gilly, I've reached the end."

Gilly gazed determinedly at his hands, which rested on his sturdy, battered cane. "You're going to desert. I knew that when I heard you had sent the girl away. You've got to get out now, or your son will starve. But where can you hope to find shelter? I know you, Clem: maybe you imagine that cow farmer would be glad to see you again, but you'll never impose such a risk on her. The local Paladins might find a use for you, but not a use you could accept. The G'deon, though, she's gone out of her way to put you in this position. What do you think? If she shelters you, will she allow you to advocate for your people without actually betraying them? That's a very difficult balance to keep—I should know."

Gilly continued to gaze at his folded hands, as though this simply was not a conversation that could have been conducted eye-to-eye. Thinking of Gilly's uneasy life of betrayal made the choice Clement was contemplating even more discomforting. Every day she would walk into this G'deon's circle of advisors, negotiate the strange Shaftali customs, and be subjected to their seething hostilities. And she would be friendless for the rest of her life.

"Gilly, I need you to come with me."

Gilly gave her that familiar sideways glance, and asked

dryly, "Are you proposing to sling me over the wall in a basket, like Gabian?"

"Oh, hell," she muttered, reminded that they were practically prisoners in their own garrison, and that her nimble-minded friend was in fact a cripple. "I'll have to come back for you somehow."

"I'll certainly be glad to see you," said Gilly. But they both knew perfectly well that the risk to Clement would be too great, and that once Clement was gone, Cadmar would make certain Gilly didn't follow her. "In the meantime," Gilly said steadily, "you can make it easier on yourself by getting the G'deon to give you some kind of assurance. It wouldn't hurt to win yourself some of her gratitude. Bring her the storyteller. That's a woman who can climb a wall, I'd wager."

Clement had scarcely been thinking, she realized, or she would have thought of this on her own.

"And do it tonight," Gilly added. "For Cadmar has ordered her executed tomorrow."

"Bloody hell! Gilly, I can't get the storyteller out of gaol—the soldiers won't let me. And if I try I'll just get myself arrested. And if I even were willing to attack my own people to win her freedom, what would I attack them with?"

Gilly raised a hand to rub his face. His calm was finally shaken. "Oh, Clem, she must not die! Just because Cadmar can't smash his fist into the one he's actually angry at, and he's using the storyteller as some kind of proxy—"

"That stupid man will assuage his injured pride even if it destroys his entire people in the process."

"Now you're sounding mutinous," said Gilly seriously.

She got up abruptly, and handed Gilly the protesting baby. "I'm going to open the window. Keep him out of the draft, will you?"

The window had not been opened since autumn, but with some banging and effort she managed to wrestle up the sash. The ice and snow that coated the shutters cracked loudly as she swung them open. The stars were coming out. The sky, that gorgeous deep blue that she loved, breathed down at her its bitter breath. She said out the window in a low voice, "Is there a raven here? I want to send a message to the G'deon."

She heard nothing. The garrison itself lay in unearthly stillness. The night bell suddenly began to ring, and she muttered, "Gods, this is a demoralized silence."

"No knives," said Gilly sardonically. "Therefore, no supper."

"Is that it? Hell!" She leaned out the window and twisted her body, so she looked up at the eaves of her own roof. "Raven!" she called, more loudly, feeling foolish, though Gilly maintained a serious silence.

She heard a scrabbling, and then, almost invisible against the sky, a head peered down at her. She heard a voice, like the creaking of old hinges. "Hold out your arm."

"Gilly, it talked!"

"Of course it talks," said Gilly. "You're still capable of surprise?"

She stuck her arm out the window. There was a dry, heavy flapping, and the raven landed—ungainly, claws digging through heavy wool cloth into skin. She brought him in, a heavy, drooping, ice-decorated bird.

"Put him by the fire," said Gilly reasonably. "Close the window. Give him something to eat."

Doing all this took a while. Clement shook the crushed remains of the rolls out of her coat pockets. Standing on the chair near the fire, the raven ate these crumbs, and drank water from her washbowl. All this was not so strange, until the bird said, "Thank you."

He flapped his wings, spraying Clement with ice water and slush. He fluffed his feathers in the warmth of the fire and looked like he would now go to sleep.

She said, "My message to the G'deon is urgent. Can you carry her a note?"

The raven said, "Emil is addressing you. Please speak your mind."

Clement looked at Gilly rather desperately. But he seemed to think that holding the baby was participation enough.

"What one raven knows, we all know," explained the bird. "Emil has a raven beside him, saying your words to him."

And what else was that raven saying to him, Clement wondered rather wildly? Would it describe her dark, disordered room, her battered face, her hunched companion and the restless, grunting baby that he awkwardly dandled on his knee?

The raven added, unnervingly, "Emil is sitting with Karis while she sleeps. The room is dark, like this one. Karis is asleep on the floor, near the fire. She has hardly slept since Long Night, and he does not wish to wake her up. He asks that you speak with him instead of her. How can he win your confidence?"

"Who *is* Emil?"

The raven said, "Emil was commander of South Hill company for twenty years, and is now a General of Paladins, and a councilor of Shaftal."

"He was the commander in South Hill?" Clement stared at the raven and demanded, irrationally, "*What happened in South Hill?* When that woman in our gaol, who used to be a warrior of the Ashawala'i—"

"*Katrim,*" corrected the raven.

"*Katrim,*" she said irritably. "She became a Paladin in South Hill, didn't she? Under Emil's command! And something happened there."

"The storyteller's name then was Zanja na'Tarwein. She came to South Hill Company wanting to kill Sainnites. But she turned her back on this war, and opened the way for others to follow her—Emil, and Medric, and Karis. Zanja became a hinge of history, an opener of doors."

"Well, she had better get some more doors opened quickly, for she is going to be executed tomorrow, at dawn."

The raven said nothing at all.

Clement stumbled on, scarcely able to believe what she was doing, even as she did it. "I'd like to save her, but I can't. Perhaps there's something you or the G'deon could do."

The raven said, "Emil asks for your patience. This is a painful problem."

Clement had been pacing the cold room, but now she sat down abruptly, in a chair near Gilly. "I make a traitor out of myself to a raven," she muttered, "And I get only silence in response. Who do I complain to?"

The raven finally spoke. "It is better that the storyteller be killed."

"What? How could it be better?"

"It is difficult to explain. Zanja na'Tarwein is no longer alive, and the storyteller's death will be a gift to her."

"Her separated spirit can be made whole by killing her?" said Gilly.

"Yes."

"This makes sense to you?" Clement asked.

Gilly shrugged crookedly. "I believe it's fire logic."

"It is fire logic," the raven said.

As the raven fluffed his feathers in the heat, Gabian watched the black bird with fixed fascination. Clement finally said, "I want to come over the wall tonight, and join the G'deon's service."

It was impossible to understand nuances in the raven's inhuman voice. But the promptness of his reply suggested a lack of surprise. "Lieutenant-General Clement, you will serve Shaftal best by remaining where you are."

"Now I'm in disgrace, there's nothing I can do except bring my son to safety before your people attack."

"There will be no attack. We are here to make peace."

"But the G'deon said her offer of peace was Cadmar's only chance."

"She said she would make peace without him," the raven said.

Something in the raven's words gave Clement pause. Gilly said, "That *is* what she said." He also paused.

"Oh, bloody hell," Clement breathed. "Gilly, where *is* Cadmar?"

Gilly said sharply, "You've got to keep away from the general! If something happens to him, you'll be blamed! Clem, listen to me!"

"Look after the baby," she said, and ran out the door.

Chapter Thirty-Seven

Garland found the kitchen's oven to be quite cantankerous, but he and his fellow cooks eventually managed to get it to produce a halfway decent tray of meat turnovers. He brought one to the Paladin who sat writing a letter by candlelight as he kept watch outside the parlor door. He took another into the parlor to give Emil. Emil, seated in an upholstered chair, flanked by a flock of extremely weary ravens, made a silencing gesture.

Karis, bolstered by feather pillows and wrapped in blankets, slept on the floor. Before J'han was half finished with her, she had fallen profoundly asleep: oblivious as he stripped her to the skin, unconscious when several people lay hands on her to help turn and arrange her nerveless form. Garland had taken Karis's clothing into the kitchen, but then lost custody of it to the people who could sew. The worn state of her relatively new clothing offered an appalling measure of how hard Karis had been working.

Garland put the plate at Emil's elbow, and then quietly added wood to the fire. Karis's big hand was outspread on the floor, as though even in her sleep she was trying to hold the pieces of a broken thing together.

Emil said in a low voice, "Raven, tell me what is happening now."

A raven spoke. "The Lucky Man has placed the baby in the basket. Now he speaks: 'I see you are a subtle people.' His tone is ironic."

The fire, rising in the fireplace, crackled softly.

"Tell the Lucky Man he can remind Clement that reluctance to take power is a virtue here. Is he following her to see what's become of the general?"

"Yes."

"Tell him it's not contagious."

The raven said, "He seems nonplused. He has left the room now."

"You birds have an astonishing vocabulary," Emil muttered. He stood up stiffly. "Garland, the storyteller is to die at dawn. How can they kill her with all their weapons broken?"

Garland felt a twist of sickness. "A heavy ax on the back of the neck."

Emil flinched. Then he took a breath and said in an even voice, "Without a sharp edge, the executioner's going to need a good aim."

"They don't miss," Garland said. "It's a point of pride. But that won't make you feel any better."

"Nothing will. Not only did I have to kill her, but I have to keep killing her. My ethical training has rarely seemed so inadequate. All I can do is endure, but to endure such an awful thing seems impossible."

Emil looked at Karis then, with a wrenching interlarding of compassion and pride. "*Must* I awaken her?"

"Don't you dare!"

"She has to be told."

"You keep away from her! Sit down and eat your supper! Leave that poor woman alone!" If Garland's rolling pin had not been in the kitchen, he would have made himself ridiculous by brandishing it.

Emil sat down and picked up the plate from the table. He took a bite of the turnover, and shook his head in amazement. "I don't know how you do it." Then he looked up, and smiled faintly at Garland's face, which must have had a strange expression. "No, I don't know how I do it either," he said. "Are you going to be up all night?"

"Yes, Emil. I expect we all will. People are out there sewing Karis a new undershirt, knitting new gloves, mending her boots, stitching up her popped seams, and patching the holes in her breeches. Other people keep dropping by to discuss recipes and where to locate ingredients. And we're cooking, of course."

"Of course. Do they mind taking orders from a Sainnite?"

"No more than you do, apparently."

Emil's grin had only the slightest twist of sorrow. "It's not obedience," he said. "It's self-interest. Do you think I could have another one of these?"

Clement pounded pell-mell down the stairs. A couple of soldiers who kept an anxious watch inside the front door leapt up, startled, from a distracted game of cards. With the pain in her face jolted back into agony, Clement had to reach for a door post for support. "Is the general in his quarters?"

"Yes, Lieutenant-General. Commander Ellid was with him for a while, and then we brought him some porridge."

"You better sit down," said the other, and guided her to his chair. She sat blinking at him, puzzled, trying to think of how or when the soldiers of Watfield had started being so thoughtful and proprietary.

"It's broken, eh?" said the soldier, gesturing at her face.

"I sure do wish I had ducked."

The soldiers grinned. And then, as the grins faded, the anxiety settled back into their faces. The entire garrison was waiting helplessly for the ax to fall; Clement doubted anyone would get much sleep tonight.

She said, "I have to talk to the general. But I don't dare go near him if he hasn't cooled off. Would one of you go ask him if he'll see me?"

The kind soldier went off down the hall, and the other one collected the cards and started shuffling them. "How are people doing?" she asked him.

"Well, I'd feel better if I had a decent blade."

Down the hall, the kind soldier uttered a sharp shout.

Clement had choreographed her share of battles, then stood back and watched them unfold with the same sense of unreality. The soldier dropped the cards. They ran to Cadmar's room.

They found him sprawled upon the floor, with his face in a pool of thick, bloody vomit.

The kind soldier grabbed Clement by the arm. "It might be the plague. Don't go in there!"

She let him pull her back from the doorway. Her panic wasn't feigned as she turned to him and cried, "Go get the medics!"

"I will, Lieutenant-General. But please, don't go in there!" He spoke wildly, and his fearful eyes said her own terrified thought: *Don't leave me with no one to stand behind!*

She took a breath. "I'll wait here until you come back. I won't go any closer to him."

Gilly arrived before the medics did, carrying Gabian in the basket, with the bottle of milk and other necessaries tucked around the baby. By then, Clement's heart had stopped its pounding, and she said to Gilly very calmly, "Get my son out of here."

They were alone in the hallway. The soldier had gone into Cadmar's room, muttering fatalistically, "First in, first dead." The door was closed now.

"Emil says it's not contagious," Gilly said.

Clement had to remember who Emil was. She cried, "And you believe him? He promised no attack! Now we're isolated from the city, with our gates and walls preventing us from infecting Shaftal, and we could all simply die in here."

"You called the G'deon a generous woman not long ago. You said she was of a woman of her word. And her words were very specific. Clem—"

"I don't want—"

"But think of what it means!"

They glared at each other by the dim light of a distant lamp. Then, in a fierce whisper, Gilly said, "Clem! Think what you can do for your people!"

He had put the baby's basket on the floor. Now, he picked it up. "I'll keep the baby in my room. Send a soldier to help me, will you?"

She nodded stiffly. Gilly's words lay in her mind like an unopened package. He walked awkwardly away, leaning on his cane, hauling the baby. A few minutes later, the medics arrived—three of them—and a half dozen soldiers.

Their faces told her they'd rather risk contact with the sick man than be in her position. She whole-heartedly agreed with them.

Clement sat at her work table with her hands cupped very cautiously over her face. She had moved the raven to a chair in a shadowed corner, because this was sure to be the kind of night that people would come barging in unannounced. What lay upon her now was the weight of silence. Clement assumed that extra watches had been placed on the wall, but there were no alarms. Gilly had sent a message assuring her that Gabian seemed quite well. Her son's absence left her room echoing with emptiness. All across the garrison, frightened captains were feigning unconcern as the terrified soldiers under their command bolstered their courage with boasting or distracted themselves with card games. Ellid would have been out making her rounds, reassuring people somehow, but the soldier bearing the devastating news of Cadmar's illness would have found her by now.

There would be no attack tonight. To defeat five hundred soldiers, even disarmed ones, would take some effort. The local Paladin company could not muster more than seventy experienced fighters, and even that would take a few days at this time of year. Of course, there was nothing to stop the Watfielders from simply rising up and throwing themselves on the Sainnites in a grand fistfight—nothing but the wall, and a gate that would not open. But, more likely they would just watch and wait while Cadmar's illness spread through the garrison, and the few soldiers who didn't die of illness died of starvation. It would be over long before spring, with not a blow struck.

Clement heard a footstep outside the door. "Come in," she said, and a soldier stepped in—an old man with a left hand so badly smashed in an old battle or accident that his fingers were now frozen in a useless claw. Clement remembered the soldier's name, and asked him in to warm up by the fire. The man handed her a note from the medics, put a log on the fire, and warmed his hands by the flames.

The note was scrawled on a torn piece of paper: "Fever, delirium, lumps in groin, one dead flea. Too early to judge outcome."

But a woman who can dole out life can dole out death just as easily. Clement dropped the note onto the coals and watched it shrivel, puff into flames, and become ashes. The soldier said, "It's bad, eh?"

"The general's certainly picked a bad time to get sick," said Clement. "Why do I remember you? Did you know my mother?"

"I knew her pretty well. We all were on the same boat, you know. You were just a little bit of a thing. Dreadfully seasick. But tough. We all told Gabian you were going to be an officer. I guess she'd be pretty proud of you right now, Lieutenant-General."

Proud of what? Clement wanted to ask. *My lousy luck?* But this was no time to be imposing her low spirits on anyone else. She said, "Thanks—I'll try to keep that in mind. How are people doing, do you think? This news about the general is going to be hard to take, I'm afraid."

The old man looked at her. "Do you think so, Lieutenant-General?" His words were neutral, but his tone had a sharpness to it. "I guess I'd better get back. Thanks for the warm-up."

Clement was left alone to think about Cadmar: a courageous, handsome, powerful man with the luck of the gods, who made a reputation for himself by barging into impossible situations and then fighting his way out unscathed. Clement had adored him once, had even indulged in fantasies of a covert love affair. That was before Gilly, before Clement watched Cadmar's casual abuse of a helpless boy, and his stupid disregard for Gilly's vivid intelligence. After Gilly had given Clement a point of comparison, she had loved Cadmar no more. In fact, she had become determined to make herself what Cadmar was not, and she had been young enough still that reshaping herself had at least seemed possible.

Yet Cadmar was a man to stand behind. An overshadowing

obstacle, he was also a substantial shield and a convenient excuse. Clement had railed against him, suffered under him, detested herself for the tricks she employed to get around him. Yet, despite the long years of repugnance, now that it seemed likely that Cadmar soon would be gone, what Clement felt was simple terror. She would be unshielded. She would be the one in front, and the lives of six thousand soldiers would entirely depend on her. If she failed, she would not have anyone else to blame.

She wanted the bloody idiot back.

She heard voices in the hallway, and lifted her head from the table. She felt empty, dazed, and then, as she stood up, dizzy.

Commander Ellid came in without bothering to knock. A soldier was standing in the hallway, with a lantern at her feet. Ellid surveyed the room, glanced at Clement, then said to the soldier, "Bring the lieutenant-general a load of wood, and find her something to eat. Kick a cook out of bed if you have to." She shut the door behind herself and added, "Well, Lieutenant-General, don't you look like hell."

"I'll take your word for it. What do you think, Ellid, is this worse than the night they burned down the garrison?"

"Much worse. There's nothing to do. Nobody to kill, no fires to fight. Sit down, will you?"

It did seem like a good suggestion. Clement sat and pushed out the other chair with her foot. Ellid sat next to her and said, "This morning, I thought I was about to initiate your demotion. And then I was thinking you were a bloody genius. By afternoon I was thinking you had gotten yourself beaten to death. And now you're about to become general. My day's been pretty lousy, but it must look good to you."

"I wouldn't want to be you either right now," Clement said truthfully. "Are the medics certain now that Cadmar's dying?"

"He's only got a few more hours, they say. They never heard of an illness moving so fast. They put themselves in quarantine, and they're desperately hoping it's the kind of illness that doesn't spread."

During Clement's solitary wait, her apprehensiveness

seemed to have consumed itself. She said, "No one else will get sick. I know it for a fact. And I don't know what's going to happen next, but I'm pretty sure it won't be what anyone expects."

Ellid looked blank. "Begging your pardon, Lieutenant-General . . ."

"Oh, for gods' sake, Ellid, we're alone in the room."

"Clement," Ellid corrected herself. And then she seemed to think for a while. "You know some things that I don't know. No, never mind—I doubt we've got time for you to explain. Tell me what you need from me."

"Whatever I do, it won't be what anyone expects, either. I need the whole garrison behind me, though: absolute obedience, no hesitation. Every last bloody soldier."

"All right," Ellid said absently, as though she were waiting for Clement to ask for something difficult.

"That's it. You better get busy."

"You got it already."

"Ellid, I commanded a garrison for five years myself. I know for a fact I haven't got it already."

"I guess you don't know everything. There was some fifty soldiers watching this afternoon when Cadmar smashed your face after you saved his worthless life. And every last one of them wanted to beat the hell out of him. And there's another fifty soldiers that just came back from a tough campaign with you, and all they've been talking about is how hard you worked to make sure they got through it without even a touch of frostbite. And there's not a soldier in the garrison who doesn't remember that you're the one who kept us all from burning to ashes this summer. You've got their loyalty, Clement. Because you earned it. Tell them what to do, and they'll do it."

Clement simply could not think of a reply. The expression on her face—what remained of her face—must have been completely blank.

Ellid got to her feet. "I'm going to assign a signal-man to you, and I'll make sure every captain in the garrison knows that when the bugle blows, that's your voice giving the orders." She paused. "A favor, Clement. A little thing."

"What?" Clement said doubtfully. It was difficult to believe any favor could be small at the moment.

"Don't put your life at risk, eh? The last thing I want is to inherit this bloody mess from you."

Clement said, "That's exactly what I told Cadmar the last time he promoted me. And now look at what's happened."

The kitchen had gradually emptied out, and Garland, too tired to go through the trouble of finding a bed, dozed on the hearth. Down the hall, he heard the Paladin's voice, and then he heard Medric saying urgently, "Emil! Wake her up! Now!"

Garland grabbed Karis's mended, cleaned, ironed, and neatly folded clothing, and ran to the parlor. Medric, standing in the doorway with a blanket trailing from his shoulders, said vigorously into the parlor, "Not only is it a mistake to try to protect her, but it's generally a good idea to keep out of her way, under all circumstances. Yes, that's a useful principle." His spectacles, reflecting fire, made his eyes into a circle of light.

Emil said, "Oh, I was just waiting for you to wake up and tell me what to do. Come in, will you? Or at least allow Garland to pass. Is there a Paladin out there?"

"Yes, Emil," said the Paladin.

"You might as well start waking up the house."

Garland went in, to find Emil kneeling near Karis, holding his watch up to the firelight. "What time is dawn in the garrison, Garland?"

"When the bell rings. Sainnites ignore Shaftali time. But we can't hear the garrison bells here; I think we're too far away."

Emil turned to the dark flock of birds. "Ravens, what time is it in the garrison?"

"An hour to dawn," a raven replied.

"What is happening there?"

"Clement is eating."

"Have the raven ask to be let out the window. I hope he's recovered enough to fly."

They waited. The raven said, "It has been done. The raven can fly."

"The raven is to fly to the gaol and watch over the story-teller." Emil sighed. "At least Karis will be able to answer her own questions." He leaned over her curled, limp form. "Karis, I'm sorry, you must wake."

This gentle approach had no apparent effect. Emil resorted to vigorously shaking her. Eventually, Karis sat up and gazed dazedly at Medric, who crouched at her feet now, talking rapidly though not very coherently. She put her arms through the new linen undershirt that Garland offered and tugged it over her head. She said, "Garland, do you know what happened to my boots?"

"A cobbler's been working on them. They're out in the kitchen."

"Can you find my coat, too? And my toolbox?"

Emil said worriedly, "Tell me what you're going to do."

She lifted her big hands, and examined them, minutely, with a certain puzzlement. "I'm going to get a tool. And I'm going to do something with it."

Medric uttered a grunt of laughter. He said to Emil, "I'm going to go put some clothes on."

"But what . . .?"

Medric looked blurrily but intently at Emil over the top of his lenses. "Oh, Emil, this is the easy part. Don't try to understand. Just follow her."

The hall outside Cadmar's room was crowded with people, none of whom had any business there. At Clement's approach, a babble of voices rose up. "Lieutenant General, we can't put an edge on the weapons." "We can't repair the guns." "The gate won't . . ." "General Cadmar . . .?"

"I've had a full report from Commander Ellid," she said. "I am entirely aware of our situation."

Someone insisted, panicky and desperate, "But they'll attack us at first light!"

"There's not going to be an attack."

"Then why are we waking up the day watch already, an hour before dawn?"

"You mean people were actually able to sleep?" She looked at them, eyebrows raised, until a few of them, at least, managed crooked smiles. "Now what are all of you doing here? You think you're the only ones who are worried? And that if you could just talk to someone in charge, something would be done about it?"

Their lingering mutter of voices fell silent. She said, "We're in a bad position; there's no doubt about that. Those people at the gate yesterday, they wanted to make an impression, and they've made one. But what kind of strategy is that? To hit us hard and then walk away? They don't intend to fight us! They'll be coming back, but now we've had time to think, they'll be wanting to talk again. Should an entire garrison go into a panic over a simple conversation?"

After a silence, one of the frightened soldiers said, "What kind of conversation?"

"Hell, I don't know. But I *can* talk—you all know that."

There was a startled silence, and then a burst of laughter. The soldiers began to leave, but they wanted to touch her first, as though she were some kind of luck charm. It took some time for the hall to empty. When they had finally dispersed, Clement opened Cadmar's door and went in. She said to the startled medics, "I just want to see him. I won't touch him."

A window had been cracked open despite the cold, but it didn't do much to relieve the ungodly stink of the room. Cadmar lay quiet in a neat bed, garishly illuminated by bright lamps. *Everyone loses at least one battle,* thought Clement, looking down at the fallen mountain of a man. Perhaps Cadmar had forgotten that, or had chosen to never know that one day he would be completely outmatched. "By a flea, eh?" she said soberly. "I guess I'll have to take that as a warning."

A medic said, "There are never any fleas at midwinter, because of the cold. It's very strange."

"Very strange," she agreed.

Cadmar struggled for a breath and then lay still again.

She reminded herself again that he had helped her, taught

her, and supported her rise. But it all seemed long ago. She turned away.

"I'll be waiting in the hall," she said.

The light was rising. The ravens flew up in a crowd, uttering sharp cries that seemed like curses. They wheeled into the paling sky. One by one, as people followed the ravens out the narrow door, they looked up to check the time and weather. Garland thought it looked to be a fair day, tolerably cold but bright for once. Leeba, still half asleep in J'han's arms, peered up at the sky like everyone else. "Where is the sun?" she asked.

"It's coming up over there." He pointed eastward.

She looked towards the east in sleepy amazement. "Why?" she asked.

Karis was already walking away down the street, bareheaded, with her coat unbuttoned. In her right hand she held a gigantic hammer, its handle worn to fit her hand, scorched black by the heat of the metal it had shaped over many years. She wore no gloves. There was no time for Garland to run back in and find some for her.

At Karis's elbows, Norina and Emil took big steps to keep up with her. The others crowded along behind: the Paladins, adjusting their weapons and tightening up their buckles, Medric, waving ink-stained fingers and talking excitedly to no one in particular, J'han, attempting to explain the sunrise to his daughter, and Garland, with his pockets crammed with apples and biscuits and a nice wedge of cheese, in case anyone became hungry.

They turned onto the main street. Citizens still in their nightclothes peered out their front doors at them. People who had kept watch on the street corners all night trotted up to talk with Mabin, and then ran off, on what errands Garland could not guess.

The city smelled delicious, of roasted meat, onions, pastry crust, cinnamon and burnt sugar.

J'han said vaguely, "But this isn't a feast day."

"It's a new feast day. The feast of following without knowing why."

"Rabbit wants to walk," Leeba declared.

"We're practically running," J'han said to her, more than a little out of breath. "Tell your rabbit to be patient."

"Rabbit *knows*."

"Well, tell the lizard, then. I don't think *he* knows."

Leeba held the wooden lizard, and the stuffed rabbit peeked out of the front of her coat. She shook the lizard roughly and told him to be patient and to stop complaining.

The trotted down the street. As they drew close to the garrison, the dawn bell began to ring.

Clement had set a chair under an unshuttered, east-facing window and had watched as the darkness became light. The signalman squatted nearby with his back against the wall. The bugle hanging around his neck began to gleam, as though it were collecting every bit of this winter dawn's sparse light.

The dawn bell rang. Clement stood up abruptly and paced down the hallway, cursing under her breath.

That Clement's first words to the G'deon would be an explanation of why and how the storyteller had died in their custody was intolerable. What Emil had said about the necessity of the woman's death had made no sense and did not matter.

Cadmar's door opened. A haggard medic looked for her. "General Clement," he said. "General Cadmar is dead."

"Come with me!" she said to the signal-man. And she ran down the hollow hall, out the door, down the ice-slippery steps and into the road.

The garrison was awake. She felt it: coiled, alert, listening.

The snow that was piled high on either side of the road made the path through seem like a cave, a tunnel, paved with extraordinarily slippery stones. Somehow, Clement managed not to fall.

In the distant yard that abutted the outer wall, four soldiers stood. In the middle of their circle, a slim gray figure knelt and obediently lay her head upon the block.

Clement shouted at the signal man, "Stand down!" It was an order that should stop even a battle-mad soldier mid-stride, mid-blow. Gasping for breath, the bugler brought the bugle to his lips, but the noise that came out was an unrecognizable spurt of sound that to any listener would seem a meaningless accident.

The sky seemed full of ravens.

"Hell!" Clement cried helplessly. "Do not kill her! Do not kill her!" Her voice echoed back at her.

The ax rose. The ax fell.

The garrison wall burst open.

Chapter Thirty-Eight

Squatting on her heels, Zanja read Medric's book until the water in her pot boiled. She had read the book many times, but it seemed different every time she read it. When the water boiled, she shut the book and steeped her tea. As she looked up from the porcelain pot with a poured cup of tea in her hand, she noticed the owl perched atop a stone, gazing at her. The owl had the passionless, infinite eyes of a god. Surely, Zanja thought, the land in which she endlessly traveled was a place in the owl's mind.

"Salos'a, is it finally time for me to die?" she asked.

The owl said, "You die painfully at every crossing. Yet you have never refused to cross. Why is that?"

Zanja said, "Because it is my duty to my people."

"Speak again," said the owl. "The truth this time."

"Because you named me a crosser of boundaries when I became a *katrim*."

"Speak again," said the owl. "More accurately."

Zanja thought, and said at last, "Because crossing boundaries gives me joy."

"That is a good reason," said the owl. "Remember it."

When Karis struck the wall, the hammer-head fractured like glass. The hammer handle shattered to splinters. Pieces of the hammer exploded out from Karis's hand, burning as they flew from shadow into sunlight. The sound of that blow reverberated in Garland's head. The feeling of it shook his joints loose, so he felt that he would collapse; that nothing could possibly remain standing.

The stones of the wall simply let loose of each other. The wall fell down before Karis, nearly obscuring her in a shimmering cloud of shattered mortar and dislodged snow. Through the dust, Garland caught occasional glimpses of her: legs straddled, hands open, feet buried in restless rubble.

Leeba shrieked wildly, "Look! Look at that! Oh!" She held the wooden lizard over her head, so that he could see. Stones crashed, cracked, and clattered. Beyond this racket, a bugle was sounding. Garland shouldered his way through the awestruck Paladins to Emil, on whose dust-caked face glowed the sunlight that broke through the widening breach in the wall.

"Emil," said Garland humbly, "that bugler is signaling the soldiers to stand down."

Emil rubbed dust and tears from his eyes. "To stand down? Well!" He grinned ferociously at the crumbling wall. "I guess even the Sainnites don't want to know what it's like for Karis to lose her temper."

The storyteller genuflected, folded neatly over her bent knees with her hands tied behind her. Her face was crushed into the shattered ice that covered the block. Across her back sprawled the spread wings of a fallen raven.

"Lieutenant-General Clement?" said the executioner. The wall was disintegrating beyond him, and he started nervously at every new crash.

"General Clement," she said. "Cadmar's dead. What happened?"

"The bird tangled with the ax."

"And what?"

"The ax hit the block, not the prisoner."

"But she looks dead!"

"I guess she's fainted. Shall I—?" He hefted the ax.

"Gods, no! Put that down."

Still gasping for breath, with the bugler still sounding his signal—half of the soldiers of the garrison seemed to have already arrived, but now stood back in a disorganized rabble—Clement unbuttoned her coat to be used as a stretcher, and suddenly a dozen soldiers were there doing what she wanted, though she had not seen them arrive and did not remember giving any orders. As the soldiers tucked the storyteller and the folded up raven into the coat, Clement called, "Signal-man: honored guests in the garrison!"

The puzzled bugler began playing the new signal. Ellid, who approached from a distance, flanked by several of her lieutenants, shouted, "General Clement! Your orders?"

"Just follow me," Clement said.

They went plowing through the snow: Clement, starting to feel the cold; the senior officers pretending they knew what they were doing; the four soldiers, carrying the storyteller between them; and the bugler blaring away at the rear. All along the edge of the field, the captains were frantically getting their companies in order. For no apparent reason, the soldiers began to cheer.

And then Clement realized they were cheering for her. It made no sense.

And then it did make sense: those shouts made her feel like she could do anything. And by the gods, she needed to feel that way, or she was going to collapse just like the wall, right there in front of five hundred soldiers.

She and her entourage reached the wall as another arm-span of it came crashing down. The breach was already as wide as three wagons, and where the wall had collapsed lay an ever-shifting and spreading field of restless rubble, of stones that rolled and rolled and did not rest until they were no longer touching any other stone.

A rolling stone bumped into Clement's foot. On the other side of the restless rubble stood a woman in a flapping red coat. At her right stood a lanky gray man with the fire of sunrise in his face. At her left stood a wiry, cool woman whose glance was like a sharp blade drawn across skin. Flanking her were a half dozen black-dressed, gold-earringed Paladins—not farmers with weapons, but the kind Gilly had once called deadly philosophers. Clement noticed Councilor Mabin, the ubiquitous runaway cook, a jumpy little man in sun-drenched spectacles, a sturdily built man with a joyous, shrieking little girl in his arms. And beyond them were gathering astonished townsfolk, with their coats thrown on over nightclothes and their bare feet jammed into boots they hadn't taken the time to strap up.

Clement started forward across the unsteady stones. Karis met her in the middle. Her unbuttoned coat revealed plain work clothes, and a belt from which small tools dangled and danced: a folding rule, a fat pencil, a utilitarian little knife. Her boots looked as if they had walked down every last one of Shaftal's godawful roads.

She offered her bare hand. Clement clasped it, and felt like she had grabbed hold of a piece of hot iron.

"The war is over," Karis said.

The stones heaved underfoot. The soldiers were shouting Clement's name. "The war is over," Clement affirmed, as definitely as she could manage to say such a preposterous thing.

The cold woman at Karis's left turned to face Shaftal. She cried, in a voice that seemed trained to carry long distances, "The war is over!"

Clement glanced backwards at Ellid, who had climbed up the rock pile behind her. "Signal peace. Make bloody sure the soldiers act happy about it."

"Yes, General."

Clement turned back to face the steady, implacable gaze of Shaftal. "Do you want to discuss some details?"

A deep humor came into the face of the man at Karis's other side. Three earrings—a Paladin general. Emil, Clement realized.

Karis said, "The Sainnites will not be harmed or attacked, and you will not harm or attack the people of Shaftal. The people of Shaftal will offer you the hospitality of strangers and eventually the hospitality of friends."

The rocks slipped away from under Clement's feet, but the powerful grip on her hand balanced her. The cold woman at Karis's left said, "General, say that you will do whatever is necessary to make these things happen."

Clement opened her mouth to speak, and then there was a great, terrible pause.

"I am a Truthken," the cold woman said, answering a question Clement had not asked.

Clement said, "I have to tell you, I don't know how to make peace. I can't be certain that all the garrisons will follow me. And I may only be general for a few months."

The Truthken's expression became distinctly appreciative. "I understand these qualifications."

Clement said, "I will do whatever is necessary to make peace with Shaftal."

"Karis, the general declares a sincere intention."

"Oh, we'll solve these problems," Karis said.

The bugler had begun sounding a sequence of notes that had never been heard in Shaftal. Clement couldn't even be certain her soldiers knew what the signal meant. But Ellid had also sent her officers in person to pass the word, and the soldiers' voices were a rising roar. On the other side of the wall there also rose up a growing wave of cheers. A bell had begun to peal.

Surely, Clement thought belatedly, *none of this is possible. It cannot possibly be so simple as this.*

Karis said, "What happened to the storyteller?"

Clement said, "A raven got in the way of the ax. It missed her entirely. But she seems to be unconscious."

The gray man uttered an exclamation. "Karis, why did you interfere? How many times must we make up our minds to kill her?"

"One last time, Emil," Karis said.

"Are you the one who's managing this business of feeding the garrison? We're ready with the bread."

Garland was being addressed by a rather floury woman, who had seen fit to tuck under her arm a hot loaf of bread, which crackled and steamed in the chill. She brought him into a wonderful conversation about butter and jam with a dozen other people. Then Medric blundered into the crowd of cooks, his vision obscured by a paste of snow and powdered lime. "Is Garland here? I've got to get to Karis. Useless bloody spectacles!"

Garland took him by the elbow, saying irritably, "If you

would just ask Karis to mend your vision, you could throw the spectacles away."

That startled Medric into a moment's silence, but then he responded firmly, "Just because she *can* fix everything doesn't mean she *should*. Get me over these rocks, brother."

As they tripped and stumbled their way across the spreading carpet of rock, Medric said, "Can you see Karis? What is she doing?"

"She's on her knees in the snow. There's a raven beside her—it looks like it's dead. She has a woman, a body, in her arms. It must be Zanja. Gods, does Karis get to feel not even a moment's triumph?"

Medric swayed wildly from side to side. "What in Shaftal's Name has she done to these rocks? This wall will *never* be finished falling! I would not have expected her, of all people, to be so immoderate!"

Garland said, "Norina's unbuttoning her coat to get at her dagger."

Medric shouted shrilly, "Gods of hell! Karis! Don't let her do it!" Arm waving wildly for balance, he added, "Did they hear me?"

Emil had turned; he noticed their approach. He lay a hand on Norina's arm. "Emil heard," Garland said.

"Of course he heard," Medric said. "He's a listening sort of man! Are we anywhere near them yet? How long do these bloody rocks continue?"

"The snow's next," Garland said. "Here we go."

They waded past Sainnite officers, who clustered intently around their rapidly talking new general. Emil had come through the snow to meet them and took Medric's other elbow. "Karis says her heart is still beating, but the spirit is gone. She says she just needed to know for herself. And now she does know."

"But she only knows what her hands can tell her," Medric said. "She can't know that the storyteller is dead because she was *expecting* to be killed. But think, Emil, think of what's possible now!"

"Think?" said Emil. "At this moment?"

"*Must* we go through this again?" said Norina impatiently as they drew up to her.

"Here's Karis," Garland said, and put Medric's hand onto her shoulder.

The limp woman lay in Karis's arms. A piece of cut rope hung from one of the woman's wrists, and a long, slender braid of her hair trailed across the snow. Garland remembered her vividly: her silence, her alert, fierce attention, her astonishing courtesy, and the extremely pared-down beauty of her sharp-edged face. But now she merely looked dead.

Karis raised her bowed head. "What, master seer?" she said. Her voice, her face, her eyes, all were terribly calm.

Medric felt blindly for the woman's head, picked up the long braid, and wrapped it several times around one of Karis's hands. "If this hair were a rope, and Zanja were dangling at the end of it, what would you do?"

Karis looked blankly at her hand. And then she closed her fist over the slender braid, and pulled.

The barren land of the unending mountains sped past below. The sun popped into the sky and popped down again. Day became night in the blink of an eye. Dizzy, sick, numb, shouting with pain, Zanja dangled by the hair from the claws of her god. Faster and faster, the owl flew. Time passed in a blur, thousands of nights. She cried, "Salos'a, when will this journey end?"

Salos'a looked down at her. The god's eyes were round circles of light. The god's feathers frayed out into blinding fire. "There is another boundary you must cross," said the owl. And then the god let her go.

She cried, "Not again!" She fell: into light, a blare of horns, a shattering ringing of bells, hoarse cheering voices, fragments of speech, torn shreds of blue and red and then an eye-burning white. She was falling, tumbling through light, through brittle air and wide spaces. She saw faces, stones, a glittering cloud, the round, blinding face of the sun.

She stared at it until a hand covered her eyes, and a beloved, racked voice said, "You'll go blind that way."

"No," she breathed. "No!" she cried in despair. More words would not come.

Voices spoke, but the words shattered into fragments. There was no pattern, no meaning, no possibility of understanding.

Zanja felt a dizzying, tilting sensation. Blinding light again, followed by impenetrable shadow. Hands gripped her clothing, voices filled her ears. She cried, "Gods—how could you— have I not served you?"

"Shaftal," a blurry voice said. "Oh, blessed day!"

Something heavy enwrapped her: a comforting warmth, and then the sensation of being held, rocked, the voice, less blurry now, saying roughly, "Zanja, Zanja na'Tarwein, oh my sister . . ."

She heard a heartbeat. She felt the rise and fall of a ragged breath. Who was calling that familiar name? "Emil?" she said in disbelief. "Is everyone dead?"

The shadow that blocked the blinding light bowed over her. "No one is dead," said Emil.

"Karis is dead."

"No."

"I heard her voice."

"You heard her living voice with your living ears."

"What," she said in bewilderment.

"Look over there. Do you see that wall?"

She peered in the glare of light. She saw stones letting go of each other and falling in a happy tumble. "Not a wall," she said. "Rubble."

"Well, it *was* the wall of Watfield garrison. And look over there."

She turned her head and saw a proud, rigid woman in Paladin's black, taking the hand of a younger, tireder, prouder woman in Sainnite gray.

"Mabin?" said Zanja.

"And Clement, General of Sainnites."

"Oh. Oh, Emil!"

Now the confusion of voices began to sort itself out: Norina, scolding as usual, Medric, making a rather plaintive speech on the difficulties of getting desperately needed assistance, and then Karis's distinct raw voice, saying, "Just take one step forward so I can reach you."

Zanja peered into the haze of light and watched Karis pluck the spectacles from Medric's nose, spit on the lenses, and wipe them clean on the tail of her shirt. She examined them critically in the sunlight, then put the spectacles back on Medric's face. He blinked at her. Then, he looked down at Zanja and cried with vivid joy, "It's you!"

Zanja felt the confusion beginning to claim her again. She did not feel certain Medric's assertion was correct. Medric dropped to his knees in the snow and grabbed one of her hands in his. "Emil, she's *awfully* cold."

"Karis, can you ask Clement if there's a place indoors, by a fire, where we can go?"

Karis looked down at them. She seemed terribly far away. Someone was energetically beating a cloud of dirt and snow from her red coat. She turned away.

Medric said giddily, "Zanja, have you heard? This is the thirteenth day of the first year of Karis G'deon! And we have a truce!"

Emil's voice rumbled in his chest, a warm vibration against Zanja's ear. "So many people will not forgive us for this peace. Peace without justice, they'll say, is not peace at all. And those Death-and-Life people, just because Willis is dead—"

Zanja mumbled into the scratchy warmth of his shoulder, "Enough worrying."

Medric snorted with amusement. "Just try to make him stop!"

"Norina is glaring at me," Emil said.

"No doubt she thinks Shaftal's councilor should do official sorts of things, rather than sit like a weeping lump in the snow with his best friend in his arms. Look, here comes J'han. He'll want to take a good look at Zanja. Oh, and I hope you're ready—though I'm sure you're not—for Leeba."

Leeba careened into them. Zanja tried to put her arms around her, but it was impossible to hold her. Might as well try to embrace a windstorm. *My life!* she thought in astonishment. And it fell on her, with all its weight and wonder, and no matter how she tried to grasp it, it eluded her, and yet it was hers.

"Little Hurricane," she cried, "I missed you!"

❖❖❖❖❖❖❖❖❖❖❖❖❖❖❖

Chapter Thirty-Nine

Herme's company had taken it upon themselves to clear out the large room that was serving them as sleeping quarters. By the time Clement arrived, the room was not only clean, but furnished with chairs, tables, even a threadbare carpet and hastily polished lamps. Unsettled dust was still swirling in the lamplight, and a fire, nursed by two attentive soldiers, burned briskly on the hearth. The soldiers who had been clustered around Clement had been dispersed by a crisp storm of commands, and now she was alone, with—astonishingly—nothing to do.

Weak-kneed, shivering with what she hoped was merely cold, she collapsed into a chair.

By a feat of soldier's magic, Herme instantly appeared before her. "General, what are your orders?"

She wanted to tell him to stop calling her "general." But she dared not disturb the illusion—it was an illusion, wasn't it?—that seemed to be held together by words alone. So she said to Herme, "Captain, please inform your company of my gratitude for their quick action."

"Yes, General."

"We'll be wanting a lot of hot tea."

"That's on its way, general."

"Tell Commander Ellid I want to speak with her."

"Yes, General."

"That is all."

He saluted and disappeared. Almost immediately, a soldier snapped open the door to admit Ellid, in a wash of cold air.

"Your soldiers are making quite a show of themselves," Clement told her.

Managing to look gratified, Ellid reported that more than half the wall had fallen, and that it continued to fall. The front gate now lay flat on its face. Watfielders were walking across it to deliver basket after basket of hot bread, fresh butter, and sweet jam.

Unable to bring herself to be concerned about the wall or the gate, Clement said weakly, "Hot bread?"

Ellid grabbed a soldier. "Get some of that bread in here for the general."

"What's delaying our guests?" Clement asked.

Ellid gave a wry grin. "Better guests than conquerors, eh? The G'deon's people wanted her to show herself to the Watfielders. You can hear them cheering out there. The local Paladin commander just strolled brazenly in, and the two Paladin generals are briefing him before he goes off with my people to discuss details of the truce here. I've told them to produce a proposal by noon and it's coming direct to me and you. I assume you'll want to use it as a model for the other garrisons. Do you want me in here, General, or out there?"

"Out there. Visible. Very visible."

"Yes, General. What else?"

"Has someone gone to fetch Gilly?"

"Yes, but you know it takes time to get that man out of bed. And I've told the company clerk to get some sleep because he'll be up writing orders all night. And you had better talk to the Paladin generals about security for our messengers to the other garrisons."

"Right," Clement said, in a daze of exhaustion.

Ellid looked gravely down at her. "You sure managed to look like you knew what you were doing out there."

"You know bloody well it was a blind charge."

"That's a secret between you and me, General. The soldiers think you're some kind of magician who pulled a truce out of the teeth of disaster. And that's exactly what they need to be thinking."

"Oh, hell," Clement said. "You mean I have to continue this pretense?"

Ellid's grin was more than half a grimace. The door opened, and this time the cold air smelled like a bakery. A crowd of people, some soldiers and some not, carried in the storyteller, with the little girl riding behind on her father's shoulders, crying imperiously at them to be careful and vehemently waving a painted lizard in the air.

A soldier deposited a glorious basket of marvelous bread in Clement's lap. Ellid said, "My lost cook gave me a distracted greeting, and promises that soup, meat, pies, and other fine foods are soon to follow the bread. If you want to make an old woman happy, you'll think of a way to make him a soldier again!"

She left to look after the garrison.

Clement breathed in the scent of the bread. She picked up a round loaf and the warmth was almost painful on her numbed fingers. She tore off a piece, and the crust shattered, and the interior let out a cloud of exquisite steam. At last, she took a bite and let out a small moan. The cold fled from her flesh, but the pain revived: face, shoulder, hip, muscle. She had been smashed, bruised, broken, depleted, and worn out by these momentous days and nights, and it seemed only right that this should be the case.

She forced herself to stand up and walk over to the one person in the room whose condition was worse than hers. The storyteller had been deposited on the hearth with a much-worn coat over her shoulders and the red-cheeked little girl tucked under her arm. The child noticed Clement's approach and said with hostility, "It's another one of those *soldiers*."

The storyteller slowly looked up at Clement. Her dark skin had turned gray with cold, her lips blue. Her muscles were still spasming with shivers. Apparently, the cold of the unheated gaol had nearly killed her before the execution squad even arrived. Clement squatted down beside her, knees cracking, muscles quivering. She proffered the basket. "Warm bread?"

The storyteller said, "Do you truly think I will break bread with you?"

Clement instinctively jerked back, lost her tenuous balance, and nearly dropped the basket in the effort to catch herself. Even the man who was unstrapping the woman's boots looked shocked. "Zanja—!"

"Why are you so mad?" the little girl asked nervously.

Clement set the bread basket securely on the floor. "Zanja na'Tarwein?"

As the woman glared, the man said politely, "Yes, General, she has been restored."

So this was the one Clement had feared: who had survived a skull fracture, a broken back, torture, and imprisonment; who had emerged from a valley populated by corpses determined to exterminate the killers of her people; who had suborned both the Sainnite Medric and the Paladin Emil; who had not merely found the Lost G'deon but had won her love; and who had finally sundered her very soul . . . all for the sake of—revenge?

"I'll just leave the basket here," Clement said. Feeling truly battered, she gathered herself to rise, but simply could not do it.

"General, you're hurt! Let me help you," said the man.

Zanja said, "No, J'han."

"It is not right—"

"Brother healer, heed me!"

Apparently perceiving something that Clement could not, the man sat back on his heels, restraining his reflexive kindness with an obvious effort. Less than a year ago, a person of his generosity and knowledge had taught the Sainnites how to save themselves from the plague. Perhaps it had in fact been this very man. Unfortunately, not all Shaftali were like him.

When Clement looked at the silent warrior, she looked into the other face of Shaftal: unbowed, unforgiving. Every attempt to overcome the people had not merely increased their resentment, but also their ability to resist. Clement's acts, and the actions of all the soldiers like her, had created this unrelenting enemy and all the enemies like her. With a great deal of effort they could be killed, but they could not be eliminated.

"What do you want from me?" Clement asked in Sainnese.

The warrior replied in the same language. "You took no risk when you put yourself at the G'deon's mercy. Karis is so fearful of doing harm that she has repeatedly refused to act at all. You had good reason to expect only generosity."

Clement protested, "My desire for peace is sincere! Ask that Truthken—"

"If you misrepresented your intentions in her presence you would not be alive now. But sincerity is not enough." Zanja na'Tarwein was speaking with an effort, yet her words were like the storyteller's: precise and devastating.

Clement urgently wished that she could get away from her. But she could not. "What *would* be enough?" she asked. "If I offered you as many soldiers to kill as we killed in your village—"

"It would not be enough."

"If I had the power to undo the past—"

"You could not help but undo the marvelous along with the despicable."

The weight of those words, the horror of them, felt unendurable. Clement's eyes were burning—a general does not weep! Yet she spoke, inadequately, words that broke even as she uttered them. "What my people did to yours *was* despicable. I am sorry—desperately sorry."

There was a silence. The warrior took a breath and looked away, as though she also were fighting tears. Suddenly, she did not seem terrible at all. She said, "The valley of my people is populated by nothing but bones. The memories of their deaths will haunt me until the day of my own death. But your sorrow—like my sorrow—is not enough."

"Then nothing can be enough."

The *katrim* looked at her. "If that is true, then lasting peace is impossible. Nothing has been gained today."

Dread replaced the last remains of Clement's relief as she realized how truly Zanja na'Tarwein had spoken. So many people had been wronged, over so many years! Somehow, reparations *must* be made, or the peace of words would never become a peace of fact. Yet Clement had nothing to offer Shaftal. Nothing.

Surely seven thousand Sainnite soldiers was not nothing!

As sometimes happens in extreme exhaustion, Clement felt a hallucinatory clarity. She understood exactly what must be done.

She said, "If my people become Shaftali, would that be enough?"

The last survivor of the Ashawala'i people turned her harshly beautiful, starkly alien face to her. "You will offer them to Shaftal?"

Every stupidity of the last thirty-five years had come from the Sainnites' unwillingness and inability to change. Certainly they had not been welcomed, permitted, or encouraged to belong in Shaftal. But neither had they tried to be anything other than conquerors. To attempt it now might be so difficult it verged on the impossible, and might take the rest of Clement's life to achieve. But wasn't her only other option to take Cadmar's well-trodden road, a coward's way of self-induced oblivion and obstinacy, to delude her people with visions of heroism as she marched them to destruction?

Clement said, half to herself, "I must do better than merely preserve the past. For I have a son." She looked up at Zanja. "So even if I fail at everything else, I will offer myself to Shaftal. And though I fear I won't live long enough to see this promise fulfilled, I'll do all I can to transform my seven thousand soldiers as well."

And then Clement felt sick with disorientation—giddy, grief-struck, light-headed—and the man had leapt up to steady her, to help her get securely seated on the floor, to bow her head between her knees until the nauseating dizziness had lifted. When her ears had stopped roaring and the cloud of her vision had cleared, Clement cautiously lifted her head.

"I am satisfied," said Zanja. Her spasms of shivering had eased. The little girl was saying to her irritably, "You talk funny! Why are you doing that?" The man spoke soothingly to the child as he returned to his examination of Zanja's feet. "You Ashawala'i are a sturdy folk," he commented.

Zanja reached for one of the loaves of bread and tore it in half. She said to the child in Shaftalese, "I have been speaking with General Clement in the soldiers' language, Little Hurricane. Look—here is some jam in this basket. Do you want some on your bread?"

With the restless child successfully distracted by bread and jam, Zanja gave Clement a serious look. "I will eat with you now," she said, and handed Clement the remains of the loaf. With the crust crunching softly in her teeth she added, "I am a crosser of boundaries . . ."

It sounded so like the storyteller's opening ritual words, *I am a collector of tales,* that Clement rubbed her face in bafflement.

"To cross is my calling—my curse—"

"Your gift!" protested the healer.

Zanja smiled wryly. "That also. And my joy."

"I thought your curse was telling stories," said Clement.

"The storyteller is gone," said the healer. "Zanja doesn't even remember her."

"Medric says the storyteller was killed—that she had asked to be killed. She must have known that she had completed her task." Zanja brushed breadcrumbs from her fine wool clothing. Clement watched her knife-scarred hand in dazed fascination. Did this woman not remember doing up those silver buttons? Did she not know how she came to be in Watfield garrison? Did she remember none of the stories she had been told? She seemed remarkably composed for a person who had awakened to find the walls falling down around her.

A crosser of boundaries, Clement thought, might be accustomed to such abrupt and inexplicable transitions—accustomed enough that she could mask her disorientation as effectively as Clement could mask her fear.

Zanja glanced at Clement, still smiling wryly. "Even to my kinfolk I always seemed peculiar," she said. "But I might be a useful friend to you, General."

"Gods of my mother!"

The little girl, jam-smeared, looked worriedly at Clement.

"Zanja surprised me," Clement explained to her. "Your mother is a very surprising person."

The girl said, "But she just wants to be your friend. Why, Zanja?"

Zanja stroked a hand affectionately down the child's tangled hair. "She needs a friend to teach her how to be Shaftali."

"She won't be a soldier any more?"

"Maybe she'll be a different kind of soldier."

"I do need your help," Clement began.

Zanja interrupted her. "In Shaftal, no one's judgment overrules the judgment of a Truthken—except the G'deon's, of course—for a Truthken represents the law. Therefore, General—"

"Won't you be one of the people who calls me Clement?"

"Yes, Clement. I advise you to do whatever Norina tells you to do."

Clement turned her head and found the Truthken standing beside her. The woman gave Zanja a keen look, then, in a swift glance at the healer, seemed to ask and receive an answer to a question. She turned to Clement and said, "General, Karis has asked to speak to you."

"Of course," said Clement.

She was able to stand and began to follow the Truthken, but then turned back to clasp Zanja's hand in farewell.

"You are becoming a Shaftali already," said Zanja na'Tarwein. In the black center of her dark eyes there was a flame.

While Clement had been preoccupied, the room had become crowded: soldiers and Paladins in what appeared to be equal numbers were standing against the walls. The Paladins, all of whom seemed to possess extraordinarily graceful manners, were attempting to engage the uncomprehending soldiers in conversation. In the center of the room, the G'deon's people formed a constantly loosening and tightening knot around Karis, who was kneeling at Gilly's feet with his hands clasped in hers. No one appeared to find her behavior unusual.

Herme hurried over when Clement beckoned him. "Tell your people to ask the Paladins to teach them Shaftalese," she said.

Herme managed to maintain his bland countenance. "Yes, General."

The Truthken murmured, "Watch Karis, General. See how he refuses, she insists—there, it's over already."

Karis had risen. Her big hands stroked down the twisted, hunched line of Gilly's back. Then, she stood talking to him casually, with a hand on his shoulder. Clement's cynical old friend stared up at Karis with an expression of bedazzled adoration.

Clement said, "Very instructive. But I think I've already studied that lesson."

The Truthken said, "Save yourself some trouble, then. Ask her what Shaftal needs of you, and promise to do whatever she says. Call her by name, look her in the eye—though it makes your neck hurt—and don't mince words."

"I will. Thank you."

Clement wiped her sweaty palms on her trousers, and stepped forward to clasp the G'deon's hand. "Karis, what have you done to my friend?"

She replied blandly, "Nothing, really. I just made his back stop hurting."

Well, for her perhaps it was nothing, thought Clement. By the gods, the woman was big, and wildly disordered, as though she had come in from a storm wind and had not yet caught her breath. But her devastatingly gentle handclasp was still warm. "I thought we should discuss Shaftal," she said, as though the problems they faced could be dispensed with in a single conversation.

"Karis, I want my people to become Shaftali. Do you think that would be possible?"

Karis gave her a very surprised look, then cast an amazed glance at the Truthken, who said dryly, "Zanja is already doing what she does best."

"Oh," said Karis. Her face crinkled up as though she were suppressing a sneeze—no, a laugh—and she said with exaggerated disgust, "Fire logic!"

"Oh ho!" cried the peculiar little man in spectacles. He peered at Clement with intense curiosity, as though he could scarcely wait to see what she did next. Councilor Mabin, who remained excessively upright under these very strange circumstances, gave the little man a look of withering disapproval—a wasted effort.

Clement bent to mutter in Gilly's ear, "You've never looked at me the way you were looking at Karis."

"Of course not, Clem. You never deserved it." He added, straight-faced, "Has anything important happened?"

Gabian announced his presence with a loud yelp. Clement lifted him out of his basket, and he flapped his arms enthusiastically. "Don't make me giddy," she admonished him. "Gilly's obviously lost his mind, and one of us must keep a clear head."

Karis held out her big hands, and Clement put her son into them. Competently cradled, Gabian blinked at Karis with dim-witted devotion.

Then Emil pushed his way in, assured Clement that they all certainly hoped the Sainnites could become Shaftali, and introduced Medric, who said cheerfully, "I imagine you hoped you'd never hear of me again. What did you make of that cow farmer, eh?"

"Watch out," Karis interjected. "You are completely surrounded by dangerous busybodies."

Clement suddenly had to sit down again: she was so dizzy with trying not to laugh, and her face hurt abominably. Karis sat next to her with Gabian in the crook of her arm. So gently that Clement could hardly feel it, Karis nudged Clement's broken nose into better alignment. The pain went completely away.

So the seven of them sat knee-to-knee, passing Gabian from lap to lap, arguing vehemently about what to do next. Medric said that transforming Sainnites into Shaftali was possible but not easy, for they would have to neither hurt the soldiers' pride or arouse the Shaftali anger. The Truthken reminded them that it was human nature to escalate conflicts and hold grudges. Emil thought they might counter old bitterness with intelligence, insight, hope, good will, generosity, self-interest, education, and wisdom.

"And coercion," Clement said.

"Persuasion," said Karis.

"Oh, persuasion," said Medric. "Like iron before your hammer? That kind of persuasion?"

"I doubt it will be that easy," said Karis.

Clement said, "If my people aren't attacked or forced to go hungry, they'll follow my orders—for a time. But eventually I've got to win their consent, not just their obedience. I think it's the same problem you've got, Karis, only worse. I have to give them a reason to surrender the only thing they're proud of, in exchange for something they've always scorned. Right now, I've got no idea how to do that."

Medric peered at her and said, quite unnervingly, "The same way it happened to you, General."

So Clement found herself thinking what had happened, really: the plague, Alrin, the fire, Kelin's death, the kidnapped children, the storyteller, Davi's rescue, Seth's embrace, Gabian's birth, Medric's book, Willis's death, Cadmar's fist, and the madness of the last two days. Each situation had been accidental or unpredictable, yet together they had changed her, so that when Zanja insisted that she confront the last, radical truth, she had been prepared to do so. Clement shut her eyes, pressing her fingers against her eyelids, trying to remember the storyteller's glyph card pattern. In the middle, there had been a wall. A pile-up of images leaned against it, one after another.

"The wall fell down," Clement said.

"Ho!" cried Medric triumphantly. "Exactly!"

Emil put a restraining hand on the giddy man's knee. "By the land, General, you do astonish me. You would not believe how many nights we spent studying those cards."

"Which cards?" asked Zanja. Supported by the healer at one side and the child at the other, she was standing shakily at the edge of their close-crowded circle. As they hastily put Zanja in the chair the Truthken vacated for her, Gilly produced the storyteller's card pack out of a pocket. She accepted the cards as if they were old friends she had feared lost, but gave him a puzzled look.

"Gilly was your—the storyteller's—friend," said Clement.

"I am sorry I do not remember you, sir. But thank you."

She handed the cards to Medric, who, declaring vehemently that he never wanted to see a glyph card again, hastily passed them to Emil. "These cards get resurrected as often as you do,"

Emil commented as he knelt on the floor and began laying down the cards.

Zanja watched intently as Emil reproduced the pattern the storyteller had made for Clement in the gaol. When he finished, Zanja let out her breath in a huff. "It's as bad as Koles."

The seer collapsed in a paroxysm of laughter. Grinning, Emil collected and handed Zanja the pack of cards. Mabin, apparently as baffled by their amusement as Clement was, commenced a speech about the historical importance of this occasion. But she was summarily interrupted by the runaway cook, who led in a parade of self-conscious townsfolk carrying steaming hot, luscious-smelling dishes. Under the influence of this extraordinary meal, seriousness became impossible. Even the soldiers, who had been dutifully but grimly attempting to say a few words in Shaftalese, began to laugh a little as they ate standing up with their erstwhile enemies.

Gilly lay his gnarled hand over Clement's. "With meals like this, the peace will last forever," he said. "What fool would fight when he could be eating, eh?"

Clement gazed fondly at her old friend, who had the sleeping baby tucked into the crook of his arm. "A lot of work lies ahead of us, though."

"Work worth doing," he replied.

"At last."

Clement looked across the table at Karis, who was poking distractedly at her beef in onion sauce over shredded potatoes. Zanja, who had eaten only some more bread and the richly flavored soup, now rested her head against Emil's shoulder. The two of them could have been lovers, so delighted were they by each other's company. But Zanja and Karis had not spoken to each other yet, had not even met each other's gaze.

This had been a remarkable morning. But much yet remained to be resolved.

Only rubble remained of the wall that had divided Sainnite from Shaftali. On one side of the fallen wall, new timber frames had been established in the snow-covered ashes of burned buildings. On the other side, the stone and slate buildings of the Shaftali town seemed almost bereft without the garrison wall to crowd up against. The stones were still rolling; the rubble piles continued to spread and flatten until no stone lay atop any other. Soldiers and townsfolk stood watching the restless rocks—fearful, curious, or amazed.

This is Watfield, Zanja reminded herself: a prosperous midland city, fortunately situated on the River Corber, which was an important route for bringing goods into and out of Hanishport, six days' journey to the east. Despite these facts, Zanja felt utterly dislocated and kept seeking the sun to remind herself that she was walking north, with the sun sinking westward and the Corber behind her to the south.

She wore a jacket of finely woven wool with silver buttons; she was wrapped in a thick cloak with a silver clasp at the shoulder. Her head felt light; her hair was gone. The people around her—her family—they also were changed. Leeba had learned some caution. Emil had become a Paladin general. Karis—

Karis and Clement had stepped onto the fallen gate piled with empty food baskets. Clement, in her begrimed leather coat and squashed hat, might have just come home from a bruising campaign. The baby Gabian was buttoned into her coat, with the top of his blue cap just under her chin and her gloved hand supporting the back of his head. Karis towered over her: her hair in a tangle, her red coat powdered with pulverized mortar. Leeba rode on her hip, asking question after question with no pause for the answers. Karis looked as ordinary as she could ever manage to look: a laborer in the midst of an exhausting building project. But her stance had a weighty dignity that spoke of the power of ten generations—the power of Shaftal's seeds, stones, wombs, hands. And the power of finally knowing what to do with that power.

Karis crouched over to kiss Clement like a sister. The hoarsely cheering people who crowded the street seemed to swallow their shouts for a moment, and the soldier's cheers also faltered. For a long moment Karis gazed gravely at the silent, frowning group that stood just beyond the gate, draped with white banners on which were painted names—the names of the dead?

Zanja's heart clenched with the old guilt and sorrow. Surely, the ghosts of the Ashawala'i people would condemn her for making peace with their killers, just like these name-draped witnesses condemned Karis for it. And surely, by refusing to satisfy them, Zanja—and Karis—were condemning themselves to the unending haunting of other people's unsatisfied angers.

What have I done to us? Oh, what have I done? Zanja dug a hand into her pocket and felt there the familiar, worn, warped pack of glyph cards. But even these could not comfort her. The storyteller's glyph pattern had seemed not merely ambiguous, but unreadable. Had life become so momentous that all her answers would now be nothing but a tangled muddle of contradictory possibilities? She almost missed the clean clarity of those empty months—years, really—of walking the mountainous wasteland between life and death.

Then, she felt the strong grip of J'han's supporting hand on her elbow. "You're awfully tired," he reminded her in his old, timely, pragmatic way.

They walked through Watfield down a street so crowded with people they sometimes could scarcely get through. At Zanja's left, Medric maintained a continuous commentary. "Here come the town elders—they're looking rather self-important, aren't they? Are they telling Emil that they've found us another place to stay? That's too bad. I rather liked that drafty, humble old house in the alley. Does Karis think she has to talk to every single person in Shaftal, starting with the people of Watfield, right at this moment? Well, perhaps she does! But surely she'll wear out her voice again? There, Norina has put a stop to that nonsense. We don't all have Karis's supernatural energy! Emil is looking pretty worn, don't you think? Still, we'll be up talking half the night, just like the Sainnites will. Greetings, Garland, you've been busy! Is it possible that you and I are now Shaftali?"

This last was addressed to the cook, who was toting a basket of wax-covered cheese, dusty bottles of spirits or wine, and highly polished apples. Medric had predicted he'd find his way to them, and here he was, no longer lost. The cook said, "Well, weren't we Shaftali already? Oh, there's the man with the bacon." He trotted off to add another package to his basket, to acquire a second basket crammed with bread, and to converse joyfully with a woman riding atop a wagon load of barrels. Everyone he talked to was left smiling in his wake, as though happiness were a contagion. His pockets were crammed with packages, and people pressed more items on him until his baskets overflowed.

Zanja stared about herself at the high slate rooftops, the extravagant lightning rods, the crowded shops of the prosperous city. And then they came to a square, with a wide park whose bare trees were exuberantly decorated with bright ribbons and paper flowers. At one end stood an ugly, looming, massive stone building. The Paladins had to press people back to create a passage. Karis followed her escort, and at least the wildly clamoring people had the sense not to mob her. So they reached their destination and climbed an impressive flight of stairs to the front door, where Karis turned and patiently let the people of Watfield look at her: a big, determined woman who knew exactly what to do. Finally, she stepped through the door, and her people followed her into an echoing, extravagant hallway.

Even Medric was astonished into silence.

Zanja said, "People live like this? Why, do you suppose?"

No one seemed capable of responding. "Here's the cloakroom," said a Paladin.

After Zanja had taken off her boots, she sat on the bench in that vast, warm, convenient cloakroom. As it filled with boots and coats, it emptied out of people, and soon she sat alone there, breathing in the rising odor of leather oil and wet wool. The puddles of slush melted into the mats. She realized abruptly that she was waiting for the short night to end, and the swift sun to rise. She rubbed her face, and pressed her fingers to her aching eyes.

The door opened, and Emil looked in at her. "There are more comfortable places to be alone, if that's what you want."

"Emil, I'm afraid."

"I'd be afraid too, if I could find the time for it."

"This house—!"

He groaned. "Not you too! Everyone tells me that they can't endure a single night here! And Karis has declared this place to be a travesty. No more complaining, please!" He entered the cloakroom and took Zanja by the hands. "If you love me—"

"If?"

"Because you love me," he corrected himself, with a smile that could not quite erase the lines and shadows of weariness from his face, "I beg you to let me spend just one night of my life on a feather bed!"

"Feather bed?" she said, incredulous.

"Oh, my dear, you can't imagine how soft—"

She began to laugh, and was still laughing as he pulled her to her feet and tugged her back into that overpowering hallway. He gave her a ragged handkerchief to mop up her tears. Her diaphragm hurt, but she felt relieved, as though she had in fact been weeping.

"Can I make a bargain with you?" he asked. "That you'll never ask me to kill you again?"

"In exchange for what?" she gasped, still out of breath.

"Well, what do you want?"

Eventually, sobered, she said, "I don't know how to answer you."

Emil's hand rested on the small of her back; she put her arm around him and they walked silently, apparently aimlessly, past clutters of dusty, grotesque furniture. The monstrous house seemed to have swallowed everyone into its echoing maze of rooms and hallways.

Emil finally said, "You are a hero of Shaftal, you know. You deserve to have whatever you want."

He turned down another hallway—their path was so complicated Zanja doubted she could find her way back to the front door—entered a self-important anteroom, and went through that, into a bedroom full of gleaming furniture, thick carpet, and rich draperies. This room, at least, seemed recently cleaned.

Karis sat near the hearth on a cushioned stool, taking tools out of her tool box, unwrapping them, examining them, testing their sharp edges, rubbing them with an oily rag to protect them against rust. She said grumpily, as Emil came in, "But I'm not going to sleep in that awful bed."

"You can stand out in the snow all night—I don't care," he replied.

Zanja found herself paralyzed in the doorway, unable to cross the threshold. Emil said to Karis, "What are you doing, anyway?"

Karis gently extricated a small plane from the box. Zanja could remember when Karis had shaped that plane's body and forged its blade, but she could not remember what this particular plane was designed for. When Karis invented a tool, she also invented the need for it, and Emil went about the country showing the new tool to carpenters, who became better at their work by buying it.

The hand that does the work creates the tool; the tool creates the work done by the hand. By earth logic, action and understanding are inseparable.

Zanja said, "The tools remind Karis who she is."

Karis looked at her. "Do *your* tools remind you of who *you* are?" Her eyes had a deep, rather dangerous brightness to them. She reached again into her toolbox, and although the tool she had removed was swathed in leather, Zanja recognized it. Karis held up the little knife that had been her first gift to Zanja.

Zanja had come into the room somehow, had dropped to her knees on the lush carpet.

Karis said, "Clement confiscated this blade from you—from the storyteller. But then she gave it to a raven, to bring to me. That one gesture made everything possible." She pressed the leather-wrapped blade into Zanja's hand.

In a moment, Zanja said, "When they took the blade from me—from the storyteller—she felt a terrible loss. She knew that she had always carried the blade with her, though she couldn't remember where it had come from or what it represented to her. But she treasured it anyway. It allowed her to keep believing that she had a past, that she was someone, and not merely a container of stories. But after they had taken the blade and the cards, she had nothing of her own."

She looked up at Emil, who had given Zanja the cards, who now wearily leaned against a chair back but seemed unwilling to sit down. "She loved the glyph cards too," she said, "for the same reason." She added, "The storyteller's memories are very strange."

He signaled with his eyes, telling her to look again at Karis. She had taken Zanja's dagger out of her toolbox and was holding it out to her.

"I left it lying on our bed," Zanja said.

"Did you? When Norina brought it to me, she didn't say where you had left it." Karis paused, and added apologetically, "I'm as stupid as ever about symbolism."

"I don't remember feeling angry, but to leave the knife in the bed we had shared for five years, that was an angry gesture. I can't believe I did such a thing."

"I do remember being angry with you," Karis said. "With you—and with our family—and with Harald. But it's gone now."

There was a long silence, during which the faint sound of Emil shifting his weight seemed awfully loud.

Zanja said, "The storyteller thought she had murdered her wife."

"Will you take the blade," Karis said impatiently. "Or not?"

"Of course I will!" Zanja took the dagger out of her hand.

Emil straightened up rather stiffly. "I'm going to bed. My only wish is that no one bother me before breakfast. Everyone else will eventually end up in the kitchen this evening, I expect, sitting on the floor and drinking beer like the rustics we are, and eating with our fingers whatever amazing thing Garland cooks up next. Oh, Karis, I suppose I should warn you that Garland has fallen in love with the kitchen."

"What? No! Emil!"

But he was gone, the relieved liveliness of his voice already swallowed by the house's maw.

"Now it's inevitable that we'll live in this ugly travesty," said

Karis gloomily. "This building is an affront—a waste of good land and good stone. How shall I endure calling it my home?"

Zanja put her head on Karis's knee. In a moment, Karis's hand stroked her head, and Zanja's skin came alive, like dry tinder catching fire. Karis gave a gentle tug to her solitary braid. Zanja murmured, "You practically pulled it out by the roots already."

"Ungrateful—"

"I am not at all ungrateful. Do you know, someone has mentioned to me that it's the thirteenth day of the first year of Karis G'deon? How did that become possible?"

After a silence, Karis said, "Thirteen days? Surely it's been thirteen years."

Zanja raised her head, for Karis's voice had been harsh in its center and ragged at its edges. "What's so awful about that bed? Why can't you bear to lie down in it?"

"Those bedposts are overbearing. The carving is grotesque. The whole thing is an ostentatious monstrosity."

Zanja looked at the bed. It truly was an awful thing; she herself couldn't imagine lying in it. "So take a chisel to it," she said.

Karis blinked at her. "By Shaftal, I've missed you." Eyes glittering, she reached for a chisel in its protective wrappings and a wooden mallet that lay nearby. Then she chose a crosscut saw, its handle darkened by oil and age. "This won't take long," she said.

Not much later, they made love on the feather bed, amid wood chips and sawdust, as the ornate bedposts burned briskly in the fireplace.

A new age in Shaftal had begun.